THE GHOST SEQUENCES

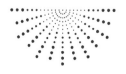

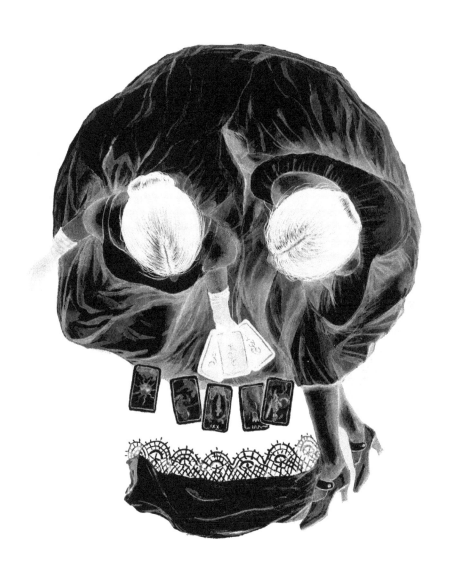

THE GHOST SEQUENCES

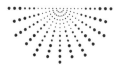

A.C. WISE

UNDERTOW
PUBLICATIONS

Even though they'll never know it—to Ray Bradbury, for making me fall in love with short stories again, and to Alvin Schwartz, for all the scary stories to tell in the dark.

CONTENTS

How the Trick is Done   11

The Stories We Tell About Ghosts   35

The Last Sailing of the "Henry Charles Morgan" in   59
Six Pieces of Scrimshaw (1841)

Harvest Song, Gathering Song   67

The Secret of Flight   91

Crossing   113

How to Host a Haunted House Murder Mystery   135
Party

In the End, It Always Turns Out the Same   149

Exhalation #10   161

Excerpts From a Film (1942-1987)   189

Lesser Creek: A Love Story, A Ghost Story   219

I Dress My Lover in Yellow   235

The Nag Bride   251

Tekeli-li, They Cry   297

The Men From Narrow Houses   311

The Ghost Sequences   325

Publication History   351

Acknowledgements   353

About the Author   355

Also by A.C. Wise   357

HOW THE TRICK IS DONE

The Magician Takes a Bow

HOW MANY PEOPLE CAN SAY THEY WERE THERE THE NIGHT THE
trick went wrong and the Magician died on stage? Certainly,
that first morning on the strip—dazed gamblers blinking in the
rising light, the ambulance come and gone, with the smell of
gunpowder lingering in the air—everyone claimed they knew
someone who heard the Magician's Assistant scream, saw the
spray of blood, saw a man rush on stage and faint dead away.

Of course very few people making the claim, then or now,
are telling the truth. Vegas is a city of illusion, and everyone
likes feeling they're in on the secret, understand how the trick is
done, but very few do.

The end came for the Magician, fittingly, during the Bullet-
Catch-Death-Cheat, the trick that made him famous. A real gun
is fired by a willing audience member. The Magician dies. The
Magician reappears alive and at back of the theater. Presto,
abracadabra, ta-da.

There are small variations. Sometimes the Magician's
Assistant fires the gun, if the audience is squeamish, or espe-

cially drunk. She revels in these brief moments in the spotlight, dreaming of being a magician herself some day. Sometimes the Magician reappears in the balcony, waving, and sometimes by the exit doors. Once he reappeared as a vendor selling popcorn, his satin-lapelled jacket smelling of butter and heat and salt. Once, he came back as a waiter and spilled a drink on an audience member who was confidently whispering that they knew exactly how he pulled it off.

Just because Houdini flashed bullets in his smile years before the Magician was born, people think they have it nailed down. Variations on tricks of every kind are a grand tradition in the magic world, and everyone knows none of it is real. The world is rational; it obeys certain rules. They hold this truth like a shield against the swoop in their bellies every time the Magician falls and gets back up again. None would dare admit out loud that deep down, a tiny part of them desperately wants to believe.

Here's the secret, and it's a simple one: dying is easy. All the Magician has to do is stand with teeth clenched, muscles tight, breath slowed, and wait. The real work is left to his Resurrectionist girlfriend, Angie, standing just off stage, night after night, doing the impossible, upsetting the natural order of the world. Her timing is always impeccable, her focus a razor's edge. Her entire will is trained on holding the bullet in place, coaxing the Magician's blood to flow and forbidding his heart from simply quitting out of shock. Death can be very startling, after all.

There is pain, of course, but by the time he died for good, it had become a habit for the Magician, and besides, the applause made it worthwhile. He never once allowed himself to think about the thousand huge and tiny things that had to go right for the trick to work, or that only one thing had to go wrong.

After all, the Resurrectionist pulled it off night after night— how hard could it be? Inside the wash of the spotlight, he couldn't see her grit her teeth, how she sweated in the shadows while he flashed his smile and took his bows. Everything always went off, just like magic, and he always managed to vanish by the time her raging headache set in, forcing her to lie in a dark room with a cold cloth over her eyes.

But she never complained. The money was good, and much like dying had become a habit for the Magician, the Magician had become a habit for her.

Maybe they could have gone on like that forever if it hadn't been for the Magician's Assistant. Not the one who fired the gun, but the first one. Meg, who died and came back as a ghost.

The Assistant Takes Flight

Meg was young when she was the Magician's Assistant, but everyone was back then. She was also in love with the Magician, but everyone was that back then, too. Even Rory, the Magician's longtime stage manager, who was perhaps the most in love of all.

Rory thought of Meg as a little sister, and Meg thought of Rory as a dear friend, but neither of them ever spoke of their feelings for the Magician aloud. They worked side by side every day, believing themselves alone in their singular orbits of longing, both ashamed to have fallen so far and so hard for so long.

All of this was before the Magician's Resurrectionist girlfriend, before the Bullet-Catch-Death-Cheat was even a gleam in the Magician's eye. Back then, before coming back from the dead to thunderous applause supplanted it all, the Magician sawed women in half, plucked cards from thin air, nicked watches from sleeves, and pulled one very grumpy rabbit out of a hat night after night. Off stage and on, the Magician called the rabbit Gus, even though that wasn't his name, and assigned him motives and personality to make the audience laugh.

Whether it was the name or the hat, the rabbit only tolerated this for so long, and one fateful night, he bit the Magician hard enough to necessitate the tip of his left index finger being sewn back on. After the blood and the gauze, and the trip to the hospital, the Magician decided he was fed up too. He needed a new act, a new assistant, a fresh start.

He didn't consult or warn Meg, but directed her to an all-night diner as she drove him back from the emergency room. Up until the moment the words "I'm done," came from the Magician's mouth, Meg harbored the hope that this trauma would allow him to finally see her, and that he'd invited her to the diner at 1:47 a.m. to confess his love.

Instead, he broke her heart and put her out of a job in the same breath. And he didn't even have the decency to pay for her half of the meal.

Meg stared at the Magician. The Magician fidgeted with his gauze, and looked at the door and the neon and the cooling desert outside.

"I'm sure you'll land on your feet, kid," he said.

Meg blinked. She dug in her purse for tissues and money for the meal. When she looked up, the Magician was gone. Vanished into thin air.

Meg dropped coins and bills on the table without counting. Colt-wobbly legs carried her into the night. The air seared her lungs, and tears frosted her lashes. All up and down the strip, everything blurred into a river of light.

The Magician's Assistant—she wasn't even that anymore. Just Meg, and her parents had drilled into her young that that wasn't worth anything at all. Who was she, if she wasn't with the Magician? What could she possibly be?

Lacking evidence to the contrary, she chose to believe her parents. On stage with the Magician, she could pretend the glitter on her costume was a little bit of his glory rubbed off on her. Alone, she was nothing at all, and her ridiculous costume was just sequins, falling in her wake as she hailed a cab.

The car stopped at a location she must have given, though she didn't remember saying anything at all. The space between her shoulder blades itched. She climbed out. Wind tugged at her hair and she took a moment to breathe in awe at the lights illuminating the vast sweep of concrete, a marvel of engineering, a wonder of the new world.

Meg left her purse on the backseat. She slipped off her shoes. The itch between her shoulder blades grew. Feathers ached to push themselves out from inside her skin.

Instead of landing on her feet, Meg landed at the bottom of Hoover Dam. A 727 foot drop that should have been impossible with all the security, except that just for a moment, Meg borrowed a little bit of magic—real magic—for her own. As she jumped, feathers burst from her skin and all the sequins in her costume blazed like stars. For just one instant before she fell, the Magician's Assistant flew.

The Stage Manager Brings White Roses

Rory remembered Meg, and it seemed he was the only one.

Before she hit the ground, before he left the diner and Meg sitting stunned in the booth behind him, the Magician had already forgotten her name. If he ever knew it at all. While Meg flew, capturing a moment of real magic without an audience or applause, the Magician was at a bar forgetting what he'd never remembered in the first place, and so Rory was the one who got the call. He sat on the floor, put his head in his hands, and sobbed.

Even though the Magician paid her a pittance, Meg

brought Rory coffee and pastry at least once a week. He taught her how to knit. She taught him how to throw a fast-ball. She invited him to her tiny apartment, and introduced him to her guinea pigs, Laurel and Hardy. They watched old movies, both having a fondness for Vincent Price, William Powell, and Myrna Loy, and popcorn with too much salt. They laughed at stupid things, and cried at sad ones, and never let each other know of their mutual ache for the Magician.

Now that it was too late, Rory saw that of course he was like Meg, she was like him, and they were both fools. He brought a massive spray of white roses to her funeral. He laid them gently atop her cheap coffin, and his heart broke all over again. There were only five other people in the tiny chapel, and the Magician wasn't one of them.

Rory hated him. Or, he meant to. Except when the Magician came to him three days later and told Rory he was putting together a new show and would Rory continue to stage manage him, Rory didn't hesitate half as long as he should have before answering. His heart stuttered, his breath caught. The word no shaped itself on his lips, and the word yes emerged instead.

He betrayed Meg's memory, and loathed himself for it, but he didn't change his mind. The best Rory could do was press a single white rose in his handkerchief, and tuck it in a pocket over his heart, listening to it crackle as he followed the Magician to start again.

Every night, under the lights, the Magician smiled. His teeth dazzled with a rainbow of gel colors Rory directed his way. Every time the gun fired, Rory felt the kick of it reverberate inside him. His blood thundered. His stomach swooped. He ached with the Magician and felt his pain as he watched him fall.

Every night as the Magician allowed himself to be shot, Rory held his breath. He clenched his teeth. His muscles went tight with hope and dread wondering if this time the Magician might finally stay down so he could be free.

~

The Resurrectionist and the Ghost

Angie is the first person to see Meg when she comes back from the dead. The Resurrectionist sits in the Magician's dressing room, applying concealer over the exhausted bags under her eyes. No one will see her in the wings, but that's precisely why she does it. The makeup is a little thing she can do for herself and no one else.

It's getting harder to hold everything together, to want to hold it together—tell the bullet to stop, to cease to be once it's inside the Magician's skin, and tell the Magician's blood to go. She sleeps eighteen-hours a day, and it isn't enough. Angie's life has become an endless cycle—wake, eat, turn back death, applause that isn't for her, sleep, repeat ad infinitum.

She smoothes the sponge around the corner of her left eye, and the ghost appears. Angie starts, and feels something like recognition.

"I've been waiting for you." The words surprise Angie; she wonders what she means. A vague memory tugs at the back of her skull, of a night in a bar long ago, but before she can grab hold it fades away.

"Who are you?" the ghost asks.

"Who are you?" Angie counters.

"The Magician's Assistant," the ghost says.

"The Magician's girlfriend." The words leave a bitter, powdery, crushed aspirin taste on Angie's tongue.

Angie laughs; it's a brittle sound. How absurd, that they should define themselves solely in relation to the Magician. The ghost looks hurt until Angie speaks again.

"I'm Angie."

"Meg." The ghost gives her name reluctantly as if she isn't entirely sure.

"So, you were the Magician's Assistant," Angie says.

Memory nags at her again, and all at once, the pieces click into place. When she and the Magician first met, he'd worn sorrow like a coat two sizes too large, but one he wasn't even aware of wearing. Angie had sensed a hurt in him, and it had intrigued her, and now she knows—the hurt belonged to Meg all along.

There's a certain flavor to it, tingeing the air. Even with the glass between them, Angie tastes it—like pancakes drowned in syrup, and coffee with too much cream.

Looking at Meg, Angie sees herself in the mirror. The Magician pulled a trick on both of them, sleight of hand. They should have been looking one direction, but he'd convinced them to look elsewhere as he vanished their names like a card up his sleeve, tucked them into a cabinet painted with stars so they emerged transformed—a dove, a bouquet of flowers, a Resurrectionist, a ghost. If Angie squints just right, there's a blur framing Meg, a faint, smudgy glow sprouting from between her shoulder blades. It almost looks like wings, but when Angie blinks, it's gone.

Well, shit, Angie thinks, but doesn't say it aloud.

Behind Meg, sand blows. Or maybe it's snow. The image flickers, like two stations coming in on the TV at the same time, back when that was still a thing.

"Can I come through?" Angie asks.

"Can you?" Meg's eyes widen in surprise.

"I'm a Resurrectionist." Angie's mouth twists on the words, but she can't think of a better way to explain. "Death and I have an understanding."

Angie reaches through the glass. The mirror wavers, and Meg's fingers close on Angie's hand.

"Is there somewhere we can talk?" Angie asks.

Meg shrugs, embarrassed. This is her death, but it isn't under her control.

"Over there?" Angie points to the neon shining through the storm.

Meg shudders, but her expression remains perfectly blank. She looks to Angie like a person actively forgetting the worst moment in their world.

As they walk, Angie learns that for Meg, sometimes death looks like a desert with a lomo camera filter applied. Sometimes it's sand and sometimes snow, but it's always littered with bleached cow bones and skulls. It's a place where you're always walking toward the horizon, carrying your best party shoes, but you never arrive. Mostly, though, Meg's death looks like a diner at 1:47 a.m., right before your boss—the man you love—tells you you're out of a job and a future and good luck on the way down.

Inside the diner, laminated menus decorate each booth. The wind ticks sand against the glass as Meg and Angie slide onto cracked red faux-leather banquettes. In the corner, a silent jukebox glows.

"I don't mean to be indelicate, but you've been dead for a while. Why come back now?"

The air is scented with fry grease and coffee on the edge of burnt, old cooking smells trapped like ghosts.

"I don't know," Meg says. "I think something important is about to happen. Or it already happened. I can't tell."

She shreds her napkin into little squares, letting them fall like desert snow. Her nails are ragged, the skin around them chewed. This time when Angie squints, Meg goes translucent, and Angie sees her falling without end.

∼

The Rabbit Returns

The first time Angie saw the Magician, he had gauze wrapped around his left index finger, spotted with dried blood. She'd just lost her job, or rather it had lost her. Donna, who sat in the next cubicle over, caught Angie uncurling the browned leaves of a plant, bringing them back from the brink of death to full glossy health. Angie's boss called Angie into her office at noon, and by 1 p.m. Angie was installed at a bar, getting slowly drunk.

The constant movement of the Magician's hands was what caught Angie's eye. She watched as he tried the same cheap card trick, only slightly clumsy with his injured hand, on almost every patron in the bar. No matter which card his mark chose, when the Magician asked, "Is this your card?" he revealed the Tarot card showing the Lovers, and smirked at the implications of flesh entwined. She watched until it worked, and someone left on the Magician's arm. Angie found herself simultaneously annoyed and amused, and the following night, she returned to the same bar, curious whether the Magician would as well.

The Magician did return, but there were no card tricks this time. She spotted him alone in a corner, his head resting on his folded arms. Angie slipped into his booth, holding her breath. If this was a performance, it was a good one. The Magician looked up, and Angie couldn't help the way her breath left in a huff. His face was stark with a grief, thick enough for her to touch.

"He's dead," the Magician said. "The little bastard bit me. He was my best friend, and now he's gone."

The Magician blinked at Angie as if she'd appeared out of thin air. Angie said nothing, and the Magician seemed to take it as encouragement to go on. He held up his gauze-wrapped finger, and poured out his pain.

"Maybe I left his cage open after he bit me because I was mad. Maybe I was distracted because I'd just fired my assistant and I forgot to latch it tight. Whatever happened, he got all the way outside, across the parking lot. I found him on the side of the road, flat as a swatted bug."

Tears glittered on the Magician's cheeks. They had to be real. If he'd been putting on a show, he would have made a point of letting Angie see him wipe them away.

"I put his body in a shoebox in my freezer. I'm going to bury him in the desert." The Magician laughed, an uneven sound. "Have you ever been to a rabbit funeral?"

The faint sheen at his cuffs spoke of wear. Despite the show he'd put on the night before—cheap card tricks to tumble marks into his bed—she saw a man down on his luck, wearing thin, a man whose deepest connection was with the rabbit who'd bit him then run away.

The Magician looked lost, baffled by grief—like a little boy just learning the world could hurt him. There was something pure in his sorrow, something Angie hadn't seen in Vegas in a long time. It looked like truth, and Angie wanted to gather it into her hands, a silk scarf endlessly pulled from a sleeve.

A shadow haloed the Magician. A death that wasn't the rabbit's clinging to his skin; he didn't even seem aware it was there. Angie caught her breath, deciding before she'd fully asked herself the question. That bigger death wasn't one she could touch, but the rabbit—that was a small thing she could heal.

"Do you want to see a magic trick?" she asked. "A real one?"

The Magician's eyes went wide, touched with something like wonder. Maybe it was his grief making him see clear, but for just a moment, he seemed to truly see her. He nodded, and held out his hand.

The Magician led Angie to his shitty apartment. As they climbed the stairs, her nerves sang—a cage, full of doves waiting to be released, a star-spangled box with a beautiful woman vanishing inside. Her skin tingled. She considered that she was about to make the biggest mistake of her life, and decided to make it anyway.

"His name was Gus." The Magician set a shoebox on his makeshift coffee table.

The rabbit lay on his side. Despite the Magician's description, he wasn't particularly flat. He might have been sleeping, if not for the cold. It seeped into Angie's fingers as she held her hands above the corpse. The Magician watched her, all curiosity and intensity, and Angie blushed. A rabbit was different than a houseplant—what if she failed? And what if she succeeded?

The rabbit twitched. His pulse jumped in her veins, a panicked scrabbling. Angie placed her hands directly on the rabbit's soft, cold fur. She meant to make a hushing sound, soothing the rabbit's fear, but the Magician's mouth covered hers. Salt laced his tongue; was she crying, or was he? She lifted her hands from the rabbit and pressed them against the Magician's back instead to still their shaking. Death clung to them, tacky and oddly sweet. She resisted the urge to wipe her palms against the Magician's shirt, pulling him closer.

She'd never brought back anything larger than a sparrow. Now she could feel the rabbit's life in her—hungry, wild, wanting to run in every direction at once. The other, larger death continued to nibble at her edges—feathers itching beneath her skin, wind blowing over lonely ground.

The rabbit's pink nose twitched; his red-tinged eyes blew galaxy-wide. He ran a circle around the Magician's apartment, and the Magician laughed, a joyous, bellowing sound. He lifted Angie by the shoulders, twirling her around.

"Do you know what this means?" His voice crashed off the cracked and water-stained apartment walls.

He scooped her up, carried her to rumpled sheets still smelling of last night's sex. Angie's teeth chattered; the rabbit was still freezing, and the Magician was warm. She dug her fingers into his back, and leaned into him.

The sex was some of the strangest Angie had ever had. The Magician touched her over and over again, amazed, as if searching for something beneath her skin. For her part, Angie kept getting distracted. She snapped in and out of her body, pulled to the corner of the room where the rabbit rubbed his paws obsessively across his face. She giggled inappropriately, her limbs twitching beyond her control. She developed an insatiable craving for carrots. The Magician, lost in his own wild galaxy of stars, never seemed to notice at all.

In the morning, she found the Magician at his cramped kitchen table. The sense she'd forgotten something nagged at the back of her mind—something sad, something with feathers —but the more she reached after it, the further it withdrew. She watched the Magician scribble on a napkin, coffee cooling beside him, burnt toast with one bite taken out of it sitting on a plate. He looked up at Angie with a wicked grin.

"How would you like to be part of a magic show?"

The Assistant Returns

The bell over the door chimes, and Meg flinches, her shoulders rising like a shield. She and Angie both look to the entrance, but there's no one there.

"We should go." Angie might be about to make the second biggest mistake of her life, but she decides to do it anyway. "Would you like to see a magic show?"

"I did magic once." Meg's voice is dreamy. "I think, but...." She frowns, then shakes her head, a sharp motion knocking the dreaming out of her voice and eyes. "I don't remember."

Hunger flickers in Meg's eyes now, tiny silver fish darting through a deep pool of hurt. Will seeing the Magician help, or add one more scar? Angie holds out her hand. Meg's touch is insubstantial, but she takes it.

Here's the secret to what Angie does: dying is easy. Being

dead is hard. And coming back hurts like hell. But it's easier if you're not alone, and Angie doesn't let go of Meg the entire time. She's come a long way since the rabbit, but it's an act of will, consciously holding space for Meg's hand, bringing her—not back to life, but back as a ghost. The act leaves Angie's vision bursting with grey and black stars. She has to steady herself against the dressing room table as she and Meg emerge.

"I've been looking all over for you." The Magician puts his head around the doorway, impatient, distracted. "We're about to start the show."

He barely looks at Angie; he doesn't see Meg at all. In Angie's peripheral vision, Meg's expression falls. She's braced, but nothing can truly prepare her for the Magician failing to see her one last time.

"I won't let go." Angie adjusts her grip, straightens, and Meg follows her to the wings off the stage.

Angie keeps Meg grounded throughout the show. The extra effort turns her skull into an echo chamber, her bones grinding like tectonic plates shifting through the eons. When the bullet kisses the Magician's flesh, Meg gasps. Once it's done, and the Magician reappears in the back of the theater—a combination of misdirection and Angie's resurrection magic—Meg finally releases her death grip on Angie's hand. Love is a hard habit to shed; Meg applauds. Angie is the only one to hear the sound, and each clap sounds like the cracking of ancient tombstones.

The Magician makes his way back to the stage, smiling and waving the whole way. Circles of rouge dot the Magician's cheeks. The lights spark off his teeth as Rory cycles through gel filters, making a rainbow of the Magician's smile. He takes his bows, gathering the flowers and panties and hotel keys thrown his way. Meg's features settle into something less than love, less than awe. She frowns, then all at once, her mouth forms a silent 'o'.

"I remember why I came back," she says.

"Come with me." Angie slips out of the theater, not that anyone is looking for her to notice.

She keeps a room in the hotel attached to the theater, and there, Angie collapses onto her bed. Meg hovers near the ceiling, turning tight, distraught circles like a goldfish in a too-small bowl.

"I don't know if it's happened yet, or if it's happening now." Meg stops her restless spiraling and sits cross-legged, upside down. Her hair hangs toward Angie; if Meg were solid, it would tickle Angie's nose.

"Can you show me?" Angie's skull is as fragile as a shattered egg, but Meg came back for a reason, and Angie wants to know.

Meg stretches. Their fingers touch. The room shifts and if Angie had eaten anything besides the ghost of bacon and coffee in the diner inside Meg's death, she'd be sick. Her body remains on the bed, but Angie's self stretches taffy-thin, anchored in a hotel room at one end, hovering above a swirl of music and laughter and brightness at the other. She isn't Angie; she isn't fully Meg either. They are two in one, Angie and Meg, Meg-in-Angie.

And below them is the Magician.

He burns like a beacon. A sour vinegar taste haunts the back of Angie's throat. Pickled cabbage and resentment, brine and regret. Angie can't sort out which feelings are Meg's and which are hers. She must have loved the Magician once upon a time. Didn't she?

The room is full of strangers, but another familiar face catches Angie-Meg's eye. Rory stands at the edge of a conversation where the Magician is the center. He sways, too much to drink, but also blown by the force of yearning, a tree with branches bent in the Magician's wind.

Angie and Meg watch as Rory orbits closer, his need fever-bright. The Magician turns. He stops, puzzled at seeing something familiar anew. After so many years of being careful in the

Magician's presence, Rory's desire is raw. Something has changed, or perhaps nothing has, and Rory is simply tired, hungry, willing to take a chance. And after so many years of looking right past his stage manager, the Magician finally sees something he needs—admiration, want, fuel for his fire. He sees love, and opens his mouth to swallow it whole.

A flick of the hand, a palmed coin, a card shot from a sleeve —the first and easiest trick the Magician ever learned and the one that's served him best over the years. He turns on his thousand-watt smile, and Rory steps into that smile. Parallel orbits collide, and their kiss is a hammer blow, shattering Angie's heart.

She gasps, coming up for air from the bottom of a pool. Meg floats facedown above the bed, a faint outline haloing her in the shape of wings. Tears drip endlessly from her eyes, but never fall.

Angie is angrier than she's ever been.

It's not the Magician's infidelity. Like the Magician himself, she's grown used to that. The Magician could kiss hundreds, flirt with thousands, fuck every person he meets, and Angie wouldn't care. The kiss means nothing to the Magician, and to Rory it means the world. That, Angie can't abide.

Rage widens cracks in Angie she hadn't even known were there. She can see what will happen next, Rory fluttering to the ground in the Magician's wake like a forgotten card. There's already forgetting in the Magician's eyes, his mind running ahead to the next show, the next trick, the thunder of applause.

Angie makes fists of her hands. She wanted better for Rory. She wanted him to be better. She wants to have been better herself. Smart enough to never have fallen for the Magician's tricks, clever enough to see through the illusion and sleight of hand. Angie meets Meg's eyes.

"We have to let the Magician die."

~

A Rabbit's Funeral

"Shit, shit, shit." Heat from the asphalt soaked through Angie's jeans where she knelt in the Magician's parking lot, the shoebox by her side.

Tears dripped from the point of Angie's nose and onto the rabbit's fur. She'd woken in the Magician's rumpled sheets, wondering if she was the first to see them twice, even three mornings in a row, and she'd found the rabbit curled next to the defunct radiator, empty as though he'd never contained life at all. Nothing she could do, no amount of power she could summon, would unravel his death again.

"Are you okay?" A shadow fell over her, sharp-edged in the light, and Angie looked up, startled.

"Yes. No. Shit. No. Sorry." She wiped frantically at her face, leaving it smeared and blotchy.

The sun behind the man turned him into a scrap of darkness. Angie wished she'd brought sunglasses.

"I'm fine." She stood and lifted her chin.

"You don't look fine." The man's gaze drifted to the box.

Exhaustion wanted Angie to drop back to her knees, but she turned it into a deliberate motion, scooping the box against her chest and holding it close.

"I know that rabbit," the man said. "The Magician—"

"The Magician. The fucking Magician." Angie couldn't help it—a broken laugh escaped her. She held the box out. "Do you know his name? It's not Gus."

"No." The man looked genuinely regretful, and it made Angie like him instantly, and study him more closely.

The air smudged dark around his shoulders, curling them inward. A shadow haunted him, like the one clinging to the

Magician, with the same flavor, but unlike the Magician, this man felt its weight.

"I'm Rory." The man frowned at the box. "I'm the stage manager, I was looking for the Magician."

"He's out. I don't know when he'll be back. He doesn't even know yet." She indicated the box again.

Guilt tugged at her briefly, recalling the Magician's grief at the bar, but Angie doubted she'd see such a display again. The Magician had already moved on, his head too full of plans for his own death and return, overfull with confidence not in her abilities, but that he was too important to properly die.

She caught disappointment in the stage manager's eyes. Angie recognized it; Rory was as big a fool as she was, maybe bigger still. Like a compass point finding North, Rory's gaze went to the Magician's window. He didn't have to count or search, pinpointing it immediately. Love was written plain on his skin, letters inches high that the Magician was too stupid to read.

"Will you help me bury him?" Angie held up the box, drawing Rory's attention back, his expression smoothed into one of weary pain.

"I'm—" Angie stopped. She'd been about the say the Magician's girlfriend. But they'd only just met; they'd fucked a few times. She'd brought his rabbit back from the dead, and that was the most intimate thing they'd shared.

"Angie." She coughed.

Her name felt awkward, a ball of cactus thorns she wanted to spit out. Now it was her turn to glance at the building, though she had no idea which window belonged to the Magician. Dread prickled along her spine.

"I have a car." Rory gestured. "We could bury him in the desert."

Angie followed Rory across the parking lot. She climbed into the passenger seat, and set the box containing the dead rabbit in her lap. The car smelled faintly of cigarettes—old smoke, like Rory had quit long ago. Angie found it oddly comforting.

"I'm a Resurrectionist." Angie tested the word. The Magician had suggested it last night, bathed in the after-sex glow. She tried it on for size. "I bring things back from the dead."

She expected Rory to slam on the brakes, swerve to the side of the road and demand she get out. He did neither. She kept talking.

"Simple things fall apart more easily—mice, sparrows, rabbits." She tapped the box, finger-drumming a sound like rain. Telling Rory her secret felt necessary, an act of defiance. The Magician didn't own her or her truths, not yet.

"Small things know the natural order of the world. Only humans are arrogant enough to believe they deserve a second chance at life."

Angie let her gaze flick to the side, finding Rory's eyes for a brief moment before he turned back to the road.

"How about here?" Rory parked and they got out.

Desert wind tugged at Angie's hair. She held the box close, sand and scrub grass crunching under her feet. Rory kept a small, collapsible shovel in the trunk of his car for emergencies, a habit held over from when he lived in a climate with much more snow. He also kept a Sharpie in his glove box, and once they'd dug a hole, and laid the rabbit inside, Angie chose a flat, sun-warmed rock and uncapped the pen.

"What should we write, since we don't know his name?"

"He was a good rabbit. His name was his own."

Angie scribed the words. The moment felt like a pact, and when Angie stood, she took Rory's hand. The sun dragged their shadows into long ribbons, and at the same moment, they turned to look behind them, as if they'd heard their names called. The city glowed in the gathering dusk. The Magician was waiting for them.

~

How the Trick is Done

This is how it goes: Meg protests; she blushes translucent. She is dead, but she is afraid.

Angie points out how many people the Magician has hurt, how many more he will hurt still. Meg comes around to Angie's point of view.

They tell Rory together, a united front. With Angie holding Meg's hand, amplifying her form, Rory can see her. His eyes go wide, and his face becomes a glacier calving under its own weight. After his initial moment of shock, something like wonder takes over Rory's face as he looks at Meg.

"You have wings."

She blinks, spinning in place to try to see over her shoulder. The wonder on her face mirrors Rory's, but the melancholy in her voice breaks Angie's heart.

"I remember," Meg says. "I think, once, I knew how to fly."

"I should have..." Rory says, but he lets the rest of the sentence trail. Meg offers him a sad smile, telling him over and over again that her death is not his fault. Angie tells him that kissing the Magician was not a crime. Rory looks doubtful, but in the end, like Meg, he agrees. They need to let the Magician die.

Angie tells herself they are doing this for the dozens of lost souls, blown in like leaves from the strip, looking for magic, and instead finding the Magician. She tells herself it is not revenge. That he failed them more than they failed themselves. She thinks of late-night coffee, and early-morning champagne. All the opportunities she had to tell Rory that she knew he was in love with the Magician, to tell him to run. She savors her guilt, and pushes it down.

The one person they do not tell is the Magician's Assistant, his current one. It is unfair, but she needs to be the one to fire the gun. Magic, true magic, requires a sacrifice, and none of them have anything left to give.

On the night the Magician dies, he asks for a volunteer from the audience. A hand rises, but the woman raising it feels a terrible chill, ghost fingers brushing her spine. She takes it as a premonition, and lets her hand fall. Rory trains the spotlight on the woman, on Meg behind her, and its brightness washes Meg away.

No other hands rise; the Magician's Assistant accepts the gun with a smile, and Angie's heart cracks for her. There is brightness in her eyes, curiosity. She believes. Not in the Magician specifically, but in the possibility of magic. She's the Assistant for now, but her faith in the world tells her that she could be the Magician herself someday.

Rory shifts the spotlight to the stage. Bright white gleams off the Magician's lapels, the Assistant's costume sparks and shines. Angie watches the Magician preen.

There is a flourish, a musical cue. The Magician's Assistant fires the gun. Angie holds her arms tight by her side. The bullet strikes home. A constellation of red scatters, raining like stars on the stunned front row. The Resurrectionist grits her teeth and trains her will to do nothing at all.

The Magician's eyes widen. His mouth forms a silent 'o'. He falls.

Dread blooms in the Magician's Assistant's stomach. The gun smokes in her hand.

Angie sweats in the wings. The Magician's death tugs at her, demanding to be undone. It's harder than she imagined not to knit the Magician back together. He is a hard habit to break, and she's been turning back his death for so long.

She considers—is she the villain in this story? The Magician is callous, stupid maybe, and arrogant for sure. Angie is not a hapless victim. She made a choice; it just happened to be the wrong one. Rory and Meg, they are innocent. All they are guilty of is falling in love.

Angie does not tell the bullet to stop, or the Magician's blood to go. She lets it run and pool and drip over the edge of the stage and onto the floor. All Angie can hope is to turn her regret into a useful thing.

Rory lets out a broken sob. His will breaks, and he runs onto the stage, folding to his knees to cradle the Magician's head in his lap. Meg hovers above them. She spreads her wings, and their translucence filters the spotlight, lending the Magician's death a blue-green glow.

Angie walks onto the stage. In the corner of her vision, the lights are blinding. The theater holds a collective breath. She thinks of a lonely grave in the desert, and a rabbit without a name. She thinks of Meg, falling endlessly. She thinks of Rory, his lips bruised with regret. Angie kneels, and looks the Magician in the eye. She knows death intimately, his most of all, and she knows he can still hear her.

"Dying is easy," she says. "Being dead is hard. Coming back is the hardest part of all. See if you can figure out how the trick is done, this time all on your own."

She leans back. It isn't much, but it assuages her guilt to think he might figure out the secret, the catch, the concealed hinge. He might learn true magic, bend it to his will, and figure out how to bring himself back to life one day.

The Magician blinks. The spotlight erases Angie and Rory's features; they blaze at the edges, surrounded by halos of light. Between them, a blurred figure occludes the lights. It reminds the Magician of someone he used to know, only he can't remember her name.

"Is this…." The Magician's fingertips grope at the stage as if searching for a card to reveal. Those are his final words.

∽

Death and the Magician

Angie lets a month pass before she tracks down the Magician's Assistant, his most recent one. They meet in an all-night diner, and Angie offers to pay.

The woman's name is Becca, and she reminds Angie of a mouse. She starts easily, all shattered nerves. A dropped fork, bells jangling over the diner door—they all sound like gunshots to her, and her hands shake with guilt.

"It's not your fault," Angie says. "You did your job."

Maybe one day Angie will admit the whole truth; maybe she'll simply let it gnaw at her for the rest of her days, until she finds herself completely hollow inside.

"This is going to sound strange," Angie says once they've finished their meals, "but how would you like your very own magic show?"

It isn't enough, certainly not after what Angie has done, but it makes her feel slightly better to think she is offering Becca the chance to live her dream. The pain is still there in Becca's eyes, but Angie sees a spark of curiosity and something like hope.

"Tell me," Becca says; by her voice, she is hungry to learn.

The act that replaces the Bullet-Catch-Death-Cheat looks like something old, as all the best tricks do, building on what came before and paying homage, while being something completely new. Every night, the Magician summons a ghost onto the stage. It must be an illusion, audiences say. Smoke and angled mirrors, just like Pepper back in the day. Only, the ghost knows answers to questions she couldn't possibly know. She finds lost things, things their owner didn't even know were gone. Sometimes she leaves the spotlight and flies over the audience, casting the shadow of wings, and creating a wind that ruffles their hair. Sometimes she reaches out and touches one of them, and in that instant, they know without a doubt that she is absolutely real.

The ghost looks familiar, and so does the Magician. The audience can't place either woman, but something about them calls to mind spangly leotards and pasted-on smiles. They look like people who used to be slightly out of focus, standing just on the edge of the spotlight, out of range of the applause. Now they've moved center stage, and their smiles are real, and they positively glow.

Angie no longer watches from the wings as the show goes on. Meg is strong enough now that she no longer needs Angie to ground her, and Becca and Rory are just fine on their own. Perhaps one day, Angie will slip away from the theater altogether, though she isn't sure where she'll go.

For now though, she sits backstage in front of the mirror and looks the old magician in the eye.

As she does, she learns what death looks like for him, and thinks about what it will look like for her when her own time comes. Sometimes it looks like the darkest depths of a top hat, endlessly waiting for the arrival of a rescuing hand. Sometimes it looks like a party where everyone is a stranger, and no one ever looks your way. Every now and then, it looks like a diner at 1:47 a.m. and a heart waiting to be broken.

But most of all, it looks like a brightly-lit stage in a theater packed with people, utterly empty of applause.

THE STORIES WE TELL ABOUT
GHOSTS

Growing up in Dieu-le-Sauveur, my friends and I told stories about ghosts—the Starving Man, the Sleeping Girl, and the House at the End of the Street. The summer I was twelve, I saw my first ghost for real. That was the summer my little brother Gen disappeared.

The first official day of summer, the day after school ended for the year, we gathered in Luke and Adam's clubhouse—me, my little brother Gen, and Holly and Heather from across the road. Luke and Adam lived next door. By the time Gen was born, Luke and I had already spent years passing through the hedge between our houses.

That didn't change immediately when Gen was born, but it changed when he got old enough to walk and my parents insisted I take him with me any place I wanted to go. Luke didn't mind, but he was the younger brother in his relationship, the one used to tagging along. He couldn't understand why I could be annoyed, and yet protective of Gen at the same time, the first to rush to him if he got hurt, or stand up for him if someone else gave him trouble.

This is what I couldn't explain to Luke: It didn't matter that I loved Gen or not, because I did; it didn't matter that he was actually pretty cool for a little brother. What mattered was I didn't have a choice anymore. I used to be just me, but for the last seven years, I'd been Gen's big brother. I would always be Gen's big brother, with all the weight and responsibility it entailed.

"This is that game I was telling you about." Adam pulled out his phone. All week while we waited for school to be out, he'd been talking about an app called Ghost Hunt!, where you collected virtual ghosts and stored them in a scrapbook. He already had 27 unique ghosts, including the Bloody Nun.

"I found her behind the church. There used to be a cemetery there, but they dug up all the bodies and moved them somewhere else."

He turned his screen to show us the Bloody Nun's picture. The clubhouse was really a cleared-out garden shed, but Luke and Adam's mom had put in a carpet for us and a mini fridge with an extension cord running to the garage. I reached to grab a soda, popping the tab before I looked at the picture on Adam's phone.

The colors were washed out and strange, like one of those filters had been applied to make it look like an old photograph. The grass had a peachy tone, but I recognized the lawn behind the church, but not the woman, who wore an old-fashioned habit, with a wimple and a big silver cross. Her face was jowly, making me think of a bulldog, and at first I didn't even notice her feet until Holly pointed it out.

"She's floating." Holly pointed at the screen.

Even though she was closer to Luke and mine's age, Adam had a crush on Holly. Even though he hadn't said as much, I'm pretty sure recruiting me and Luke to play Ghost Hunt! was Adam's way of trying to impress her.

I leaned in for a closer look. Holly was right, below the nun's full skirt, her feet just sort of vanished. Instead of standing flat on the ground, she hovered, casting a dark stain of shadow.

Gen jostled my shoulder. I glanced back, moving so he could see better, but he edged away from the screen as Adam continued to scroll. Heather looked doubtful, too. She and Holly were only eleven months apart, practically twins. Like me and Gen, they came as a set. Wherever Holly went, her sister followed.

"Certain ghosts show up more in certain places." Adam continued flicking through his catalogue. "Like the Nun and the church, but regular haunts and ghouls can show up anywhere."

He paused on the picture of a haunt, a black and white photograph made to look all harsh and full of contrast, so the boy in the picture appeared to have no eyes, only dark staring pits where his eyes should be. The ghouls Adam showed us looked like they'd been shot in night-vision, emerald-tinted blurs hinting at tooth-filled mouths and legs bending the wrong way.

"We should all play together." Holly searched for the app on her phone, setting it to download, and Adam sat a little straighter. "I know some places where I bet we'll find ghosts."

Even though I didn't know Holly all that well, I knew she considered herself an expert on ghosts. I looked back at Gen. He had his phone out, but he hadn't downloaded the app yet. Our parents had gotten him his own phone just this year. They didn't care if he used it to play games and watch videos as long as he kept it with him in case of emergency.

"It won't be scary. I promise," I said, taking his phone.

Gen scrunched up his mouth; I hadn't played the game yet, so I had no way of knowing if it was scary, but I could tell he wanted to believe me.

"There are add ons," Adam said. "EVP Mode, Night Vision, Auto Detect, but they cost extra. The game's still fine without them."

He led us outside, and we swept our phones around the yard.

"I don't see anything." Holly sounded impatient.

"Ghosts don't appear everywhere." Adam put his phone away. "Anyway, I have soccer practice now, but we'll go on a proper hunt tomorrow."

He tried out a grin, seeing whether anyone would challenge his self-appointed role as our leader. Holly fake-pouted a moment, but no one else said anything, other than agreeing we would meet up again tomorrow. I couldn't tell whether Holly liked Adam the way he liked her, or just considered him a means of finding ghosts. I couldn't tell whether I liked Holly, not as a girl, but as a person. But the best place to hang out was Luke and Adam's clubhouse, which probably meant I'd have to put up with her either way.

I ducked through the hedge, pausing when I realized Gen wasn't following me. He stood framed by the gap we'd made over the years, the ground worn by our feet so the grass didn't grow. I crouched, so I could see him fully. He had the look of concentration he got when he was trying to solve one of the math problems my parents gave him to practice while I was doing my homework, so he wouldn't feel left out.

"What's wrong?"

"What if I don't want to see a ghost?" Gen fidgeted with the pack around his waist. It held his phone and his inhaler; he wasn't allowed to leave the house without it.

"You don't have to play."

"But then you won't play with me if you're all doing it and I'm not."

Gen pushed his lower lip out. Guilt stung me, making the hope that flared for the briefest of moments feel ugly and cruel. I couldn't help the thought: would it really be so bad if Gen stayed at home and played with his own toys some days while I played Ghost Hunt! with Luke and Adam? At the expression on Gen's face, I tried to push the thought away.

"Hey." I crab-walked through the hedge and put my arm around his shoulders.

His bones poked at my arm, even through the fabric of his shirt. He'd always been small. Reminding myself that Gen needed my protection chased away the last bit of hope so that I could almost convince myself I'd never felt it in the first place.

"It's just a game." I tightened my grip into a one-armed hug. "If it gets too scary, we'll both stop playing, okay?"

"Promise?" Gen looked up at me through his lashes.

I held out my hand. Our dad had once sealed a promise to take us out for ice cream if we cleaned up the yard with a hand-shake. Gen had been three-years-old, and the idea of a hand-shake had stuck with him as the gold standard for a really serious deal you couldn't ever go back on.

"Promise." I said it loudly and clearly, making sure I believed it, too.

"I have a good one," Holly said.

The six of us sat shoulder to shoulder in the clubhouse. We'd been hunting ghosts all morning, but only Holly and Adam had caught anything, a regular haunt and a ghoul each. After a while, it had gotten too hot out, and we'd retreated to the shed with a fan run from the same extension cord as the mini fridge, and freezies from the corner store.

"It's one you haven't heard."

At the edge in Holly's voice, I looked up. She was looking straight at me and I blushed, realizing I must have rolled my eyes. She held my gaze for a moment longer, then launched into her story.

"Before Dieu-le-Sauveur was a real town, it was just a bunch of houses and a general store. A man named Martin St. Jean lived in the last house at the end of town, and everything after that was fields and forest. Everyone knew everyone back then, and neighbors looked out for each other, except for Martin St. Jean.

"He didn't go to church on Sundays. He would grunt instead of saying hello to his neighbors. His wife was even worse. If she came to the general store with him, she would sit in the wagon and wait, or walk behind him with her head down, never looking at anyone. She never spoke at all.

"The last time they came into town together, Martin's wife was pregnant. They were there to get supplies before a big snow storm. The shopkeeper's wife tried to talk to Martin's wife about the baby while their husbands loaded up the supplies, but Martin came back into the store and grabbed his wife's arm saying they were done."

Holly paused, looking around to make sure we were all paying attention. Seeing nobody was looking away or playing with their phones, she gave a half-smirk of satisfaction, and continued.

"When the storm came, all of Dieu-le-Sauver was snowed in for weeks, but no one thought to check in on Martin St. Jean and his wife, even with the baby on the way. Or maybe they did think of it, and they chose not to go because he didn't smile and nod at them and because his wife looked so small and afraid all the time.

"Once the snow thawed, people started to feel guilty. They got a party together to check on Martin St. Jean. No one answered when they knocked, but they heard a sound like a wild animal inside his house. It took three men to break down the door."

Holly dropped her voice, leaning forward. I found myself leaning forward, too, and Gen's shoulder brushed mine.

"When they got inside, they found Martin St. Jean crouched in the corner, covered in dirt and blood. He snarled, and when one of the men spoke to him, Martin St. Jean tried to bite him and tear out his throat.

"Another man tackled him, and they dragged him outside. That's when the men who were still inside found Martin's wife. She'd been tied to the bed, and pieces of her had been carved away. In the fireplace, they found bones. Some were too small to belong to anything but a baby, and they all looked like they'd been gnawed on."

Beside me, Gen flinched. Holly grinned.

"Martin claimed a wolf got into the house. He said he killed it and survived on its remains, even though he was too late to save his wife and child. No one believed him. They locked him up and he howled night and day, never stopping except to say how hungry and cold he was. In the end, they couldn't take it anymore, and they strung him up from a tree without waiting for a trial."

Holly paused again, making a point of meeting each of our eyes before delivering her last line in a dramatic whisper.

"And that's how the Starving Man was born."

I caught my first ghost in the high school parking lot after we'd been playing for a week. The six of us rode our bikes over together, then split up. I went to the far side of the lot near the trees, Gen sticking close as my shadow.

There was nothing, nothing, nothing, then suddenly a girl crouched on the asphalt right in front of me. When I looked away from my screen, I couldn't see her, but through my phone she looked as real as Gen. She wore a bathing suit. Water ran from her skin, pooling beneath her and soaking into the ground. I didn't remember animations from Adam's phone, but then he'd only showed us the still pictures. I wasn't prepared for how real she looked, the dripping water, or the way her lips seemed tinted blue.

"She's talking," Gen said.

I'd almost forgotten he was there. The girl's lips moved, but I couldn't hear anything.

"It's okay." I didn't look away from my phone.

I centered the girl and clicked the app's camera button. The girl's blue-tinged lips and the multi-color stripes of her bathing suit resolved into a black and white picture like the ones Adam showed us. I breathed out.

"I got one!" I raised my voice.

"Where'd you find her?" Holly was the first to reach me, everyone crowding around.

I pointed. Holly lifted her phone, but her screen only showed only asphalt and painted lines.

"Spawn must have timed-out." Adam shrugged. Holly looked annoyed.

"She was talking," Gen said.

A small line dented the skin in-between his eyebrows, his math problem look again.

"If you download the EVP add-on, you can play that back. Sometimes you can make out words," Adam said. "Here. Listen."

He tapped a button and held out his phone out. A garbled sound emerged.

"What's that?" Heather's eyes widened.

"Ghost voices." Adam played it again.

"It's just noise." Holly's mouth crimped, and Adam's shoulders slumped.

"I'm going to keep looking." Holly followed the border to some trees to the left, Heather trailing after her.

"Why was she dressed like that?" Gen asked.

Adam was still close enough to hear and answered.

"There used to be a swimming pool here. Maybe she drowned."

"Seriously?" I couldn't tell if Adam was messing with us, but he didn't have that look.

"I took swimming lessons here when I was really little. They filled it in right before Luke was born. I'm sure hundreds of kids drowned here."

Gen made a small noise, and I leaned down to whisper in his ear. "It's okay, we don't have to play anymore today."

I straightened, pitching my voice louder so Holly and Heather would hear, too. "We have to go home now. Our aunt is coming over for dinner."

I put my hand on Gen's shoulder, squeezing so he wouldn't give away my lie. I was proud of myself, not for the lie, but for keeping at least part of my promise to Gen.

Later that night, I downloaded the EVP add-on, and pulled up the picture of the ghost girl in the bathing suit. Green lines scrolled across the screen, jittering up and down with the volume. I didn't have the add-on installed when the ghost girl's lips moved, so there was no way I could have captured real sound.

Even though I knew it was just a trick to make the game feel more real, I couldn't help the tightness in my chest as I listened. The noise on Adam's phone sounded like someone talking with marbles in their mouth, or a recording slowed way down so you couldn't make sense of the words. The sound on my phone was nothing like that at all.

It reminded me of how when we visited our grandparents, Gen and I would sink to the bottom of their pool and take turns saying words and trying to guess what the other was saying. Gen was always better at it than me. The sound on my phone was like that, a wet sound. I listened five times in a row, and after the fifth, I crept down the hall. Gen's door was open a crack; he lay on top of the covers with his back to me, the lights off.

"Hey. I downloaded the EVP mode. Will you help me figure out what the girl is saying?"

His shoulders might have twitched, but it might also have been a trick of the shadows as a car passed by outside. I waited, listening to his breathing, but I couldn't tell if he was really asleep or faking.

"Gen?" I tried one more time. No answer.

Before I could decide whether to barge into his room anyway, the screen lit up on Gen's phone. Wavy green lines scrolling, just the way they had on mine, the wet sound, but louder so I could almost make out a word.

I stepped back. Gen hunched his shoulders. I couldn't hear his breathing at all now, but I couldn't make myself move. Was he holding his breath, waiting for me to go away? Trying to pretend I hadn't seen anything at all, I retreated to my own room, closing the door behind me.

I woke to the sound of Gen's screams. Disoriented, my legs tangled in my covers and I hit the floor with a crash trying to get up. I made it into the hall at the same time as my parents.

Gen stood at the top of the stairs, his heels hanging over the top step like he was about to do a back flip off a diving board. His eyes were blank, his mouth a perfect circle of darkness. He looked like one of the ghost pictures on Adam's phone.

No one moved. Up until he turned five, Gen had suffered night terrors. The sleep specialist my parents took him to said to let Gen wake up on his own, no matter how bad it seemed. I never understood that, and my mom looked doubtful now, too.

"Gen, honey?" She took a cautious step, one hand out like she was trying to catch a nervous dog. "It's okay. You're safe."

Her fingers sketched the air near his arm, but she didn't touch him.

"Gen?"

He turned toward her, his mouth widening impossibly, and let out another shriek. He leaned back, like he was trying to get away from her, and his arms pin-wheeled as gravity snatched him. My mother threw her arms around him, yanking him back. They hit the floor together, Gen's limbs flailing in panic and hitting my mother in the nose.

"Get his inhaler." My father spoke without turning around.

I found it in his bedside drawer. My father still didn't look at me as I handed it over, concentrating on Gen. When Gen's eyes finally focused, he reached toward my mother's face.

"Mommy, you're bleeding."

"It's okay. Just a nosebleed." She smiled, her eyes bright with more relief than pain, but it still made Gen cry.

He buried his face against her shoulder, exhaustion and fear coming out in a rush. She held him, rubbing his back and reminding him to breathe. My dad stayed nearby, watching them. There was nothing else I could do, and everyone seemed to have forgotten about me.

I crept back to my room and opened Ghost Hunt!, thinking of the green wavy lines scrolling across Gen's screen. I hadn't seen him download the EVP app, or take a picture of a ghost. As far as I knew, he hadn't caught any at all. I pulled up the ghost girl again. Nothing had changed. Some part of me expected to see Gen's picture instead, his mouth open like a circle of darkness, bruised eyes staring at me from the screen.

The next morning, I looked up the swimming pool before I went down to breakfast. Adam hadn't lied, but he'd exaggerated. Hundreds of kids hadn't drowned, just one. Her name was

Jenny Holbrook, and she lived right behind the pool so she could get there by cutting through her backyard. I read through the stories about her, piecing together a narrative. Gruesome as it was, I had a vague idea in my head that the next time we all gathered in the clubhouse, that would be the ghost story I would tell.

Jenny used to sleepwalk when she was little. She hadn't done it in years, but one night when she was almost twelve, she got up, put on her swimsuit, and went outside. She cut through the yard and somehow got inside the fence around the pool even though the gate should have been locked. A lifeguard found her floating in the deep end the next day. Jenny had climbed the high dive board, jumped, and hit her head on the way down. She might not have even woken up before she drowned.

Another story published a few months after Jenny died said how she'd been planning to try out for the diving team. She'd been practicing for days. In the follow up report, the coroner revealed Ambien had been found in her system during the autopsy. Jenny must have been so nervous that she wouldn't sleep before the tryouts, she'd taken a pill.

The scent of my dad making banana pancakes wafted up from the kitchen, Gen's favorite, but it made me feel sick. I abandoned the idea of telling the story in the clubhouse, imagining the hungry expression on Holly's face if I did. Jenny Holbrook had been a real girl, and she'd died in Dieu-le-Sauveur. Why would the makers of the Ghost Hunt!, who had probably never even heard of our town, have put her in the game?

"I have a story," Adam said.

He slid a glance sideways at Holly. She put her phone down,

and Adam struggled with a smile. I wondered if he'd been reading up on ghosts and the history of Dieu-le-Sauveur.

"In the 1960s, there was a girl in Dieu-le-Sauveur named Candace Warren. She disappeared and no one knows what really happened to her. Candace lived in the House at the End of the Street."

Adam grinned, waiting for the startled look of recognition. Of course we all knew the House at the End of the Street. There's a cul-de-sac at the end of our street, and a set of wooden steps leading up to street running parallel. At the end of that street is the House. There's an empty lot beside it, and a park with a big willow tree, but nothing else around.

"There used to be another house there a long time ago, and that's the house where Martin St. Jean lived." Adam's grin widened, and Holly smacked his arm.

"Shut up. That isn't true."

"It is."

Holly crossed her arms; she was supposed to be the expert on ghosts. Despite her frown, it was clear she was still interested. After a moment, she relented.

"Okay, keep going."

Adam took a breath and continued.

"Candace spent most of her time with her babysitter, Abby. Her parents fought a lot and sometimes Candace would have bruises on her arms. She never talked about it with Abby, but Abby knew what the bruises meant. Because of that, Abby and Candace spent a lot of time away from the house, and one of their favorite places was the park across the street. They would have picnics under the willow tree, and Abby would tell stories."

It had taken him a few moments to recover from Holly's interruption, but he'd fallen back into a rhythm. In fact, it was the same rhythm she used, like he'd been studying the way she told her stories. I caught movement out of the corner of my eye. Gen looked uncomfortable, like he was trying hard not to squirm. I'd taken him away from the parking lot, and after his night terror, I thought for sure he'd want to stay home, but he'd crossed through the hedge right after me. I'd briefly considered turning back, but a nagging voice in the back of my head spoke up—why should I have to give up my summer and my friends just because he was scared and too stubborn to stay home?

Gen met my eyes, and I looked away, concentrating on Adam's story.

"One day while they were having one of their picnics, Abby showed Candace a secret. There was a certain spot under the willow where if you squinted just right, it looked like winter on the other side of the branches even in the middle of summer.

"Candace asked how it worked, but Abby said she couldn't tell her. The magic wouldn't work if it was explained. Instead, she told Candace to close her eyes until her lashes and the willow branches made a crosshatch pattern. When everything was hazy and glittery, Abby took off her shoe and threw it. They saw it pass through the branches, but they never heard it hit the ground. They made a full circle around the tree, but Abby's shoe was gone. When Candace asked where it went, Abby would only say one word: winter.

"That night, Candace disappeared."

"That's not a ghost story." Annoyance edged Holly's tone. This time, Luke was the one to answer her.

"Shut up. He's not done yet."

Holly opened her mouth, but Luke and I both shot her a look, and she closed it.

"This is the part with the ghost," Adam said. He glanced at Holly as if for approval. She didn't say anything, and he went on.

"A couple years after Candace disappeared, another family moved into the House at the End of the Street. Everyone had forgotten about Candace by then, and even Abby had moved away. The new family didn't have any kids, but people would sometimes see a little girl standing at the upstairs window. Then one day, a whole pile of drawings appeared around the oak tree in the House's yard.

"They were a kid's drawings, in bright crayon, hundreds of them. They showed a stick figure family—a mother, father, and little girl. The parents always had red smiles, but the girl's face was blank, with no mouth or eyes at all. There were also pictures of a tree that looked like it had been drawn over something else, and a house with its windows scribbled out.

"No one could figure out where the drawings came from. They thought it was a prank until they noticed something weird. Every picture had a figure in black ink somewhere on the page. Sometimes it was so small you could barely see, and sometimes it would fill the entire page, like it hadn't been there before and suddenly spread. It was a tall, thin man, so thin he looked like he was starving. He had no eyes or nose, but he always had a mouth, full of sharp teeth, and it was always open."

Adam sat back; he wore a satisfied look, but he looked at Holly while trying to pretend not to.

"Was it the Starving Man?" Heather asked. "In the pictures?"

"Yup." Adam nodded.

"How do you know it's true?" Holly asked.

"How do you know your stories are true?" Luke countered.

A low-level argument broke out. I ignored it, turning toward Gen. I felt guilty for looking away before, pretending I couldn't see he was upset. I caught my breath. Tears rolled down Gen's cheeks, his shoulders hitching. I grabbed his pack, which he had taken off, and dug out his inhaler, but he shook his head.

"Come on, let's go," I whispered.

Luke and Holly were still arguing. Gen took my hand and squeezed it so hard I felt my bones shift, but I didn't pull away. I let him hold onto it as we crossed through the hedge and back home.

~

Gen forgave me. When I asked, he said he'd never been mad, but he also didn't want to talk about it. I tried to make it up to him by staying away from Ghost Hunt!, and from Adam and Luke's house for a whole week. Everything went back to normal for a bit, and Gen didn't have any more night terrors. I started playing Ghost Hunt! again on my own without mentioning it. If Gen knew, he didn't say anything.

Three weeks after Adam told the story about Candace Warren, Gen and I were on the swings in the park near the school. I'd just finished baseball practice, and we were waiting for our parents to pick us up to go to our grandparents' for the weekend.

"Push me?" Gen asked.

I dragged my feet to stop my own swing.

"Think I could push you all the way around?" I asked as I pulled his swing back.

"Don't!" He squealed as I let go, kicking his feet, but laughing. It was an old game between us. I pushed as hard as I could.

"Higher!"

I pushed again and as the swing came back toward me, Gen's phone pinged. It was the Auto Detect sound Ghost Hunt! made. Gen yelped, jumping. The swing's chains jangled as he hit the sand.

"Hey! You okay?" I caught the swing before it cuffed him.

His phone had fallen when he did. Green lines scrolled across the screen. I froze. The sound coming from Gen's phone was cold wind and the rattle of chains.

Gen whimpered. I inspected his hands. No scrapes. I brushed dirt off his palms.

"You're okay."

The sound from Gen's phone changed. The chains rattled

more violently, and underneath came a noise like someone struggling to breathe.

I reached for the phone, and Gen yelled, "Don't!"

I rocked back, startled. I pulled out my own phone. Gen shook his head.

I ignored him, and opened Ghost Hunt!, panning across the park. In the empty swing at the far end of the set, a girl sat with her hands wrapped around the chains. Her lips moved, breath trickling out in a cloud despite the summer day.

Gen turned to look over his shoulder, leaving his phone where it lay. He scrambled back, almost knocking me over.

"Gen!"

I reached for him, and he twisted away. Grabbing his phone, I ran after him. At that moment, our parents pulled around the corner. If they saw him running, I would be the one to get in trouble. Gen slowed at the park's edge, and I caught up. His breath rasped, but he wasn't having an attack.

"What happened?" I touched his shoulder, but he shrugged me off, climbing into the car.

He tucked his fingers in his armpits; goosebumps rose on his skin. I held his phone out and he shoved it into his pack without looking at it.

"Everything okay?" Mom glanced in the rearview mirror, looking between us.

Gen's face was pale, but blotchy with high points of color. He pressed his lips together. I shrugged. Her gaze lingered, doubtful, but she pulled away from the curb.

That night, I lay awake for a long time, watching the unfamiliar shadows slide across the ceiling of my grandparents' spare bedroom. I woke to Gen peering over the side of my bunk bed with no memory of falling asleep. I always slept on top, because Gen was afraid of falling off.

"What's wrong?" I sat up.

Gen didn't answer. I made room for him, and he scrambled

up. A nightlight by the door gave off a bluish glow, and orange-tinted streetlights seeped through the window. Gen had been crying. He shoved his phone into my hands, the case damp like he'd been clutching it in sweaty palms. Ghost Hunt! was open to the scrapbook page.

It took me a moment to recognize the girl from the park. On Gen's phone, the swing she'd been sitting on hung from one chain, empty. The other chain had been cut, a length of it wrapped around the girl's throat so she dangled from the cross-bar, her bare feet high above the ground.

"She can't breathe." Gen touched his throat.

I dropped the phone, then picked it up again, stabbing the button to close the app. It didn't feel like enough. I turned the phone all the way off, and shoved it under the pillow. Then I pulled Gen closer. He shivered against me. I imagined the sound of cold wind and chains, the sound of someone struggling to breathe.

"We should go to the House at the End of the Street for real and hunt ghosts there," Holly said.

Gen drew his knees up against his chest. After what he'd shown me at our grandparents' house, I'd thought for sure he would stay home when I mentioned going over to the club-house. I don't know why I'd suggested it, why I was still playing Ghost Hunt! when I'd promised him we'd quit.

I hadn't even been playing that much since catching the first ghost in the parking lot, but no one else had quit yet, and I didn't want to be the first. If it wasn't for Holly, I'm sure Adam would have quit long ago. Same thing with Heather. But there was no way Holly was giving up.

As for Gen, I don't know if he was being stubborn, or in some weird way he was trying to shame me into keeping my promise. Surely, if he got scared enough, I would quit, right? Until then, he wouldn't stop, no matter how miserable he was, which left us in a weird standoff. Every time I didn't shut the app down, or suggest doing something else, it made me angry at myself, which inevitably turned into being angry at Gen. Why couldn't I have this one thing? Why'd he have to be such a baby about it? When I wasn't looking at the pictures on his phone, or hearing the sounds, I could forget how terrible they were. I could convince myself it really was just a game.

"We should go tonight," Adam said.

"Mom and Dad would never let us." Heather spoke without looking at her sister, but Holly still turned to glare at her.

"So we don't tell them."

"I know how we could do it," Gen said.

As small as the clubhouse was, his voice was almost lost. I stared at him, but he ignored me, looking at Holly and Adam instead.

"All our houses are on the same security system. If we trick them into doing a maintenance cycle, we can sneak out and our parents won't know we're gone. I saw how to do it on the internet."

It was simple once I thought about it, but I hadn't thought about it, and Gen had. How long had he been planning this? Gen finally looked at me. Some trick of the light made his eyes as dark as the ghosts in my scrapbook, a stranger staring back at me.

Maybe Gen's asthma made him vulnerable, or maybe it was his night terrors. Maybe being afraid is what let the ghosts in. Martin St. Jean's wife was afraid. Jenny Holbrook was afraid. Candace Warren was afraid, too.

Or, what if Candace Warren's parents did more than just

leave bruises one day? What if Jenny's parents gave her the Ambien because they just couldn't take her nerves and wanted her to shut up? What if there's a reason we tell so many stories about ghosts?

What if we need an excuse.

Or maybe, Dieu-le-Sauveur really is haunted. Maybe a bad thing happened here long ago, and it keeps happening, and there's nothing anyone can do to stop it. It's a comforting thought in its own way.

Every town has their version of the Starving Man; The Bell Hook Witch; the Weeping Woman; Drip, Drip, Drag. Ghosts have always known how to get inside people's mouths, using them to tell themselves over and over. Before everyone had smartphones and creepypasta, and Normal Paranormal, they had nursery rhymes, and clapping games, and campfire tales.

There have always been ghosts.

And even if there weren't ghosts, kids would still disappear all the time.

It's not my fault. Just because I wanted Gen to quit the game. Just because he got more attention than me because he was sick and small and afraid.

There's a reason we want to believe in ghosts. We need them.

Luke, Adam, Holly, Heather, Gen, and I gathered in the middle of our street and walked together to the cul-de-sac. At the top of the stairs, we turned right. Shadows jittered through a stand of trees, and Heather's phone pinged. She jumped, but stopped and snapped a picture. I didn't look at her screen. I didn't want to see. Holly whispered something in her sister's ear, and jabbed her with her elbow.

We kept walking, stopping at the edge of House at the End

of the Street's lawn. The streetlights threw harsh patches of darkness across the empty lot next door. I imagined the Starving Man folded away in one of those patches, waiting.

The House looked perfectly normal, even in the dark. It was two stories, painted a pale yellow like cold butter, the door and windows edged in white trim. The yard bore a scar where the oak tree had been pulled up, roots and all. The worst thing about the House was that it felt empty—hollow all the way through—the kind of loneliness that goes with a place where no one has lived for years.

"Well?" Holly nudged Adam. "You're the leader."

Adam didn't move. I could just make out the willow in the park across the street, its branches swaying even though there was no wind. A glimmer of light showed through the leaves, sparkling and hard-edged, then it was gone.

"Gen, let's go." I caught my brother's sleeve.

Gen glared at me, but didn't move. It was my fault he was here, and he wanted me to know. I wanted to tackle him to the ground like my mother had when he was gripped with a night terror. I wanted him to bloody my nose. It would be easier than admitting I was wrong, saying I was sorry. Gen spun on his heel, brushed past Adam and Holly, and kept walking right up to the House's front door.

It shouldn't have opened, but it did. I can't remember whether he looked back before he stepped over the threshold, daring me to follow, giving me one last chance to keep my promise.

From where I stood, it looked like he fell into a solid wall of darkness, visible one moment, then gone. I hesitated; it was only a split second, I'm sure. My chest tightened; my heart kicked against my ribs. I hated Gen for everything he had and hadn't done, then I loved him again, and I sprinted up the porch steps.

I caught myself on the doorframe. Musty and still air greeted me. My upper body leaned inside, while my feet stayed planted outside the door.

A staircase stretched up to my left; a hallway receded to the right. Doorways opened in either direction, revealing furniture-less rooms. Blank walls, nowhere for Gen to hide.

I must have shouted his name, because it echoed back to me. I caught a flash of movement, a small face peering over the railing at the top of the stairs, but it wasn't Gen.

I took the stairs two at a time, wheezing the way Gen did in the middle of an asthma attack. In room after room, my feet kicked up dust. My footsteps overlapped until it seemed like a whole herd of ghosts running with me. I searched, going through more rooms than the house should have, but Gen wasn't in any of them.

Finally, I pulled out my phone. Fumbling, I got Ghost Hunt! open. Nothing. Nothing except green lines briefly skittering across my screen, accompanied by a sound like snow ticking against windows, building up and sealing away the inside like a tomb.

I shouted Gen's name over and over, but no one answered me. In the end, I folded myself onto the top step. I wrapped my arms around my legs, my knees pressed against my chest, and struggled to breathe.

∾

Before we moved away from Dieu-le-Sauveur, before my parents got divorced, one more thing happened. On a rainy day, I crossed through the hedge and knocked on the clubhouse door. Moisture spotted my shirt and dampened my hair. I heard shuffling inside, hesitation, then Luke opened the door. An uncomfortable glance passed around the room like they'd just been talking about me. I didn't blame them.

Luke sat back down, and I sat beside him. Holly put away

her phone, her expression guilty. I suspected they'd been comparing ghosts like nothing happened.

No one said anything. It was clear they wished I hadn't come; everything would be so much easier if I'd just disappeared along with Gen. I didn't disagree. The truth was, I didn't know why I was there either. Except it was better than listening to my parents shout or staring at the walls while my eyes stung.

In that awkward silence, while everyone searched for something to say, my phone pinged.

I hadn't opened Ghost Hunt! since Gen disappeared, but the sound was unmistakable—Auto Detect kicking in. It was so quiet I could hear everyone breathing. Then Holly spoke, her voice barely more than a whisper and rough around the edges.

"Aren't you going to look?"

Her eyes were bright, but for once it wasn't with eagerness. She looked like she regretted her words, but couldn't stop herself.

I picked up my phone. Green wavy lines scrolled across the screen. At first, all we could hear was wind blowing and an old house creaking. Then the sound of breathing. Louder than any of us, and getting more strained. Someone struggling, someone running out of air. I thought of Gen touching his throat. I wanted to scramble in his pack for an inhaler that wasn't there.

Before I threw my phone against the clubhouse wall. Before it shattered and tears gathered in my eyes and my own breath hitched in response to the terrible noises coming out of my phone, one more thing happened. We heard a voice.

It was a bare whisper, but I would recognize it anywhere—Gen saying my name.

THE LAST SAILING OF THE "HENRY CHARLES MORGAN" IN SIX PIECES OF SCRIMSHAW (1841)

1. SPERM WHALE TOOTH, LAMPBLACK

The first scene depicted is the whaling ship *Henry Charles Morgan,* beset by a storm. The waves are stylized curls, the wind traced as spirals battering the masts and tearing the sails. A series of dots arranged diagonally across the image stand in for rain. The lampblack is worked most deeply into the ocean bearing the ship up and tossing it around. The ship itself is second in darkness, with the spirals of wind touched most lightly, giving them a ghostly feel. Spaces of blankness within the waves suggest the presence of hands, shapes of absence rather than definitively carved things. It is possible the artist meant to metaphorically represent the storm, the ocean as a malignant force actively trying to pull the whalers from the ship and cause them to drown.

2. SPERM WHALE TOOTH, RED SEALING WAX

This piece depicts the immediate aftermath of the storm that struck the *Henry Charles Morgan.* In contrast to the high, vicious curves of the first piece, the waves here are represented by small triangles with concave sides, indicating the water calmed. The *Henry Charles Morgan* is clearly damaged, sails limp and torn, the mainmast cracked and listing. Debris lies scattered upon the waves. In the forefront, two human figures float face down. A third figure hangs limply from a rope secured around his chest and under his arms as three of his fellows haul him back aboard. The artist took care to include the minute detail of water dripping from the man's toes. Again, the absence-marked shape of a hand is suggested, reaching after the half-drowned man as he is pulled from the sea. Perhaps this is meant to represent the sea's jealousy, and its unsated hunger, despite the lives already claimed. The red hue of the sealing wax calls to mind waves darkened by blood.

3. Right whale baleen

The third piece shows the *Henry Charles Morgan* repaired, but becalmed. The water is not depicted at all, the absence of waves underscoring the utter stillness. The natural arc of the baleen is used to good effect, suggesting the vast sweep of sky above the ship. The artist has taken care to illuminate the scene with a scatter of stars etched into the baleen, and the faintest crescent of a moon. It seems likely the choice of material for this particular piece was made specifically to represent a scene taking place at night.

In the midst of the becalmed sea, the *Henry Charles Morgan* lies still, yet motion is suggested in a singular figure, scaling the ship's hull. The figure is shown from the waist up only, legs swallowed by the invisible water. The arm muscles stand out with the effort of the climb, while the tips of the fingers taper to points fine enough to suggest claws sunk into the wood. A faint pattern of scales, so slightly drawn it might be missed, covers the skin. Ropes of wet hair hang over the figure's shoulders. Seen only from behind, the figure's sex is indeterminate.

THE LAST SAILING OF THE "HENRY CHARLES MORGAN... | 61

To stretch the metaphor applied to the earlier pieces, here the artist gives physical form to the whalers' anxiety. Even though their ship has been repaired, they cannot leave. The sea still has a grip on them, creeping up the very boards, intent on doing them harm.

4. THREE JOINED RIGHT WHALE VERTEBRAE (COLLECTIVELY KNOWN AS THE VERTEBRAE TRIPTYCH), VERDIGRIS

Even though three separate scenes are depicted on each of the three bones, the piece, taken together, is counted as one entry in the series. The first bone shows a group of three men. One holds a lantern aloft, and finely drawn rays of light illuminate a fourth figure, crouched in front of them. It is reasonable to assume this is the same figure depicted on the baleen climbing the ship.

The figure is shown in profile, the sex still indeterminate, with much of the body hidden behind a wet mass of hair. The features in evidence are thin haunches, accentuated by the crouched position; jutting hipbones; wiry arms, the muscles still in evidence though less defined; and fingers splayed upon the deck to show a hint of webbing between each. The figure is poised to spring.

The expressions on the faces of the three whalers are, if not identical, at least similar. Each clearly shows a man frozen in his own private moment of surprise, terror, or disgust.

The second vertebrae shows the moment after an attack. The lantern lies on its side, projecting rays of light upward. The man holding it now clutches his face. The darkness of his hands is emphasized, suggesting blood from a wound he is trying to staunch. The other two men are sketched more lightly, having withdrawn a pace, and putting their wounded fellow between themselves and the creature. The creature itself now crouches on the opposite side of the men, as though it leapt clear over their heads, tearing at the face of the man formerly holding the lantern as it passed.

The third and final vertebrae shows four men holding the creature restrained. Impressionistic lines—like the ghost outlines of hands reaching up for the ship—cloud the background suggesting all hands on deck after being raised by an alarm. The creature's arms are pinned behind its back; the taut lines of its body imply motion, a struggle. At last, the creature can be seen head-on. The chest is flat, faint contours marking a dip inward at the waist. No sexual organs are in evidence, although this may be a choice of modesty on the part of the artist, rather than a factual report. Diagonal slashes heavily darkened with verdigris suggest gills along the creature's sides, or the extreme protrusion of its ribs. Its mouth is open, revealing rows of needle-like teeth.

Aside from the creature, the clearest figure in the third piece of the triptych is the captain, marked by the fine cut of his clothes. He stands apart from his men, elevated on the forecastle deck while the crew holds the creature on the main deck. A concentration of verdigris suggests the captain's face is largely in shadow, with stark contrast given to the whiteness of his eyes. The ultimate effect is a staring expression, the roundness of his gaze foreshadowing mania, or obsession, as it fixes firmly upon the creature.

It is in the vertebrae triptych that the allegory of the sea's hunger begins to break down. The details are extremely specific. Perhaps the artist chose to give the capricious cruelty of storm and sea a concrete and monstrous form. Or perhaps an inhuman being actually crawled from the sea and onto the deck of the ship. No written records from the *Henry Charles Morgan* remain to support either position.

5. WALRUS TUSK, INDIA INK

The length of this piece measures twenty inches, the entirety of it carved from base to tip. The scene is a rolling one, composed of several moments in time marked by the phases of the moon etched in miniature above each instance. The work is extremely delicate, yet rich in detail. In total, the events depicted cover a span of just over a month.

Beginning at the base of the tusk, the first moment shows only the creature's face in close up, struck through by bars, indicating imprisonment.

The next scene shows the creature at full length, secured by a manacle about its ankle. Although the phase of the moon etched above it points to the passage of time, the artist still shows the creature's hair as ropes of wetness, coiled against its skin. The pattern of scales is shaded more subtly, and the gills are less pronounced. Accentuated, however, is the narrowing of the creature's waist, giving the illusion at least of the slight swell of breasts and a roundness to the hips. The captain holds a lantern aloft to study the creature. A faint pattern of cross-hatching behind the captain, but separate from him, suggests a shadow watching from an unseen distance.

The third scene depicts the captain's stateroom, a small table illuminated by candle-glow and laid with a rich meal. The captain sits opposite the creature. Thick chains bind the creature about the legs and waist, but its upper body and arms are left free. Bones litter the plate in front of the captain, while the creature's plate remains full, piled high with food untouched. The captain's expression is one of slack fascination; the creature is watchful, tense, its mouth open ever so slightly to show the edge of its teeth.

Next, three men—one bearing a bandage partially covering his face—study the creature from a safe distance. Shadows partially obscure the creature. Perhaps it is a trick of the lighting which eliminates the curve at hip and breast, returning the creature to a more neutral form? Though the face itself is inhuman, the creature wears a very human expression—hatred as it glares from its chained position at the watchful crew.

Following this, the same three men are shown wrestling with the creature, then restraining and leading it by a rope. The creature's forward progress is ensured by means of a harpoon. A wound upon the creature's side—just below the slit of its lowest gill—leaks blood, highlighted by the artist through the heavy application of ink.

The creature is next seen secured to the deck, ropes binding each wrist and each ankle, holding it splayed. The wound upon its side is longer in evidence—either sealed of its own accord, or merely omitted by the artist. The three men stand with their heads bowed in conference. The creature's face is turned towards them, lips skinned back to show its needle-sharp teeth.

A fourth man joins the next scene. He carries a surgeon's kit. The bound figure of the creature appears smaller in this scene, more childlike in appearance, though the bonds remain tight.

In the next vignette, the skilled hand of the artist manages to capture a keen intelligence in the creature's eyes, the growing unease of the three men standing watch, and the heartsickness of the surgeon at his work. Even restrained against the deck, the creature is imbued with a sense of watchful waiting, hatred rolling from its being in a way that is nearly palpable. Also palpable, even carved, is the fear-stench of sweat from the men. It is a remarkable achievement, and testament to the power of art that it can evoke these sensations for all that it is only lines etched upon dead matter, darkened by ink.

The scene itself shows the surgeon cutting into the creature's flesh. The curve of what appears to be a rib bone lies bloody upon the deck. There is a gaping wound in the creature's side, and yet it unquestionably remains alive.

In the next scene, the men are surprised at their ghastly work by the captain. His face is livid, brimstone and fire. The creature's lips show a hint of teeth, either a grimace or a smile.

Next, the four conspirators are clapped in chains. They stand below the main yard, four sturdy lengths of rope depending from it, the end of each done up in a hangman's bow. The conspirator's eyes are downcast, all save the surgeon whose face is raised as if to implore God. The creature, unwounded, stands at the captain's side, hands unbound. A length of rope tied lightly about the creature's waist leads to the captain's hand.

The final scene upon the tusk shows four men hanging from the main yard, bodies swollen with rot. Beneath this grisly frieze, the captain and the creature stand facing each other, their hands clasped. The creature is dressed, or clothing has been put upon it—a dress such as a modest woman might wear. The creature's shape once again suggests a shift to the feminine, though it may be the garments providing this illusion. The captain wears a look of rapture. On the part of the creature, no such expression is in evidence.

6. Substance unknown

The final piece of scrimshaw resembles the curve of a rib bone. It was found, along with the other pieces, in a canvas sack likely made from sail cloth. The sack was found in a lifeboat evidently cut free from the *Henry Charles Morgan* and left to drift.

This last piece in the collection is delicate in size, yet sturdy in nature, harder than most calcium-based bone, yet carved upon nonetheless. It possesses a nacreous quality, its coloring a grey-purple sheen like an oncoming storm. Where lines have been carved into the surface, the bone—if that is what it is—shows silver-white, like the full moon.

The etching on the final piece is cruder, with none of the artistry of the other pieces, suggesting it might have been rendered by a different hand. It shows the *Henry Charles Morgan* sailing toward a horizon marked by the curve of the setting sun.

Debris, including what appears to be human remains, litter the water in its wake, along with two lifeboats, one carrying three men, the other appearing empty.

Of the *Henry Charles Morgan* itself, no further record exists. Both lifeboats eventually reached separate shores, one bearing a lone corpse, the other the canvas sack containing these six pieces of scrimshaw. The ultimate fate of the ship, the remaining crew, and their strange captive or guest, remains unknown.

HARVEST SONG, GATHERING SONG

Our first night out on the ice, we traded war stories. Reyes, Viader, Kellet, Martinez, Ramone, McMann, and me. We were all career military, all career grunts, none of us with aspirations for command. Captain Adams hand-picked us, brought us to the top of the world—a blue place all ice and snow and screaming wind—with only the vaguest idea of our mission. And none of us had cared. We'd signed on the dotted line, and had ourselves ready at 0500 on the tarmac, as expected.

The plane had dropped us at a base camp that used to be an Artic research station. We were all too restless for sleep yet, so we sat around the table and the remains of our meal, and talked.

"Why do you think Adams chose us for the mission? Why us in particular?" Reyes asked.

"To hell with that," Viader said. "What is the mission? Does anyone know?" She looked around the table.

"Extraction?" Martinez shrugged, underlining it as a guess. "We're here to get something top secret the military wants very badly."

"Okay," Reyes said. "So my questions again. Why us? None of us are anything special."

He looked around for confirmation; our silence agreed.

"My guess?" Kellet leaned back as she spoke, balancing her chair on two legs. "Because we're all fucked up."

When she leaned forward, her chair thumped down hard. The table would have jumped if Martinez and McMann hadn't been leaning on it. Kellet pointed at me first.

"You. What's your story? Syria? Iraq?"

"I was in Al-Raqqah." My stomach dropped, but I kept my voice calm.

"And?" Kellet's eyes were a challenge, bristling like a guard dog in front of her own pain.

"I was working an aid station on the edge of a refugee camp, distributing food, medicine, the basics." Under the table, my palms sweated.

Kellet leaned forward; Ramone fidgeted. Six pairs of eyes gave me their attention, some hungry, and some looking away in mirrored shame.

"I was handing a package of diapers to a young mother with a little boy on her hip, and another by the hand. Then the world turned black and red and everything went upside down."

I paused; instead of the room, the world flickered briefly, black and red.

"I was blown off my feet and ended up across the street, but I saw the second supply truck go up in a ball of flame. The first thing that came back was the smell."

"Burning hair," Viader said.

"Burning skin." This from Ramone.

I looked down. Snow ticked against the windows. Wind— cold and sharp as a knife—sighed around the corners of the research station. It sounded like teeth and nails, trying to get in. But I felt heat, the blooming fireball pushing me back, death breathing out and flattening me to the ground.

"The woman's legs were gone," I said. Silence, but for the snow. "But she kept crawling toward her baby, even though there was no way it was still alive. The other kid, her little boy, was vaporized on impact."

"You thought about killing her." Martinez's voice was soft, the intonation not quite a question. I raised my head, the muscles at the back of my neck aching and putting dull pain into my skull. "Putting her out of her misery?"

"Yes." The word left my throat raw. I'd never admitted it out loud; I'd barely admitted it to myself. Until now.

McMann produced a bottle. I didn't even look to see what it was before shooting back the measure he poured me and letting him refill my glass. My hands shook; they didn't stop as I swallowed again and again. The bottle went around, and so did the stories, variations on a theme. An IED tearing apart a market square, a hospital blown to smithereens instead of a military base; a landmine taking out three humanitarian aid workers.

We lapsed into silence, the answer to Reyes' question sitting heavy in our stomachs. Adams wanted us because we were broken. Because none of us had anyone at home who would miss us. We were expendable.

"Is that about right?" Kellet asked, looking over my shoulder.

I twisted around to see Adams watching us with her arms crossed. Her posture put a physical shape to something I'd been feeling as the stories and bottle went around. The seven of us had fallen into thinking of ourselves as a unit. Adams was outside of that—us against her. We'd follow her, but we didn't trust her. She'd drawn our pain to the surface; that made her our enemy.

"I'll tell you a story," Adams said, instead of answering.

There was one chair left against the wall. She dragged it over, turning it backward and sitting with her arms draped over the back, another barrier between us and her.

"There was a map," she said. "A soldier in Kandahar sold it to me. He claimed it would lead us to bin Laden, back when we thought he was hiding out in a cave like some desert rat."

Adams snorted. Without asking, she reached for the bottle, and drank straight from the neck, killing what remained before setting it down with a heavy thunk. The wind chose that moment to pick up. The walls of the station were solidly-built, but the wind still rattled the door

"The map was hand-drawn, and we were idiots to follow it. I think my commander only humored me to teach me a lesson."

Adams twirled the empty bottle. The noise of the glass rolling against the wood made my skin crawl.

"A few clicks out from where the cave was supposed to be, our equipment went haywire. Our radios burst out with static, mixed with echoes of conversations from hours and days ago. Our compasses spun, never settling on north.

"We should have turned back. But there was a cave, right where the map said it would be, and if there was even a chance..." Adams grimaced.

"Ten of us went in. I was the only one who came out."

Adams pulled a small bottle out of her pocket, thick glass, stoppered with a cork. The air around it shivered, humming with the faint sound of wings. I sat forward, and saw the others all around the table do the same thing, a magnetic pull drawing us towards the glass.

"This is why we're here," Adams said.

I stared at the bottle, filled with honey, viscous and bright. It glowed. Martinez reached out, but Adams' look stopped him. He dropped his hand into his lap. Adams held the bottle up, turning it so we could watch the honey roll.

"They found me two days later, half a click from the cave entrance, or where it should have been, except it was gone. I was severely dehydrated, puncture wounds all over my body, half-dead from some kind of venom they couldn't identify. They got a med-evac copter to pull me out."

There was more she wasn't telling us, knowledge stored up behind her eyes. She honestly didn't seem to care whether we knew, even if it meant walking blind into the mission she still hadn't explained. The bottle disappeared, neat as a magic trick. The humming stopped, its absence so sudden my ears popped.

Adams reached into her pocket again, and I couldn't help flinching, mirrored by Reyes and Ramone. Instead of a bottle, Adams set her smart phone on the table, a video cued up.

"I had the honey with me when I came out of the cave. It saved my life." She didn't explain. Doubt flickered from Martinez to McMann to me, a spark jumping between us.

"If I'd been in my right mind, I wouldn't have told them about it. But." Adams shrugged, let the word stand. She tapped play.

The video had been shot on another camera phone, one struggling to decide between focusing on a glass cage or the rat inside it. Thin wires ran from multiple points on the rat's body.

"Lowest voltage," a voice off camera said.

"This is what happened when the doctors at the military hospital fed a rat the honey." Adams tone was non-committal, unconcerned. Only the set of her shoulders said different.

Following the voice was a distinct click like a dial being turned. I imagined the snap of electricity, the scent of ozone popping blue-white in the air. The rat showed no reaction.

"Next level," the voice on the phone said. "Sustain it longer this time."

Again the thunk of the dial, the ghost of electricity. I felt it shoot up my spine, wrapping around my bones. The rat cleaned its whiskers with its paws.

"What's the point of this?" Kellet said. "Why the hell would they feed a rat honey, then electro-shock it?"

"Because apparently I told them to," Adams said. She wasn't looking at the screen. "I told them it was the only way they'd understand."

"Maximum voltage." The camera lost focus briefly, coming back as the dial clicked again.

The scent of singed fur had to be my imagination.

"Jesus Christ." McMann breathed out.

Adams retrieved the phone as the video ended. She swiped from video to a photo and turned the screen so we could all see. Reyes covered his mouth before the screen angled my way. The rat lay on its side, one of its front limbs missing, the lining of its cage sodden and red.

"After they unhooked the wires, the rat gnawed its own leg off. It did it so quietly, they didn't notice until it was already dead."

Adams slipped the phone into her pocket.

"The cave is out there on the ice now. I can see it." Adams tapped the side of her head. There was no air left in the room; none of us could have questioned her even if we'd dared. "I'm sure it's obvious why the military has a hard-on for this honey. It's our job to bring it to them."

We set out at dawn. Thermal gear blanked our faces so we might have been the same person repeated eight times, not separate individuals. Spikes on our boots crunched against the ice, a raw sound with crystalline edges. The ice itself groaned, like bones breaking, the vast sound of massive trees cracking deep in a forest.

Trapped between the padded mask and my skin, my breath rasped. The holes to let it escape clotted with frost, leaving my face clammy. I kept my eyes on Viader ahead of me, and put one foot in front of the other. I was the tail of the party, Adams, the head.

The sky lightened, a blue so searing my eyes watered even behind the reflective goggles protecting them. Then just as suddenly, clouds rolled in, dark and heavy. Adams led us between two walls of ice, high enough to slice the sky into a thin ribbon and erase everything else. Sheltered from the wind, she called a halt, told us to eat protein bars to keep our strength up. I unwrapped mine, clumsy with my bulky gloves, lifting my mask just high enough to get the food into my mouth. Even so, the cold stung.

As I swallowed the last bite, my radio burst out in static. I jumped at the squawk so close to my ear. It was the snow made auditory, a grey-white flurry of noise. Then, in its wake, my grandmother's voice. And simultaneous with my grandmother's voice, the storm broke, howling down on us in our trench. Kellet caught my arm, and tugged me into a crouch. The others were doing their best to wedge themselves against angles in the ice.

I made myself as small as I could, pulling extremities close to the center, conserving heat while my grandmother chattered in my ear. Seven years dead, but her voice was clearer than Kellet's shouting over the storm. She sang, the way she used to while cooking Sunday dinner. I caught snatches of Slavic fairy tales, the rhythms she'd used to lull me to sleep as a child. As the storm's fury rose, she called my grandfather's name in the same high, panicked tone she used in her last days, not seeing the hospital room, but a long-ago village torn apart by war.

Martinez tapped my shoulder and I almost hit him.

"Adams says move."

My grandmother fell silent. The wind died a little, and I forced my legs from their awkward crouch. We edged forward. The fresh layer of tiny ice pellets skittering over the hard-packed ground made the going even rougher. Despite the spikes in our boots, we slid. The wind pushed at us, and the cold crawled under our clothes. Behind my mask, my teeth chattered.

"Hold here." Adams' voice cut over the storm.

Instinct made us gather around her in a half circle. The honey appeared in her hand, last night's magic trick in reverse.

Everything else wavered in the dying storm, but it was bright and clear.

"It's the only way we're getting out of here alive," Adams said.

I didn't understand what she meant, but my body folded nonetheless, knees hitting the hard-packed snow. In my peripheral vision I saw Viader, Ramone, and the others do the same. Had Adams ordered us? The air hummed. I couldn't hear it over the wind, but I could feel it in my bones.

Adams didn't lower her mask, and goggles still blanked her eyes as she moved down the line. Despite the bulky gloves, her pour was deft. One by one Viader, Kellet, Martinez, Reyes, McMann, and Ramone lowered their masks and received Adams' honey on their tongues.

I should have felt frost burn immediately, but the proximity of the honey was enough to unleash the effect. I felt it sliding down my throat before it ever touched my tongue. Time bent, and the world went sideways. I had swallowed the honey, would swallow the honey, was always swallowing it. Then Adams tilted the bottle and let a drop touch my tongue.

Her limbs bent strangely, and there were too many of them. I saw myself reflected a dozen-dozen-dozen times in multifaceted eyes. The honey was liquid fire. It was like holding a burning coal in my mouth, all heat and no taste. It was like swallowing stars. But as soon as I did it, I felt no pain.

The storm raged, but I couldn't feel it anymore. The wind became a hush, a lullaby. I thought of my grandmother, but it was someone else singing now. The words weren't Russian; they weren't even human.

Adams lowered her scarf. Her lips were cracked and bloody, but light clung to her. She was holy, we all were, and I watched in wonder as she used her teeth to pull her glove free, ran her finger around the inside of the bottle, and rubbed the last of the honey on her gums.

It should have been crystallized with the cold, rough against her skin, but it was as liquid as it had been when she'd poured it down my throat.

"Come on," she said. "Let's go."

Everything was sharp and bright after the honey. Adams walked on gravel and broken glass, fallen leaves. Each pellet of ice under her boots cracked inside my bones so I felt it as much as heard it. My blood thumped; eight of us breathed. I heard the crystals growing where my breath froze on my scarf—fractal ice patterns, branching and branching. Forming hexagons. Forming a structure like a hive. Rewriting my cells; instead of bones and blood, guts and liver, there were only endless chambers, dripping honey.

And under it all, the song. A lullaby, a nursery tale. Limbs like needles tucked me in, sealed me in wax and left me to dream. A girl with wild, tangled hair stood under a tree, its trunk lightning-struck and smelling of scorched woods. Bees swarmed the air around her, a steady hum, and liquid gold dripped down the seared bark.

Only she wasn't a girl, she was much older. Ancient. Her bones were already buried beneath the roots, her skin peeled from her ribs, her insides hollowed to make room for a hive. Raised welts dotted her skin, a secret language I could almost read. History a billion, billion, billion years old. A map. Bees hummed while her bones fed the tree and she stood in its shadow, buried and not buried, dead and alive.

All of it echoed through the song, inhuman concepts crammed into human form. The girl wasn't a girl, but a god, a seed, a splinter of history forced under my skin. I wanted to scream. Instead, I hummed, my whole body vibrating to the frequency of wings beating. I didn't feel the cold. None of us did. And together we walked, a segmented body with too many limbs, and Adams as our head.

~

Night fell, the sky darkening from plum twilight to deep blue-black. I didn't care where Adams was leading us. I could have walked forever. Ahead of me, Ramone stripped back his protective gear, exposing his arm to the elbow. Kellet pulled a folding knife from her pocket and cut open her palm. I listened to the blood plink-plink-plink on the snow.

The eight of us were joined, bound by an invisible cord. Reyes and McMann, Martinez and Viader, they were my skin and bone.

As we walked, something walked with us. Vast and impossible, just on the other side of a sky that was a blue-dark curtain, painted with stars. Long, thin limbs. Taller than the Empire State Building. Moving slowly. Singing. The song wanted something from me. It wanted me to change.

I wanted to.

I wanted to let the honey stitch my veins with threads of liquid gold. I needed it, more than I'd ever needed anything in my life. I wanted it to subsume me.

Al-Raqqah had been folded into my skin. The world torn apart, gone black and red; the flash-point explosion vaporizing a child. Those things lived between my bones, branched through my lungs. The honey was bigger than that. It could eat my pain whole.

Because it wasn't just honey, it was a civilization too old and terrible to comprehend. More had been lost than I could fathom. That was in the song. That was in the honey. It was too big to hold, and that gave me permission to let go.

Tears ran on my cheeks. They should have frozen, but the honey left my skin fever hot. It kept the moon from setting and the sun from coming up. I couldn't tell how far we'd gone, but it was still dark when Adams called a halt. We pitched tents from

the packs we carried—packs whose weight we no longer felt—
and built wind-blocks out of snow.

I watched the street in Al-Raqqah torn apart, an endless film
reel flickering and superimposed on the night. I watched the
mother crawl towards the burned remains of her child. I saw
her other child caught in a loop of instant incineration, his
mouth open in a wail. And none of it mattered.

In the here and now, I watched Reyes kneel to clear space for
a fire. There was an old hunting trap buried under the snow. I
saw it an instant before it happened. He put his hand into the
drift, and metal jaws closed around his arm with a wet snap.
Reyes saw it, too. The scene hung inverted in his eyes, playing
out like the film reel of Al-Raqqah's destruction. And Reyes
stuck his hand into the snow anyway.

He didn't scream. I thought of the rat in the cage, cleaning its
whiskers as electricity sang through its body. I imagined teeth
sunk into flesh and the rat tearing its leg off, bleeding out and at
peace with the world. Reyes held his arm out, staring at torn
cloth, red nerve, and splintered bone. He smiled.

Kellet and Viader moved to either side of me and together
we pried the trap loose. Ramone sat by, watching his flesh
redden, then go dead-white with the cold. McMann broke out
the first aid kit, cleaning and bandaging the wound as best he
could. Adams watched us, arms crossed, her expression saying
we were wasting our time. Then Reyes sat down, still smiling,
staring in wonder at the flames as Martinez built up the fire.

I don't remember sleeping. Light crept over the horizon,
staining the snow pale gold and carving deep shadows in the
hollows. We found Reyes' clothing, shed like skin and frozen
into the ground. There were footprints, spaced farther and

farther apart until they simply stopped. But no Reyes, not even his remains.

"It's like the story of the wendigo." Ramone's voice made me jump. His gazed was fixed on the last footprint, dragged long and impossibly sharp into the snow.

"It comes in the wind to snatch people into the sky, making them run faster and faster until their feet burn to ash. Sometimes, you can hear their voices in the sky, still screaming."

I didn't know the story they were talking about, but I tilted my head, listening for Reyes. I didn't hear anything except the low vibration of wings.

I don't remember sleeping, but before we woke to find Reyes gone, I woke with Adams' hand over my mouth. Or maybe it was after, or during. Time was funny on the ice.

"It's here," Adams said. "Come on."

She led me out of the tent and into the dark. I didn't ask where we were going. I could feel it—a vast system of caves under our feet, the earth gone hollow and strange. Juts of ice stabbed at the sky. I followed Adams through a maze of crystal spikes like crazed, broken teeth. There were steps cut into the frozen earth. We descended into an amphitheater for giants. One bowl below us, the other above us, the sky spattered with stars. Then we were underground.

I crawled behind Adams. Shadows moved on the other side of us. Echoes. Memories. Cracks in the real. The groove worn into the earth was a record. Adams and I were the needle, playing the sound. Occasionally, the record skipped, and we caught flickers of ancient things, impossibly out of time. Somehow, I knew: we were in the blind servants' tunnels, crawling out of sight of the masters. Wingless. Broken at birth so we couldn't flee.

There were bones in the ice around us. Australopithecus. Neanderthal. Hives hung in their ribcages, hexagons in place of hearts, dripping with honey.

"Here." Adams' voice jolted me into the present.

The ice wasn't ice anymore, but rock, a slick purplish-grey, like a thin layer of mica spread over slate, but the wrong color—night instead of gold. Or it was both. Ice and stone and rock the color of desert sand. Here and now and on a planet billions of years ago.

"Dig," Adams said.

My hands moved. I knew the patterns, written into my bones with the gathering song. I was born for this, scraping honey from the walls until my skin tore. Adams kept handing me bottles, which I filled before they disappeared into her coat, more than the folds of fabric should have been able to hold.

The cave buzzed. And all the while, the song echoed. The song like the one my grandmother used to sing while cooking Sunday dinner, calling ingredients and flavors together and compelling them to be a meal. A making song. It mellified my bones. It mummified me, rewriting me in a different language. I was the god-child beneath the tree, curled at its roots. The beginning and the end, the seed of the world. Bees thrummed the air and wrote maps onto my skin. Words. Commands, compelling me to be ancient, to be terrible, to change.

A harvest song. A blinding song. A binding song.

I obeyed.

A day later, or a million years later, we climbed out of the dark. The stars turned in dizzying motion overhead. If I kept going, I could climb right out of the world into the night. Like Reyes, pulled screaming into the sky. Adams caught me by the ankle and hauled me back down. I hit the ice, scrabbled and fought her, weeping and babbling incoherently.

She dragged me back over the snow, tucked me into my tent like a worker bee sealing up a little queen in a cell of wax. She whispered in my ear, a continuation of the song, that humming buzz, and this one said *sleep, sleep.*

I obeyed.

~

We packed our gear and left without Reyes. I thought about what we'd tell his family. We didn't have a body to bring home, no explanation to offer. He disappeared and we didn't look for him, because we knew he was gone.

The honey still sang in my veins. Had we accomplished our mission? Adams hadn't said a word about the tunnels. Only the abraded skin on my hands suggested I'd been under the earth, under some earth, gathering.

I had no sense of where we were in relation to the base camp. Like Adams' story, our compasses spun, and our GPS was useless. We'd given up on the radios long ago.

That night, we pitched our tents next to a wicked-blue crevasse, a scar in the ice so deep we couldn't see past a few feet even with our lights.

"Do you know where we are?" I asked Martinez, keeping my voice low.

He shrugged, unconcerned, and I moved to help him with the tents. I wanted to ask if he'd heard anything during the storm, or what the honey felt like on his tongue. Maybe Adams had taken him under the earth, too. Maybe she'd taken us all one by one. Maybe what Reyes had seen was too much. Enough to make him stick his hand in a trap. Enough to send him screaming into the sky.

Behind us, Viader and McMann built a fire. In the back of my mind, Reyes played on a loop, the trap closing on his arm. Each strike driving the tent peg into the ice became the snap of bone.

I smelled Viader's burning flesh an instant before it began to burn. And in my mind, the street in Al-Raqqah went red-black, and the woman crawled. I turned just in time to watch Viader walk into the flames. She made no sound. Her clothes went up in an instant. Then she stood there, eyes closed, humming. I recognized the song, felt the echo in my bones. Sparks kissed her cheek, ate away the skin and heat-cracked her jaw.

"It's beautiful," she said. Or maybe she said, "I'm beautiful."

Heat seared my cheeks, leaving salt-tracks dried to crystal. When had I started crying? I agreed with Viader; she was beautiful.

She was necessary.

Patterns had to be repeated. Viader burning wasn't really Viader, she was cities turned to ash, wax melting and the sound of wings, all the queens burning in their cells, keening, and the low, sad song as the tall creatures behind the sky moved from the beginning to the end of time.

None of us tried to stop Viader when she went to the crevasse. None of us tried to catch her as she dropped, plunging into the blue. She was a meteor, streaking into the abyss, never hitting the ground.

I woke to the sound of propeller blades, and the spray of ice and snow they whipped up as the tiny plane landed. Panic slammed through me. I couldn't hear the song over the engine, then the shouting as the team sent to pull us out hit the ground, boots too loud on the snow. Hands on me; I thrashed against them, all fists and elbows. A curse, muffled, as I landed an unintentional blow.

Three sets of arms now, restraining me. A needle snapped in my arm as they tried to give me a sedative. The ice fell away beneath me. I'd been wrestled into the plane and we were leaving. I looked around for Adams in a panic. I couldn't see her, then someone pushed my head back, strapped me down with more restraints.

A high, wild keening, like the sound of the queens in their cells as the city burned. I didn't realize until much later the sound was coming from me.

It's been almost a year since the ice.

A year of therapy, of convincing myself I couldn't possibly have seen what I thought I saw. Enough time for one honorable discharge, zero contact from Adams, and three hundred and sixty-five, give or take a few, nights of dreams—cities burning, honey dripping from bones, vast shadows crossing the sky. And all that time, the song, just on the edge of hearing. Last week, it started getting louder. Yesterday, I could feel it reverberating inside my skull.

Today, I got an email from Kellet. No subject line, all lower-case: *martinez is dead. funeral at st. john redeemer, des moines, iowa. saturday 1100.*

Light slanted over the church steps, leaving Kellet and Ramone in shadow as they stood in the doorway. Ramone had his empty sleeve pinned up against the wind snatching at our clothing and hair, blowing a storm of petals around our feet. I'd either forgotten or never known that he'd lost his arm after they pulled us off the ice. What had the past year been like for him, for Kellet? Had the edges of their hearing been haunted by inhuman voices, did they dream?

"What about McMann?" I asked.

"I tried to contact him, no response." A frown touched

Kellet's lips, and I felt a twinge, a certainty that McMann was gone, and none of us had been there to witness it.

I didn't bother to ask about Adams.

Our footsteps echoed as we entered the church. A trio of women—Martinez's sisters? Cousins?—occupied the front-most pew on the left-hand side. A few others were scattered through the rest of the church, but the room was emptier than it should be.

"He shot himself." Kellet nodded toward Martinez's casket as we slid into a pew in the back.

A framed picture of Martinez, younger than when we'd known him, sat where his head would be. Draped over the middle of the casket, a spray of purple flowers gave off a sweet scent on the edge of rot.

I thought about Martinez in his tiny bathroom, knees bumping the edge of the tub as he sat on the toilet lid, lips puckered around the barrel of a gun. I'd never seen Martinez's apartment, or his bathroom. Certainly I hadn't been there when he died. Except I was there, now, bound as we had been on the ice. A unit. A hive.

Martinez's shoulders twitched, even as he fought to steady the gun. His cheeks were wet, the tears leaving glistening tracks in a face already carved by pain.

Shoot up. Shoot up, not in.

For a moment, I thought I'd spoken aloud. But the priest behind the lectern didn't pause, and neither Kellet nor Ramone looked at me. Were they seeing the coffin, or were they seeing Martinez's bathroom, too?

Martinez jerked, like he at least heard me. Like I was there and then, not here and now. He jerked, but he still fired and the bullet did its job, spraying blood and bone and brain onto the wall.

"I'm going to look for her," I said, as we stepped out of the church into the too-bright sunlight.

"We're with you," Ramone said; neither he nor Kellet had to asked who I meant, and of course they were coming with me. It was never a question.

~

"Why now?" Ramone leaned forward to be heard over the plane's engine. We'd tracked Adams to a small fishing village in the Yukon. Through the tiny windows, a network of rivers gleamed below us, the patchwork slowly resolving into detail as we descended. "Why did we wait almost a year?"

"We were scared." The engine drone swallowed my voice, but it was still just loud enough to be heard.

Kellet shot me a look, but didn't object. The look on Ramone's face was one of relief, like he was grateful someone had finally said it aloud. It was easier to breathe when I leaned back. The plane circled lower. After a year of sweat-soaked sheets and night terrors, we were going home.

We found Adams drinking in a bar converted from an old canning plant—corrugated metal walls, plain wooden furniture, the whole thing crouched on a pier jutting out over the water. It still smelled of fish, the odor laden over with sweat and beer. Peanut shells cracked underfoot. I thought of the ice cracking and tiny bones.

Adams kept her back turned, her shoulders hunched until we were close enough to touch her. Heavy cable-knit sweater, thick rubber waders, her hair cropped jagged-short. She didn't even look up when she spoke.

"I have a small plane," she said. "I can fly us out anytime."

She'd been waiting for us. Waiting while we gathered our courage. Waiting until Martinez died, the breaking point to push us into action. She finally turned, and I heard Kellet catch her breath, the smallest of sounds. Adams' eyes were gold, the color of honey, the color of fire and the stars we'd swallowed on the ice. All this time with the dreams, and she hadn't fought them. The blind things in the tunnels, the girl under the tree, the shadows, vast and slow moving behind the sky—they'd gotten inside her, and she'd changed.

The base camp Adams flew us to was smaller than the one we'd left from a year ago. Curtains divided cots set along the walls for the illusion of privacy. There was a stove, and stores, but none of us were hungry. Unlike the first base camp, the wind didn't howl outside. Only silence, the vast stretch of snow waiting beyond the walls, and the stars pricking the darkness. The ghosts were already in the room with us, the spaces of absence carved in the shadows for Reyes, Viader, Martinez, and McMann.

Kellet and Ramone retreated to their cots soon after we arrived. I was too jittery for sleep. As for Adams, I couldn't tell. I'd always found her hard to read. With her golden eyes and the new angles of her bones, it was even harder. Her impatience, her anger, seemed to have burned away. Instead, she was literally worn thin, almost flickering, like it took all her effort to stay in this world.

A fat candle sat on the table; its light sharpened the planes and hollows of Adams' face and spread the illusion of wings behind her. She retrieved a bottle of whiskey, tilted it toward me in a silent question. I nodded and watched her fill two glasses. She'd been waiting for us for a year, the strain evident in her movements. I still didn't understand why.

"What happened a year ago?" The question came out more plaintive, more broken than I intended.

Adams swallowed from her glass, lips peeling back in a grimace.

"You'll have to be more specific." Her honey-gold eyes pinned me, testing.

I didn't know how to ask about the tunnels and the gathering song. I came at it sideways.

"The mission. Did we succeed?"

"You kidding?" Adams knocked back half of her remaining drink; this time when she showed her teeth, it was wholly feral. "Soldiers who feel no pain, who keep fighting even with massive wounds, or missing limbs, soldiers who can go days without eating or sleeping? The honey was never for them. I thought you understood that."

So, she had run, when the plane came for us, and she'd never turned over the honey.

"Then why?" Why bring us on the mission at all? The map was in her head. She never needed us.

The look Adams returned was pitying. She surprised me further, covering my hands with her own. Her palms were rough, calloused, like she'd spent a year hauling nets in the cold.

"They need us to remember." Her words sparked something, a twinge of recognition. "We need them to forget."

Them. Where her hands covered mine, her skin hummed. Those things from beyond the stars, they'd fought and died and torn themselves apart. When the tall things from beyond the sky had come, signaling the end of their time, with the last dying breath of their civilization, they'd made a song. They'd flung their ghosts across the stars, casting their tattered remains into the void, hoping to find something for those echoes to hold onto, someone to remember. And like Adams said, we, the eight of us, had needed them in order to forget.

Those tall, attenuated creatures. Their footsteps extinguished stars, put out of the light of worlds. What did it mean that I'd seen them in the sky? Were they an echo of the past, or a glimpse at our future? Maybe it didn't matter. Maybe all that mattered was letting go.

I thought of Viader, falling, Reyes, vanishing into the night. Cities burning, a child buried under a tree. The seeds of a civilization that required blood and sacrifice to grow.

Adams reached into her pocket, and set a bottle on the table. Honey, the same color as her eyes. It sang, and my blood sang back. The harvest song, the lullaby. *We'll seal you up, but you'll dream, and all your years of darkness will be worthwhile.*

Gold dripped from my bones, written with history. I could taste it, curling my tongue with its sweetness so sharp it drowned everything else.

Adams touched the bottle with one finger. I shivered.

She unfolded a knife from her belt, and used the blade to nick the meat of her palm. Honey oozed to the surface. She didn't need the cave anymore. She licked the wound, glancing at me. I pressed a hand against my chest. Under my breastbone, a hollow space waited for a hive.

Adams stood, skinning her shirt over her head. Her dog tags gleamed as she turned around. Her back was covered in raised welts, smooth and white, old scars.

"The map," she said.

I stood, palm outstretched. The heat of her skin beat against me like a flame. Her scars met my touch, pearls stitched into her skin, the puncture wounds she'd received in Afghanistan. I traced my hands over the pattern. Stars, arranged in configurations eons old.

"It was never meant to show where we were going," Adams said. "But where they had been."

History, written on her skin. She guided me to one of the two remaining cots and pushed me down gently. The light from her eyes cast shadows on her cheeks. The bottle of honey appeared in her hand. Straddling me, Adams pulled the cork from the honey with her teeth. Liquid the color of a full harvest moon—ripe to bursting.

Adams dipped a finger in the honey and held it out to me. I

pictured light leaking from her eyes like tears, seeping from her pores. The harvest song howled in the dark. Shadows bent over us, long fingers needle-sharp and venom-tipped, ready to stitch through skin and bone.

I sucked her finger clean.

It wasn't sex, it was more like farewell. Adams flickered, her translucence overwhelming her solidity. My hands closed on empty air, but the memories kept flowing through me, hers and theirs.

I was in the cave in Afghanistan. Thousands of hexagonal cells covered the walls. Needle-thin legs brushed my skin, then the first stinger entered me. My body arched, my flesh trying to escape my bones. I was being torn apart, threaded back together. Adams' map wrote itself onto me, stars burnt into my being in a pattern from before the world. But there was no pain. Bones dripped honey, skeletons embedded in the walls, but still living. They remembered. Everything. Wings beat inside the remains of their papered skin, a steady hum. A whole lost world, resurrected inside the dead, calling them—calling me—to sing.

There's a certain quality of cold where temperature becomes color. Ramone, Kellet, and I walked into a solid wash of it, thick enough to feel. I'd shown them the map on my skin, and they'd agreed, we had to finish it out on the ice where it began.

We didn't go far, just enough to be alone with the wind. Out here, we would hear Reyes when he screamed. We'd see Viader when she rose like a meteor out of the dark.

"I dream about Viader sometimes," Kellet said as we huddled around a Coleman lantern in our tent. "Her flesh is still burning. She's only got one eye. There are holes in her skin and she's holding embers in her jaws."

"Reyes came to see me," Ramone said. His right sleeve hung by his side, his left hand held a mug filled with vodka. I'd never noticed the paler band of skin on the fourth finger before.

"He came to my bedroom window. His breath fogged the glass, so I knew he was really there. His hair was all matted. His teeth were broken, and his eyes were the color of dried blood. He tapped on my window."

Kellet put her hand on Ramone's knee. I could feel myself spreading in the wind. Still here, already gone.

"I didn't know what else to do, so I let him in. He crawled under the covers with me. I thought he'd be cold from being out on the ice for so long, but he was warm. He smelled like red meat and wet dog.

"He put his head on my chest." Ramone touched his knuckles to the spot. "And then he just lay there, listening to my heart."

Ramone swallowed the rest of his drink, squeezing his eyes closed.

"The next morning, he was gone. That was the first time I tried to kill myself. I took pills, but then I chickened out and called 911."

I put my hand on his other knee. Outside, the ice sang.

"I watched Martinez kill himself," I said, my own unburdening. I'd already given the honey Al-Raqqah, everything else I had to give. This was the last thing.

"I wish we knew what happened to McMann," Ramone said.

"He's probably waiting for us," I gestured at the tent flap.

Kellet reached for my hand across Ramone's knees. She tangled her fingers with mine, and our joined hands covered Ramone's one good hand. My lips brushed the corner of Ramone's mouth. He closed his eyes again. We went soft, slow, all three of us together. It still wasn't sex. It was a map, a shared history, a surrendering of our pain.

When they left in the dark, I didn't hear them go.

I cut a bottle of honey from my veins, bled it into the glass, then drank it whole. Burning like Viader, I walked out into the cold.

My body is going up in flames, bits of me flaking away to ash. Martinez is here. I can see the stars through the hole in his skull. Reyes lopes beside me. Viader is an angel. Adams' footsteps crunch through the snow, getting farther and farther apart. Ramone and Kellet, even McMann, they're all here. We're separate, but together, strung across vast distances, never alone.

There are tall, vast shapes moving across the sky. They have no faces. Their skin blushes like the aurora borealis, studded with stars. They are the beginning and the end. They harvest the honey; they sing the song. The wind dies down, and it's the only thing I can hear. History, writing itself onto my bones. The dead being reborn.

Harvest. Gather. Change.

Open your bones, they sing. *Make space inside your skin.*

Let us in.

THE SECRET OF FLIGHT

The Secret of Flight
Written by Owen Covington
Directed by Raymond Barrow
Prologue
Act 1
Scene 1

SETTING: THE STAGE IS BARE EXCEPT FOR A BACKDROP SCREEN showing the distant manor house.

The lights should start at 1/8 and rising to 3/4 luminance as the scene progresses.

AT RISE: The corpse of a man lies CENTER STAGE. POLICEMAN enters STAGE RIGHT, led by a YOUNG BOY carrying garden shears. The boy's cheek is smeared with dirt. The boy points with the shears and tugs the policeman's hand. POLICEMAN crosses to CENTER STAGE and kneels beside the corpse. BOY exits STAGE RIGHT.

POLICEMAN puts his ear to the dead man's chest to listen for breath or a pulse. His expression grows puzzled. POLICEMAN straightens and unbuttons the dead man's shirt.

He reaches into the corpse's chest cavity and withdraws his hands, holding a starling (Director's note: use C's, already trained). POLICEMAN holds starling out toward audience, as though asking for help. Starling appears dead, but after a moment stirs and takes flight, passing over the audience before vanishing. (Director's note: C assures me this is possible. C concealed somewhere to collect the bird?). POLICEMAN startles and falls back. (BLACKOUT)

~

LEADING LADY VANISHES!
Herald Star—October 21, 1955
Betsy Trimingham, Arts & Culture

Last night's opening of *The Secret of Flight* at The Victory Theater will surely go down as one of the most memorable and most bizarre in history. Not for the play itself, but for the dramatic disappearance of leading lady Clara Hill during the play's final scene.

As regular readers of this column know, *The Secret of Flight* was already fraught with rumor before the curtain ever rose. Until last night, virtually nothing was known of *The Secret of Flight* save the title, the name of its director, Raymond Barrow, and of course, the name of its playwright, Owen Covington.

Raymond Barrow kept the play shrouded in mystery, refusing to release the names of the cast, their roles, or a hint of the story. He did not even allow the play to run in previews for the press. Speculation ran rampant. Was it a clever tactic to build interest, or was it a simple lack of confidence after the critical and financial failure of Barrow's last two plays?

Whatever Barrow's reasoning, it is now inconsequential. All that is on anyone's lips is the indisputable fact that at the culmination of the play, before the eyes of 743 witnesses, myself included, Clara Hill vanished into thin air.

For those not in attendance, allow me to set the scene. Clara Hill, in the role of Vivian Westwood, was alone on stage. The painted screen behind Hill was lit faintly, so as to suggest a window just before dawn. As the light rose slowly behind the false glass, Hill turned to face the audience. It appeared as though she might deliver a final soliloquy, but instead, she slowly raised her arms. As her arms neared their full extension above her head, she collapsed, folding in upon herself and disappearing.

Her heavy beaded dress was left on the stage. In her place, a column of birds—starlings, I believe—boiled upward. Their numbers seemed endless. They spread across the theater's painted ceiling, then all at once, they pulled together into a tight, black ribbon twisting over the heads of the theater patrons. You can well imagine the chaos that ensued. Women lifted their purses to protect their heads, men ineffectually swatted at the birds with their theater programs. There were screams. Then there was silence. The birds were gone. Vanished like Clara Hill.

Was it all a grand trick, a part of the show? The stage lights snapped off, the curtain fell abruptly, and we were ushered out of the theater, still dazed by what we had seen.

As of the writing of this column, neither Barrow nor any other member of the cast or crew has come forward to offer comment. Dear readers, as you know, I have been covering the theater scene for more years than I care to name. In that time, I have seen every trick in the book: Pepper's Ghost, hidden trap doors, smoke and mirrors, misdirection. I can assure you, none of those were in evidence last night. What we witnessed was a true, I hesitate to use the word miracle, so I will say phenomenon.

Prior to last night, no one save those directly involved with

The Secret of Flight had ever heard the name Clara Hill. Last night, she vanished. Her name will remain, known for the mystery surrounding it, but I do not think the woman herself will ever be seen again.

∾

Personal Correspondence
Raymond Barrow

December 18, 2012

Dear Will,

I know it's absurd, writing you a letter. But a man my age is allowed his eccentricities. 88 years old, Will. Can you imagine it? I certainly never intended to be this old. The young have a vague notion they will live forever, but have any of them thought about what that really means? To live this long, to outlive family and friends. Well, since I *have* lived this long, I will indulge myself and write to you, even though it's old fashioned, and there's no hope of a response. Forgive an old fool. Lord knows I feel in need of forgiveness sometimes.

It's been 57 years since Clara disappeared. Aside from you, she was my only friend. I wish you could have met her, Will. I think you would have got along—comrades in your infernal secrecy, your refusal to let anyone else in, but somehow always willing to listen to me go on about my problems.

I'm all alone now. The only one left besides the goddamn bird, the one Clara left me. It's still alive. Can you fucking believe it? Starlings are only supposed to live 15, 20 years at the most. I looked it up.

Rackham. That's what Clara called him. I didn't want to use him in the play, but Clara insisted, and now I'm stuck with the damn thing. He's not...natural. He's like Clara. I don't think he *can* die.

I'm ashamed to admit it, maybe you'll think less of me, but I've tried to kill him—more than once. He speaks to me in Clara's goddamned voice. Starlings are mimics, everyone knows that, but this is different. I tried to drown him in a glass of brandy. I tried to wring his neck and throw him into the fire. Do you know what he did? He flapped right back out into my face with his wings singed and still smoking.

To add insult to injury, he threw my own goddamn voice back at me, a perfect imitation. He said, "Leading ladies are a disease. You breathe them in without meaning to, and they lie dormant in your system. Years later, you realize you're infected, and there's absolutely nothing you can do about it. You spend the rest of your life dying slowly of them, and there's no such thing as a cure."

Do you remember? I said that to you, years ago. At least it sounds like the kind of pretentious thing I would say, doesn't it? I was probably trying to be clever or impress you. Did it work?

Pretentious or not, it is true. I'm infected, and Clara is my disease. She's here, under my skin, even though she's gone. Everyone's gone, Will. Even you.

Well, goddamn you all to hell then for leaving me here alone.

Yours, ever,

Raymond

Items Displayed in the Lobby of the New Victory Theater

1. Playbill—*The Secret of Flight* (1955)—Good Condition (unsigned)

2. Playbill—*Onward to Victory!* (1950)—Fair Condition (signed—Raymond Barrow, Director; William Hunter, Marion Fairchild, Anna Hammond, cast)

3. Complete Script—*The Secret of Flight* (1955)—Good Condition (signed, Owen Covington)

4. Press Clipping—*Herald Star*—June 17, 1925

"Victory Theater Under New Ownership"

A staged publicity photo shows Richard Covington shaking hands with former theater owner Terrance Dent. Richard's brother, Arthur Covington, stands to the side. The article details plans for the theater's renovation and scheduled reopening. The article provides brief background on the brothers' recent immigration to America from England. A second photograph shows the family posed and preparing to board a ship to America. Arthur Covington stands toward the left of the frame. Richard stands next to his wife, Elizabeth, his arm at her waist. Elizabeth rests both hands on the shoulders of their three-year-old son, Owen, keeping him close. None of the family members are smiling. To the right of the frame, standing with the luggage, is an unidentified young woman with dark hair thought to be Owen Covington's nanny. A shadow near the woman's right shoulder vaguely suggests the shape of a bird.

5. Press Clipping—*Herald Star*—August 7, 1976

"Fire Destroys Historic Victory Theater"

A half-page image shows the burned and partially collapsed walls of the Victory Theater. Dark smudges above the ruins show a sky still heavy with smoke. Certain patches might be mistaken for a densely-packed flock of birds. The article offers scant detail beyond that the fire started early in the morning of August 6, cause unknown. The blaze took several hours to bring under control. No casualties reported.

6. Press Clipping—*Herald Star*—December 1, 2012

"A New Life for the Victory Theater"

The image at the top of the page shows the exterior of the New Victory Theater. A brushed stainless steel sign bears the theater's name, and below it, an LED marquee screen shows the word Welcome. The article discusses the successful fundraising campaign leading to the construction of the New Victory Theater at the site of the original building. Brief mention is made of the architects' intent to incorporate elements salvaged from the old theater into the new design, however all the historic pieces are held by an anonymous collector who was unwilling to donate or sell them. The majority of the page is given over to pictures of the gala opening. The article notes that Raymond Barrow was invited to serve as honorary chair of the event, but he declined.

～

Incomplete Draft of *Murmuration* by Arthur Covington— typed manuscript with handwritten notes

(CLAIRE glances over her shoulder before hurrying to EDWARD's desk, rifling through the drawers.)

CLAIRE (to herself): Where is it? Where is he keeping it?

(As her search grows more frantic, she fails to notice EDWARD entering the room. EDWARD grabs CLAIRE by the arm.)

EDWARD: Are you trying to steal from me?

CLAIRE: You stole from me first. Where is it?

EDWARD: Stole from you? You live in my house. You eat my food. Everything you *own* is mine.

(CLAIRE tries to strike him. EDWARD catches her hand. He leans close, his jaw clenched in anger.)

EDWARD: Show me how it works, and I might forget about your attempted thievery.

(CLAIRE doesn't answer. EDWARD grips her harder, shaking her.)

EDWARD: There's some trick to it. Look at this.

(EDWARD rolls up his sleeve and shows CLAIRE a long gash on his arm.)

EDWARD: I shouldn't be able to bleed anymore. I shouldn't be able to die.

CLAIRE (her voice hard): It was never going to work for you, Edward. You can't steal a feather from a bird and expect to fly, or steal a scale from a fish and breathe under water. You can't change the nature of a thing just by dressing it up as something else.

EDWARD: Then tell me. Tell me how it works, and I'll let you go.

(ANDREW enters STAGE RIGHT, freezing when he see CLAIRE and EDWARD. Unnoticed, ANDREW hangs back, watching. EDWARD strikes CLAIRE. CLAIRE doesn't react. He knocks her down, pinning her, and puts his hands around her throat.)

God, this is shit. The whole thing is shit. It isn't enough. It doesn't change what happened. It doesn't make up for the fact that Andrew *just stood there and did nothing. I stood in the hall and listened to them yell, and then when I finally got up the courage to go into the room, I froze instead of helping Clara. Not that she seemed to need my help. Speaking of which, what about the birds? How the hell do I stage the birds? No one would believe it. I don't believe it, and I was there. The room filling up with beaks and feathers and wings. Hundreds of birds coming out of nowhere while Clara lay there, and Richard throttled her, and I did nothing.*

What the hell am I doing, writing this thing? Shit.

**SUICIDE ATTEMPT THWARTED AT THE VICTORY
THEATER!**
Herald Star—**April 19, 1955**
Betsy Trimingham, Arts & Culture

There is a hero in our midst, dear readers. One, it seems, who has been hiding in plain sight at the Victory Theater. For months now, the theater scene has been buzzing with speculation over the Victory's latest production, all of which is being kept strictly under wraps.

Last night, however, one cat escaped the bag. Owen Covington, son of late theater owner Richard Covington, prevented an unknown woman from leaping to her death from the theater's roof. As it so happens, not only is young Mr. Covington a hero, he is the author of Raymond Barrow's mysterious new play.

Although he declined to comment upon his heroic actions, I was able to unearth one piece of information at least. Owen Covington's play, scheduled to open at the Victory later this year, is titled *The Secret of Flight*.

As for the young woman whose life Mr. Covington saved, could she be a member of the cast? Has Raymond Barrow unearthed the next darling of the theater scene? Or is she merely some poor seamstress working behind the scenes? More scandalously, could she be Raymond Barrow's lover? The only clue Mr. Covington provided during my repeated requests for comment was an unwitting one. He said, and I quote: *Clara is none of your business.*

Who is Clara? Rest assured, dear readers, I intend to find out!

Personal Correspondence
Raymond Barrow

December 20, 2012

Dear Will,

Here I am, at it again. The old fool with his pen and paper. Did you know they reopened the Victory Theater earlier this month? Not *the* Victory Theater, of course, a new one with the same name where the old one burned. They wanted me to be on their godforsaken Board of Trustees or some bullshit. I almost wish I'd taken the meeting in person just to see the look on their bootlicking, obsequious little faces when I said no.

God, I'm an ass, Will. I was an ass back in the day, and I'm an ass now, just a donkey of a different color, as they say.

Maybe it's the new theater that has me dredging up all these memories. It's like poking an old wound, though there were some good times mixed in with the bad. There was Clara. And of course, there was you. If you could have seen.... Well, it doesn't matter. I cocked it all up in the end.

I was so excited when Owen Covington brought me the script of his new play. He was a virtual unknown, this snot-nosed kid who couldn't hold his liquor, but God help me, I thought he would save my career. Old money and all that. I didn't know his family had fallen into ruin. His father murdered, his uncle a suicide. All their lovely money pissed away. I should have done my research, but live and learn.

The whole thing was a disaster from beginning to end. Even before Clara, before.... The press was at my throat from the get-go, desperate to see me fail. Then goddamn Owen Covington goes and tries to kill himself. Like nephew like uncle, I suppose.

Clara saved his life. She stopped him from jumping off the Victory's roof, though the newspapers reported it the other way around. Made Covington out to be a hero. What was that horrid woman's name? Betty? Betsy Trimblesomething? She was the one who gave you that absolutely scathing review as my leading man in *Onward to Victory!* God I hated her.

But there I go, rambling. I was telling you about Owen and Clara. After she saved him, Clara told me how much she wanted to let Owen jump. She showed me her palms. They were all cut up where she dug her nails in trying to stop herself from grabbing him. But she couldn't. She told me she couldn't help saving Owen, no matter how much she hated his family.

That was the closest she ever came to telling me anything about herself. Of course, I knew bits and pieces from Owen, not that I believed half of it. But then here was Clara, someone I trusted, saying the same thing. She said she'd known Owen as a child, that she'd been his nanny, and he was the only good thing to come out of the Covington family.

I asked her what the hell she was talking about, she and Owen looked exactly the same age. I thought maybe she'd finally open up all the way, maybe I'd finally get the truth out of her. Hell, I'd have settled for knowing her real name because I'm sure as shit it wasn't *Clara Hill.*

Instead of answering, Clara pointed out a flock of starlings. We were up on the roof of the theater, smoking, the way you and I used to do after rehearsals. That was the first place you kissed me. Do you remember? I was certain my mouth would taste like ash and whatever rotgut we were drinking and you'd be disgusted, but you weren't.

Are you angry that I spent time with Clara up there? There wasn't anything between us. We were friends. Actually, we became friends because of the roof. We'd both been going up there separately to smoke, and then we banged into each other one day and started taking our cigarette breaks together. It's a lucky thing we never burned the goddamn theater down.

I suppose that's how she found Owen, snuck up for a quick drag on her own and ended up saving his life.

Anyway, the birds. The sun was just starting to rise, and the birds were winging back and forth across the sky like one giant creature instead of hundreds of little ones. Clara watched them for a while; then she said, "Can you imagine what it's like, Raymond? Being part of something larger than yourself, knowing exactly where you fit in the world, then having it all ripped away from you, and finding yourself utterly and completely alone?"

God, Will, it's been years, and I can still hear her asking it. Even when she asked it, it had been two years since you'd been gone. When you died, Will…. Well, I knew exactly what Clara was talking about. You were everything, and I couldn't even be with you at the end. I couldn't tell anyone how my heart had been ripped out, or cry at your grave.

Things are different now, but there's no one I want to cry for the way I wanted to for you.

Maybe that's why Clara and I got along so well. We were alike in our loneliness. We both had things we couldn't tell anyone about ourselves. Not all ghosts are about guilt. That's something else Clara told me once, and I understand her now. Some ghosts are about sorrow, and loss. But God, Will, of all the ghosts to have haunt me, why did it have to be hers, and not yours?

Ray

Incomplete Draft of *Murmuration* by Arthur Covington— typed manuscript with handwritten notes

(EDWARD and CLAIRE face each other in EDWARD's office, the same setting as their earlier confrontation. Light flickers through a screen painted to look like a window, suggesting a storm. CLAIRE holds a gun pointed at EDWARD.)

EDWARD: Give me the gun, Claire. We both know you won't shoot me.

CLAIRE: You don't know the first thing about me. You have no idea what I'll do.

EDWARD: Elizabeth is upstairs. She'll hear the shot and call the police. There's nowhere for you to go. You'll be caught, and you'll hang.

CLAIRE (laughing bitterly): It doesn't matter. They can't kill me. It doesn't matter what you took from me, I still can't die. But you can.

(CLAIRE steadies the gun. EDWARD finally shows a hint of fear.)

EDWARD: Claire, be reasonable. I can—

CLAIRE: No, you can't. You can't do anything. You tried to steal from me, but my life can't be stolen, not that way. When you couldn't steal it, you broke it, and now I can't fly away either. I can't leave this place, not while you're alive.

(EDWARD reaches for CLAIRE. OWEN enters STAGE RIGHT, dressed for bed. He looks between CLAIRE and EDWARD, confused, and takes a step toward CLAIRE.)

OWEN: Will you tell my bedtime story?

(CLAIRE fires. EDWARD falls, and OWEN puts his hands over his ears and screams. CLAIRE stands still for a moment, then drops to her knees. Running footsteps can be heard from offstage.)

CLAIRE (barely audible): It didn't work. I'm still here. Oh, God, it didn't work.

This is still shit. That's how it happened, but no one will believe it. The truth is too strange.

Clara shot Richard while Owen watched, and she didn't run away. She let them arrest her. She confessed, but there was never a trial. She vanished out of the cell where they were holding her. The police were mystified.

Shit. I could write my play closer to the truth. No one would know the difference except Elizabeth. Then she'd start asking questions. What's the point? I can never produce this goddamn play, for her sake and for Owen's.

Clara shot Richard with Owen standing right there watching. He doesn't remember, at least not consciously. His young mind couldn't cope, so he shuttered the information away, but something like that doesn't go away completely. It changes a person. It leaves a stain.

I took Owen to see a hypnotist. Elizabeth doesn't know. Dr. Samson put Owen into a trance, and Owen recounted word for word the whole exchange between Clara and Richard. In real life, Owen didn't walk into the room the way I wrote it in the play. He was hiding under Richard's desk, playing a game. He wanted to jump out and scare Clara. He saw the whole thing.

That's not the worst of it though. After describing his father's murder, Owen started laughing. Dr. Samson thought it might be some sort of defense mechanism, his mind, even hypnotized, trying to protect him. He asked Owen about it, and Owen said he was laughing because the bird-lady was making pictures in the sky. She was telling the starlings which way to fly, like she used to on the boat from England.

God help me, he was talking about Clara. I'm more sure now than ever—she isn't human.

~

TRAGEDY STRIKES THE VICTORY THEATER!
Herald Star—October 10, 1955
Betsy Trimingham, Arts & Culture

Owen Covington's life was cut tragically short yesterday when he was struck by a subway train. As regular readers of this column know, Mr. Covington was both a playwright, and a hero. I spoke with a police officer who was "unable to comment on an ongoing investigation." He declined to say whether foul play was suspected, but I do wonder how a young man in the prime of his life could simply slip from the subway platform in front of an oncoming train.

Keep your eyes on this column, dear readers. The truth will out eventually, and I will report on it.

Personal Correspondence
Raymond Barrow

December 22, 2012

Dearest Will,

Here I am again with my pen and paper. I've been thinking a lot about paper lately, the pages Owen had from his uncle when he first pitched me the idea of his play. He wouldn't let me read them for myself, he just sort of waved them around in front of me and said he was going to use them as the basis for his script. He only had fragments, Arthur Covington killed himself without ever finishing the play.

Of course I read those fragments eventually. It wasn't snooping, just protecting my investment. Besides, it was Owen's fault for passing out drunk on my couch with the damn pages still in his jacket pocket.

It was all there—Owen's father Richard, his uncle Arthur, and Clara. Of course in the play they were Edward, Andrew, and Claire, but it's obvious who they were supposed to be. Except it was fiction. Fantasy. Or maybe I was too stubborn to see what was right in front of my face.

This is what I think now: Owen's father did something terrible to Clara a long time ago. Clara murdered him, and Owen witnessed the whole thing. Of course, Owen didn't remember it happening, not consciously. Trauma and all that. But on some primal level he did remember. He was in love with Clara, or he thought he was. It was all tangled up in guilt and her killing his father, like some goddamned soap opera, but real.

Clara loved Owen too, in her own way. Not the way he wanted her to, but like a mother bird that hatches an egg and realizes a cuckoo has snuck its own egg into her nest. Her baby is gone and she's accidentally raised the cuckoo's child, but she defends it and she cares for it because that's her nature, and it's not the baby's fault after all.

It's why Owen tried to kill himself. He thought it would set her free. And it's why Clara couldn't let him.

At first I didn't believe it, any of it, but the more time I spent around them, the more time I spent with Clara…. God, Will. You were gone, and I didn't have anyone else. I thought I could help Clara, do one good thing in my life and save her. I started thinking maybe Owen was right. Maybe if no one in his family was left alive, she could finally leave. I didn't…I just bumped him, really. He lost his balance. He was so utterly piss drunk, he probably didn't even feel it when the train hit him.

I never told Clara, but I think she knew. She was the one who insisted the play go on, in Owen's memory. I tried to convince her to leave. I'd just killed a man. I couldn't think straight. I was raving, shouting at her. I think I almost hit her. But Clara just looked at me with this incredible pity in her eyes. She put her hand on my arm, and said, "Grief can change the nature of a person, Ray, when nothing else can. Enough loss, and it weighs you down, you forget how to fly."

She told me everything I needed to know, Will, but I didn't know how to listen.

I didn't know how to listen when you told me you needed help all those years ago. The empty bottles, the needles; I refused to see it because I didn't want it to be true. I should have listened. I miss you, Will.

Yours, always,

Ray

Personal Correspondence
Raymond Barrow

October 20, 1955

Dear Ray,

This is it, our big night. *The Secret of Flight* opens, and I don't know what will happen after that. There's something I'm going to try, Ray, and if it doesn't work, I might not see you again. So I wanted to say thank you for everything you've done for me, and everything you tried to do. You're a good friend. I don't have many of those, so believe me when I say our time together meant a lot to me even though I couldn't tell you everything about me. Instead, I'm giving you this story. It's the best I can do, Ray. I hope you'll understand.

Love,

Clara

The Starling and the Fox

Once upon a time, there was a fox, and there was a starling. They weren't really a fox and a starling, they only looked that way from the outside, but for the purposes of this story, those names will do. This happened far away, in another country, many years ago.

The starling was flying, minding her own business, when she spotted a tree with lovely branches. She landed on one and discovered a fox lying across the tree's roots, crying piteously.

"Oh, they have killed me," the fox said. "I shall die if you don't aid me."

The starling couldn't see anything wrong with the fox, but she didn't see the harm in helping him either.

"What is it you need, sir fox?" she asked him.

"Only a feather from your beautiful wing, and I will be well again," the fox said.

The starling was doubtful. She looked again and she couldn't see any blood on the fox's fine fur, but he continued moaning as she looked him over, and it certainly sounded as if he might die.

The starling chose one of the small feathers near the top of her wing. She didn't think it would hurt to pull it out, and she didn't think she would miss it either. As she took hold of it in her beak, the fox cried out again.

"Not that feather! Only the long feather at the tip of your wing will do. The straight and glossy one that shines like a still pool at midnight, even when you think there is no light at all."

The starling thought the fox sounded a little foolish with his poetic language and the way he carried on, but the fox rolled on his back, weeping, and put a paw over his eyes. His tongue lolled from his mouth, and surely he would die at any moment if she did not help him.

The starling took hold of her longest and straightest feather with her beak, and pulled. It hurt, worse than anything she had ever felt, like the stars and the moon and the sun going out all at once.

"Good. Now bring it down to me, quickly!" the fox said, jumping to all fours, even though he had been at death's door a moment ago.

Dazed with pain, the starling hopped down to him, half tumbling as she went. She presented the feather to the fox.

"Are you saved now?" she asked him.

"Very much so," the fox replied, and his eyes were bright.

"Then I will take my leave," the starling said.

She spread her wings, but when she tried to take flight, she found she could not. Without her longest, straightest feather, she couldn't fly. She leapt toward the sky again and again, but crashed back to the ground every time.

The fox watched her impassively through all her attempts.

"Help me, sir fox," she said when she had finally exhausted herself.

"Surely I shall," he said, and stepped forward, snapped her up in his jaws, and swallowed her whole.

This is the moral of the story: You should never trust a wild animal. A fox cannot change its nature no matter how it dresses itself up, or what fine words it uses. It will always hunger. If you let your guard down, even for a moment, it will devour you whole.

~

iPhone Audio and Video Recording
Raymond Barrow

December 26, 2012

[The image swings, showing the floor, a man's feet, and a desk cluttered with papers. A starling perches on a corner of the desk, briefly visible before the camera turns to show the face of Raymond Barrow.]

BARROW: There, you see, Will? I've been dragged kicking and screaming into the 21st century after all. My great niece, Sarah's daughter, gave me one of those infernal iPhone things. They were all over for Christmas yesterday, and spent most of the day showing me how to use it. Sarah suggested I might like to record some of my personal recollections of the good old days, something to preserve for generations to come. Ha! If the future is interested in a washed up old has-been who failed at every important thing he ever turned his hand to, then I pity them. But there is something I want to show you, so maybe this thing will be good for something after all.

[The camera turns to face outward again, the image bouncing while Barrow holds the phone in front of him as he walks. The camera catches glimpses of an ornate entryway, a crystal chandelier, a sweeping staircase. Carvings, hangings, sketches, and paintings on the walls depict birds of all kinds. The camera approaches a massive grandfather clock standing next to a door set beneath the curving staircase. The wooden case is chased with mother of pearl, showing a heron standing placidly among a cluster of reeds.]

BARROW: You see, I did all right for myself in the end. Not that I deserved to, but life isn't fair, is it?

[Barrow reaches for the door, holding the phone steady in his other hand. A flight of stairs leads down. There's a rustle from behind the camera, and Rackham, the starling, flies past Barrow's shoulder, disappearing down the stairs. Barrow stumbles, catching himself against the wall, but doesn't fall.]

BARROW: Damn bird will be the death of me.

[The image is dark as Barrow gropes his way to the bottom of the stairs, and flicks on a light. The camera shows rows of red velvet seats on a raked floor, facing a stage. The curtains are open, the set bare save for a painted screen backdrop, meant to look like a window.]

BARROW: It's the Victory Theater. I bought up everything they could salvage after the fire, and had it all restored. What they couldn't restore, I had rebuilt, exact replicas.

[The image wavers again as Barrow moves to a row of seats halfway to the stage. He sits, steadying the camera against the back of the chair in front of him.]

BARROW: I salvaged too much, Will. I was right, all those years ago when I said leading ladies are a disease. I've been carrying Clara in my blood for fifty-seven years, and there isn't any cure. All I ever wanted to do was help her, Will, but I think I know why she chose me. It's what she said about ghosts, and loss, and sorrow. A man can't change his own nature, but the world can change it for him if he lets his guard down. I let my guard down. I fell in love with you. I left myself open, and where did it get me?

[Barrow doesn't move, but the house lights in the theater dim, and the lights begin to rise slowly on the stage. As the lights reach full, they reveal a woman with dark hair, wearing a beaded gown, standing center stage.]

BARROW: That's her, Will. It's Clara.

[There's a faint translucence to Clara's form, but the starling flies from behind the camera and lands on Clara's shoulder. She smiles.]

BARROW (softly): That's what all my love earned me, Will. A ghost, but the wrong one.

[Clara turns toward the camera, and the man behind it. Her expression is sad, but fond. She smiles, but it's pained. Clara raises her arms. As they read their full extension, birds pour forth from the spot where she stands. Her dress falls, crumpled, to the floor. Dozens, hundreds of starlings boil up toward the ceiling like a cloud of smoke. When they reach the ceiling, they spread outward.

Barrow tilts the camera to show the birds as they pull together into a tight formation and fly toward him. He nearly drops the phone, and the view swings to show him in profile as the birds stream around him. Their wings brush his hair, his skin. His cheeks are wet.

The murmuration flows through the theater. The birds make no noise in their flight. Barrow steadies the phone, turning the camera to face him again. The birds are gone. He is alone.]

BARROW: It's the same thing every night. Every goddamn night for fifty-seven years. I tried to set her free, and she came back. She came back, Will, so why the hell didn't you?

[Barrow fumbles with the camera for a moment. The rustle of wings sounds and the starling lands on Barrow's shoulder. The recording ends.]

CROSSING

EMMA ROSE IS FOUR YEARS OLD THE FIRST TIME SHE ENTERS THE
ocean alone. All her life, she's lived with the beach at the end of
her street. Her parents carried her into the waves the week she
was born. When she learned to stand, they taught her to float.
Older still, they showed her how to stretch her body out long,
how to reach, and turn her head to breathe, letting the water
guide her like a friend.

Now, her parents watch from towels on the shore. Sun
reflects off the Dover chalk cliffs so they shine brilliant white.
The wind plays with Emma Rose's curls, and the tide garlands
her toes with foam. She steps carefully and the water swirls up
to her knees, her waist. There's a small moment of doubt, but
surely the water will keep her safe. She knows it as well as she
knows the sound of her father's voice, the touch of her mother's
hand.

Goose-pimples fade as she adjusts and the water shapes
itself around her. Squinting, she pretends she can see all the
way to France. Her parents showed her pictures in a book
holding frozen moments of their lives before her. Her mother
with curls so much like Emma Rose's, her father with a

smudge of flour on his nose, each of them proudly holding up a tray of pastries they made in the cooking class where they met.

Looking toward the land of her parents' stories, Emma Rose knows she will cross the water one day. Not in a boat; she will swim.

Emma Rose stands on her tippy toes, then lets the water take her. She floats, lying on her stomach, putting her face in the waves. She opens her eyes.

Through the salt sting, the world blurs blue and grey. She lets a few bubbles escape to rise around her like pearls. Just as she's about to turn her head to breathe, a face appears below her.

The eyes are grey, like Emma Rose's, the color of waves under a sullen sky. The woman's hair floats around her head, long and straight, tinted green like she's been under water a long time. She smiles.

Emma Rose is so startled, she screams, and cold saltwater rushes into her mouth. Panicked, she forgets everything her parents taught her. Her limbs won't cooperate. She can't lift her face out of the water. She can't remember which way is up.

Then hands catch her. Her father lifts her out of the water, and maybe the woman pushes her from below. Her father pats her back and she coughs water.

"Shhh," her mother whispers. "It's okay."

They make a protective circle around her with their bodies, standing knee deep in the waves. Emma Rose cries, shock and fading fear. She clings to her father, her head on his shoulder, while her mother strokes her back. When her sobs turn to hiccupping coughs, her father carries her back to the shore.

"What happened out there, jellyfish?" her father asks.

His eyes are blue, like the water when the sun is bright and borrows pieces of the sky to wear like a gown. Her mother's eyes are deep brown, like the water under the moon. No one has ever been able to explain to Emma Rose where her grey eyes come from.

Except once, her mother told Emma Rose she dreamed of the ocean the night she was born. Sometimes Emma Rose secretly believes she's a princess from under the sea. Her parents found her on the shore, curled up in a giant oyster shell. The woman under the water must be a princess, too, a secret one, just like her.

"I…" Emma Rose hesitates. "I saw a fish. It surprised me."

Emma Rose doesn't dare peek to see if her parents believe her. The lie fizzes in her stomach, making her feel bad and good at the same time.

"Okay, jellyfish." Her father smoothes her water-wet curls. "That's enough for today. We can try again tomorrow."

Her parents have always taught her not to quit when something is hard, but to keep going until it isn't scary anymore. Emma Rose takes her father's hand on one side, and her mother's on the other. She walks between them up the path leading toward home. Next time, she promises herself she won't be frightened, no matter what she sees.

Emma Rose is eleven years old the next time she sees the woman in the water, even though she swims in the ocean almost every day. Her bones have grown long under her skin, her body stretching like taffy. She wears her curls pulled back now, making herself sleeker.

She's on the cusp of turning twelve. Tomorrow is her birthday, and she's celebrating with friends. Her parents sent them to the beach with a hamper stuffed with food. Cold chicken. Home-baked bread. Lemonade in a glass bottle. A cake, layered with sponge and jam and frosted white, topped with the reddest strawberries.

Best of all, the girls are allowed to be alone. No parents to supervise them. They shriek and run, daring the edge of the waves. They splash each other, and pretend to be mad, then make up again. They braid strands of seaweed, making bracelets and necklaces and crowns.

None of the other girls know the water the way Emma Rose does, but she pretends to be like them. Rather than swimming, she stands waist-deep, dunking the other girls under the water and allowing them to dunk her in turn. She plays chicken, Bethany's legs draped over her shoulders as they charge toward Sara and Maureen.

When they grow tired, they troop to the blanket spread on the shore, falling on the picnic like locusts. Then they lie for a while with their heads in each other's laps, forming a lopsided circle as their stomachs settle.

Emma Rose ends up with her head in Corinne's lap. She's only known Corinne for two years; Corinne's parents moved from Cornwall and she had to join their class halfway through the year. Sara, Maureen, and Bethany, she's known since they were all five years old.

"Are you going to cut the cake?" Maureen asks after a few minutes, growing bored and fidgety.

Maureen has red-gold hair that Emma Rose has always admired, and freckles scattered across the bridge of her nose. Her eyes are bluer than Emma Rose's father's—like the ocean in pictures where the beaches are white sand and palms trees cast angular shadows on the ground.

Maureen sits up, upsetting the circle. Corinne's legs twitch under Emma Rose's head, but Emma Rose doesn't move for a moment, just to see what happens. Corinne's shadow falls over her as Corinne sits up, and Emma Rose feels the muscles of Corinne's legs, imagining what they would feel like stretching and bunching through the water.

Corinne peers down at her. Her eyes are a color Emma Rose

can't quite name. Not brown, but not green either. Like the water when it's choppy, sand stirred into the waves and catching the light, glinting with flecks of gold. Corinne drapes the seaweed crown she braided over Emma Rose's brow. It's damp and cold and smells of salt, but Emma Rose doesn't shiver.

"Now you look like a fairy queen," Corinne says.

She doesn't quite smile, but her lips do something that changes her face, and it brings a fluttering tightness to Emma Rose's stomach. She sits up too quickly, and the seaweed crown falls into her lap with a wet splat.

Maureen hands Emma Rose the cake knife, and Bethany passes plates around. Corinne touches Emma Rose's wrist.

"You have to make a wish."

Emma Rose pretends her face is underwater, seeing how long she can go before she turns her head to breathe. She's still holding her breath when the last slice of cake is cut, and only then does she let it go.

After the other girls' parents collect them, Emma Rose stays on the beach alone. Wind stirs the sea grass and wildflowers dotting the path leading home. Emma Rose thinks about France. She thinks about Corinne. She touches her forehead where the seaweed crown rested, and the skin is warm.

Emma Rose does what she always does when she's frightened or sad or confused. She swims. She launches herself into the waves, thinking for a moment that perhaps the time is now, she will swim all the way across the Channel. But that's stupid, and she knows it. Instead she flings her arms out as far as she can and kicks her legs hard, crossing back and forth parallel to the beach.

She isn't fighting the sea, never that. She's fighting herself. Exhaustion, that's what she wants, bone-deep. She'll sleep through her birthday, sleep for a whole week. It's what she's thinking when she sees the woman beneath her, her eyes grey and her hair drifting just the way Emma Rose remembers. Her hair seems a little greener, though, almost black, and the bones of her cheeks are sharper.

This time, Emma Rose doesn't scream. She stills herself, sculling water to stay in place. The woman flashes pearly teeth, a sheening purple color like the inside of an oyster shell.

Emma Rose's skin prickles. The woman's eyes are a mirror for her own, even if everything else about her is different—the length and curves of her body, the dip of her waist, the prominent line of her ribs, the pallor of her skin. After a moment, it strikes Emma Rose that the woman is naked, and her skin flushes so hot she fears the water around her will turn to steam.

Emma Rose reaches down and the woman reaches up at the same time. Their fingertips touch, then their palms. The water keeps Emma Rose from telling whether the woman's skin is cold.

Their lips meet next, the woman rising, Emma Rose falling. The woman's mouth tastes of salt, of seaweed, the grit of sand, and the smoothness of a pearl. She tastes of everything but drowning. As long as their lips touch, Emma Rose can hold her breath forever.

With her mouth against the woman's, Emma Rose thinks of Corinne. By the time she climbs back to the shore, her skin is so wrinkled it feels like it will slide off her bones, and her legs are trembling. Emma Rose turns to look at the water one last time, scanning it for a shadow beneath the waves, any glimpse of the woman. There is nothing, only the sun sinking and painting the water bright gold.

After her second encounter with the woman, Emma Rose begins swimming at least twice every day. She swims first thing in the morning before school, and first thing in the afternoon when she gets home. Days and weeks at a time pass where the woman keeps herself to a constant flicker of motion at the corner of Emma Rose's eye. But other times, she glides close as a shadow, her face inches from Emma Rose's own. When Emma Rose's muscles burn and she wants to quit, the woman brings her lips close, closer, until they touch. Until they share a heartbeat, share breath, and Emma Rose feels she could swim forever and never stop.

Other times, the woman is nowhere to be seen. On those days, Emma Rose swims purely for herself. She comes to love the solitude as much as the company, but it's a different kind of love. On those days, the water is hers and she knows one day she will cross it. Her name will be written alongside Gertrude Ederle, Amelia Gade Corson, Mercedes Gleitze, and Florence Chadwick.

She can't be first to cross the Channel, but maybe she can be fastest? The most crossings? Maybe she'll be the one to swim across and never come back. She'll find another sea, another ocean, another crossing and just keep going, swimming her way around the world.

Emma Rose spends so much time in the ocean that her father jokes she will turn into a fish. Emma Rose can't remember what wish she made before cutting her birthday cake, so she wishes for her father's words to come true.

Emma Rose is sixteen the first time she kisses a girl outside the water. Her name is Martha. Corinne has long since moved away, and Emma Rose barely even thinks about her anymore.

The kiss with Martha happens on the bleachers at school. Martha runs track, her legs flashing graceful and long the way Emma Rose's do in the water. She is faster than anyone else on the team.

Emma Rose and Martha have been friends for seven months when Emma Rose starts regularly watching track practice. Martha lives just a few streets over, so it only makes sense for Emma Rose to stay so they can walk home together.

The sun warms the bleachers, heat soaking through Emma Rose's uniform to the back of her thighs. She watches Martha, her brown skin gleaming with sweat, even though her motions seem effortless. Gravity doesn't apply; she pushes off the ground, and the earth pulls her along. Practice ends, and Martha comes over to the bleachers, grinning. Her frizzy hair is tied back in two poofs, and even they glisten with sweat, the black overlaid with droplets like a net of diamonds.

"That was brilliant," Emma Rose says, then blushes. She's been watching Martha run for weeks, why should this be any different?

Martha sits beside her, their knees almost touching, catching her breath. They talk about nothing for a while, then somehow they're kissing. Emma Rose isn't sure who started it, but she doesn't care. Martha's mouth tastes like the orange sports drink she says is her secret weapon—sugar-brightness exploding on Emma Rose's tongue. The kiss goes on for so long, Emma Rose is sure she's drowning. And when it ends, it's far too soon.

When they finally break apart, Martha rests her forehead against Emma Rose's, dampening it. Grey eyes meet deep brown, and they giggle. The laughter runs out, and they kiss again. The nervous fluttering in Emma Rose's stomach calms; instead of butterflies, she's full of sunlight, bursting out through her pores.

Emma Rose and Martha have been secret-not-so-secret official girlfriends for three months when Emma Rose brings Martha to the beach for the first time. She hasn't been swimming as much lately, her afternoon sessions melting into time watching Martha practice, or going to the shops together, or pausing to kiss by the side of the road, around the corner of buildings, anywhere and everywhere they can. Emma Rose and Martha are constantly amazed by each other, discovering all the things they have in common, wondering how they managed to grow up so close to each other without ever knowing it because they didn't go to the same school until now.

They play the 'what if' game. *What if you'd never transferred schools? What if I'd transferred years ago and we'd known each other since we were five? What if we walked right past each other on the street one day when we were twelve and we never knew?* And they both agree now that they've found each other, they need to make up for lost time.

"You never came to the beach when you were little?" Emma Rose asks, leading Martha down the flower-lined path.

Martha shakes her head. "My dad's little brother almost drowned when they were kids. He's been terrified of the water ever since."

"My grandfather used to race sailboats," Emma Rose says. "My dad always loved being out on the water. My mom wanted to be a marine biologist until she discovered a passion for baking and became a pastry chef. They've been bringing me here since I was a baby."

The sun is setting, tinting the water shades of peach and coral. Standing on the shore, Emma Rose feels the tug of France, gentle, yet ever-present at the edge of her mind. There's a pang of guilt. She's been neglecting the water. And there's something else that isn't guilt; it's almost fear. Emma Rose hasn't seen the woman in the water since she first kissed Martha. It isn't unknown for her to disappear for months at a time, but this feels different somehow.

"Fancy a swim?" Emma Rose pushes her doubt away and

pulls her shirt over her head, revealing the swimsuit underneath.

"It's getting late." Martha looks at the water with unease.

"We won't go in deep." Emma Rose kicks off her shorts. "I promise I'll hold your hand the whole time."

That does the trick. Martha skims out of her clothes, and it turns out she's wearing a swimsuit underneath her clothes too, which makes Emma Rose's chest squinch in a complicated way.

She's been thinking about telling Martha she loves her for days. The words are always on the tip of her tongue, but she keeps swallowing them down. She's pretty sure Martha will say it back, but what if she doesn't? What if she says it but doesn't mean it? What if it comes out all wrong, or she scares Martha away?

They walk to the water's edge. Martha hisses at the temperature; the waves tangle lace around her ankles. They take it slow. To their mid calves, their knees, their thighs. Waves surge around their waists, and Emma Rose lets herself fall backward. The water catches her and plays a soft game of tug of war. She smiles at Martha, in up to her armpits now. Emma Rose sees she's standing on her tiptoes, afraid to cede the last bit of control.

Martha has never been anything but graceful; there's something comforting in seeing her out of her element. It makes her more human.

Emma Rose holds out her hand. Martha takes it, letting Emma Rose guide her until the ground no longer supports her. In a moment, Emma Rose will put her arms around Martha's waist. She'll kiss her. She'll finally say what she's been longing to say.

Then, sudden as a blink, Martha is gone. All Emma Rose can do is stare. The water froths, Martha thrashing, and Emma Rose dives, trying to pull Martha to the surface. Something holds Martha down. Emma Rose catches a glimpse of a face beside

Martha's. Grey eyes meet grey. A flash of teeth. Emma Rose wants to pretend it's a trick of churned water and flashing limbs, but she cannot. The woman's face is undeniably there, and in this moment, she looks more like Emma Rose than ever, mocking her.

Emma Rose uses all her strength, and Martha pops to the surface like a cork, gasping.

"Are you o–" But Emma Rose doesn't get any farther.

The sky bruises purple, the first pale stars beginning to appear. Martha's pupils are impossibly wide, dark like the ocean where it's deepest and coldest. She scrambles for the shore, trips, bangs her knee on the stones. A thin strand of watered blood runs down Martha's leg like a ribbon as she picks herself up again. She must have cut herself on the stones, Emma Rose thinks, and she tries not to picture sharp teeth like mother of pearl.

Emma Rose wades for the shore, trying to quell the thoughts spinning through her head. The water resists her so she's breathing hard by the time she gets to Martha's side. Martha shivers, her teeth clenched so hard the vein below her jaw protrudes.

When Emma Rose touches Martha's shoulder, Martha jerks away.

"Don't," Martha says, her voice fraying.

She gathers her clothes, and when she turns, she reveals a mark like a bruise, the faint outline of a hand upon her skin. More than that, it spreads dark tendrils through Martha's veins, flushing them the color of ink and the darkening sky. Emma Rose blinks, but the mark refuses to disappear. She reaches for Martha again, but Martha steps back, holding her clothes against her in a wet bundle like a shield.

"Just stay away from me."

Martha's eyes are wide; they are hurt and afraid. Afraid of Emma Rose. She pivots, heels striking the ground hard and when she reaches the road, Martha runs. Her track star legs carry her away without a backward glance.

Emma Rose's heart cracks, and it keeps cracking. The words she never got the chance to say lodge in her throat like barbs. Martha isn't coming back. She'll never talk to Emma Rose again. This is her fault. The woman tasted Martha on Emma Rose's skin, and now she's punishing her, hurting Martha to hurt Emma Rose.

The sky is full dark when Emma Rose flings herself back into the waves. She beats at them, letting her body rage. Salt water stands in for her tears. The ragged, horrible rhythm of her breath stands in place of screaming until her throat is raw and coughing up *I love you* in blood.

And when that is done, when her muscles tremble with exertion, she keeps swimming. If she's only allowed to have one thing, then she chooses this. Hollow, numb, her skin wrinkled and every part of her hurting, she refuses to leave. The waves can't frighten her away. Even though they took Martha, she won't quit. This ocean is hers, and one day she will force it to carry her all the way to France.

Finally, exhausted, Emma Rose puts her face in the water and drifts. Her eyes sting. She holds her breath, and waits. She thinks of all those days with the woman gliding just beneath her, lending her strength to Emma Rose's own. Will she come to share this heartbeat, too, to lessen the burden, ease the pain?

Emma Rose loses track of time. Her chest aches with the desire to breathe before the woman appears. The sharpness of the woman's cheekbones and ribs is even more pronounced now. The grey cast to her skin makes Emma Rose think of sharks and hunger.

Emma Rose is hungry, too. The woman looks like her. Maybe they have always been the same. Maybe they are both monsters, unfit for the love of any but their own kind.

Emma Rose lets out the last of her breath, bubbles escaping

in a silent scream. The woman rises and Emma Rose falls, a tangle of arms. Coldwater lips crush against hers and Emma Rose bites down. Mouths and saltwater. Love on the cusp of violence. Desire that tastes like drowning. Release. It's almost as good as crying.

Emma Rose goes back to swimming twice every day. She doesn't speak to Martha. She avoids her in the halls. All she needs is the water.

There's a story Emma Rose remembers from when she was very young, from a big book of fairy tales, thick like an old-fashioned telephone book, with different colored pages. In the story, a rich man is visited every night by a ghost, or a water fairy. She stands at the end of his bed, dripping. She claims to love him, but he gets sick from lack of sleep and always being wet and cold. Finally, he tricks her into following him outside in winter so she freezes and never bothers him again.

The story both fascinated and terrified Emma Rose as a child. There was an illustration of the woman, glittering and perfect, frozen for all time, with no sense she would recover at winter's end. Emma Rose could never work out who the villain was supposed to be—the man who only wanted a good night's sleep, or the ghost who only wanted to be warm and loved. Maybe they were both monsters in their own way, perfect for each other.

It's nearly a year before she allows herself to kiss another woman on land. Her name is Joan. She's in her second year at university, and when Emma Rose meets her, she's home on summer holiday. She has a ring through her eyebrow, and one through her nose, and others Emma Rose will discover later, hidden by her clothing. Joan's laugh is almost a bray, unapologetic and full of joy. Her hair is red, not like Maureen's long ago, but dyed and cut short, spiked like the crest of an exotic bird.

Emma Rose doesn't love Joan; Joan is safe. She'll be back at school soon. In-between, they go to cafes and music clubs. Once, they go to a traveling funfair. The Ferris wheel carries them high up and then stops, suspending them over the twinkling lights below. The car rocks when they kiss. Joan's hands move under Emma Rose's shirt, and for just a moment, Emma Rose feels like she is the exotic bird, the one who might take flight. For just a moment, she feels like everything might be okay.

She doesn't take Joan to the beach. She never mentions the ocean at all. She leads a secret, double life, because she never stops swimming either.

She showed Martha her heart, the ocean, and she ran, so now Emma Rose keeps it locked inside. Instead of making time for the water in-between seeing Joan, she makes time for Joan by pulling herself away from the water—from the woman—as long as she can, which is never long.

Emma Rose is twenty-one when she attempts to cross the English Channel. Gertrude Ederle, the first woman to make the crossing, did it at nineteen. It was her second attempt, and she did it in fourteen hours and thirty-one minutes. Emma Rose has memorized the times and ages and number of attempts of every one of the women to cross the Channel, and some of the men, too. She will carry them with her when she steps into the water. If she succeeds, she will carry them with her all the way to the other side.

Emma Rose's parents are both in the boat accompanying her. Like her grandfather's sailing, like their love of cooking and baking, they understand her passion even if it doesn't exactly match their own. The whole way across, they will be there to feed her sugar cubes and protein blocks, to give encouragement, and gather her in their arms whether she succeeds or fails.

Emma Rose enters the water at 6:09 a.m. Scraps of cloud cling to the sky, the moon forgetting to clean up after itself. The water is a deep blue, brushed with hints of purple and grey. Her hair is short, curls flattened under a swim cap. Emma Rose lowers her goggles, rolls her neck, shakes her arms out so they hang loose and long.

Breathe. She reaches as far as she can with each stroke. The waves don't fight her, and she allows herself to hope. She keeps her rhythm steady. Stroke, stroke, stroke, turn, breathe. She kicks. She counts in her head, reciting names to keep time. Webb, Ederle, Toth. Breathe. Chadwick, Corson, Gleitze. Breathe. She sights by the boat so she doesn't go off course. Her parents speak encouragement, but mostly she is alone with the water, with her lungs and her heartbeat. France waits for her on the other side.

At seven hours, the water grows choppy, but Emma Rose doesn't stop. Her legs and arms burn. She has to fight a little harder against the weight of the water, but she won't quit. She thinks about the woman, about the times she pressed her lips against Emma Rose's, breathing for her. Doubt creeps in. What if she can't do this on her own?

As she turns her head to breathe, Emma Rose catches a flash of long limbs, blue-grey skin and mother of pearl teeth. A wave of panic rolls through her. She tries to push the doubt away, but it nags, sapping her strength. Just past eight hours, a cramp hits, hot and bright as though a hand slapped against her muscles. She thinks of Martha on the beach years ago and the not-bruise blooming on her skin.

No.

Emma Rose's heart fractures infinitely and intimately, branching patterns reaching all through her bones. She bites down hard on her lip, tasting salt blood and tries to swim through the pain.

Please, let me go.

Her legs won't cooperate, dead weight dragging her down.

A face glides just beneath hers, hair all twisting seaweed ribbons. Nothing about it is human except for the eyes—they are Emma Rose's own. The woman opens her mouth, but no bubbles emerge. Her smile is gloating, mocking.

Don't touch me, Emma Rose pleads silently. *I want to do this on my own.*

The woman reaches for her, and Emma Rose jerks upright. She signals the boat, the cramp stitching through her side, knotting her until she nearly screams. Hands pull her in, and maybe one hand lifts from the water, but whether it is to push her higher or pull her down, she cannot tell.

Emma Rose's lips are blue, bruised, as though someone has pummeled them. She can't stop shaking. Her mother wraps a thermal blanket around her shoulders. Her father brings her a thermos of tea, holding the cup because her hands are trembling. Her parents put their arms around her. They tell her it will be okay. They can try again. Exhausted, Emma Rose leans against them and sobs her broken heart out. She is four years old again, and her parents encircle her with their bodies until there are no tears left, until she finally stops shaking, until she is warm.

Emma Rose tries again at twenty-three, and twenty-five, her confidence wearing thin. The first time, a mechanical failure in the boat turns them back; the second, an unexpected storm. She will never know whether she could have made it across. If she simply accepts the woman's help, will all these problems go away? But if she does, will she really be the one making the crossing? Maybe she isn't even meant to. The certainty she's carried since she was four weights her like a stone. How many times can she try and fail? How many times can she stand to have her heart broken?

Emma Rose is twenty-seven years old when she meets her first serious girlfriend. Her name is Elizabeth. They move in together after three months, which seems both fast and far too long to wait. Emma Rose wants to be touching her all the time, brushing her fingertips across the back of Elizabeth's hand, kissing her shoulder, pressing their legs against each other while they watch old movies and eat popcorn. It's like she has to constantly remind herself Elizabeth is real and not just a story she's told herself. That she won't vanish, or run away.

They've been living together for almost nine months when Emma Rose wakes to rain pummeling the windows. Briefly, Emma Rose mistakes the wet hush of traffic outside their apartment for the sound of the tide. She sits up, counting the space between flashes of lightning and growls of thunder. For just a moment, she swears there's a face in the water droplets, the outline of a woman's cheekbones, sharper than any human's should be, and a smile too wide. Emma Rose starts back. Is it her reflection? Is she imagining things?

"You okay?" Sleep-warm, Elizabeth sits up and wraps herself around Emma Rose, fitting her chin against Emma Rose's shoulder as if it was purpose-made for just that thing.

Emma Rose shivers. There's nothing outside but lightning and rain.

"Do you think it's possible for a person to be haunted?" Emma Rose asks, thinking of the fairy tale from long ago.

"You mean like sheets and chains? Rattling doors and disembodied voices?"

The questions aren't mocking. Emma Rose allows herself to sink back into Elizabeth's embrace. It's like the water long ago—holding her, knowing her, keeping her safe.

"Sort of." She takes a deep breath. "When I was little, I saw something in the water."

The whole story tumbles out. Elizabeth listens, never interrupting. The storm dies down until only the sound of rain dripping from the gutters remains. Emma Rose lapses into silence. She meets Elizabeth's eyes, which are pale blue with a ring of darker blue around the edges.

"Do you believe me?" Emma Rose asks.

"Yes." There is no hesitation. Elizabeth majored in English Literature and Comparative Mythology; Emma Rose shouldn't be surprised she understands about fairies and ghosts.

"You don't...I mean, you're not..." Emma Rose stops, unsure how to ask Elizabeth if she'll stay.

"Hey." Elizabeth catches Emma Rose's hands, pressing them between her own. "I'm not going anywhere."

"Why?" Emma Rose breathes out, afraid of the hope wanting to grow inside her.

"I don't scare that easily." Elizabeth smiles. "Besides, we all have our things, right? I support you, you support me."

"Yeah?" Emma Rose allows herself to relax just a little bit. "What's your thing?"

"Well, when you're rich and famous for crossing the Channel, I'll let you pay for everything while I go back to school. Then you can suffer through endless stuffy dinners with my fellow academics. It'll be a glamorous life, but it'll be ours."

Ours. The word beats inside Emma Rose, timed with her heart. It is echoed by words never spoken aloud, which she's long imagined spoken by blue-grey lips, slipping through teeth like mother of pearl. *You need me, just like I need you.*

She's always thought it meant a choice, to take the ocean

into her heart and nothing else, or give up on her dream. But maybe there's more.

"There are creatures that can't cross running water, right?" She tests the words out loud, feeling her way through them as she speaks.

"Sure." Elizabeth's eyes are bright, curious.

"What if my ghost, or whatever she is can't step onto dry land without me."

It sounds silly, but Elizabeth puts her head to the side like she's considering Emma Rose's words. Maybe her ghost just wants to be warm and loved. Maybe neither of them are monsters. Maybe they can help each other somehow.

"If I try the crossing again, will you be there with me?" Emma Rose holds her breath. She looks into Elizabeth's eyes with all their myriad shades of blue.

"Of course," Elizabeth says. She wraps her hands around Emma Rose's. When they kiss, Emma Rose is light, buoyant, completely safe and surrounded. Elizabeth is the ocean that keeps her afloat.

Emma Rose is twenty-eight when she and Elizabeth walk down an aisle of strewn rose petals in her parents' garden. Emma Rose promises herself she won't cry, and breaks her promise in the first five minutes. Her father is there with a tissue, his eyes bright and teary as well. They stumble through their vows, and even though Elizabeth cries too, when they kiss, somehow it doesn't taste like salt at all.

There's cake afterward, and champagne, and dancing, and the garden is strung with fairy lights. Over the music, Emma Rose hears the hush of waves. As they slow dance their last song, Emma Rose listens to Elizabeth's heartbeat, her breath, timed to Emma Rose's own. A sudden thought hits her, and it's like being bowled over by a wave. Needing someone else doesn't mean that she isn't also strong.

"I'm ready to try again," she says in a whisper so low she almost hopes Elizabeth won't hear.

"I know." Elizabeth brushes her lips across Emma Rose's brow. "I've already arranged for the boat and a hotel. We'll honeymoon in Paris when you get to the other side."

Emma Rose's breath catches. She looks at Elizabeth with the fairy lights gleaming in her hair. Elizabeth smiles, and Emma Rose falls in love all over again. She will keep Emma Rose safe; they will keep each other safe. If Emma Rose falters, Elizabeth will be right there to pull her from the waves, into her arms.

They set out at dawn. Emma Rose's belly is a knot of nerves. The sun rises as she steps into the water. Up to her calves, to her knees. Breathe. She has known the water all her life, in all its moods, and all of hers. She will cross it. They will carry each other, all the way to the other side.

Emma Rose lets the ocean take her weight. Elizabeth is by her side, waiting to feed her sugar cubes and protein, to speak encouragement. Emma Rose stretches her arm as long as it can go, and reaches for the opposite shore.

Stroke, stroke, stroke, breathe. Her feet kick in time with her heartbeat. A shadow glides beneath her, her twin. The face isn't remotely human anymore. Bones like blades press against grey skin; mother of pearl teeth gleam in a mouth too wide. Gills slit the sides of the woman's throat, and there are webs between her long fingers and toes. After all this time, Emma Rose knows her the way she knows the waves, and she refuses to be afraid.

If the woman is part of her, so be it. This is still her journey. They will be each other's guide. The woman lifts a hand, palm flat, facing Emma Rose and waits.

Emma Rose is twenty-eight when she lets go of doubt and fear. She reaches out and presses her palm flat against the webbed hand waiting below her. She lets her love for Elizabeth flow through her, lets the woman taste it from her skin. Here is a little piece of dry land inside the ocean, a little bit of warmth and love. Emma Rose forgives her, and is forgiven in turn. The woman rises, Emma Rose does not fall. When their lips touch, it tastes of nothing but goodbye.

HOW TO HOST A HAUNTED HOUSE MURDER MYSTERY PARTY

Choose Your Setting

Find a large house with lots of rooms. One where the light switches are far enough away from each door that your guests will have to step into the room to turn them on. If possible, find a house where the electricity is fragile. (Keep an eye on the weather report and schedule accordingly.) A basement and an attic are essential, the former with a woodpile and a cast iron stove, the latter with dress forms, an old hobby horse, dolls no one has thought about in years, and at least one antique steamer trunk large enough to hold a body.

There should be mirrors in odd and unexpected places. Let your guests catch their reflections as they're groping for the light in a darkened room and feel for a moment that they are not alone. Eventually, they will realize it's only a mirror, but that moment of pure terror is enough to set the mood. From that point on, they will continue to glance in the direction of the glass, wondering whether the reflection in the corner of their eye could really be them.

There should be plenty of bedrooms, but few bathrooms. Of

these bathrooms, one should contain a claw-foot tub deep enough that you cannot see the bottom of it while standing in the door. Showers should have their curtains pulled tightly closed before the evening begins.

The kitchen should be incongruously bright, a break in the tension, a place where your guests will feel they may be safe for a while.

A dining room table to seat at least thirteen. Chandeliers. Narrow staircases requiring guests to ascend and descend one at a time. That one room you never go in, no matter what, even though the door has never been locked.

Ideally, your house is already haunted and only minimal preparation will be required.

Creating Your Invitations

Use thick, good quality paper. Consider a scent—nothing crass like lilac or vanilla. Use something subtle, like wood smoke, reminding your guests of tales told around a campfire, or more obscure still, the scent of old books, that one book in particular with the gruesome illustrations their parents warned would give them nightmare, but which they could never resist. The book they returned to again and again for the awful, delicious and terrible thrill, reading it by flashlight under the covers, and later waking screaming, betrayed by those same covers meant to keep them safe. That smell.

The invitations should be done in calligraphy to add a touch of class. Deliver the invitations by hand. No postmark. No return address.

Invite extra guests. Invite at least one person liable to turn up late. Provide at least one guest with the wrong address so they become lost along the way. They will consider themselves lucky, once all is said and done. Every tale needs a survivor.

Don't be concerned if you don't have thirteen close friends. The evening will work better if your guests are unacquainted with each other (at least on the surface). Do not be concerned that your guests will refuse. There is no doubt they will attend. They always do.

Not for the secrets you know about them, and you do, but for what they have come to know about themselves in the long, lonely years they have spent waiting for just such an invitation to arrive. When the invitation comes, it will be a relief. They will be able to let go of the sense of dread, the one they have never been able to name. They will breathe out and say, *Ah, yes, here it is at last.*

Most of them are long past thinking they can be forgiven. Some are even past believing they deserve this. No, they *need* this. A ghost to give shape to their pain, a physical manifestation of their loss and guilt. They will come because the ghosts you can offer them are the only way they can make sense of their worlds.

(A better question to ask before your evening begins: Why are you compelled to invite strangers to participate in your game? Do you still believe you can be forgiven? Do you believe ghosts are a communicable thing, able to be passed off to an unwitting individual stepping through your door?)

Making the Introductions

No real names will be used.

The first guest shall be called Madame Edamame—the near palindrome delicious, yet slightly unsettling. It will show your guests you have a sense of fun, there's no real harm to be had here.

Next will be Miss Foster. Not Mrs. Not Ms. *Miss.* It is old fashioned and infantilizing. It is also cruel. None of this is without intent. Where Madame Edamame's name is meant to put your guests at ease, Miss Foster's is meant to pull the rug out from beneath them. Everything is uncertain here. They are on dangerous ground.

Miss Foster has been in and out of homes where she was never entirely welcome her entire life, always the changeling, never the adopted child. For all intents and purposes, she is still a child, hungry for acceptance and love, desperate to fit in. Did her families hurt her? Did she hurt them? Does she smell faintly of ash and the ghost of old fires? A little mystery in the guests adds to the mystery in the game.

Some names will be more common. This is Mr. Evans. Just that. Nothing less, nothing more.

There is also Mr. Espadrille, Young Mister Cleeves, Mrs. Hanover, Father Crispin, Elizabeth—no last name given—Mr. James, Mr. Otterly, and Captain Frank. There must always be a military officer invited to such affairs, though Captain Frank prefers her given name of Jane. She's put the war behind her, after all, even though she will show up to your party wearing every medal she's earned.

Don't forget to count yourself. You are a part of the game as well.

Cocktails to Set the Mood

Start with the classics—Old Fashioneds, Sidecars, Manhattans. These will give the party a timeless air, and help disconnect your guests from place and time. Strengthen the illusion that they have been lifted from the world they know and set adrift in some past. But not *their* past, mind you. It is still safe here. Still fun.

Even those guests who do not usually partake, or who have been known to imbibe too much and therefore have sworn to abstain, may feel compelled to accept your hospitality on this particular night. One drink, so as not to be rude. One drink to ease the pressure of being among strangers in an uncertain situation. Drinks to loosen tongues and smooth the way. It is easier to mingle with a drink in your hand. A drink, or two, or many, will allow your guests to leave their baggage behind. At least for as long as it takes them to reach the bottom of each glass.

Dinner is Served

Dinner will be tense, despite the alcohol, or perhaps because of it. At this point, your guests will begin to questions their decision to play along. They have always known they would, yet self-doubt will leave them restless. Do not be concerned. All is going according to plan.

There will be wine brought up from cellars the house doesn't have. Scotch, whiskey, brandy, and vodka in well-chilled glasses.

This is when the first ghost will appear. It will be no more than a flicker of movement at the corner of the eye. Perhaps Mrs. Hanover will be the one to spot it, and her hand will fly to her mouth. Perhaps it will be Mr. James; he will start, jerking his chair back from the table as though pulled by some unseen hand. A fork will be dropped, or a glass may break. If you are especially fortuitous, the power will choose this moment to blink, but it will remain on.

Nervous laughter will follow. *Dear me, aren't we all so silly here? Jumping at shadows. Tsk, tsk.* None of your guests will admit to the ghost they've seen, the one they've always known to be waiting for them here. One can only outrun their past for so long.

Smile. Get through the meal despite the tightness in all

throats, the lack of appetite, the sense of some worse blow about to fall. Everything will be fine.

The Late Arrival (aka The Thirteenth Guest)

He's a motorist whose car has broken down. Or perhaps you invited him. Who can be sure? Let's call him Mr. Perkins. His name is not important. Now your quota of thirteen guests is complete.

Rain will drip from the hem of his coat, and his over-shoes will leave puddles on your floor. His arrival is heralded by a crash of thunder. Maybe one of the other guests lets out an involuntary gasp. Despite the lingering sense of unease, the other guests—consciously or not—have come to think of your party as their own. There is a proprietary sense, they are survivors thrown together to persevere against all odds. Mr. Perkins is an outsider. They have been in this together since the beginning. He has not. How can they trust him? He does not belong.

Your party is going swimmingly so far.

Dealing with Potential Pitfalls

The problem is, your house is actually haunted. This was never a game. There is a strong likelihood someone will die in earnest before the evening is done. There is no known solution to this pitfall. Do not be concerned. This is a feature, not a bug.

Entertainment (Variant #1)—The Séance

After dinner, bring out the Ouija board. There is no need to procure one beforehand. There are many closets in your house of many doors. One of them has a board; it is wrapped in your great-aunt's favorite table cloth, tucked away on a top shelf behind a pair of boots no one has ever worn.

Ask your guests to join hands. Dim the lights. (Perhaps the power is already off by now.) Light candles, either out of necessity or to set the atmosphere.

Before the game begins, ensure no one is touching the planchette. It will move regardless. It will spell a name, which none of your guests claim to recognize, though at least two of them do. Mr. Otterly, or perhaps Elizabeth-with-no-last-name, will leave the table in disgust. They will consider departing the house all together, but something will compel them to stay.

There is a pressure, not visible but certainly tangible, standing just before the front door. To pass through it is to drown. To pass through it is to have all your worst experiences dredged up from the bottom of your soul and wrapped around you like a second skin. No one ever notices it coming into the house. Everyone notices when they try to leave. You have ceased to notice it at all.

Entertainment (Variant #2)—Blind Man's Bluff

This game is traditionally played outdoors, however your sitting room is more than large enough to serve. (Perhaps it was once a ballroom?)

Draw the curtains against the lightning. Madame Edamame will wear the blindfold. Have your guests stand around her in a circle and spin her until she is dizzy and nearly falling down. (The alcohol will help in this regard.) As she reaches to steady herself, your guests will scatter and hide themselves away— beneath the grand piano, behind the tight-drawn curtains, inside the curio cabinet where the good china and glass figurines used to be displayed, the one with the shelves taken out long ago.

Madame Edamame will stumble. She will call a name, possibly the name of one of your guests, but not the name they have been given for the game.

Inside the curio cabinet, where shelves used to be, there will be one heartbeat and two sets of breath. Behind the curtains, a stifled laugh. Beneath the piano, two sets of eyes peer out at the game, even though the guest hiding there hid alone.

Madame Edamame will pretend not to be afraid. She will feel someone touch her hand. By the time your other guests think to help her, it will be too late. She will already have left bloody gouges on her cheeks tearing the blindfold away.

Entertainment (Variant #3)—Exploration

This is the most popular variant. It always comes down to exploration and isolation in the end. A ghost for every guest, and each to their own.

Divide the party into pairs and send them out in different directions. Your guests may be reluctant, there is safety in numbers, after all. Remind them that none of them will be alone. If this isn't exactly comforting, remind them that they came here of their own free will. What happens from here on out is out of your hands.

First Exploration Team: The Library

Miss Foster and Young Mister Cleeves will proceed to the library. Young Mister Cleeves will grope his way toward the light, or where he believes the light ought to be. He will trip over a pile of books, cursing softly. He will lose track of Miss Foster right away. He will be terrified simultaneously that he is alone and no longer alone.

Something will break. Don't worry. Material things can always be replaced.

When Young Mister Cleeves finds the light, it will illuminate Miss Foster standing in front of one of the floor to ceiling bookshelves. In all her un-rooted childhood, books were her constant. Her sole anchor in the dark. Her lips will move, but Young Mister Cleeves won't be able to make out the words. He will be profoundly grateful for this fact. Blood, a single drop, will fall from Miss Foster's palm.

She will not turn when Young Mister Cleeves calls her name. He will be profoundly grateful for this as well. The idea of seeing her face fills him with blank dread. He has begun to suspect she is not so young as she seems. At the same time, the fear that she is unable to move, will never move again, haunts him. He cannot leave her here, but he cannot bring himself to touch her shoulder either, as if a haunting could be passed along like a disease.

He will be forced to admit to himself that he was hoping for something more, exploring a dimly-lit house with a lovely and fragile young woman (girl). He will feel small, seeing his impulse to chivalry for the base thing it is. His pulse will slow. It will slow continually, each beat more distant from the next. Paradoxically, his breath will speed with the waiting, which will seem interminable, waiting to see whether the distance between one beat and the next becomes too vast and they stop.

Second Exploration Team: The Basement

Mr. James and Captain Frank will make their way to the basement. They will reach the bottom of the steps before they find the light. The basement smells of dust and the memory of rain, something sweet and sharp and long buried underlying both.

The woodpile and the glowering pot-bellied stove will greet them. Mr. James will be reminded inexplicably of his father.

He will pick up the ax, even though the blade is sunk deep into one of the logs, abandoned mid-chop, and it will require a great amount of effort to pull it free. He will not understand why he does these things, but he will be compelled.

The blade is rusty; the handle fits his grip like an old friend. Mr. James will swing the ax, just once (in his mind) to test the heft, but his arms will ache as though he swung it again and again.

Captain Frank, Jane, as she prefers to be called, will think, *fuck, no, I am not dying this way. I did not survive two wars to buy it in a moldy basement.* She will see, again, buildings torn apart, hear the screams following an IED explosion, every IED explosion. She will taste plaster and cement blown to dust as her mind struggles to rearrange a puzzle of scattered limbs. She will think, *yes, this is familiar. This I know.* And she will do what needs to be done.

Captain Frank will limp when she climbs the stairs back into the light. She will be alone. Her hair will be disheveled, and one of her medals missing. Behind her, the basement will be dark. Even if she did look back, she wouldn't be able to see a thing.

Third Exploration Team: The Garden

Father Crispin and Mr. Evans will take the brick path to the shed at the end of yard, a straight line from the house's back door. There is no light in the shed, which is scarcely bigger than a tomb, and why should there be? Most people don't garden in the dark.

Father Crispin will prop the door open with a brick. It will take a moment for his eyes to adjust, and a moment longer to realize he is alone. Mr. Evans vanished somewhere between the shed and the back door.

Or perhaps he has always been alone.

Father Crispin will breathe in the scent of turned earth and old clay. Trowels, rakes, and clawed instruments hang from the walls. Bottles of fertilizers and weed killer and rat poison line the shelves. Everything in the shed can be used to kill.

Even though he isn't a man of the cloth, not outside of this evening and the role you have assigned him, Father Crispin will whisper a prayer. As he does, he will suddenly remember the monastery where he took his vows, a place he has surely never been. Yet he will know how his days there smelled of earth, and how he spent long hours in the garden, weeding rows of tomato and cucumber plants by hand.

Water will drip from the hem of Father Crispin's cassock. A voice at the back of his head will suggest he kneel. Not to pray, but to see better into the corners of the shed.

He will find a bundle wrapped in burlap and tied with twine. He will not want to open it. He will dread opening it with all his soul. And he will open it all the same.

The bones inside are too small, too light to be human, yet too perfect to be anything else.

He will know, he has always known, this was waiting for him here. Father Crispin will cradle the bones close against his chest, murmuring the words of a long-forgotten lullaby, weeping softly the whole while.

Evaluating Your Party's Success

There are more rooms and more pairings. There is no need to enumerate them all. Some things are better left unseen, as

Father Crispin well knows. Besides, it would take all the fun out of your party to know every detail in advance.

As the evening unwinds, there are several ways it might go. You could find yourself with a house full of final girls, or a house full of final boys. You could find yourself with a mix of both, or neither. You might find yourself all alone.

It has happened many times before.

Ideally, this is the part of the evening when you gather your guests to reveal how and where and who and why. However, it seems there is no one left to gather. You aren't even certain anyone has been murdered, or whether there is any crime to reveal. There are human remains in your house, to be sure, but it is highly like those have been there all along.

All that remains is your own exploration, a foray through the empty rooms of your house to take stock of the evening's game. You may delay, hesitate, hem and haw, but sooner or later you'll have to climb the attic stairs and throw open the steamer trunk that is large enough to fit a body inside. You will have to descend to the basement, return the ax to its place, and use your fingernails to pry up the floorboards. You will have to go to the library, and the garden shed, the kitchen and the conservatory. You will have to stand on your tiptoes in the bathroom door and hope that just this once you'll be able to see inside the claw-foot tub without entering the room.

As the host, it is your duty to search every last nook and cranny to be sure. But to be sure of what? That you are alone? That you have never been alone?

Sooner or later, you'll have to go into the room you swore you'd never enter again. The door stands an inch ajar, waiting for you. You will stand in the hallway for as long as you can, then you'll grope for the light and there will be a moment of panic before you remember—all the switches are far away from all the doors. You must step into the dark.

This darkness is physical, like dropping into a pool. It closes over your head, and maybe this time, just this once, you really will drown. Maybe it's better not to reach for the light. If you do, you'll *know* the faceless thing in the corner isn't just a shadow. You'll *know* that in the closet, there's a hanged girl. Someone is waiting in the corner, by the crib, by the old hobby horse, by the rocking chair where no one has sat for years. They were in the room a moment before you. They just left. They must have passed you in the hall, close enough to touch.

If you reach for the light now, a hand will reach back for you. Fingers will brush across your skin. But if you wait long enough, if you refuse to act, the decision will be made for you. Your eyes will adjust; the shadows in the corner, in the closet, under the bed, by the chair, will coalesce. You will see, even if your eyes are closed.

There are so many ways to host a haunted house murder mystery party, but there is only one way this can end.

This room, this house, your life, have all the hallmarks of a haunting. You should know by now—you cannot be forgiven. By now, you should no longer need a ghost to make your pain real. But standing paralyzed in the door, counting the space between one heartbeat and the next, you can't help but ask yourself over and over again—what did you do to deserve this?

IN THE END, IT ALWAYS TURNS OUT THE SAME

Five children have gone missing since the school year began. The youngest, only six; the oldest, no more than ten. They all went to school together, but all in different grades. The only thing they have in common is that they all rode the school bus together every day.

Richard McGinty reported the first child missing. And the second. And the third. He's the bus driver, it makes sense he would notice, but even so, the police chief can't help but wonder. There's just something about him, the police chief has always thought so. Sunnydale is a nice town, a safe one, but there are some people, like Richard McGinty, who just don't seem to belong. It isn't anything the police chief can put his finger on, but he's learned over the years that if someone looks suspicious it's most likely because they are. So the police chief writes McGinty's name at the top of his suspect list, then he does what he always does. He gives the Super Teen Detective Squad a call.

Helen is the pretty one. Everyone says so. Her hair is long and red and flips over her shoulders just so. She isn't quite rich, but she isn't poor either. She always has money for new clothes when she wants them, but she tends to wear the same ones day after day. Pretty is something she is, not something she does.

She's been a Teen Detective as long as she can remember. Along with Greg, Tricia, and Rooster, she's solved more mysteries than she can remember. They blend together in her mind—the Old Mill, the Haunted Cemetery, the creature in the pond, or the river, or the swamp. There's always a ghost, or a demon, or a monster, one that always turns out to be someone in disguise. Helen has never met a real monster. She's almost eighteen, but she still hopes she will grow up to be a monster someday.

In her time as a Teen Detective, Helen has learned that most people only think they know what monsters look like. They walk past real monsters every day and never see them at all, which is why the monsters she meets go around in disguise. It's the only way anyone will ever recognize them, and they are all so desperate to be seen.

Helen thinks a lot about disguises. She thinks about putting on a hundred pounds, or losing fifty, and paying someone to beat her up so badly it will utterly transform her face. She'll get a crummy apartment, one with a roach problem, and a door that doesn't properly lock. It will be the kind of place a girl like her would never live. She'll spend her days walking right up to people who know her, or think they do, and laughing behind her hands when they don't recognize her. And it will be absolutely glorious.

This future, alternate, unrecognizable version of her will get a dog. A big one who slobbers. One who growls at everyone who isn't her. The dog will know her and love her unconditionally; it won't have any idea she's supposed to be the pretty one.

It will know her by her smell, and the fact that she feeds it, and it won't care a thing about her face, her shape, or the color of her hair.

By unofficial consensus, Greg is the Super Teen Detective Squad's leader. Helen thinks she might have slept with him once, because they are both pretty and that's the way it's supposed to go. Though it's also possible that they got drunk together once and he told her that he's gay.

Lately she's been having recurring dreams about murdering Greg. In fact, she's dreamt about murdering every single member of the Teen Detective Squad. More than once, she's woken with blood on her hands. She has no idea where the blood comes from. The only thing she knows for certain is that it isn't hers. Sometimes she wonders if she's spent so much time thinking about becoming a monster that she's turned into one after all.

He didn't start driving the school bus until after he retired. Maybe that's why all the kids on the bus call him old. *"Better behave, or Old Man McGinty will get you." "I heard Old Man McGinty's face is just a rubber mask." "I dare you to pull it off and see what he looks like for real." "I heard he crashed a bus on purpose once." "I heard he locks bad kids inside the bus and hurts them."*

There are so many rumors, none of them true. He doesn't even really mind; it's just the way kids are. It comes with the job, it comes with being "old", with being a little too quiet, a little lonely, a little odd.

The kids are right about one thing at least. He does look like someone in his disguise, his face and clothing all wrong. The clothes are hand-me-downs from his father. Never throw a good piece of cloth away, his mother always said. They don't fit him right. They smell of mothballs and smoke, though he's never touched a cigarette in his life. His father died when he was eight-years-old, but his mother kept the clothes in a trunk in the attic, waiting for him to grow.

He doesn't remember the growing part. As far as he knows, he's always been old. What he does remember is the day his mother pulled his father's old clothes out of the chest and presented them to him. He remembers climbing into them, all shades of umber and brown, sienna and burnt orange. It was like wearing his father's ghost. He looked in the mirror and saw a man with hound dog eyes, with shadows in the seams of his skin, and hair fading to the color of a mouse's fur. He was only eighteen at the time.

Tricia is the smart one, but no one ever tells her so. They simply take it for granted. She is the reliable one, dependable, boring. She is so predictable that even she catches words coming out of her mouth before she's had time to think of them sometimes. It's like someone else living inside her, speaking through her skin.

Every morning when she gets dressed, Tricia finds dog hairs on her clothes. She finds them even though she hasn't been anywhere near a dog, ever, as far as she knows. Her parents have always told her she's deathly allergic, even though the dog hairs on her sweaters don't even so much as make her itch. It's the greatest mystery she's ever encountered. Even with the ghosts, the pirate treasure, the naiad inhabiting the old pond. This is the thing that will haunt her, the unsolved puzzle that will follow her to her grave.

There are times Tricia wishes she could be the pretty one. Even better, she wishes she could be both pretty and smart, even though everyone knows that's impossible. There are other times she knows it's that she wants to be *with* the pretty one. She dreams of kissing Helen, running her fingers through her fiery hair. She imagines trying on Helen's clothes, and she imagines them shopping together. They take turns in the dressing room, like a movie montage, holding up dresses and jeans and sweaters, saying "What do you think about this one and this one and this one?" Tricia knows it will never happen. She and Helen don't spend time together unless they're solving a mystery. She doesn't even think they're friends.

Sometimes Tricia wonders whether she would rather be with Greg, or be like him. So smooth, so confident, always ready with a quip and a smile. Always up for anything. Other times she knows with absolutely certainty she doesn't want to be with or like any of them at all. In fact, she hates them. They terrify her, and she wants to run as far away as she can and never see any of them again.

Every day, after he picks up the last child at the last stop, before he turns onto the road leading to the school, Old Man McGinty counts the children's faces. He counts them once in the rearview mirror, and once again when he turns around. There is always one more or less than there should be, but he can never be sure which way around. His school bus is haunted; he knows this with certainty, but he has never told anyone. The school itself is haunted, but he's the only one who knows.

Once the ghost children realize he can see them, they start coming to him all the time. They press their hands against his skin, never blinking, never breathing, silently asking why. "Tell me how to help you," he begs, but they cannot answer him.

At night, when he's making soup from a paper packet, they

hover around his stove. When he's watching TV, they drape themselves over the top of the set. When he's brushing his teeth, they crowd the mirror beside him. When he sleeps, they stand at the foot of his bed, and they are there again when he wakes in the morning.

"Please," he says. "Please tell me how to help you."

The ghosts' voices have been stolen, so they show him instead. Old Man McGinty dreams about the school grounds. He dreams about a particular patch of trees, so far away at the edge of the property that it isn't even visible from the school. There's an old shed under the trees where a wheelbarrow and other unused equipment is stored. It's a bad place. Nobody goes there. It's just another one of those things that everyone knows.

Rooster is the dropout, the burnout, the one everyone knows will amount to nothing. They tell him so all the time. In turn, he tells them nothing. Not about the nightmares, or how he wakes screaming and shaking with a head full of memories that couldn't possibly be his.

He's a soldier in a far away country where the air thumps with mortar fire and helicopter blades, and all around him foliage burns. He knows the memories cannot be real. He's only ever been a member of the Super Teen Detective Squad. They solve mysteries and unmask fake monsters, and nothing is dangerous or scary at all.

The four of them drive around in an old jalopy painted the blinding-bright color of the sun. He isn't sure where it came from. Like the Squad itself, it's always been there, a fifth member of their team. Except didn't there used to be a dog? Rooster thinks so. At least he remembers burying his fingers and face in thick fur, holding on like he was drowning.

Rooster has never asked any other members of the Squad

about the dog. The only thing they ever talk about is mysteries. Like the Squad isn't just what they do, it's everything they are. They've met other Teen Detectives in their time—the sheriff's daughter who is a little bit psychic and her pudgy, brown-haired friend. The murder-solving twins. He's always wondered which one of them is the evil one and if they'll grow up to be a killer after all they've seen, if they even grow up at all. There have been others, a blur of faces over the years. Every time they encounter another team, he can't help thinking "Aren't they too young for this? Aren't we all?"

The case he remembers the most clearly is the Civil War ghost haunting the old graveyard. Of course, he wasn't really a ghost, though he was a soldier, only in a different war. He felt more at home among the dead, he told them when they unmasked him, but no one other than Rooster seemed to hear.

He wanted to hug the man, or hold his hand, but he was afraid to even look him in the eye. He wanted to say he could understand the appeal of wearing a mask, of being someone else for a while. He could understand wanting to hide. But he didn't say anything at all, silently thinking about the days he wakes with a name in his mouth that tastes of mud, and cold beans, and rain. Which one is he? Is the soldier or the Teen Detective Rooster's real disguise?

"It's the ghost who killed them," Old Man McGinty says. "Not the little ones, the big one. Except he wasn't a ghost at the time. He was a man, and he worked at the school a long time ago."

The ghosts showed him, the ones with the blue skin, sad eyes, and tiny hands. The ones who curl up on top of his refrigerator and slide in under his door. They showed him what happened to them, and he tries to tell everyone, but no one listens.

"Please," he says. "Just let me show you, just let me explain."

He digs in the dirt until it forms rinds under his nails and streaks his arms. He unearths skulls and cradles them in his hands. He kisses them, whispering lullabies as he weeps into the empty sockets of their eyes. They're his ghosts. The ones who ride his bus. He knows them, he tries to say. But the parents who didn't even notice their children were missing until he told them—the men who smell of scotch and expensive cologne, and the women who smell like chalkboards and wear skirts that brush their calves and pillbox hats on Sundays—click their tongues.

"There's no such thing as ghosts," they say. "And everyone knows what monsters look like anyway. They look like you." Wrong. Sad. Old.

After all, how else would he know where to find the bodies? And there are so many rumors about him. He must be the one.

Greg is the rich one. Definitively rich, disgustingly rich, not just a little rich like Helen. He lives in a mansion, surrounded by grounds that have a whole team of people to take care of them. There is a tennis court, a swimming pool, and more water features than he's ever cared to count.

Greg isn't certain how his father made all his money. He thinks it might have something to do with weapons and a military coup in a far away country. All he knows is that his father is not a good man. His father was the first man who ever hurt him, but he wasn't the last one.

There's a place on the grounds where Greg never goes. It's a little cabin, barely more than a shed really, where the groundskeeper used to live. There's no groundskeeper now. The lawn and all the water features are maintained by a team who arrive once a week in a fleet of vans with neat green lettering on the side. Their logo is a broad-shouldered silhouette, standing under a tree.

Something happened in that cabin. But no matter how much he wants to forget, he still hears and smells and feels it, like jagged fragments lodged in his skull. He remembers screaming, his throat open and raw. The handles of the garden shears dry and splintery in his hands. The knowledge that once the terrible, ragged breathing stopped, no one would ever hurt him again.

He tried to tell his mother, then it was like someone came down out of the sky and scooped all the bad things out of the world like they'd never happened. Nobody said they were sorry, or that everything would be okay. There was never any body, no police ever came, then the cabin on the grounds was empty so maybe there was never a groundskeeper at all.

Just in case, though, he doesn't go there anymore. Because maybe the rind of dirt he remembers under the groundskeeper's nails was real. The calluses on his hand the first time they met. His father had just hired new staff, and he presented Greg to each of them like a trophy, not like a son. The groundskeeper is the only one who winked at him. "Don't let Greg be a bother," his father had said, like Greg was a troublesome lump of stone that might be run over with a lawnmower. "Oh don't worry your head, Mr. B," the groundskeeper had said. "I used to keep the grounds at the school. I love children." And that's when he winked. He leaned down so Greg would see, and his breath smelled like wintergreen.

There was a dog, too. A big one, with black and tan fur. It had a spiked collar and mean teeth. Greg remembers how one time it barked at him, and lunged against its chain. He was so scared he wet himself. The groundskeeper laughed; the dog belonged to him. But he told Greg not to worry, it would be their little secret. He wouldn't tell anyone, especially not Greg's father. Greg could even change his pants in the groundskeeper's

cabin so no one else would see, and then he would help Greg
bury the old ones when he was done. The groundskeeper told
Greg he was very good at burying things so no one would ever
find them.

Eventually, Greg realized the dog probably wasn't mean at
all. It had been hurt too. But by then the damage was done. He's
been scared of dogs ever since.

There was another dog later. At least Greg thinks so, but he
isn't sure. He stole a bottle of liquor from his father and went
driving in the sun-yellow jalopy. He'd driven too fast, top down,
even though it was raining. The headlights made tunnels of
light, then something jumped out in front of the car. Or maybe
he'd already been veering for the side of the road, foot crushed
down against the pedal. Maybe whatever he hit saved him.

Once he'd stopped the car, shaking, afraid to look at the
shape lying in the road, a man appeared. A boy, really, except he
looked much older—his hair long, his beard scruffy, his clothes
covered in mud. He shaved the beard later, and he turned into
Rooster, but he had it the first time Greg met him, when he
picked him up hitchhiking and they drove through the rain.
Rooster had a guitar case and he smelled like incense. He looked
like he'd been through a war, and he was crying.

The dark bundle still lay at the side of the road, all limbs
bent and pointing the wrong way. Greg didn't look at it as they
pulled away, while Rooster couldn't stop looking, staring in the
rearview mirror like he was leaving his best friend behind. Or
maybe Greg imagined that part. He was drunk and it was raining, after all.

"This isn't right," Greg says. Or that's what he tries to say, but
what comes out as Old Man McGinty weeps and clings to
Greg's shoes is, "I bet you thought you could get away with it,

too. Meddling with those kids." The real words, the ones he wants to say, stick in his throat. He smells wintergreen, and feels the splintery handles of garden shears gripped in his hand.

"Stop sniveling," Helen says. "You're pathetic. You're not even a real monster." Her teeth are very bright when she says it; her lipstick very red. It's hard for Old Man McGinty to see her. He's on the ground, looking up, and she's haloed by the sun. It sets her hair on fire and casts her face in shadow. She doesn't look human.

"I'm sorry," Rooster whispers, but he isn't sure anyone hears. He feels sorry for the old man, babbling about ghosts. Rooster knows a thing or two about ghosts. They are terrifying.

"Fuck you," Tricia says. She screams it behind a locked jaw, so all that comes out is a moan.

She never asked for this. She never even wanted to be a Teen Detective. She had never touched alcohol in her life, but right now, she wants to drink and fuck and take drugs over and over again until she forgets everything, even her own name. She won't be Tricia anymore. She'll be Karen. She'll be the kind of girl who smokes half a cigarette, then grinds the rest under her heel before lighting up another one. No one will ever think of her as the smart one again.

It's all gone wrong, and he isn't sure how. He only tried to help. Now there's a rope around Old Man McGinty's wrists, and the Super Teen Detective Squad is being congratulated on another job well done. Everyone who matters is happy; the monster has been revealed, justice has been done.

The ghosts watch Old Man McGinty with heart-broken eyes. The bodies he dug up are old. Theirs are still missing. But no one seems to have noticed except for him. They've already moved on. Sunnydale has a remarkably short memory, it seems.

The sun sets, the slate wiped clean, and the Super Teen Detective Squad go their separate ways. Old Man McGinty listens to gravel crunching under three pairs of feet, and two sets of wheels. And just before he's led away, very far off in the distance, he thinks he hears a lonely dog howl.

EXHALATION #10

IT'S NOT A SNUFFFILM, AT LEAST NOT THE TRADITIONAL KIND. THE single MiniDV cassette was recovered from the glove box of a crashed beige Ford Taurus. The car had passed through a metal guardrail and flipped at least once on its way down the incline on the other side. No body was found. The license plate had been removed, the VIN sanded away, no identifying information left behind.

The handwritten label on the cassette reads *Exhalation #10*. The film it contains is fifty-eight minutes long; fifty-eight minutes of a woman's last breaths, and her death finally at the 56:19 mark.

Henry watches the whole thing.

The padded envelope the tape arrived in bears Paul's handwriting, as does the tape's label—a copy of the original, safely tucked away in an evidence locker. It's no more than a half-hour drive between them; Paul could have delivered the tape in person, but Henry understands why he would not. Even knowing this tape is not the original, even touching it only to slip it into a machine for playback, Henry feels his fingers coated with an invisible residue of filth.

Expensive equipment surrounds him—sound-mixing boards, multiple screens and devices for playback, machines for converting from one format to another. Paul warned him about the tape over the phone, and still Henry wasn't prepared.

During the entire fifty-eight minutes of play time, the woman's body slumps against a concrete wall, barely conscious. She's starved, one arm chained above her head to a thick pipe. The light is dim, the shadows thick. The angle of her head, lolled against her shoulder, hides her face. The camera watches for fifty-eight minutes, capturing faint, involuntary movements —her body too weak for anything else—until her breathing stops.

Henry looks it up: on average, it takes a person ten days to die without food or water. The number ten on the label implies there are nine other tapes, an hour recorded every day. Or are there other tapes capturing every possible moment to ensure her death ended up on film?

"Just listen," Paul had told him. "Maybe you'll hear something we missed."

Henry's ears are golden. That's what his Sound Design professor at NYU said back in Henry's college days. As a kid, Henry's older brother, Lionel, had called it a superpower. By whatever name, what it means is that as Henry watches the tape, he can't help hearing every hitch, every rasp. Every time the woman's breath wants to stop, and every time her autonomic system forces one more gasp of air into her lungs.

He never would have agreed to watch the tape if he hadn't been a little bit drunk and a little bit in love, which he's been more or less since the day he met Paul in film school. Paul, whose eye for framing, for details, for the perfect shot is the equivalent of Henry's golden ear. Paul, whose cop father was shot in the line of duty three months short of graduation, causing him to abandon his own moviemaking dreams and follow in his footsteps by becoming a cop as well.

Henry has always known better than to chase after straight boys, what he knows intellectually and logically has never been a defense against Paul. So when Paul called at his wit's end and asked him to just listen to the tape, please, Henry agreed.

After fifty-six minutes and nineteen seconds, the woman dies. After another minute and forty-one seconds, the tape ends. Henry shuts down the screen and stops just short of pulling the plug from the wall.

~

"Jesus Christ, Paul, what did I just watch?"

A half-empty bottle sits at Henry's elbow in his bedroom, his phone pressed to his ear. He locked the door of the editing suite behind him, but the movie continues, crawling beneath his skin.

"I know. I'm sorry. I wouldn't ask if...I didn't know what else to do."

Henry catches the faint sound of Paul running his fingers through his hair, static hushing down the line. Or, at least, he imagines he hears the sound. Even after all this time he's not always sure if what he thinks he hears is just in his head, or whether he really does have a "superpower."

After watching the video of the dying woman, he's even less sure. He watched the whole thing and didn't hear anything to help Paul. But he can't shake the feeling there *is* something there —a sound trapped on the edge of hearing, one he hasn't heard yet. A sound that's just waiting for Henry to watch the video again, which is the last thing in the world he wants to do.

"I'm sorry," Paul says again. "It's just...It's like I hit a brick wall. I have no goddamn idea where this woman died, who she is, or who killed her. I couldn't see anything on the tape, and you can hear things no one else can hear. You can tell which goddamn road a car is on just by the sound of the tires."

In Paul's voice—just barely ragged—is his fear, his frustration. His anger. Not at Henry, but at the world for allowing a woman to die that way. The ghost of the woman's breath lingers in the whorls of Henry's ears. Do the shadows, carving the woman up into distinct segments, stain Paul's eyelids like bruises every time he blinks?

"I'll try," Henry says, because what else is there to say? Because it's Paul. He will listen to the tape a hundred times if he has to. He'll listen for the sounds that aren't there—something in the cadence of the woman's breathing, the whirr of an air duct he didn't notice the first time, something that will give her location away.

"Thank you." Paul's words are weary, frayed, and Henry knows it won't be a stray bullet for him, like the one that took his father. It'll be a broken heart.

The drug overdoses, the traffic accidents, the little boy running into the street after his ball, the old man freezing to death in an alleyway with nowhere else to go. They will erode Paul, like water wearing down stone, until there's nothing left.

Closer than Paul's sorrow is the clink of glass on glass as Henry pours another drink. The bottle's rim skips against the glass. Ice shifts with a sigh. He pictures Paul sitting on the edge of his bed, and it occurs to him too late that he didn't bother to look at the clock before he called. He listens for Maddy in the background pretending to be asleep, rolling away and grinding her teeth in frustration at yet another of duty's late-night calls.

Henry likes Maddy. He loves her, even. If Paul had to marry a woman, he's glad Maddy was the one. From the first time Paul introduced them, Henry could see the places Paul and Maddy fit, the way their bodies gravitated to one another—hips bumping as they moved through the kitchen preparing dinner, fingers touching as they passed plates. They made sense in all the ways Paul and Henry did not, even though their own friendship had been instant, cemented when Paul came across Henry drunkenly trying to break into an ex-boyfriend's apartment to get his camera back, and offered to boost him through the window.

At the end of that first dinner with Maddy, Henry had sat on the deck with her, finishing the last of the wine while Paul washed dishes.

"Does he know?" Maddy had asked.

Her gaze went to the kitchen window, a square of yellow light framing Paul at the sink. There was no jealousy in her voice, only sympathetic understanding.

"I don't know."

"I won't tell if you don't." Maddy reached over and squeezed Henry's hand, and from that moment, their relationship had been set, loving the same man, lamenting his choice of career.

Henry wants to tell Paul to wrap himself around Maddy, take comfort in the shape of her, and forget about the woman, but he knows Paul too well.

"I'll call you if I hear anything," Henry says.

"Henry?" Paul says as Henry moves to hang up.

"Yeah?"

"Are you still working on the—"

"The movie? Yeah. Still."

His movie. Their movie. The one they started together at NYU, back when they had dreams, back before Paul's father died. The one Henry is now making, failing to make, alone.

"Good. That's good," Paul says. "You'll have to show it to me someday."

"Yeah. Sure." Henry rubs his forehead. "Get some sleep, okay?"

Henry hangs up. In the space behind his eyes, a woman breathes and breathes and breathes until she doesn't breathe anymore.

～

Sweat soaks thirteen-year-old Henry's sheets, sticking the T-shirt and boxer shorts he sleeps in against his skin. His mother left the windows open, but there's no breeze, only the oppressive heat they drove through to get to the rental cabin. His brother snores in the bunk above him, one hand dangling over the side.

The noise comes out of nowhere, starting as a hum, building to a scream, slamming into Henry full force. Henry claps his hands to his ears. Animal instinct sends him rabbiting from the bed. His legs tangle in the sheets, and he crashes to the floor. The sound is still there, tied to the heat, the weight and thickness of the air birthed in horrible sound.

"Henry?" Lionel's voice is sleep muffled above him.

Henry barely hears it over the other sound, rising in pitch, inserting itself between his bones and his skin. There's another sound tucked inside it, too, worse still. A broken sound full of distress and pain.

Footsteps. His mother's and father's voices join his brother's. Hands pry his hands from his ears.

"Can't you hear it?" Henry's voice comes in a panicked whine, his breath in hitching gulps.

"Henry." His mother shakes him, and his eyes snap into focus.

"It's just cicadas. See?" His father points to the window.

A single insect body clings to the screen. Lionel trots over and flicks the insect away before pulling the window closed.

"What's wrong with him?" Lionel asks.

Even with the window shut, the noise remains, filling every corner of the room.

"Can't you hear?" Henry's hands creep toward his ears again.

His mother gets him a glass of water. His father and brother watch him with wary eyes. They don't hear it. They hear the cicadas' song, but not the broken, stuttering sound that digs and scrapes at Henry's bones. No one hears it except for him.

Later, Henry learns that the sound is the cicadas' distress call, the noise they make when they're threatened or in pain. And over the course of the two weeks at the lake, Henry learns his hearing is different from the rest of his family's, possibly from almost everyone else he knows. There are tones, nuances, threads of sound that are lost to others. It's as though he's developed an extra sense, and he hates it.

Lionel, however, turns it into a game, dragging Henry around to various parts of the lake, asking him what he hears, getting Henry to challenge him to see if he can hear it, too. Henry's big brother grins, amazed at every sound Henry describes—birds murmuring in distant trees, small animals in the burrows, dropped fishing lines, an aluminum rowboat tapping against a dock all the way across the lake.

Henry almost allows himself to relax, to have fun, until on one of their excursions he hears the crying girl.

Henry and Lionel are deep enough in the woods surrounding the lake that the dense, midsummer foliage screens them from the road, the water, and the other cottages. Henry scans the tree trunks, looking for shed cicada shells. The sound comes, like it did the first night, out of nowhere—a ticking, struggling sound like hitching breath. Except this time it's not hidden in cicada song but stark and alone, somewhere between mechanical and organic, full of pain.

Henry freezes, cold despite the sweat-slick summer air. Lionel is almost out of sight between the trees before he notices Henry is no longer with him.

"What's wrong?" Lionel trots back, touching Henry's arm.

Henry flinches. He's sharply aware of his own breath. His chest is too tight. Underneath the insect sound there is something else—distinctly human, horribly afraid. He tries to speak, and the only sound that emerges is an extended exhalation, a "hhhhhhhh" that goes on and on.

Lionel's repeated questions fade. Henry stumbles away from

his brother, half-blinded by stinging eyes, catching tree trunks for support. He follows the sound, its insistence a knife-sharp tug at his core. He needs to find the source of the sound. He needs....

Henry crashes to his knees, nearly falling into a hole opened up in the ground. The edges are ragged and soft, the forest floor swallowing itself in greedy mouthfuls. There's a caught breath of alarm from below him, wet with tears, weak with exhaustion, fading.

"There's someone down there," Henry pants, the words coming out between clenched teeth, his whole body shuddering. He's doubled over now, arms wrapped around his middle, where the sound burrows inside him.

"What—" Lionel starts, but then he looks, seeing what Henry sees.

The girl is barely visible. The tree canopy blocks direct sunlight, and the hole is deep enough that the child is a mere smudge at the bottom.

"Get..." Henry's voice breaks. Tears stream on his cheeks. "Mom. Dad. Get help."

Lionel sprints away, and despite the pain, Henry stretches out flat on his stomach. Leaves crackle, branches poke at him. Things crawl through the earth underneath him, worms and beetles and blind moles further undermining its integrity, impossible things he shouldn't be able to hear. He stretches his arm as far as he can, pressing his cheek against the ground. He doesn't expect the girl to be able to reach him, but he hopes his presence might comfort her.

"It's okay." His shoulder feels like it will pop out of its socket. "I'm not going to leave you."

From the dark of the earth, the girl sniffles. Henry stretches further still, imagining small fingers reaching back for him.

"It's okay," he says again, terrified the girl will die before rescue comes. Terrified it will be his fault, his failure, if she does. "Just hold on, okay? Hold on."

The second time, Henry listens to the tape with his eyes closed. It scarcely matters. He still sees the woman, slumped and taking her last shallow breaths, but inside the theater of his mind she is so much worse. She's carved up by shadow, her skin blotched as though already rotting from within. At any moment she will raise her head and glare at Henry, his powerlessness, his voyeurism.

He stretches after any glimmer of identifying sound, wondering if his unwanted superpower has finally chosen this moment to abandon him. Then, all at once, the sound is there, sharp as a physical blow.

A faint burr, rising from nothing to a scream. The cicada song he can't help but hear as a herald of doom. It knocks the breath from his lungs, bringing in its place the heat of summer days, air heavy and close and pressed against the window screens. He shoves his chair back from the desk so hard he almost topples, and stares, wide-eyed. The image on the screen doesn't change. After a moment, he forces himself to hit rewind. Play.

Ragged breath, stuttering and catching. There's no hint of insect song. Even though Henry knows exactly when the rise and fall of the woman's chest will cease, he holds his own breath. Every time her breath falters, he finds himself wishing the painful sound would just stop. It's a horrible thought, but he can't help it, his own lungs screaming as he waits, waits, waits to hear whether she will breathe again.

Then, a sound so faint yet so distinct Henry both can't believe he missed it and isn't certain it's really there. He reverses the tape again, afraid the sound will vanish. Sweat prickles, sour and hot in his armpits. He barely hears the woman breathing this time, his strange powers of hearing focused on the almost-imperceptible sound of a train.

A primal response of exaltation—Henry wants to shout and punch the air in triumph. And at the same time, the woman on the screen is still dying, has been dead for days, weeks, months, even, and there's nothing he can do. Henry forces himself to listen one last time, just to be sure. The train is more distinct this time, the lonely howl of approaching a crossing. Goose bumps break out across Henry's skin. His body wants to tremble, and he clenches his teeth as though he's freezing cold.

He must have imagined the cicadas, even though the noise felt so real, a visceral sensation crawling beneath his skin. The train, though, the train is real. He can isolate the sound, play it for Paul. It's an actual clue.

He thinks of the summer at the lake when he was thirteen years old, Lionel snoring in the bunk above him. That first terrible night where it seemed as though all the cicadas in the trees around the lake had found their way into the room. Then, later, how their song had led him to the almost-buried girl.

Henry reaches for the phone.

"I'm going to send a sound file your way," he says when Paul answers. "It's something. I don't know if it's enough."

"What is it?" Water runs in the background, accompanied by the clatter of Paul doing dishes. Henry imagines the phone balanced precariously between Paul's ear and shoulder, the lines of concern bracketing his mouth and crowded between his eyes.

"A train. It sounds like it's coming up to a crossing."

"That's brilliant." For a moment there's genuine elation in Paul's voice, the same sense of victory Henry felt moments ago. And just as quickly, the weight settles back in. "It might give us a radius to search, based on where the car was found, and assuming the killer was somewhat local to that area."

There's a grimness to Paul's voice, a hint of distraction as though he's already half forgotten Henry is on the other end of the phone, his thoughts churning.

"Thank you," Paul says after a moment, coming back to himself.

The water stops, but Henry pictures Paul still standing at the sink, hands dripping, looking lost.

"I should—" Paul starts, and Henry says, "Wait."

He takes a breath. He knows what he's about to ask is unreasonable, but he needs to see. Without the safety and filter of a camera and a video screen in the way.

"When you go looking, I want to go with you."

"Henry, I—"

"I know," Henry interrupts. His left hand clenches and unclenches until he consciously forces himself to relax. "I know, but you probably weren't supposed to send me the tape, either."

Henry waits. He doesn't say please. Paul takes a breath, wants to say no. But Henry is already in this, Paul invited him in, and he's determined to see it through.

"Fine. I'll call you, okay?"

They hang up, and Henry returns to his computer to isolate the clip and send it to Paul. Once that's done, Henry opens up another file, the one containing the jumble of clips he shot with Paul at NYU. Back when they had big dreams. Back before Paul's father died. Back before fifty-eight minutes of a woman breathing out her last in an unknown room.

Henry chooses a clip at random and lets it play. A young man sits in the back seat of a car, leaning his head against the window. He's traveling across the country, from a small town to a big city. The same journey Henry himself had taken, though he'd only crossed a state. There are other clips following a boy who grew up in the city, in his father's too-big shadow, but both boys' heads are full of dreams. Two halves of the same story, trying to find a way to fit together into a whole. Except now, the film will always be unfinished, missing its other half.

Even though he knows he will never finish the movie without Paul, Henry still thinks about the sounds that should accompany the clip. It's an exercise he engages in from time to time, torturing himself, unwilling to let the movie go. Here, he would put the hum of tires, but heard through the bones of the young man's skull, an echo chamber created where his forehead meets the glass.

The perfect soundscape would also evoke fields cropped to stubble, the smell of dust and baking tar and asphalt. It would convey nerves as the boy leaves behind everything he's ever known for bright lights and subway systems. Most importantly, it would also put the audience in the boy's shoes as he dreams of kissing another boy without worrying about being seen by someone he knows, without his parents' disappointment and the judgment of neighbors' faces around him in church every Sunday.

Henry watches the reflections slide by on-screen—telephone poles and clouds seen at a strange angle. His own drive was full of wind-and-road hum broken by his parents' attempts at conversation, trying to patch things already torn between them. Henry had gotten good at filtering by then, shutting out things he didn't want to hear. Maybe he should have given his parents a chance, but love offered on the condition of pretending to be someone else didn't interest him then, and it doesn't interest him now.

Between one frame and the next, the image on the screen jumps, and Henry jumps with it. Trees, jagged things like cracks in the sky, replace the cloud and telephone pole reflections. The car window itself is gone, and the camera looks up at the whip-thin branches from a low angle.

Then the image snaps back into place just as Henry slaps the pause button. He knows what he and Paul shot. He has watched the clips countless times, and everything about the trees cracking their way across the sky is wrong, wrong, wrong.

When the phone rings, Henry almost jumps out of his skin. He knocks the phone off the desk reaching for it, leaving him sounding weirdly out of breath when he finally brings it to his ear.

"I'll pick you up tomorrow around ten," Paul says. "I have an idea."

"Okay." Henry lets out a shaky breath.

His pulse judders, refusing to calm. He needs a drink and a shower. Then maybe a whole pot of coffee, because the last thing he wants to do is sleep. When he blinks, he sees thin black branches crisscrossing the sky, and he hears the rising whine of cicada song.

There is a legend that says cicadas were humans once. They sang so beautifully that the Muses enchanted them to sing long past the point when they would normally grow tired, so they could provide entertainment throughout the night while the gods feasted.

But the enchantment worked too well. The singers stopped eating. They stopped sleeping. They forgot how to do anything except sing.

They starved to death, and even then the enchantment held. They kept singing, unaware they'd died. Their bodies rotted, and their song went on, until one of the Muses took pity on them and fashioned them new bodies with chitinous shells and wings. Bodies with the illusion of immortality that could live for years underground, buried as if dead but wake again.

Cicadas are intimately acquainted with pain, because they know what it is to die a slow death as a spectacle for someone else's pleasure. But they do not die when they are buried. They merely dream, and listen to other buried things, things that perhaps should not have been buried at all. They remember what they hear. When they wake, they are ready to tell the secrets they know. When they wake, they sing.

~

Paul drives, Henry in the passenger seat beside him, a bag of powdered donuts between them, and two steaming cups of coffee in the cup holders.

"Isn't that playing a bit to stereotype?" Henry points. Paul grins, brushing powdered sugar from his jeans.

"So sue me. They're delicious." He helps himself to another. Henry's stomach is too tight for food, but he keeps sipping his coffee, even though his nerves are already singing.

Paul mapped out a widening radius from where the car with the MiniDV in the glove box was found, circling the nearby railroad crossings. It isn't much, but it's something. They're out here hoping that whoever killed the woman crashed his car on the way back to his home, which might be the place he killed the woman. Maybe they'll find her body there, or maybe he was on the way back from burying her somewhere else. Maybe they'll find him. Henry is both prepared and unprepared for this scenario.

Right now, he's not letting himself think that far ahead. He's focusing on the plan, tenuous as it is, driving around to likely locations where he will *listen*. Henry feels like a television psychic, which is to say a total fraud. He wants to enjoy the relative silence of the car, the tick of the turn signal, the engine revving up and down. He wants to enjoy spending time with Paul, catching up, just old friends. He doesn't want to be thinking of snuff films and ghosts, and on top of that there's a nervous ache in his chest that keeps him conscious of every time he glances at Paul, wondering if his gaze lingers too long.

Trees border the road. It's early fall, and most are denuded of their leaves. Henry peers between the trunks, looking for

EXHALATION #10 | 175

deer. The sound, when it comes, is every bit as unexpected and violent as the last time. A reverberating hum, rising to a scream —cicada song, but with another noise tucked inside it this time, one he remembers from when he was a child.

That hitching, broken sound. Like gears in a machine struggling to catch. Like a baby's cry. A wounded animal. Henry jerks, his body instinctively trying to flee. His head strikes the window and pain blooms in his forehead above his right eye.

"Are you—"

Concern tinges Paul's voice, but Henry barely hears it. The sound has hooks beneath his skin, wanting to drag him in among the trees.

"Turn here." Henry bites the words out through the pain, the song filling him up until there's no space left for breath.

Paul looks at him askance but flicks the turn signal, putting them on a road that quickly gives way to gravel and dust. The trees grow closer here, their branches whip-thin, the same ones he saw in the corrupted clip of their film.

"Pull over."

Henry's breath comes easier now, the pain fading to a dull ache like a bruise. The cicada song forms an undercurrent, less urgent but not completely gone. Paul kills the engine. His expression is full of concern. Henry wants to thank him for his trust, but whatever waits for them in the woods is no cause for either of them to be thankful.

He climbs out of the car, buries his hands in his pockets, and walks. Leaves crunch as Paul trots behind him. Nervous energy suffuses the air between. Henry hears the questions Paul wants to ask, held trapped behind his teeth. It's nothing Henry can explain, so he keeps walking, head down.

When Henry stops, it's so sudden Paul almost trips. Tree branches cross the sky in the exact configuration Henry saw in the film, only the angle is wrong. Henry should be seeing them from lower down. From the height of a child.

The burr of cicadas grows louder, the steady drone rising to an ecstatic yell. Henry forces himself to keep his eyes on the trees, turning to walk backward. He pictures a girl being led through the trees, a man's hand clamped on her upper arm. Her death waits for her among the trees, and so does a camera on a tripod.

Henry is thirteen years old again, listening to the crying girl, lost and frightened and in pain. The hours after her discovery blur in his mind, though certain moments stand out sharp as splinters beneath his skin. The scent of leaf rot and dirt, his cheek pressed to the forest floor. His parents lifting him bodily out of the way as the rescue crew arrived, and Henry scrabbling at the earth, refusing to let go, terrified of leaving the girl alone.

He remembers seeing the girl's face for the first time but not what she looked like. In his mind, her features are as blurred and indistinct as they were at the bottom of the hole—eyes and mouth dark wounds opened in her pale skin.

There were endless questions from his parents, from the rescue crew—how had he found the girl, did he see her fall, was it an accident, did someone hurt her? They called Henry a hero, and he wanted none of it. He remembers burying himself under the blankets on the bottom bunk in the cabin, wishing he could stay there for years like a cicada, only emerging with everyone long gone.

Now, as then, the insect song times itself to the blood pounding like a headache in Henry's skull. He's sharply aware of Paul watching him, eyes wide, as Henry stops and turns around.

The shack is half-hidden in the trees, scarcely bigger than a garden shed. There's a catch in Paul's breath, and Henry glances over to see Paul's hand go to his service revolver.

The door isn't locked, but it sticks, warped with weather and clogged with leaves. Henry holds his breath, expecting a stench, expecting a horror movie jump scare, but there's nothing inside but more dead leaves and a pile of filthy rags. A small wooden mallet rests up against one wall.

Paul uses a flashlight to sweep the room, even though they can see every corner from the door. A seam in the floor catches the light, and once Paul points it out, Henry can't unsee it. Paul kneels, prying up boards with a kind of frantic energy, using the edge of a penknife.

"It's another tape." Paul straightens. There's dirt under his nails.

"He killed more than one person." Henry swallows against a sour taste at the back of his throat. He knew, the moment he saw the corrupted bit of film, the moment he heard the cicadas scream, but he'd wanted desperately to be wrong.

Paul holds the tape in a handkerchief, turning it so Henry can see the handwritten label—*Exsanguination*.

"I brought my camcorder. It's in the car." Henry feels the beginning of tremors, starting in the soles of his feet and working their way up his spine. Adrenaline. Animal fear. Some intuition made him pack film equipment before leaving the house, and Henry loathes that part of himself now.

Back in the car, Paul runs the heater, even though there's barely a chill in the air. Sweat builds inside Henry's sweatshirt as he fumbles with the tape, wearing the cotton gloves Paul gave him to preserve fingerprints. He flips the camcorder's small screen so they can both see, but hesitates a moment before hitting play, as if that could change the outcome. Henry knows all movies are ghost stories, frozen slices of time, endlessly replayed. Whatever will happen has already happened. The only thing he and Paul can do is witness it.

Static shoots across the screen, then the image steadies. The girl can't be more than ten years old. Her hair is very long and hangs over her shoulder in a braid. She stands in the center of the shack, dressed in shorts and a T-shirt. Dim light comes through a single grimy window. She shivers.

A man in a bulky jacket and ski mask steps into frame. He picks up the mallet leaned against the wall in the shed, now in a plastic evidence bag in the back of Paul's car, and he methodically breaks every one of the girl's fingers.

The image cuts, then the man and girl are outside. The camera sits on a tripod, watching as the man leads the girl to the spot framed by two stubby trees. The girl is barefoot. She sobs, a sound of pure exhaustion that reminds Henry of the little girl in the hole. This girl's ankles are tied. Her hands free, but useless, her fingers all wrong angles, pulped and shattered.

The man unbraids the girl's hair. He employs the same care he used breaking her fingers. Once it's unbound, it hangs well past the middle of her back. The man lifts and winds strands of it into the spindly branches of the trees growing behind her, creating a wild halo of knots and snarls and twigs.

The girl cannot flee when the man pulls out a knife. She thrashes, a panicked, trapped animal, but the knots of her hair hold her fast. He cuts. Long slashes cover her exposed thighs, her knees, her calves, her arms.

How long does it take a person to bleed to death? Henry and Paul are about to find out.

After what seems like an eternity, long after the girl has stopped struggling, the man steps out of frame. The camera watches as the trees bow, the girl slumps. Branches crack, freeing strands of her hair, but far too late.

Henry gets the door open just as bile and black coffee hits the back of his throat. He heaves and spits until his stomach is empty. Paul places a hand on his back, the only point of warmth in a world gone freezing cold. Henry leans back into the car, and Paul puts his arms around Henry, holding him until the shaking stops.

"I'm sorry," Paul says. "I shouldn't have dragged you into this."

The expression on Paul's face when he says it is a blow to

Henry's freshly emptied gut. The pain in Paul's eyes is real, yes, but what accompanies it isn't quite regret. Instead, guilt under-lies the pain, and Paul's gaze shifts away.

In that moment, Henry knows that Paul wouldn't change a thing if he could. He would still ask Henry to watch the tape, no matter how many times the scenario replayed. This death, among every other he's witnessed, is too big to hold alone. He needs to share the burden with someone, and that someone couldn't be Maddy. Because that kind of death spreads like rot, corrupting everything it touches, like it corrupted Henry and Paul's film, their past, their shared dream. Henry understands.

If Paul shared that pain with Maddy, it would become the only thing he would see anytime he looked at her, and the only thing he could do to save himself would be to let her go. And Maddy isn't someone Paul is willing to let go.

"I'm sorry," Paul says again.

"Me too." Henry reaches for the passenger-side door and pulls it closed. He can't look at Paul. His face aches, like a headache in every part of his skull at once. Paul shifts the car into drive.

"Are you…" Paul's words fall into the silence after they've been driving for a few moments, but he stops, as if realizing the inappropriateness of what he was about to say.

Henry hears the words anyway. *"Are you seeing anyone now?"* Bitterness rises to the back of his throat, even though his stomach is empty. Paul could have asked the question any time during the drive, if he really wanted to know, if the question was genuine curiosity and not born of guilt. Paul asked Henry to share his burden, and now it hurts him to think that Henry might have to carry it alone in turn. Henry hears the words even when Paul doesn't say them, his golden ear catching sounds no one else ever would.

"I hope you find someone," Paul says finally as he pulls back onto the road. "You shouldn't be alone. No one should."

Henry knows what Paul is saying; he should find someone to share his burden, too. Henry can't imagine someone loving him enough to take on that kind of pain; he can't imagine ever wanting someone to. He knows what that kind of love feels like from the other side.

The heater makes a struggling, wheezing sound, and Paul switches it off, rolling his window down. Air roars through the cabin, and cold sweat dries on Henry's skin. If it weren't for Henry's golden ear, the wind would swallow Paul's next words whole.

"I'm sorry it couldn't be me."

It's a good two days before Henry brings himself to check the other clips he shot with Paul. The rot has spread to every single one of them. There's an open barn door looking out onto a barren field, rising up to block the buildings of Manhattan, a water stain on a ceiling spreading to cover the boy's face as he gets his first glimpse of the city, a crack of light under a closet door instead of the flickering gap between subway trains. Each new image is a hole punched in an already fragile structure, unwinding it even more.

Henry understands what the scenes are now, after watching *Exsanguination*. They are films made by ghosts, the last image each of the killer's victims saw before they died. What he doesn't understand is why he is seeing them. Is it because he had the misfortune to hear what shouldn't have been there for him to hear? The cicadas, linking him to the woman whose last sight was of trees through a grimy window. Her death linking him to the deaths of the other ghosts.

Henry shakes himself, thinking of his and Paul's drive home from their aborted attempt to find answers. Awkward silence reigned until Henry stood outside the car, looking in through the driver's window at Paul. Then their fragmentary sentences had jumbled on top of each other.

"You don't have to—" from Paul.

And, "Next time you go—" from Henry.

Standing there, trying not to shiver, Henry had extracted a promise.

"Call me before you go looking. I mean it. I'm coming with you." He almost said, *whether you like it or not*, but Henry knows it isn't a matter of like; it's a matter of need. He saw the gratitude in Paul's eyes and his self-loathing underneath it, hating the fact that he should need to ask Henry to do this thing, that he should be too cowardly to refuse and demand Henry stay home. One way or another, they will both see this through to the end.

Henry doesn't tell Paul about the images corrupting their film. But he watches them again, obsessively, alone, until each is imprinted on his eyelids. His dreams are full of doorways and trees and slivers of light. At the end of the week, Paul finally calls, his voice weary and strained.

"Tomorrow afternoon," Paul says.

Henry barely lets him get the words out before saying, "I'll be ready."

They drive away from the city. Henry's stomach is heavy with dread and the sense of déjà vu. He clenches his jaw, already braced for the sound of cicadas, and speaks without looking Paul's way.

"We're looking for a house with a barn."

From the corner of his eye, Henry sees Paul half turn to him, a question and confusion giving a troubled look to his eyes. But he doesn't ask out loud, and Henry doesn't explain. They drive in relative silence until they reach the first railroad crossing on Paul's map, intending to circle outward from there.

It takes Henry some time to realize that the sound he's been bracing for has been there all along, a susurrus underlying the tire hum and road noise, a constant ache at the base of his skull. How long has he been listening to the cicadas? How long have they been driving?

Fragments of conversation reach him. He realizes Paul has been asking questions, and he's been answering them, but he has no sense of the words coming from his mouth, or even any idea what they're talking about. Suddenly the noise in his head spikes and with it, the pain. Henry grinds his teeth so hard he swears his molars will crack.

"Here." The word has the same ticking, struggling quality as the cicada's distress call.

Henry is thirteen years old again, wanting to clap his hands over his ears, wanting to crawl away from the sound.

"What—"

"Turn here." Henry barks the words, harsh, and Paul obeys, the car fishtailing as Paul slews them onto a long, narrow drive. The drive rises, and when they crest the hill, Henry catches sight of a farmhouse. Paul stops the car. From this vantage point, Henry can just make out the roof of a barn where the land dips down again.

Henry is first out of the car, placing one hand against the hood to steady himself. He closes his eyes, and listens. He's queasy, breathing shallowly, but there, as if simply waiting for him to arrive, the mournful, unspooling call of a train sounds in the distance.

"You hear it, too, right?" Henry opens his eyes, finally turning to Paul.

Paul inclines his head, the barest of motions. He looks shaken in a way Henry has never seen before.

"This is the place." Henry opens his eyes, moving toward the front door.

A sagging porch wraps around the house on two sides. To the right, straggly trees stretch toward the sky. Without having to look, Henry knows there is a basement window looking up at those trees.

Paul draws his service revolver. The sound of him knocking is the loudest thing Henry has ever heard. When there's no answer, Paul tries the knob. It isn't locked. Paul leads and Henry follows, stepping into the gloom of an unlit hallway. The stench hits Henry immediately, and he pulls his shirt up over his nose.

Stairs lead up to the left. Rooms open from the entryway on either side, filled with sheet-covered furniture and windows sealed over with plywood boards. Paul climbs the stairs, and again, Henry follows. Up here, the scent is worse. There are brownish smears on the wall, as if someone reached out a bloody hand to steady themselves and left the blood to dry.

At the top of the stairs and to the left is a door bearing a full bloody handprint. It hangs partially open, and Paul nudges it open the rest of the way. Henry's view is over Paul's shoulder, not even fully stepped into the room, and even that is too much.

The corpse on the bed is partially decomposed, lying on rumpled sheets nearly black with filth. There are no flies, the body is too far gone for that, but Henry hears them anyway, the ghostly echo of their buzz. But just because the flies are gone doesn't mean there aren't other scavengers. A beetle crawls over the man's foot.

Henry bolts down the stairs before he realizes it, back in the kitchen where unwashed dishes pile on the countertops, with more in the sink. Garbage fills the bin by the door. The air here smells sour, but after the room upstairs, it's almost a relief.

Henry thinks of the wrecked car, and imagines the killer somehow pulling himself from the wreck, somehow managing to make it back home, only to die here, bleeding out the way the girl in the woods did. He wants to feel satisfaction for the strange twist of justice, but there's only sickness, and beneath that, a hollow still needing to be filled.

Henry turns toward the basement door. It seems to glare back at him until he makes himself cross the room and open it. Wooden steps, the kind built with boards that leave gaps of darkness between, lead down.

He finds a light switch, but he doesn't bother. Light filters in from the high basement window. It matches the light on the tape where the woman breathed and died and so it is enough.

Beneath the window, a pipe rises from the unfinished floor. There's a tripod aimed at the pipe, a camera sitting on the tripod, the compartment where the tape was ejected standing open. At the base of the pipe, there are marks on the floor. When Henry bends close to see, they resolve into words. *Find me.*

Henry's breath emerges in a whine. For once, his ears fail him. He doesn't hear Paul descending the stairs until Paul is beside him, touching his shoulder. Henry can't bring himself to look up. He can't even bring himself to stand. He stays crouched where he is, swaying slightly. When he does finally look up, it isn't at Paul, it's at the window. On the other side of the dirty glass, stark, black branches crisscross the gray sky. Henry looks at them for a very long time. And he breathes.

There are twelve more tapes. They arrive in a padded envelope, each one labeled like the originals, copies written in Paul's hand —*Exhalation 1–9, Contusion, Asphyxiation,* and *Delirium.* Henry didn't ask, but Paul knew he would need to see them. Even so, it's several weeks before Henry can bring himself to watch.

In *Asphyxiation,* a man hangs from the rafters of the barn, slowly strangling to death under his own weight. In *Contusion,* a little boy is beaten within in an inch of his life and locked in a dark closet, only the faintest sliver of light showing underneath the door. In *Delirium*, an old man is strapped to a bed, injected with a syringe, and left to scream out his life with only the water spot on the ceiling for company.

Paul informs Henry by email that four bodies were unearthed on the property—the old man, the young boy, the hanged man, and the girl. But not the woman. Paul informs Henry that the search is ongoing, her body may have been dumped in the woods somewhere, buried or unburied. It may even have been on the way back that the killer crashed and crawled free of the wreck, leaving the tape behind.

What made her special? Or is she special at all? Perhaps the killer was afraid of burying yet another body so close to his home. Maybe he was planning to dig up the others and move them, too, but he never got the chance. Or maybe, just maybe, he woke in the middle of the night to an insistent cicada's scream and tried to get the woman's corpse as far away as he could. As if that would ever make them stop.

Henry watches the clips one last time, the ones he and Paul shot, the ones corrupted with ghosts. The frames are back to normal, only the footage he and Paul shot of city streets and subway rides—no stark trees, no water-stained ceiling. Henry sees those things nonetheless. He will see them every time he looks at the film. The only thing he can do to save himself is let them go.

After he watches the clips for the last time, he deletes every last one.

When Henry finally makes his movie, his great masterpiece, it's no longer about a boy leaving the country for the city and finding his true home and meeting a boy from the city who grew up in his father's shadow. The city no longer belongs to the boy Henry used to be, and the boy who grew up in his father's shadow never belonged to him at all.

Before he begins work on the movie, Henry moves to a city on the other coast, one smelling of the sea. The trees rising up against the sky there are straight and singular; their branches do not fracture and crack across the sky. That fact goes a little way toward easing his sleep, though he still dreams.

While working on the movie that is no longer about a boy, Henry meets a very sweet assistant director of photography who smiles in a way Henry can't help but return. Soon, Henry finds himself smiling constantly.

Even though the movie Henry makes isn't the one he thought he would make when he first dreamed of neon and subways and fame, it earns him an Oscar nomination. He is in love with the assistant director of photography, and he is loved in turn. He is happy in the city smelling of the sea, as happy as he can be. The love he has with the assistant director of photography—whose eye is good, but not quite golden—isn't the kind of love that would willingly take the burden of death and pain from Henry's shoulders. For that, Henry is grateful. He would crack under the weight of that kind of love, and besides, half his burden already belongs to the man he willingly took it from years ago.

At first, Maddy sends a card every Christmas, and Henry and Paul exchange emails on their respective birthdays. But Henry knew, even on the day he packed up the last of his belongings to drive to the other coast, when he said *see you later* to Paul, he was really saying *goodbye*. Paul chose, and Henry consented to his choice. Maybe Paul's relationship with Maddy could have survived the weight of his pain, but sharing his burden with Maddy wasn't a risk Paul was willing to take.

Henry is the one to drop their email chain, "forgetting" to reply to Paul's wishes of happy birthday. When Paul's birthday rolls around, Henry "forgets" again. It's a mercy—not for him, but for their friendship. Henry can't bear to watch something else die slowly, rotting from within, struggling for one last breath to stay alive. Perhaps it isn't fair, but Henry imagines he hears Paul's sigh of relief across the miles, imagines the lines of tension in his shoulders finally slackening as he lets the last bit of the burden of the woman's death go.

For his part, Henry holds on tighter than before. The movie that earns him his Oscar nomination is about a woman, one who is a stranger, yet one he knows intimately. He saw her at her weakest. He watched her die. The words scratched in the floor where the woman breathed her last, *find me*, are also written on Henry's heart.

He cannot find the woman physically, so he transforms the words into a plea to find *her*, who she was in life or who she might have been. Henry imagines the best life he can for her, and he puts it on film. It is the only gift he can give her; it isn't enough.

When Henry wins his Oscar, his husband, the assistant director of photography, is beside him, bursting with pride. They both climb the stage, along with the rest of the crew. The score from their film plays as they arrange themselves around the microphone. Henry tries not to clench his jaw. A thread winds through the music, so faint no one else would ever hear— the faint burr of rising insect song.

Paradoxically, it is making the movie he never expected to make that finally allows Henry to understand the movie he tried to make years ago. Even though he destroyed the clips, that first movie still exists in his mind. He dreams it, asleep and waking. In the theater of his mind, it is constantly interrupted by windows seen at the wrong angle, water stains, and slivers of light, and scored entirely by insect screams.

The movie that doesn't exist isn't a coming-of-age story. It isn't a story about friendship. It's a love story, just not the traditional kind.

Because what else could watching so many hours of death be? How else to explain letting those frames of death corrupt his film, reach its roots back to the place where their friendship began and swallow it whole? What other name is there for Henry's lost hours of sleep, and the knowledge that he wouldn't say no, even if Paul asked for his help again. Even now. When Henry would still, always, say yes every time.

Every time Henry looks back on the film in his mind, all he sees is pain, the burden he willingly took from Paul so he wouldn't have to carry it alone. Even so, Henry will never let it go. The movie doesn't exist, he destroyed every last frame, but it will always own a piece of Henry's heart. And so will the man he made it for.

EXCERPTS FROM A FILM (1942-1987)

Silver Screen Dream Productions, August 1987

ALONE IN HIS OFFICE GEORGE HARWOOD WATCHES THE DAILIES. She's there in the background. After so long, he almost dismisses it as a trick of his imagination, or maybe the Laphroaig at his elbow, ice warming and cracking in the glass. But no, she's there, his Mary.

George still does things the old-fashioned way, running 16mm film through his Bell and Howell projector. He leaves space on his office wall blank, the furniture cleared to give a clean line of sight. Mary Evelyn Marshall. Sometimes Mary, sometimes Evelyn or Eve. Eva. Lillian. A myriad of names to slip into like a different dress every day.

He comes around his desk, moving closer to the images on his wall. Black and white, a recreation of another time, all high silver and sharp-edged night. The women smile with lips like coal; the men watch them through eyes like high-beams beneath their hats. A bar scene. Couples dancing in the foreground, men and women sipping cocktails in the middle ground. In the background, Mary, Evelyn, Eva, stands almost out of the frame. She isn't watching the band or the couples, she's watching him.

~

She's been dead for over forty years. A shallow grave is the best he can hope for, because the other options are her body crammed into a storm drain, rolled into a tarp alongside the highway, scattered in pieces across defunct rail ties. In the dark, in an alley, in a rain-slicked dead-end.

Or she isn't dead at all. The truth is, he doesn't know what happened to her, but she's here now, blooming like a stain across his latest film. He stops the projector, pulls free a ribbon of celluloid, and holds it to the light. Not just one frame, all of them. Always in the background, smudged-hollow gaze fixed on him.

There are other dead girls, too, fitting themselves into the spaces between actors. As George fits the film back into the projector and runs it again, the ghosts are so obvious he can't believe he missed them, spreading outward from the point that is Mary Evelyn Marshall. Like mushrooms, fruiting after a hard rain. Their skin soft, born on the edge of rot, and so easy to bruise. Once he's seen them, he can't un-see them, until the rest of the film blurs and they're all he can see.

George reaches for his drink. He fumbles, knocking the glass to the ground. Leaving the amber liquid to soak into the carpet, he pulls canisters of film from the safe in the corner of his office instead. 1973—*The Lady in Green*. 1967—*Blue Violet Girls*. 1959 —*Bloody Rose*. 1946—*The White Canary Sings*. A whole rainbow of his sins. He runs them through the projector one by one, even though he already knows. She's there, in all of them.

Shaking so he can barely thread the film, he opens the last canister, the first canister from the bottom of the safe. 1942. Mary Evelyn Marshall is there again, but not dead this time, not yet. She's on the beach, a screen test from a lifetime ago. Wind tugs her curls, and she lifts a hand to push them away. There's no sound, but he hears the question anyway.

"What do you want me to say?"

He answers from behind the hand-held camera, and from decades away in his movie studio office, here and now.

"You don't have to say anything. You're perfect. You're going to be a star."

She doesn't answer, but her eyes and her smile say, *I know.*

Waves crash silently, and she turns to look at the ocean. She'd claimed to be eighteen; he hadn't believed her. Another runaway with dreams of being a big star. A dime a dozen. She'd come miles and miles. He could smell it on her skin—the road, the desert, pine trees, crossing the whole country chasing her dream, or running away from whatever was chasing her.

He hadn't lied about making her a star. She had *it.* Like hunger, but the opposite somehow. The kind of thing men, and even some women, wanted without being able to name. The kind of thing audiences would tear through meat and bone to get their hands on.

George watches the film, spools it back, and watches it again.

There's another film that isn't in the safe. One that arrived nearly forty years ago, wrapped in brown paper, delivered to his office with no return address. Amateur. Full of skips and jumps, cutting off before the end, the last frames ragged and burned.

He finished the job, putting the rest to fire, as if destroying the evidence could undo the crime.

As if reducing it to ashes could bring Mary Evelyn back from the dead.

It occurs to George—far too late—that the only kind of magic he ever needed was this. Watching his films backward to arrive here, on the beach in 1942. This is *his* Mary, better than resurrected, not yet dead, bright and terribly alive. She flashes her teeth as she flickers on the blank space of his wall like she wants to devour the world.

George smells the ocean, licks the tang of salt spray from his lips.

"I'm sorry," he whispers.

He puts his face in his hands. It isn't enough. After forty years, he finally understands. She isn't here for him. This haunting isn't about forgiveness, or offering redemption from the cheap thrills he put on screen. She isn't even punishing him. All she ever needed from him was to *see*, and stop trying to reshape her story and make it his own.

The weight of it crashes down on him. George's chest tightens. Pins and needles tingle up and down his left arm. He's cold. It takes him a while to notice. That's always been the way. He never sees what's in front of his eyes until it smacks him in the face. Too late for apologies or goodbyes.

His vision narrows. A pinpoint, a tunnel. He's not rushing toward the light, it's coming at him. A train. When it hits, the impact bruises across his entire body and he goes down. His legs fold. He grasps wildly and gets only a handful of film canisters. They clatter to the floor and he goes with them. Ribbons of film flutter and crackle, tangling in his fingers and around his legs. Thousands of frames of her, over and over again. Mary Evelyn Marshall. Lillian. Eve. His last thought as the screen fades to black is, *Finally. Finally, at last, thank God.*

Monument Valley, Utah, April 1942

The land here is like something out of a dream. Or a nightmare, depending on your perspective. The sky is huge; the rocks are impossible colors that would look like a mistake if someone tried to paint them that way. There are whole cities carved out of the land by the wind. From a distance, they look like castles in a fairy tale. The kind where ogres live.

I wish Mama had stayed to see this. She turned back in Nebraska. I knew she would. Just like she must have known I would keep going. Nothing in the world could make me go back home.

Because here's the first thing I remember—in my life, I mean. I couldn't have been more than two years old, standing up in my crib, looking out into the hall. A lamp had fallen over, and the light was shining on Mama and Daddy, casting their shadows on the wall like a picture show.

Daddy had his hands around Mama's neck, choking her. She was smaller than him, weaker in every sense of the word. He got her down on her knees before he finally let go, and left her there, crumpled on the floor.

At the time, I was too frightened to cry. If I made a noise, any noise at all, he would strangle me, too.

That moment right there was when I knew. Even if I didn't understand it fully at the time, the knowledge was burned right onto my soul. That's what happens to girls. If you don't fight back, if you don't run away, someone bigger and stronger will chew you up and just walk away. They'll leave you crumpled on the ground like so much trash, and the world will never know you existed at all.

So, no, I'm not going home.

I thought maybe when we saw the dead girl Mama would change her mind. That was proof right there of the same thing I'd seen standing up in my crib, watching shadows projected on the wall. But of course she already knew, and despite that knowledge, she'd made up her mind long ago.

The summer I was twelve, I broke my arm trying out the brand new pair of roller skates my neighbor Wilma Jean got for her birthday. Mama sat with me in the doctor's office and held my hand while I cried. When I was done, she leaned over and wiped my tears. *There are worse things than pain,* she told me. *Like what,* I asked her, because right then all I could think about was how much my arm hurt. I'd heard daddy screaming at her the night before; no matter how I tried to block it out, it kept on coming right through the walls. He said if she was so unhappy, she should just leave. I heard him throw her suitcase on the floor. He must have started throwing her perfume bottles next, because I heard glass breaking and the scent of them all mixed together—rosewater and violets and lily-of-valley—coming through the wall, strong enough to make me gag. But even after that, in the doctor's office, Mama looked me in the eyes and whispered like she was telling me the greatest secret in the world. She said, *Like being alone.*

We first saw the dead girl in a little roadside diner just outside of Ogallala. We'd been driving all night. Well, Mama drove and I helped keep her awake by finding songs on the radio so we could sing along. To her, we were still on vacation, on a lark of a trip to visit Cousin Joyce in Hollywood. That's what she'd told daddy at least. Neither of us ever said the words *running away* out loud.

I ordered a big breakfast: eggs, bacon, sausages, and toast. All that grease was delicious, and I just wolfed it down, but Mama only picked at her food. She'd ordered scrambled eggs, pushing them around her plate. Her shoulders were hunched the whole time, like she was waiting for something heavy to fall.

That's when a man at the counter started talking about the dead girl. He was loud, like he wanted everyone in the diner to hear, not just the waitress refilling his coffee. He'd known the dead girl, you see. Nancy. A real looker, but sweet, innocent, the girl next door that everyone knew. Her family owned a gas station, and sometimes she would help her daddy at the pumps. The man at the counter sounded so proud, like he was special by association now that Nancy was famous, now that she was dead.

He waved around a newspaper with her picture. The killer hadn't been caught, and other dead girls had been found in other towns, like the killer was working his way from coast to coast. Just like me and Mama on our road trip. Look at the pattern, he said, a big jagged line like a bloody smile right across the face of America.

Some kids found Nancy dumped by the side of the road. Another girl had been found in a storm drain, and one inside an empty rail car. Nancy's body had been rolled into a tarp with a few rocks and dirt thrown over top, but whoever killed her didn't bury her. He wanted her to be found.

When I looked up, Mama was staring over my shoulder. I twisted around to see what she was looking at and there was Nancy, the dead girl, in the booth behind ours.

I don't think anyone saw her except Mama and me, and Mama looked down so fast I knew she'd never admit it out loud. The thing about dead girls is once you see them, you can't unsee them, and you realize they're everywhere. If Mama admitted to this one, she'd have to admit what might happen to me, what might happen to her, and she couldn't bring herself to do that.

So she looked away, and I kept looking at Nancy. There were none of the cuts and bruises the man at the counter had talked about, but I could tell she was dead. She looked me right in the eye, and I knew what had been done to her.

I touched Mama's hand so she'd have to look at me, but she pulled away like she'd been burned.

"I can't do this," she said.

There were tears in her eyes. No matter how many times daddy hit her, she didn't know how to be without him.

"I'm sorry," she said.

She dropped money on the table, then she was out the door. A plume of dust kicked up behind her wheels, and she was gone.

I should have been scared, or sad, but I was only relieved. All I could think as I watched her drive away was *finally*.

I know how it all sounds. How many girls run away with the same silly dream of going to Hollywood and becoming a star? But I'm not stupid. I have a plan. My cousin Joyce, the one Mama and I were going to stay with, she's had a few small parts in films. Not speaking parts, but she's up on the big screen. She can introduce me to people, take me to the right parties. And there are *things* a girl can do to get noticed at those parties. You see? Like I said, I'm not stupid.

It isn't about being famous, not really. The way I see it, the camera sees people in a way we don't see each other. The camera doesn't lie. Sure, there are movie tricks, but those are all man-made. The camera sees what it sees and it remembers. So that's me. That's my plan, my dream. I'm going to live forever, up on the big screen.

~

Grauman's Chinese Theater, September 1946

Cameras flash, pinning their shadows to the red carpet like the splayed out wings of a butterfly. This is it, Mary's screen debut, *The White Canary Sings*. George shouldn't be nervous; he's done this before. Mary—except she's Eva today—should be, but she's perfectly poised, lightly holding his arm so he feels like he's the one clinging so he won't fall.

Her curls have been tamed into gentle waves. Lips red, teeth white, dress sleek, and heels impossibly thin. Yet she never stumbles, despite the champagne in the car on the way over. Her eyes are bright and hard. She smiles in a way that seems to light up her whole face. Only he knows she's baring her teeth.

He stumbles, right at the door, but Mary keeps him upright. She should let him fall. This whole thing has been a mistake, nearly four years from beginning to end—from a year of stalling and putting Mary off while he found *just the right project* for her, to conceiving *The White Canary Sings* as her debut feature, to production problems, delays in shooting, to just now in the car on the way here. Three glasses of champagne for her, two of whiskey for him, his hand on her leg, the silky sheen of her dress under his palm. Her head turning, her hand firmly lifting his and putting it back in his lap.

"We're not doing that anymore, George, I told you." Barely twenty to his thirty-five, but she sounded like his mother, scolding him as a naughty child.

He'd flushed shame-hot, but his hand moved to her arm, gripping harder than he intended. "Please, for old times' sake," on his lips. This is exactly what he'd expected. Why else put her off for so long?

At the same time, he'd expected her to comply, fold as she had when they first met at the party on the beach, the taste of salt on her mouth and then his. In his mind, he was already guiding her to his lap, feeling the warm wetness of her wrapped around him. Picturing her carefully reapplying lipstick afterward, smoothing her hair.

She pulled her arm from his hand. "No," once more, final and firm.

The ghost of his fingers remained, fading by the time the car pulled up in front of the theater. She hadn't even needed to dust on powder to cover the marks, like they'd never been there at all. He hated himself, and he hated her, the resilience of her skin, resisting him, and the sickness roiling in his stomach with the aftertaste of whiskey.

And now she's guiding him into the darkened theater like a little boy who can't find his own way. They take their seats in the front row. Mary, Eva, Lillian, Eve. The taste of all her names coats his throat as he glances at her out of the corner of his eye. She's rapt, sitting forward, waiting to breathe in the silver screen ghosts and hold them in her lungs. He might as well not be here at all. Except, no. She needed him to see her first, to see that hungering thing inside her and put her up on screen.

He holds onto this, even though she's changed since those first moments in front of his camera. Did he change her, or did she do it on her own? Was she always dry tinder and he only the spark that finally let her burn?

George wants to take her hand. He wants to apologize. It was supposed to be different. *She* was different. Not like the other girls, but he treated her just like one of them anyway. He's always hungry, starving for more. Mary, Eva, Evelyn melting on his tongue like cotton candy. All spun sugar, at least the parts he can reach. Her core, whatever it is, lies beyond him.

The curtains rise and Mary is there, larger than life, filling the screen. He cast her as a young ingénue, of course, a want-to-be star. She wears a dressing gown, waiting to go on stage, her curves tantalizingly visible through the sheer material. A little titillation for the audience, as though she's something they can have. And oh, did he deliver up the satisfaction.

Even as the opening credits roll, George can feel the end of the film rushing toward him. Her discovery, her meteoric rise, her jealous lover, her obsessed fan. Her body splayed in a cold alley-way, arranged as though death was a beautiful thing. Her throat opened like a bloody smile beneath lips painted jet and ash. The curves of her still a buffet; her body an invitation for appetites of another kind. A cautionary tale and an object lesson—this is how we break our girls and make them tame. This is how we keep them fresh and young. This is what happens when you run away.

It's all wrong. George bolts for the bathroom. He brings up whiskey and his breakfast from hours ago. He brings up guilt and bile and slides to the floor, resting his head against the wall.

He killed her. He killed her because he couldn't have her. He killed her because he doesn't know what else to do with girls. His head pounds. Mary Evelyn Marshall is inside the darkened theater watching herself up on screen and he can't shake the feeling something terrible is coming for her, for him. Like a train, barreling down a tunnel, and there's nothing he can do to stop it. Nothing at all.

～

Hollywood Hills, May 1942

I'm up above the city, smoking. All the glamorous women smoke in Hollywood, that's what Joyce told me, so I figured I'd better get on board. I can see so many lights, and it's peaceful. I've never been this far from home. Back in Detroit, nothing ever changed. Here, the air tastes like rain and electricity and everything waiting to happen.

There's a big party tomorrow at some producer's house on the beach. Joyce promised to take me. There's a swimming pool, and there'll be lots of alcohol, and maybe even drugs. Joyce said I don't have to do anything I don't want to, she'll look out for me. She's lying, though not on purpose. The only person Joyce'll be looking out for is herself. I don't blame her. We all do what we have to do.

Girls like me, and Joyce even, we're a dime a dozen. There's so many of us, but there's only so much room we're allowed to take up in the world. So it's every girl for herself.

I'm thinking of introducing myself as Lillian, just to see how it sounds.

Anyway, the dead girls followed me here. Unlike living girls, ghosts don't take up any room. They can fit themselves in anywhere, spread themselves out and multiply, on and on. It's more than just Nancy. There are dozens of them now. It's like the man in the diner where I met Nancy said. There's a monster killing his way across the country. I guess I followed behind him and cleaned up the mess he made. This whole damn country is haunted, every single step of the way.

Silver Screen Dream Productions, January 1947

George looks up from his desk as Mary Evelyn barges into his office. She's unsteady; she's been crying, and he can smell alcohol on her—something much cheaper and harder than champagne—as she slams a newspaper onto his desk.

"We did this, George."

He recognizes the picture under the headline: Killer Sought in Brutal Murder. Elizabeth Short. She's been all over every newspaper for days. Her mutilated body was found in Leimert Park just under a week ago.

He looks up from the black and white portrait of the smiling girl with curls in her hair, the want-to-be star. It could be Mary Evelyn, but it isn't, because she's leaning on his desk, her hands in fists, shaking.

"We did this to her," Mary says. "It wasn't supposed to be this way. The movie was supposed to help them, give them a face, a name, so people would finally see."

"What are you—?" He stands up, but before he can get the words out, her hand cracks across his skin, hard enough to leave the ghost of her fingers behind.

Then she crumples, sinking to the carpet in front of his desk, and putting her head in her hands. Her fingers muffle her words.

"We put it up on screen, my body in the alleyway, so people would see."

George almost corrects her, telling her Elizabeth was found in a park not an alleyway, and that some want-to-be starlet's death has nothing to do with her. The movie they made, *The*

White Canary Sings, all they did was make a crime flick, something to put behinds in seats and make a quick buck. But deep down, George knows it's a lie. He made a crime flick, Mary made something else. Despite his best efforts, on screen, she transformed. So Mary is right; this is their fault, even if he doesn't fully understand how. Movies are a special kind of magic, playing with make-believe and blurring the line between real and unreal. Humanity is the other half of the equation; they have to be willing to believe, take the ghosts flickering up on screen into their very souls and allow themselves to be changed.

He looks at the newspaper again. The dead girl. He looks back at Mary. Evelyn. Eve. So many names. So many girls all rolled into one, and the dead girl on the front page could be her. He pours a measure of whiskey from the bottle in his desk and holds it out to her even though a drink is the last thing she needs.

Mary downs it in two long swallows. He watches her throat work as the liquid goes down. She stands, a fawn on unsure legs. Her eyes are pinpoints of light, coming out of the shadows straight at him. She takes one unsteady step, bringing the raw sweat-and-alcohol scent right up to him. Her fingers graze the buttons of his shirt.

"For old times' sake." Her words slur.

Her mouth lands hot on his skin, and she murmurs words he can't hear against his throat. His fingers move to help hers even though he wishes they wouldn't. In his haste, in his regret, his shirt rips, buttons scattering. This isn't about him; it's about Mary and he's caught up in her wake somehow. He should say no. He should be stronger, but she's always been the strong one.

She pushes him hard against his desk. Pain jars from his tailbone up his spine. Script pages and a letter opener and a heavy glass paperweight scatter. Every part of her is furnace hot, burning like a fever. George lets himself sink into the dark and the heat, the slick sweat of her, praying he'll fall all the way through to the other side where light will shine again.

~

Hollywood Hills, February 1947

I saw her last night, Elizabeth Short. She came and sat beside me and we looked out at the city together. I offered her a cigarette, the one I was halfway through smoking. She put it to her lips, took a deep drag, and I watched the smoke go right through her and swirl beneath her skin. Part of her was as blue as the sky above us. Part of her was silver, like a goddess up on the screen. Part of her looked just like me.

That was only if I looked at her head-on though. If I looked out of the corner of my eye, I could see what had been done to her. The smile extending to the edges of her face, the cuts all along her body, the line bisecting her.

I wonder if some mortician stitched her up before they buried her, tried to make her look pretty and presentable. Just like George cut up *The White Canary Sings* to make my death beautiful up on screen. Did someone do that to Nancy, too, and all the other dead girls?

The world should have to see what happens to girls like Elizabeth and Nancy. They shouldn't be able to look away.

All the dead girls without names stood behind Elizabeth. The girls who followed me across the country and stuck to my skin. Vague outlines in starlight, the way ghosts are supposed to be. Only Elizabeth was sharp and clear.

I figured it out pretty quick. They made her that way, all those newspapers and cameras, her image everywhere, repeated again and again. They made her a star. Elizabeth Short, the Black Dahlia.

I didn't tell her I was sorry. What would be the point? Sorry never brought anybody back from the dead. I swear I thought I was helping, but of course it doesn't work that way. Dead girls up on the big screen are a thrill. My body filtered through the lens was a lie. It's like I said—the camera tells the truth, but the tricks, those are all man-made. In the dark, it's easy to bend the truth into something safe. When the lights go on, people can step back into the sun knowing a girl didn't really die in an alley, it was all a show.

I have to do more. I can't just be a face or a name, I have to be every face, every name. I have to be all of them in one. If I can put all those ghosts up on screen with me, people will have no choice but to see.

Dead girls aren't lovely. The media tries to make them so, but they're only dead, clogging storm drains and rotting on railway ties.

I have an idea though, or at least the beginnings of one. The way Elizabeth died, and the way she'll never die because her picture is on every newspaper page—there's something there. I was always going to live forever in camera shots, in flashbulb lights, up on the big screen, but now it's going to mean something. I'm going to bring the other dead girls with me. We're going to show the world what we really are.

Silver Screen Dream Productions, October 1965

"What the hell are you saying, George? You want to make a snuff film?"

"No, Jesus, no. Aren't you listening?" George's hands tremble, so he shoves them under the desk as he looks across it at Leonard, his sometime business partner.

He can't help thinking of a film, one that doesn't exist anymore, wrapped in brown paper and delivered to his desk. He sees it when he tries to sleep, playing on the screen of his eyelids. There's something there, something Mary was trying to tell him. He needs to drag the horror out into the light. All those dead girls, he owes them an apology.

"I want to recreate a snuff film." George is aware he's slurring his words, but if he doesn't get them out fast enough he'll choke.

"The movie is about a guy who fakes snuff films, it doesn't matter why. But the more he makes, the harder it gets for him to tell reality from fiction, until he crosses the line. Or maybe he doesn't. Who knows? The whole idea is the audience can't tell because the guy in the movie can't tell. He's gotten lost inside his movie. It's a cautionary tale."

"I can't sell a cautionary tale." Leonard frowns.

George wipes sweat from his palms.

"Okay, how about this, then? It's a movie within a movie, so the audience is two layers removed. It's safe. It's okay for them to be titillated by the sex and the violence. It looks real, but it can't possibly be real."

George hears the words like someone else is speaking, and he wants to punch that guy right in the face. He wants to hear bone crunch, watch blood spill down a crisp, white shirt.

Leonard's expression changes, a smirk edging out the frown. George wants to punch him, too, but he keeps his hands where they are.

"You're not a director, George. You're a producer, that's what you've always been." Leonard chomps on an unlit cigar; George sees the dollar signs spinning behind his eyes. It's all show when Leonard throws his hands up. "What the hell. If that's the movie you want, and you're putting up the lion's share of the cash, who am I to say no? I'll get you some hot-shot kid to write it, find you your ingénue...."

The word *no* sticks in George's throat.

"I want to see headshots," George says.

"Fine." There's a sour note in Leonard's voice, like George has admitted something shameful. He tries not to blush.

Leonard stands, but doesn't leave.

"What time's your shindig tonight?" Leonard asks with a twist to his mouth, as if the thought of spending time with George socially is suddenly distasteful somehow. Did George invite Leonard to a party tonight? He doesn't remember.

"It's an open house, come whenever you want. Someone will let you in." George takes a guess; it sounds right. That's the way his parties have always been, free-flowing, an endless succession of strangers, names and faces he doesn't bother to remember. They all want something from him, feeding off him like parasites, and he feeds off them in turn.

The door opens and closes. Leonard is gone and George is alone. George wonders briefly if anyone would even miss him if he failed to show up at his own party. But he squares his shoulders. It's his duty to be a good host. Tonight, there will be a party. Tomorrow, Leonard will arrive at his office with a handful of glossy 8x10 photographs, a whole bouquet of girls for George to choose from.

He imagines shuffling the headshots like a deck of cards, using them to tell the future. Except George already knows his future; it's the same as his past.

He's tried this before, with *Bloody Rose* in 1959. It was a movie about a disappearance or a sensational murder, the line between the two all blurred. His ingénue was a girl calling herself Lily, a girl lying about her age, a girl with the sense of running away tucked under her skin. So much like Mary, but without the scent of desert and pine trees clinging to her from all the distance she'd run. Oh, her eyes were bright enough, pupils all blown with drug-fueled desire, but they were nothing like Mary's eyes.

Blue Violet Girls will be different; George swears it. Leaning back at his desk, he closes his eyes and watches it unfold. The ring of bruises left around the victims' throats after the killer is done with them. The metaphor extended with flowers scattered on their graves. He reaches for his drink. There won't just be one starlet this time, but a whole string of beautiful dead girls. Too many to ignore. His film will be a mystery and an apology. Maybe, just maybe, it'll be enough this time.

Behind his eyelids, the imagined movie changes. It's Lily with contusions around her throat, Mary with flowers on her grave. George's eyes snap open. Violets aren't bruises. Death isn't lovely, but he's trying to blur the line again, sugar around a bitter pill so the audience will swallow it whole.

He scans the corners of his office, half expecting to find Mary there, or Lily. He can't tell whether he's disappointed to find himself utterly alone.

After the baby—he paid to take care of it—Lily went home, back to Kansas, or Texas, or wherever the hell she was from. *Bloody Rose* was a critical success, but she didn't even stick around for the preview. Audiences ate it up, and it left him sick, as sick as he knows *Blue Violet Girls* will make him feel, but he can't stop.

Every time he watched *Bloody Rose*, he kept looking for things that weren't there, flickers of movement shivering across the screen. He wants Mary to haunt him. He wants it so badly it hurts. If he could just see her again, maybe he could make it okay. Maybe she would forgive him.

George reaches for his drink and finds it empty. He takes a swig straight from the bottle rolling around at the bottom of his desk drawer instead. Almost empty, too. He lets the bottle fall, and it clunks uselessly to the floor.

Mary Evelyn has been gone for almost twenty years, but how can he be sure she's dead? There's a headstone in Mountain View Cemetery, the same place Elizabeth Short is buried, but there's nothing underneath. No body, only a film that cuts off before the end, a film he burned. Some days he knows beyond a doubt what he saw. Other days, the line is blurred; there's room for death to be clean and beautiful again.

He has to know. George stands, holding onto the edge of his desk. He fumbles open the drawer opposite from the one with the bottle, then goes to his knees to dig beneath layers of paper. Good old George, he never throws anything away unless it's a living, breathing girl.

He pulls the film canister free and hugs it to his chest. A séance. He'll call Mary, Evelyn, Eve back from the dead with the ashes of her last film. He'll fall on his knees and beg her to forgive him. It'll be like it was always meant to be, Mary at his side, his ingénue, his star.

He looks around his office for something. What? What does he need to conduct a séance? George's mouth is dry, the back of his throat fuzzed and aching. He needs another drink, is what he needs. He needs witnesses. An audience. His party.

He makes his way to the door, clutching the film canister under one arm. The sky is dark, but lights burn all along Holly-wood Boulevard, smearing in his unsteady vision. The night is crisp, clear, a breeze ruffling his hair and tugging his clothes. He considers walking all the way home, but his feet won't agree on a direction. He calls a car, slumping into the backseat and holding tight to Mary Evelyn's remains.

George dozes; he must have, though he doesn't remember falling asleep. He comes to himself as someone presses a drink into his hand. Everything is lit like the inside of a silver screen, a movie seen the wrong way around.

Panic slams him for a brief moment, but no, the canister is still tucked under his arm. A bright, beautiful girl swirls past him, dropping a kiss on his cheek as she heads toward his pool. She's wearing stiletto heels. She doesn't bother to take them off before she dives into the water, splashing with all the other bright, beautiful nymphs.

George doesn't recognize anyone. Did he invite them? He

downs the drink in his hand, and comes up coughing and sputtering. Champagne.

Empty bottles are scattered on tables and chairs. Some even float in the water. Broken glass crunches under George's feet. He's kicked over a thin-stemmed flute, and crushed it.

"Swell party, George," someone says.

Bare feet. He's worried she'll cut herself on the glass, but she's already gone, a shooting star off to drown herself.

"It's not a party," he says, or tries to say. "It's a wake."

The garden is dark. The only light is from the pool's depths, leaving the swimmers shadows lit from below. They all seem to be girls, they always are, dying to be discovered, desperate to be made. But in the half light they might as well be sharks or mermaids, selkies or sirens, or something more terrible by far.

George watches them glide in the dark, liquid motion. Is Lillian among them? Mary, Eva, Evelyn, Eve? No. She's dead: he has the proof in his hands. He pries opens the canister. The world tilts and he tilts with it, emptying the ashes of the film—Mary's film—into the water. He's keeping his promise to make her a star, just not in the way he originally intended. He watched the film, and it infected him. Every movie he's made since then, whether he means it to or not, contains a piece of this one. Now he's spreading it even farther. The starlets swimming beneath him, he's infecting them, too. Mary Evelyn is not just one star, she is all of them.

"Time to come home," he says.

He sways, perilously close to falling in, but he keeps his balance. Or something pushes him back. He isn't wanted here. He isn't needed. This sacred communion is between Mary and the girls. Her ashes swirl through the impossibly blue water, and all the pretty little wannabes swim in the ghost of her, soaking her through their skin.

George desperately wants to join them. He wants to throw himself into the water. He wants to drown. What the hell has he done? The empty film canister slips from his fingers to the ground. George follows, his legs folding beneath him. He puts his face in his hands and weeps beside the pool while all around him fey starlets, nightmares, and unreal creatures, swim.

Hollywood Hills, March 1947

I've been reading a lot lately. On set, there are long stretches with nothing to do except smoke and drink and wait. So I've been reading history and religion, mythology and astronomy, weather patterns and agriculture. It's all connected. Everything.

I was on to something with Elizabeth, and why her ghost is clearer than the rest. The cameras made it so, all those pictures of her plastered everywhere. The image becomes the thing, and the image gets passed on and on, and she's resurrected over and over again.

It's like sympathetic magic. A black goat is sent out into the desert carrying the sins of the entire village; communion wine and wafers become the blood and body of a man nailed to a cross; the chief of a tribe consumes the flesh of his enemy to gain their power. Symbols have power.

The man killing his way across America, that's a kind of magic too. One killing begets more killings, copycats spreading outward from a single gruesome death. How do you stop something like that?

I stop it by becoming a symbol, too. A woman dies up on screen, and she stands for all women everywhere. A woman who already has other women folded up inside her, ghosts stitched onto her skin. The film gets passed on, the image endures, and no one can ever forget those ghosts or pretend not to see them ever again.

Silver Screen Productions, December 1972

George switches on the projector. Drawn shades darken the room as he watches the rough cut of *Lady in Green*. He's made a ghost story this time. A story about a man haunted by the death of his lover, a married woman killed in a car crash on the way back to her husband, even though they both knew he was no good for her.

He's trying again.

Flickering against the blank space on his office wall, rain slicks the LA streets. Windshield wipers sling it out of the way, but it isn't enough. His lady in green strains forward to see, but she's crying. This is the scene where she dies. In the next scene, she returns as a ghost, a phantom hitchhiker causing drivers to veer off the road and have crashes of their own.

George holds his breath, leaning forward like the actress. He peers through the same rain she does, straining to see, heart beating hard, the electricity of the movie set storm telling him something terrible is about to happen. A shape appears in the road, and George's heart nearly stops. A glitch in the film, a splice cutting in a later scene where the ghost causes a crash. But, no. The sweep of headlights illuminates the figure through the pouring rain. Mary Evelyn.

Mary. Eva. Lillian. Eve. The lady in green slams on the brakes. The car slews. She takes her hands off the wheel, throws her arms across her face. Shattered glass flies everywhere; metal and his leading lady both scream. Through it all, Mary Evelyn continues staring directly at him.

George is halfway to reaching for the phone on his desk, calling down to his director, his AP, someone, anyone to find out if—oh god—he's killed his leading lady. His hand hangs in the air, not touching the phone. He sets it back on his desk, and lets out a shaky breath.

They never shot that scene, not that way. The lady in green dies and becomes a ghost, not vice versa. Time does not fold in this film. His lady in green is not her own haunting. George was there when they shot the scene, just as he has been on set every single day, hovering over the director's shoulder, peering through the camera lens, judging every shot as it is set up and framed. The scene playing out on his office wall is impossible; it isn't real.

He rises, tripping over the edge of the carpet as he reaches for the projector. Instead of hitting the stop button, the whole thing goes over and George with it, tangling and crashing to the ground. The projector jams, devouring celluloid even as he tries to pull it free. Faint wisps of acrid smoke sting his nostrils.

The film is burned in half, edges bubbled and crisped, the entire car crash scene gone, so he can never know for sure. This is what he wanted, isn't it? This is what he tried to do seven years ago. But no. That can't be right. Mary Evelyn is waiting for him at home. Or he hasn't met her yet.

He tries to cram the burned halves back into the projector, but his hands shake too badly. Defeated, George holds the ends of the film in either hand. They'll have to reshoot. No one will know the difference except for him.

But the difference will be an important one. Mary Evelyn won't be there next time. She was never there. He let her slip through his fingers, and there's no getting her back again.

Harwood Estate, May 1942

"Do you really think you can make me a star?" She props herself on one elbow, looking down at him.

Her curls are mussed, her lipstick chewed off, leaving her mouth mostly clean. Pure, he thinks. Bruised. Only faintly stained. The thoughts drift through his post-pleasure haze, teetering on the edge of sleep. Lovely. She still smells of salt spray and beach air. When he closes his eyes, he sees her through the camera lens, waving, her lips shaping words he can't hear.

"Of course I can. It's what I do." He lights a cigarette. It takes him two tries. He lights one for her too.

There's a glint in her eyes, something hungry as she watches him. She shouldn't be here, he thinks. This is all wrong. She flops back against the pillow, hair spread in a halo around her.

"My name isn't really Lillian," she says.

"Hm?"

Sleep tries to tug him down. He wants to sink into it, into a place where he doesn't have to think or feel anything but this warm, sated glow.

"It's Mary," she says. "But I go by Evelyn because Mary was my mother's name."

"Was?" Something in her tone snags at him, pulls him upward and now it's his turn to prop himself on one elbow to look at her.

"She died. I found out yesterday. An accident. She fell down the stairs." Mary, Evelyn, Lillian, whatever her name is blows a stream of smoke toward the ceiling.

Then the girl in his bed stubs out her cigarette and stands, pulling the bedclothes with her and leaving him exposed. She holds the sheet against her body, draping her like an ancient Roman goddess. She looks straight at him, fixing him so he can't help feeling everything he's seen up until now has been a lie. A performance. The camera never switched off for her.

"I suppose that's what happens, isn't it?" Her eyes are hard.

He doesn't know what to say. There's no air left in the room. He can only stare at her, at the line of her mouth. Hungry. Burning. He's touched her, been inside her, but he doesn't know a thing about her. The sickly sweet taste of spun sugar melts on his tongue, tinged with salt from the sea. He turns away, swinging his legs over the side of the bed.

"I'll call a car to take you home."

"Yes," she says, and the chill of her voice sends ice up his spine. "I imagine you'll do."

~

Hollywood Hills, December 1947

This is it, make or break time. By the end of the week, I'll be a star, burning brighter than any other light in the sky. I haven't slept, not since I left the Christmas Eve party at George's. I've been up, smoking.

Elizabeth sat with me. She was at George's party, too. All the dead girls were. They floated in the pool. They stood at guests' elbows while they drank champagne. They watched everything, and no one saw them but me.

We shared cigarettes and watched the sunrise, me and Liz. Eliza. Beth. Betty. We all have a dozen names here, a dozen skins we can wear over our own when we want to hide, when it gets to be too much, when we're tired.

Sometime around 4 a.m., the sky got perfectly blue. A blue I've never seen before. Like velvet, like a bruise before it starts to heal. Like the shadows at the bottom of the Grand Canyon, or my mother's favorite dress, the one my daddy bought her to say he was sorry. The dress he buried her in, at least that's what I heard.

The color matched Eliza's skin exactly.

I bought a gun. It's easier to do than I imagined. I have knives in my kitchen, the kind people use to debone things. Stockings can be used as garrotes in a pinch. Any number of objects in my apartment can inflict blunt force trauma. There are so many ways to die in Hollywood, so many ways to die no matter where you are, as long as you're a girl.

I should be afraid, but I'm not.

I have a camera I stole from George. The raw footage will be delivered to his office tomorrow. He was my first, the first one to see me and put me up on the big screen. It seems only fitting that he should be my messenger as well. He'll be my ground zero, the point of impact spreading out ripples of ghosts around the world. I have to believe he'll hold up his end of the deal. How could he refuse a death this sensational, after all?

I'm not afraid. After he's seen my film, it'll be up to him whether he keeps his promise from the day we met, whether he makes me a star.

Silver Screen Dream Productions, December 1947

It's the day after Christmas. George stares at the package sitting in the center of his desk, wrapped in brown paper, bearing his name and no return address. The shape of it is clear—a canister for a film reel.

It's barely 10 a.m., but he pours himself a measure of scotch, neat, and swallows hard against the sour taste in his throat. The projector is already set up, aimed at the wall. He threads the film, kills the light, and seats himself to watch ghosts come to life just for him.

A man lies on a bed in a tiny apartment. He looks a lot like George. He looks hungry, and more than a little drunk. He's poorer, more rundown, rougher around the edges, but the longer George watches the more he thinks they could be twins. Pitch perfect casting.

The scenery is spot on, too. He's never seen Mary Evelyn's

apartment, but he's certain he's looking at it now. The sheets on the bed are silk, or a reasonable approximation. There's a lamp on the bedside table with a beaded shade. Brass bedposts, draped in lengths of scarves and stockings. The way they hang implies violence. Everything in the room is fraught; tension fairly crackles across his skin.

The base of that lamp could crush someone's skull. Those stockings could so easily be wrapped around someone's throat. Where are these thoughts coming from? He isn't a violent person, but he can't help picturing it, running the film ahead to its inevitable end. There's a straight razor on the bedside table. The drawer beneath it is ever so slightly open, and inside, George is certain he sees a gun.

A woman steps into the frame. Her back is to the camera, but her shape is achingly familiar. George's breath catches. The woman lets her sheer dressing gown fall; it might be the very same one from *The White Canary Sings*, the first time Mary Evelyn was up on the silver screen.

George leans forward. For just a moment, a heartbeat, a frame, there's someone else in the room. Where shadows pool in the corner behind the beaded lamp there's a woman with bruise-colored eyes. Her smile is too wide, extending all the way across her cheeks, bleeding off the edge of her skin.

The film jitters. A splice stitched badly in, and there is the woman lying splayed in the park, her body cut right in two, torso here and legs over there, her intestines coiled beneath her. Sickness rises in George's throat, nearly choking him.

Cut, back to the bedroom. The space all around the bed is crowded with ghosts, cramming every available inch and not taking up any room.

Cut. Railway tracks, and a woman's body beaten to a bloody pulp.

Cut, and the man on the bed shifts in anticipation.

The cuts begin to blur, one scene, one location bleeding into another until he can't tell what is happening where.

A small dark space, the mouth of a storm drain clotted with rotten leaves. Grainy. Dim. A shape, indistinct. He can barely see. He doesn't want to see. An arm bent at a terrible angle. A thigh, a knee, a body folded up like fetal origami and shoved into the concrete opening.

How is Mary doing this? Why? Why can't he look away?

Splice. George wants to reach through the image flickering on the wall and shake the man on the bed by the shoulders, tell him to run. The woman's reflection hangs, caught like a glint in the man's eye as she moves closer to the bed. George thinks of an old wives' tale he heard once, where the last image a person sees is printed onto their retina at the moment of death, like a photograph.

Jump. Wind stirs a tarp, sifting dust and garbage and revealing a hand, pale fingers curled inward like a dead spider.

No, George thinks, please no, no more. He can't take it, not this, but he can't close his eyes either, he can't help but see.

On screen, Mary, Evelyn, Eva, Eve pulls the bedside drawer open all the way, leaving the gun within easy reach. George's heart beats through his skin. He rubs a hand over his face, stubble rasping against his palm. He needs a shave. He needs to sober up, leave town. He needs to turn the projector off and not watch the end of the film.

He pours himself another drink instead.

Cut, and the angle of view changes. A rain-slick street, which looks terribly familiar. A woman, running, dark curls bouncing. He tells himself she could be anyone. It doesn't have to be Mary Evelyn in *The White Canary Sings*, even though the shot, the pacing, the beats are all the same.

The woman's heels strike the pavement, loud as a gunshot. Her breath is ragged. She never once turns to look over her shoulder, but there's something behind her. *Someone* behind her, except George knows he's the only one here, watching her run straight for the dead-end of an alleyway.

And that's where the scene should end, where *The White Canary Sings* cut to black, leaving the wannabe-starlet's death to the imagination. This time, the camera doesn't turn away. It follows the woman into the alley. No lights, only the faint, murky glow coming from overhead between the two buildings. Almost like it's real. George strains to see through the pouring rain.

Cut, back to the bedroom scene. Dead girls everywhere. Ghosts between each frame. Sex wrapped up with the violence as the woman straddles the man on the bed, rocks her hips, tilts her head back so her dark curls spill between her shoulder blades, but never quite far enough that her face comes fully into the frame.

In the alley, flesh collides in a different way. A ragged scream, a wet, heart-rending sound.

Black. The image on the wall judders and disappears. The film spins on the reel, making a hollow click-click-clicking sound.

George jumps to his feet. There has to be more. He has to know how it ends.

He catches the reel, slicing his hand as the metal edge spins past him. He yanks and the projector falls over with a crash and the pop of shattered glass. The end of the film on the reel is burned. The final scenes, whatever they were, turned to ash. Did he do that, or was it always that way?

He lets the reel fall, film crackling and fluttering its way to the ground. The movie remains, all around him, bleeding off the celluloid and into the real. His office is filled with ghosts. Women with hollow eyes, bruises and cut skin. Women sliced open, their throats purpled with crushing thumbprints, their tongues ripped out and their fingers chopped off.

George tries to back away, but there's nowhere to go. His

heels strike the desk behind him and he whirls. He pulls open drawers, smearing the handles with blood from his cut palm until he finds the silver lighter monogrammed just for him. The wheel hisses, thuds dully. A spark. He falls to his knees and holds the edge of the film to the hungry flame.

The acrid smell of burning celluloid fills the room. George chokes on it, and he's never smelled anything more beautiful. Tears stream down his cheeks, but he's laughing, too. Laughing and weeping and breathing in the smoke as Mary, Eva, Lillian, Eve, and all her ghosts burn.

∽

Hollywood Hills

It's blue up here, in the dark, and everything below me is stars. No one ever sleeps in Hollywood, but they dream. I wonder what Mama would have thought of it if she'd stayed, if she'd kept running instead of turning back home.

It's peaceful up here with the wind and the smell of pine, cool water, and the desert—all those haunted places I passed through to get here. Down in the valley, down among all the glittering lights, I'm there, too. I'm up on the screen, caught in a thousand camera flashbulbs, pinned and framed and famous, just like I said I would be. There are whole constellations spread out in the dark, and I'm a star. I'm going to live forever. Just you watch. Just you see.

LESSER CREEK: A LOVE STORY, A GHOST STORY

ON THE TRESTLE BRIDGE, A BOY AND GIRL STAND SIDE BY SIDE. They can just see the water through the trees. Directly below the bridge, abandoned rails curve gently to their vanishing point. Weeds grow between the cracked ties, and two children walk, kicking stones along the track.

On the bridge, the girl looks at the water. Lesser Creek. It seems familiar somehow. The greenery does its best to swallow the sparkle and shine, keeping the light at bay. But all along the bank, running parallel to the tracks, muddy paths cut through the growth, and run down to the water's edge. Hoof-paths, paw-paths, and foot-paths, carve gaps in the green. They are made for stolen sips and stolen kisses, midnight swims, and midnight drownings.

She remembers fireflies.

Maybe it wasn't this bend of the creek, but some other. She wants to remember blue shadows between the trees, and the secret-wet smell of earth, bare feet trailed in cool water, and luminescent bugs flashing Morse-code transmissions from another world. And so she does. Who's to say her truth is wrong?

"It wasn't always like this, was it?" Memory nags, and she asks the question, wishing she didn't have to break the silence that has stretched between them for so long.

The boy beside her watches the children's dwindling figures, following the rails.

"Do you think we could catch them all?" he asks.

For a moment she thinks he must be talking about the fireflies she wants to badly to remember. But his past isn't her past; his memory is other-wise, and as inconsistent as hers. Who knows what meaning the creek and the rails hold for him?

Side by side on the bridge, the boy and girl are roughly the same age: fifteen, sliding backward to ten and upward to twenty, depending on who is looking. It is the age they've always been, for as long as they can remember. Which isn't very long.

She remembers fireflies, and sometimes, she remembers drowning.

She looks at the boy side-wise, wondering how he died. *If* he died. Have they had this conversation before? She picks up a stone, weighing it a moment in her palm before letting it fly. It pings the steel, reverberating like the memory of trains.

Maybe one of the children looks back at the sound, and maybe they don't. Everyone knows these woods, that bridge, these rails, that water, are haunted.

The girl picks up another stone, frowns, and closes it in her hand.

"Will we bet, then?" she says. This seems familiar, too.

"Yes, a bet," the boy agrees. "And a tally, on that big rock in the water."

He points through the trees; she knows the stone—a big boulder planted firm in the creek's middle, dividing the current.

"At the end of the summer, we'll count up the marks, and see who wins," the boy says.

A cicada drones. The sound means heat to her, summer-sweat and irritation so sharp she can taste it. She shivers all the same. It won't take much for the boy to win, between the airless nights and the far worse days, the sun beating down on everything and pushing people to the edge. She bites her lip, but she's already nodding.

The rails, stretching one way lead to the horizon, and in the other, they lead to a town. It nestles around a vast crossroad, and maybe, for that alone, it's cursed.

Could it be the town that calls them, again and again, this boy, and this girl, in their myriad forms? Or does the town exist because they come here again and again to stand on this bridge, over these rails, beside that water, to bet on the town's souls?

The town has never borne her any love, the girl thinks. Not for the boy at her side, either. She should take joy in the reaping, but she never does. There is a hunger in her, a hole deep at her core; it is in her nature to wish that hole full.

She isn't greedy. One soul, just one soul, ripe and sweet as the last summer peach, might last her all winter long. She looks side-long at the boy beside her, and breathes out slow.

"Deal," she says.

"Deal." The boy spits in his hand.

The devil's own twinkle shines in his eye. They shake on it, and go their separate ways.

And so the summer begins.

The first time you see her, you think: *She isn't real.* Because you've lived in Lesser Creek your whole life, and you've never seen her—never even seen a girl *like* her—before.

Your second thought is: *She's a ghost.* Because everyone knows these woods are haunted, and didn't a girl drown here years ago? All the stories say so.

She's sitting on a wooden bridge over the narrowest part of

the creek. Her legs dangle over the water; one hand touches the topmost rail, fingers curled as if to haul up and flee at any moment. Her hair screens her face, but you know she's chewing her lip in concentration. Just like you know exactly what color her eyes are, even though you haven't seen them yet. They are every color you can imagine, and so is her hair. Because even looking at her full-on in the sunlight, you can't tell anything about her for sure.

She is definitely a ghost.

You sit next to her, legs dangling beside hers, close, but not touching. Your mismatched laces trail from scuffed shoes. She doesn't flee, and so you say, "Hey."

You say it carefully, not looking her way. You think of a deer, ready to be startled, though she's nothing like that at all. She could swallow you whole.

Where she sits, the air is cooler, like the deepest part of the creek, where the sunlight doesn't touch. Viewed side-wise, you can see right through her. Her skin is blue, her hair moonlight, and you just *know*, when she finally turns your way, her eyes will be stones, and her will lips stitched closed. And you decide that's okay.

Then she *does* turn, dropping her hand from the top rail to the sun-warmed wood, almost touching yours. And she's as real and solid as you.

"Hey," she says, and smiles.

Nothing changes. She isn't real. She can't be. Because girls like her don't smile at you. They frown, and they're suddenly very busy, always with somewhere else to be when you're around.

This girl smiles at you. So she must be a ghost, even though the sunlight catches the fine down on her legs and turns it crystalline. You know it's a lie. The hair brushing her shoulders, the shadow in the hollow of her throat, the peach-fuzz lobes of her un-pierced ears, and the scab on her left knee—these are all a skin stretched over the truth of her. She is a hungry ghost, and she will devour your soul.

And you decide that's okay, too.

She tells you a name that isn't hers. You give her one in return. The water murmurs, and you talk about nothing. Time stretches to infinity.

Maybe, just maybe, her fingers brush yours when she finally stands up to leave.

"Will I see you again?" you say, hoping your voice isn't too full of need.

She doesn't answer, but her teeth flash bright in a nice, even row.

And so your summer begins.

The first murder occurred on a Tuesday. Or rather, it was discovered on a Tuesday, but the body had been cooling over two weeks, based on the flies buzzing over the sticky blood, and the discarded pupa cases nestled in the once-warm cavities.

Crime of passion. Scratches, bruises, evidence of a struggle, but none of a break-in. Spouses—one dead, one fled.

On a Thursday, the missing spouse turns up two counties over. A confession ensues.

Outside the county Sheriff's Office, the boy from the bridge leans against sun-warmed brick, and smiles. He chews bubblegum, shattering-hard, packaged flat in wax paper with trading cards. Collectors throw away the gum, keep cards. Not him. He savors the dusty-blandness, the unyielding material worked by teeth and tongue until it bends to his will. He throws the cards away, precisely because he knows they will be collectors' items one day.

He listens through an impossible thickness of brick, plaster, and glass to the blubbered admission of guilt. There are tears;

he can smell them, even over the cooked-hot pavement crusted with shoe-flattened filth. It smells of summer.

Sweat and stress and a tipping point—all the ingredients he needs. A beery night, a whispered word, a suggestion of infidelity. A death born of rage. This is the way it's always been. His finger, the feather, the insubstantial straw snapping the camel's spine.

The boy pushes away from the wall. Struts, hands shoved deep in too-tight, acid-washed pockets. Hair, slicked-back. He might have a comb tucked into one pocket, or a pack of cigarettes rolled in one white sleeve, depending on the slant of light that catches him.

He commands the sidewalk. Dogs, children, old men, fall into step behind him. Old women *tsk* from the safety of their porches. Young girls, well, it's best not to say what they do.

He heads west, strolling past scrub-weed and abandoned lots to the fullness of wild fields, cuts left to the creek.

He shucks shoes, wades in, and lays a hand against the massive boulder splitting the water. It is graffiti-strewn, perfect for sunbathing. Perfect for other things, too.

The boy chooses a sharp-edged stone from the current, and makes a single mark on the boulder's side—a white line on the grey.

His summer has just begun.

This is what the world tells us about girls: They are always hungry.

They are cruel.

They will suck out your soul, and leave a dead, dry husk behind.

They will laugh at your pain.

That's why we stitch up their mouths with black thread. We

cut out their eyes, and replace them with stones to stay safe from their tears.

This is what the world tells us about boys: They are hungry, too.

They grab food with both hands, stuff it in their mouths, careless of what they eat, never bothering to chew.

They are too loud.

They break everything around them, without even noticing it is there.

That's why we catch them by the tail, so they won't turn around and bite. That's why we cut off their heads, fill their mouths with dirt, and bury them at the crossroads. That's why we burn their hearts, because unlike girls, we know they'll never feel a thing.

It is all true, and every word is a lie. Don't believe anything anyone tells you about ghosts or devils.

The second time you see her, you think: *This can't be real.*

Because it's too perfect. It's the Fourth of July, and you're at yet another bend in the creek. (With her, it's always water.)

The grass is dry, but it remembers rain. The creek—angry here—smells of mud, death, and time. Things have drowned here. Things have been swept away and forgotten. Things sink, and sometimes they rise. But you take the water for granted; you always have.

A bonfire leaps high, smelling of meat and burnt sugar and wood. There are fireworks, fractured light captured and doubled, each boom-crack echoing your heartbeat, and reverberating in your bones.

You are surrounded by people you see every day. They live behind counters in the local stores; they line porches, and spit tobacco; they drive the bus carrying you to school. Except tonight, they are strangers. Tonight they are demons. And in a world of strangers and demons, you latch onto the only girl you've never seen before. The only one you know for sure isn't real.

She is solid and warm. The fireworks stain her with cathedral window colors. She smiles, and her teeth turn crimson, emerald, and gold. She is fierce and wild, too hard to hold. But you take her hand.

She leans her head on your shoulder. Her hair tickles your skin, and you smell her above and beyond the campfire, which is black powder and pine needles. She smells of soap and smoke, but also of water, of deep and sunken things. It's a creek smell, and breathing it is drowning, but you do it just the same. You think: *This is love.*

It's the Fourth of July, but *this* is where summer begins.

There's a story they tell in Lesser Creek about a girl who drowned. She had just turned fifteen, or seventeen, or twenty-one.

Just shy of fifteen, she was sad all the time, without ever knowing why. There was nothing wrong with her, other than being fifteen—a world of tragedy in its own right.

The girl was hungry constantly, and never full. When she simply couldn't stand it anymore, she went down to the creek, filled her pockets with stones, and lay in the deepest part of the water with her eyes open until she drowned.

If you go to just the right spot, where the water is the coldest and your feet don't quite touch, you'll hear her. It's hard to be still, treading water, but if you hold your breath, make your limbs only a fish-belly flash in slow motion, never rippling the surface, she'll whisper your name.

These woods are full of ghosts.

Near twenty-one, she was a farmer's daughter. She got in the family way, and her parents locked her up, and forced her to carry the child to term. Maybe the baby was still-born, and maybe she delivered it screaming, bloody, and alive. Either way, she ran away the night it came.

She ran to the trestle bridge, and threw the baby off just as a train went howling past. Who can say which wailed louder, the baby or the train? Overcome by guilt, she threw herself after the child. Her body rolled down the slope, and the creek carried it away.

If you stand at the very center of the bridge and drop a penny, when it lands, you'll hear a baby cry. Except sometimes it's the lonely mourn of a train vanishing toward the horizon. And sometimes it's a girl, just shy of twenty-one, weeping for her sins.

At seventeen, she was murdered. Her killer cut out her eyes, and replaced them with smooth stones. He stitched up her lips with black thread, and left her in the shallowest part of the creek where the water barely covered her.

The stories say her killer was a drifter, or the devil himself. They say he confessed the same day the murder was done, screaming it all over the town square. When everyone came to see what all the fuss was about, he wept, inconsolable.

He cut her eyes out, because she wouldn't stop looking at him. He sewed her lips shut, because she wouldn't stop whispering his name. They hanged him just the same.

All of these stories are true. Every one of them is a lie.

The girls of Lesser Creek leave flowers for the hungry ghost at the water's edge, and burn candles in her nameless name. The boys bring pretty toys, and line them up all in a row. The old women bake oat cakes, sweetened with blood, and the old men mumble prayers. Each brings their hopes and fears, and such desperate love.

No matter what they bring, the ghost is hungry still.

~

The second murder comes late July. In-between, there are a string of assaults, a petty theft, one count of grand larceny, and a host of undocumented sins.

The boy follows the hoof-paw-shoe-hewn path through the branches to cross the shallow water near every day. He can do that, no matter what the stories say. The wavelets glitter bright, wash sweat and grime from his skin. His toes grip slick stones, and he never falls.

He makes another mark on the boulder's side. They multiply like rabbits, like flies. They turn the grey stone dense and arcane. There is power here not found in the other graffiti. And the stone itself is rife with meaning, too —stolen kisses, secrets trysts. Oaths are sworn here, fated for breaking. It is all his doing. Or so the oath-breakers and kiss-stealers say. He drove them to it; it's what devils are for.

He has a tally of at least a dozen-dozen, and it is only July. The girl's space is empty.

He watches her, sometimes, courting her soul slow, taking her time. She is hungry; the boy sees it in her eyes. But sometimes she smiles.

And when she does, he realizes his belly is empty, too.

The marks on the stone don't fill him like they should.

Once upon a time, he was a musician. Once upon a time, he was good at cards. He was driven out of town, beaten with a stick, hung at midnight. His heart has burned countless times. He has tricked and been tricked, loved the wrong man and the wrong woman. It is always the same in the end.

Once upon a time, he walked the rails. Once upon a time, a canvas strap bit his shoulder, soaking sweat, gaining dirt. Walking, he ran. He trusted wrong, sleeping in open box cars, warming his hands by vagrant fires. He gave too much of himself away. He swapped stories, and accidentally told the truth.

He found himself dead, spit dirt from a shallow grave, and walked again.

He jumps on stumps, and has a quick hand. Dice and cards always fall his way.

Even though the marks crowding the stone aren't as triumphant as they should be, the boy makes another one, and drops the sharp stone. The creek vanishes it, a card up a magician's sleeve.

This is what the boy and the girl both know, even when they made their deal: It isn't fair. They have been given roles to play —ghost and devil, hungry to the very end.

The summer ticks past, far too slow.

There's a story they tell about the time the devil came to Lesser Creek. The townspeople chased him all along the rails. They caught him, and killed him, cut off his head and buried it upside down. They drove a spike through the ground to make sure he couldn't pick it up again.

But will-o-wisps still drift under the trestle bridge in the dead-black of night, the devil's own lanterns, leading the damned to the water's edge. And if you walk along the ties at midnight and count thirteen from the moment you pass under the bridge, you'll hear the devil breathing behind you. If you take one step back, you'll find the twelfth tie missing and he will reach up and drag you down to hell.

The first time the devil came to Lesser Creek, he was just a boy, no more than seventeen. He committed a crime, or maybe folks just didn't like the way he looked at them. Maybe the summer was too hot, and tempers were too short.

Even though he looked just like an ordinary boy, they pulled

up rail spikes, and nailed them right back down through his feet
and his hands. When they came back after three days, the body
was gone.

No one brings flowers or blood-sweetened cakes to the old
rail line. When old women pass, they spit, and old men still
drive an iron spike between the twelfth and thirteenth ties on
moonless nights to this very day.

It is a lonely place.

When the devil came to Lesser Creek the second time, he
made a deal with a drifter who dared to skim stones along the
steel rails just to hear them sing. If the man brought the devil
twenty souls by summer's end, his own would be spared, no
matter how he sinned.

It was a mass-murder summer. A fire and brimstone
summer. Preachers thundered through the churches of Lesser
Creek, damnation heavy on their tongues. The air clotted thick;
wasps drowned in sweat, humming between the pews and
banging their heads against the stained glass. Birds fell from
trees, hearts baked within the delicate cages of their bones.

All the fans stopped turning. Ice cream sizzled before it
could touch the cone. Soda went flat in every fountain. Cold
water forgot to flow, except in the creek where no one dared go.
Wives beat their husbands; fathers cursed their daughters. Boys
burst into tears for no reason, and kicked their dogs.

And the drifter came, and the drifter went, and bodies piled
like leaves in his wake. No one could ever say if it he did the
killing, or not. But every man, woman, and child in town swore
up and down they heard laughter echoing along the train tracks,
and it was the devil's very own.

The next time you see her, you *know* she is a ghost, because she
kisses you. And girls like her don't kiss you.

You are sitting side by side, hand in hand, by the creek, always by the creek. Her feet are next to yours, relaxed where yours are tense. Your footprints sink into the mud. Hers are ephemeral, and disappear.

You grip her hand too tight, and sweat gathers between your palms. Planted in the dirt, feet in the current, you look toward the rock snagging the center of the stream. Graffiti scores it. It is a magical, mystical thing; a totem centering all the summer days in danger of flying off the edge of the world.

How un-solid these liminal years of your life are. At any moment, at every moment, you are in danger of losing cohesion. The rock in the center of the stream is eternal. It says *X was here*, and that is real—tribal and shamanistic. Written in stone it can't be denied. If you vanish, the rock will remain, a record of your being.

Here and now, she kisses you, and it grounds you, too. It is the culmination of a summer's worth of desire. It is the inevitable consequence of bridges and fireworks and the muddy banks of creeks. It is the only outcome of frog-song and bug-drone, and all the other milestones of the season.

And she says, or doesn't say, but you hear, "All I want is one little piece of your soul. It won't hurt, not yet. You won't even know it's gone until much later. One day, you'll wake up, not in love with me anymore, old, and looking back on your life, and wonder where that part of you went. It'll sting for a moment, and you'll move on. Is that so bad?"

Her fingers lace yours, and the whole time she looks at the water, not you.

She says, "I'll fill you up with me, so you'll never know anything is missing."

She pauses so you think she regrets what comes next. It's what you've always known was coming since you saw her on the bridge.

She is a hungry ghost.

Here and now, you love her for her pity. You pity her for her love. It isn't fair. And so you forgive her, because you've been hungry, too.

She says, "Before you agree understand that if you give me that piece of your soul, it's mine forever. That's how love works. It consumes you. The moment it ends, you can't see past it to a day down the road when you won't be split open and bleeding for the whole world to see. In the wound, you can't see the scar, or even the scab. Memories and hindsight belong to the future. This is here, this is now."

You know how this will end. You have always known how this will end.

You hold her hand, tighter than you've held anyone's hand before, and you agree. You give her your soul.

The summer seems very short now. You have so little time.

A third murder rolls around mid August, but it holds no joy. The boy is winning by default. He longs for a reversal, a revolt, a turn of fortune. He longs for a trick to grab him by the tail.

He never asked for this, no more than she did. He is a ghost, and she is a devil. The woods have always been haunted, and so have they.

Vandalism. Arson. A near-murder that doesn't quite take. He whispers temptation. He pours jealousy, hate, venom, all into willing ears. In the end, he's powerless. So is she. They only take what the world gives them.

He makes another mark, drops the stone in the water. The creek chills him. He wades to shore, wishing the summer would end.

She tells you it is over.

She told you; she is telling you; she will always be telling you. And. It. Is.

Welts rise on your skin. Psychological, but so real.

Of course, it had to happen this way. Nobody loves you, ever loved you, ever will. And part of you knows, bitter, that you are being oh so dramatic, so you laugh. But you cry, too. She warned you, told you what she was doing as she did it, but you handed your soul over anyway, because you wanted it so goddamned bad.

Even though, deep down, you know, godfuckingdamnit, you will never be good enough to be loved. Someone else will always win, always be better than you. You will always be hungry, while everyone else is full.

So you walk the trestle bridge, where you can just see the water. You think about the summer, all the people who died, lied, cheated, and stole. The whole fucking town is going to shit, but what do you care? And what would they care if you jumped right now?

They probably wouldn't even notice you'd gone.

But you don't. You won't. And you turn away.

And maybe someone looks back at the sound of something heavy never hitting the rails. And maybe they don't. Because everyone knows these woods, that water, those trees, these rails, are haunted anyway.

She makes a mark on the stone, one shaky line. He stands on the shore, arms crossed, watching. He wants to smile, but it makes his cheeks hurt, as if the rock-hard bubblegum left splinters in his skin. His feet, planted in the mud, ache. He remembers running; she remembers drowning. In the end, it is the same.

In this moment, he loves her for her pity, and he pities her for her love. Could she, would she, ever pity him?

By the stone, she wants to weep, but she smiles, and it tastes of tears. She looks at him, standing in a slant of sunlight, watching her.

One soul, her tally.

He reaches for her, their fingers almost touching.

It is never enough.

His side of the stone is crowded; she has one single soul to her name. It is sweet, oh so sweet, but it won't sustain her to winter's end. His souls, crowded thick as they are, are candy-floss, melting on the tongue and never touching his belly.

They have played this game before, and no one ever wins.

She is sick to death of hunger and drowning. He is sick to death of treachery and spit-sealed deals. But they are what they have always been, and what they always will be.

These are the stories they tell you about hungry ghosts, and hungry devils. Every one of them is a lie, and all of them are true.

He reaches for her; she takes his hand. His fingers pass right through hers, leaving her hungrier still. His sigh is the echo of a lonely train running the rails out of town; hers, cold water running over stones.

The season ticks over to fall. A leaf drifts down, caught by the current and swept away, and they look to the bridge just visible through the thinning trees. They know, they both know, next summer they will stand there and start all over again.

And they ache, hoping next time they will remember, next time, they'll get it right.

I DRESS MY LOVER IN YELLOW

Enclosed are the documents deemed most pertinent to the ongoing investigation into the disappearances of Rani Alam and Casey Wilton. In addition to one photocopied document are several handwritten copies of original documents from the Special Collections of St. Everild's University Library. These documents have been compared to the originals, and have been found to be faithful and unaltered. The primary handwriting has been confirmed as that of Ms. Wilton. The interstitial and marginal notes on both the photocopy and the handwritten reproductions are confirmed as being written by Ms. Alam.

∾

Excerpted from "The Phantom Masterpiece: Blaine Roderick's Lost Painting", *Great Artists of New England*, A. Jansen and Tucker Cummings, eds, University of St. Everild's Press, 1984.

It is likely Blaine Roderick's career as an artist would be largely unremembered today if it were not for one extraordinary painting or, rather, the lack of a painting.

Little is known about Blaine Roderick. His earliest surviving works date from 1869, just six years before his disappearance. These works consist primarily of commissioned portraits, along with the odd landscape, and are considered largely derivative of his contemporaries while lacking their best qualities. It is known Roderick supplemented his portrait work with irregular teaching stints, the last of which was his position at St. Everild's University.

One painting falls completely outside the pattern established by the artist's early works. This is Roderick's famous (or infamous) lost masterpiece, "Mrs. Aimsbury in a Yellow Dress," known colloquially as "I Dress My Lover in Yellow, I Dress My Lover in Ruin."

By most accounts, "Yellow" is not only Roderick's masterpiece, but far surpasses those contemporaries he is so often accused of imitating, though many claim the painting is elevated solely by the mystery surrounding it. Alas for history, judging the matter is impossible. All that remains of the work is the original frame and a handful of accounts written prior to its disappearance.

Even these primary descriptive sources are considered problematic among scholars, going beyond the subjective and ranging from extreme praise to outright condemnation. Their unreliability, in all cases deemed to be tainted by personal bias, has led many scholars to believe some accounts may be deliberately false.

Regardless, the majority of these accounts focus on the feelings evoked by the work, rather than its content, making them of questionable value to begin with. An example of one such account was penned by Giddeon Parson, one of Roderick's aforementioned contemporaries. Parson calls "Yellow," "a vile piece of filth fit for nothing but the fire, though I suspect even flame would disdain to touch it."

A slightly more tempered account is offered by Vincent

Calloway, a frequent contributor to the society pages of the *Tarrysville Herald*, who had occasion to see the work at a fundraiser to benefit the university:

Regardless of what one thinks of Blaine Roderick's skill as a painter, the mastery of his brushwork, his use of light, and the startling effect of his palette cannot be called in to question here. However, one must question his powers of observation. As a personal friend of both Mrs. Aimsbury and her husband, Dean Howard Aimsbury, the portrait struck me as executed by someone who had never laid eyes on its subject. From whence did Roderick draw the wan coloring of Mrs. Aimsbury's cheeks? Never have I known her features to be so sharply sunken. It is most unsettling; one can almost see the skull beneath the flesh.

If the effect is meant to be satirical, it misses the mark, and is furthermore an unwise choice for an unknown artist relying upon the Dean not only for his commission, but his continued employment at the university. The less said about the lewd manner in which Roderick paints the dress slipping from Mrs. Aimsbury's shoulder, the better.

Colorful descriptions aside, a few incontrovertible facts remain. The subject of the painting was Charlotte Aimsbury (nee Whitmore). The portrait, commissioned by Charlotte Aimsbury's husband, Dean Howard Aimsbury, was full-length, oil on canvas, measuring 103 3/4 by 79 7/8 inches. That is where the certainty ends.

The supposed masterpiece either depicts Mrs. Aimsbury clothed in a formal yellow gown, partially clothed in the same, or nude, having just stepped out of the gown pooled at her feet. She either faces the viewer, stands in profile, or looks back over her shoulder. Her expression is one of fear, as though she intends to flee; surprise, as if the viewer has intruded upon her private chambers; or suggestive, as though the viewer is fully expected and welcome.

Most accounts describe the background as largely obscured, as though prematurely stained by a patina of smoke. Those descriptions that purport to be able to make it out chiefly describe indistinct figures, or a city shrouded by fog or blowing sand. However other accounts have the backdrop as nothing but a series of doors receding down a hallway, all closed save for one.

One account—most outlandish and therefore likely false— claims the backdrop depicts an abattoir. This description, as preposterous as it may be, has led some to speculate Roderick reused his canvas, painting Mrs. Aimsbury atop a wholly different scene meant to be a commentary upon the deplorable conditions faced by immigrant workers in America's slaughterhouses.

Beyond its physical appearance, the ultimate fate of "Yellow" is a matter of much debate as well. Later in his life, long after the disappearance and presumed deaths of both Blaine Roderick and Charlotte Aimsbury, Dean Aimsbury admitted to cutting the portrait from its frame and burning it. However, when questioned, the Dean's housekeeper, Mrs. Templeton claimed if evidence of such a burning existed she would have found it. She is further reported to have said the Dean was "poorly" and "prone to confusion and fits of imagination" at the time of this confession.

Amidst this confusion, one thread of commonality does exist across all accounts of the painting: the mention of the artist's use of color, in one form or other. Here again we find equal parts praise and damnation, everything from "brilliant, pure genius" to "having the appearance of a palette mixed by a blind imbecile, producing an effect not unlike physical illness." But every account does mention color, with at least one calling Roderick's use of it "near-supernatural, for good or for ill."

Casey—Before you get pissed at me for writing on your research notes, I submit for your consideration this: You have not taken your nose out of your books in almost three weeks. There's more to life than studying. I am officially kidnapping you for a movie night. No excuses. It's a double-feature: House of Wax *and* Dementia 13. *I promise, you'll love it. I'll even make dinner. Kisses, Rani.*

"Toward a New Understanding of Color Theory" by Blaine Roderick (incomplete draft), St. Everild's University, Special Collections, 1877.02.01.17.

[Appended note from Robert Smythe, Head of Special Collections, 1923-1947: *The following selection from the papers of Blaine Roderick represents an early draft of an unpublished treatise on color theory. It is remarkable for the way it mixes scholarly writing and personal musings, lending credence to the theory Roderick suffered from an undiagnosed mental illness at the time of his disappearance and presumed death.*]

If we are to follow slavishly in the footsteps of Isaac Newton, Moses Harris, and Johann Wolfgang von Goethe, we are left with only the primary, secondary, and tertiary colors upon the wheel, leaving no room for the creation of truly transcendent art. While theirs are serviceable models, they admit no space for *otherness*, for the ethereal, the cosmic, that which goes beyond the veil.

What of ecstatic experience? What of true *seeing*, but also in the act of seeing, *being seen?* What is needed from a new theory of color is a way to go between the shades we accept as representing the full spectrum. There are cracks through which we must pass to appreciate the fullness of the universe.

But yellow is problematic. *What* yellow? Not the color of daffodils, sunlight, or the delicacy of a canary's wing. No. The yellow of bruises, aged bone, butter on the cusp of spoiling. There's a taste to it. Slick with rot just starting to creep in. Yellow is joy, hope, life, but its underbelly is cowardice, madness, pestilence. They are not mutually exclusive; they are but two sides of the same skin. Pierce one, and you pierce the other as well.

There are shades between shades, hues which exist on the periphery of common understanding. Purple bleeds if you slice it deeply enough. I have seen such a color, printed on my eyelids. It is an infection, this color, a fever. Hungry. It means to devour me whole.

~~I want~~

Yellow remains problematic.

Why yellow? Because she *must* be dressed so. She is saddled with a husband she cannot possibly love. Too old. The yellow in the pouches under his eyes is common age, weariness. Is the shade I offer any better? Aging slowly toward death would be far kinder. More natural, certainly. But we are not natural creatures, Charlotte and I.

I've seen bones in the desert, scoured by sand. A shadow walks from the horizon, tattered by the wind. His darkness is the space between stars. It is not black. It is a color for which I have not yet discovered a name.

The wheel, were we to rearrange it, swap red for orange, yellow for the lighter shade of blue, would at first seem an affront to the artistic eye. But it brings us closer to what is needed for a *true* understanding of color. One must break to build. See how the meaning of color is changed as it is brought into contact with its opposite and its mate?

It is not simply a color, it is a door. *She* is a door. I know she has dreamed as I have. She has seen the lost city, where we are all hungry. She has seen our king in terrible rags, fluttering like flame in the wind. I tried to speak of it to her, but Charlotte looked so frightened when I touched her shoulder. (Yet I fear she understands far better than I. She will run ahead and I will be left behind.) I only meant to rearrange her into a better angle of light. It left an imprint on her skin, an oval the size and shape of my thumb. I have dreamed the dress in tatters, like the wrappings of the dead.

Casey—I'm sticking with what works. You can be mad at me later. So, movie night take two? I'm sorry I fell asleep last time. I haven't been sleeping well. I wish I could say I was out getting laid, or even being responsible and studying like you. But it's just bad dreams. My dad prescribed me some pills, but they didn't help. Seriously, this shit is supposed to knock you out, put you under so deep you don't dream. But fucking every time I go to sleep I see this fucking city. It's creepy. I don't believe in that reincarnation shit my parents do, but I'm always the same woman and she's me in this city that burns and drowns and is washed in blood. I don't like her. Us. The city. Fuck.

See? I'm so tired I'm not making sense. But I've got my coffee and I'm good to go, so tonight it's your turn to cook. We still have wine from when my parents visited. You can even pick the movies this time. Kisses, Rani

P.S. The sketch you left in the hall? I don't know if you meant me to see it, maybe it just fell out of your bag, but it's really good. Is it supposed to be me?

From the diary of Charlotte Aimsbury, St. Everild's University, Special Collections, 1877.02.21.1.

August 10, 1874

I met Mr. Roderick today, the artist my husband has commissioned to paint my portrait. First impressions do count for something so I will say this: I do not care for him. The whole time I sat for Mr. Roderick, he never touched charcoal or paper. He simply stared at me in the hideous dress he.... Well, I cannot imagine where he found it, whether he had it made, or whether he purchased it somewhere. Whatever the case, how is it that the dress fits me so well? Mr. Roderick would not answer my questions. He only insisted I wear it, and that I have always worn it. I could not make sense of him.

He was so insistent, growing flushed and agitated, I finally agreed, though I did not enjoy wearing the dress. There is a weight to it. The feel of it is wrong. It is...unearthly. I cannot give it a better word than that. It is compelling and repulsive all at once, and yet, for all the madness of Mr. Roderick's words, it is familiar. I do not pretend to understand how such a thing could be possible, but I do believe the dress is mine, and that Mr. Roderick has it in his possession because I must wear it. I have always worn it.

Yet, I felt horrid with it on my person. The silk whispers each time I moved. At times it is like the wind, or sand moving over stone. Other times, I feel there are actual voices inside the dress.

Even if it were not so, Mr. Roderick's gaze alone would be bad enough. I felt like a cut of meat, sitting so still while Mr. Roderick examined me, and he the butcher. Finally I asked him if something was wrong, and he snapped at me, commanded (his word, not mine) me not to speak.

I would be tempted to cancel the entire undertaking, but

Mr. Aimsbury is set on this idea and it would displease him greatly if I were to protest. As for myself, I have no desire for formal portraiture. Such paintings survive long after one has passed on, and all future generations will know of you is the expression you happened to be wearing that day, the way you tilted your head or lifted your hand. Everything *you* were is gone.

August 14, 1874

I expressed my aggravation concerning the portrait to Mr. Aimsbury. He convinced me to reconsider.

September 23, 1874

It has been weeks of sitting, and I know nothing more of Mr. Roderick than I did the first day. It's as though he's a different person each time we meet. One day he is moody and sullen, the next all charm. Two days ago he kissed my hand and spent the whole sitting contriving excuses to touch me, arranging my chin this way, my hair that. Yesterday he seized my shoulders as if to shake me, then immediately stepped back as though I'd struck him.

Yet my own sensibilities concerning Mr. Roderick are conflicted. I say I do not know him, but there are times I feel I know Blaine very well. But it's not a comforting sort of knowing. Or being known.

Today I asked him about it. "Of course we've met," he said. "The color can only be painted on you. Don't you remember? In the desert? In the city?"

It seemed he would say more, but he stopped as though he'd forgotten how to speak entirely. There was an intensity about him, as though he were in a fever.

He leaned toward me. I thought he meant to kiss me, but he only put his hands on either side of my face and said, "There are colors that hunger, Charlotte. There is a word for them the same shade as hearts heavy with sin."

I hadn't the faintest idea what he meant. Except, I almost did.

October 13, 1874

Today, Mr. Roderick spoke barely a word. We sat in silence and I felt I was being crushed to death under the weight of all that horrid silk. It does not breathe. I feel as if I will suffocate And why yellow? At times, I feel as though the color itself is draining the life from me. Is that possible, for a color to be alive? No, alive is not the correct word. There is nothing of life about it. I am not even certain it *is* yellow. I cannot explain it, but there are moments when the dress gives the distinct impression of being some other color, merely masquerading as yellow. Whatever color it may be in actuality, I do not believe there is a name for it....

October 14, 1874

How can I explain the horror of something that seems so simple by daylight? There was nothing monstrous *in* the dream. The dream itself was monstrous.

I dreamt of a hallway going on forever. I was terrified. But of what? A door opening? A door refusing to open?

It is irrational to be afraid of nothing. But in the dream, it was the very nothingness that frightened me. The unknown. The sense of waiting. Wanting. Is it possible fear and desire are only two sides of the same skin? To pierce one with a needle is to pierce both. Then one only needs follow the stitching to find the way through.

October 30, 1874

Blaine forbade me from looking at the painting until it is finished. But I caught a glimpse today. It was an accident, only a moment. Perhaps it was my imagination? A trick of my over-tired mind? I haven't been sleeping well, after all.

I saw the hallway. The one full of doors. The one from my dreams. Blaine painted it behind me. I never breathed one word of it to him, but still, there it was.

He means to leave me in that terrible place, a doorway to step through and never think on again.

I will not let him. After dreaming that hallway every night, I know it far better than he ever can. I will learn its tricks and secrets. I will run its length forever, if I must, but he will not catch me and pin me down.

Casey—About last night. Look, you know I like girls. And I like you. I'm just not looking for anything super-serious right now. I thought you knew that. I'm sorry if I gave you the wrong idea. I'm just sorry. Talk to me? Rani.

From the papers of Dean Howard Aimsbury, St. Everild's University, Special Collections, 1879.03.07.1.

November 18, 1877

Gentlemen,

It is with a heavy heart that I tender my formal resignation from St. Everild's University. I have had occasion to speak with each of you privately, and I am certain you understand this is in the best interests of all concerned.

I have given over twenty years of my life to this institution, but I cannot—

I cannot.

It is said time heals all wounds, but I have yet to find a thread strong enough to sew mine closed. The past two years since my wife's disappearance have taught me hauntings are all too real. They exist between heart and gut, between skin and bone. No amount of prayer can banish them.

I believed the dismissal of Blaine Roderick would purge any lingering pain. But all it did was limit his access to me and slow the tide of unpleasant—and occasionally quite public—altercations he attempted to instigate.

As I'm sure you know, gentlemen, throughout this ordeal, I have had no care for my personal reputation. I care only for the reputation of St. Everild's. Upon my resignation, I trust you will do your best to repair any damage I have done to the good name of this fine school.

As for myself, what could Blaine Roderick say of me that I have not thought of myself? He made me complicit. He was ever the shadow, the puppet master, steering my hand. I am not blameless, but his will always be the greater share of the blame.

I am not without heart. Nor am I so vain that I cannot sympathize with the notion of a younger woman, married to a man nearly twice her age seeking companionship amongst her peers. If Charlotte...I would not blame her. Whatever the truth of their relationships, whatever Blaine Roderick may have felt for Charlotte, I do believe this: He hated her by the end. He feared her. Yet he was ever the coward. He could not bear to do the deed himself, and so he drove me to it.

Gentlemen, you know me. You know I did not, *could* not, commit violence against my wife. I cherished her.

And yet, in the depths of my soul I *know* there might have been a chance for her to, somehow, return. If the painting still existed.

Charlotte's hope for life, for return, is now in ashes. My hand did the deed, but Blaine Roderick bears the blame.

I am weary, gentlemen. If this letter seems improper, I am certain you will forgive me.

Yours, etc.,

Howard Aimsbury

∼

I'm scared, Casey. I can't remember everything that happened that night. I know we both got pretty fucked up. It was a mistake. I'm sorry.

I wanted to tell you...I don't think I can stay here. I know I haven't been around the past few days, but it isn't enough. I can't stay in that house with you. When the semester ends, I'm going to call my parents and ask them to take me home.

It's not your fault. We were both....

We fooled around. I shouldn't have let it happen, knowing how you feel, and I'm sorry.

But I don't remember everything else that happened. I have bits of it, but there are pieces missing.

All that wine. Everything was so hot, like I had a fever. I remember the color flaking, and falling like ash around me. Then there were colors running down the bathtub drain. I was scrubbing my skin so hard it hurt, and you were pounding on the bathroom door.

There are bruises.

Fuck.

Please don't finish the painting, Casey.

I know it's of me. Even though it isn't done, I can tell. It's fucking with my head, and I'm scared. I'm sorry....

I came back to the house just to get my stuff. I looked at the painting again, and it's still wet. I don't remember putting on that dress. Where did you even get it? The way you painted the shadows in the folds of the fabric. They're hungry. Like mouths that have never known kisses, only pain. All those smudges of blue-gray around my throat. You painted me like I'd been strangled.

I don't even understand some of the colors you used. They're...I don't know the names for them. But I can taste them at the back of my throat, slick and just starting to rot. I keep finding paint caked under my nails, like I've been scratching—rust, dirt, bone, a color like the texture of a shadow under an owl's wing, like the sound of things crawling in the earth, like angles that don't match and....

I don't know what I did to you. I know. But I'm sorry, Casey. Just take it back, okay?

I can smell the smoke from when the city burned, the tide from when it drowned. It's sand-grit when I close my eyes, rubbing every time I blink. The dress is in tatters, and he is ragged where his shadow is stripped raw from the wind. He is walking from the horizon. I don't want to go. I can't. I have to go.

~

From the collected papers of Dr. Thaddeus Pilcher (Bequest), St. Everild's University, Special Collections, 1891.06.12.1

Physician's Report: Patient Charlotte Aimsbury, November 1, 1874

Called to examine Charlotte Aimsbury today. Cause of condition uncertain.

(I have known Charlotte since she was a little girl, and I have never found her to be prone to fits of hysteria like so many of her sex. She has a good head on her shoulders. She is a most remarkable woman.)

Patient claims no memory of collapse. Can only surmise exhaustion the cause.

(I do not blame Charlotte. While I make a point of rising above such things, talk, when persistent enough, often cannot be avoided. Being the subject of so many wagging tongues would be enough to weary even the strongest spirit.

Not that I believe there's any truth to even half of what is said. Having met Mr. Roderick, I cannot imagine Charlotte succumbing to his charms, few as they are. Roderick is brusque, rude, and highly distractible. I see little to draw Charlotte's eye. Yet, I suppose it is no great wonder that many would gossip.

In my own admittedly biased opinion, Charlotte is a very moral and upstanding woman. I refuse to believe her the faithless type.)

Final diagnosis: Exhaustion. Odd pattern of bruising evident on patient's skin determined to be symptom of collapse, not cause. Other physical signs bear out diagnosis—pallor, shading beneath eyes indicating lack of sleep; prominence of bones may indicate a loss of weight. Patient complained of nightmares. Calmative prescribed.

(I pray that will be the end of it.)

Appended Case Note: *The enclosed documents were turned over to authorities by Kyle Walters, a librarian at St. Everild's University, following his report of Ms. Wilton's disappearance in January 2014. The painting described by Ms. Alam in her addition to Ms. Wilton's notes was not among the effects in their shared residence following Ms. Wilton's disappearance, nor was it reported as being present at the time of the initial investigation into Ms. Alam's disappearance in November 2014.*

Mr. Walters admitted to removing the documents from Ms. Wilton's residence, but provided a sworn statement that nothing else had been removed or altered. Mr. Walters is being charged with interference in a police investigation, but at this time is not a suspect in either disappearance. Investigations are ongoing.

THE NAG BRIDE

"Now it's your turn to tell one." Sophie swipes a piece of candy from Andrew's pile.

He has more peanut butter cups, and they're her favorite. When he doesn't stop her, she takes a second one, giving him a mini Snickers in return.

Andrew thinks for a minute, then glances around as if afraid of being overheard. They're alone at the edge of the small plot of corn, planted equidistant between his grandparents' house and their barn, where their annual Halloween party spills music and laughter into the night.

"Have you ever heard of the Nag Bride?" Andrew licks his lips.

Something in the way he asks it draws a shiver up Sophie's spine. Just the name is evocative, and she wonders—has she heard the story before? No, she would remember something like that. She shakes her head.

"It happened right here," Andrew says, "a long time ago."

He holds the flashlight under his chin. Shadows cut angles into his cheekbones and make the freckles spread across his nose look darker. His hair sticks up every which way like a scarecrow. Sophie grabs the flashlight from him, shining it into his eyes like a police interrogation.

"Just tell the story."

Andrew squints and they tussle for a moment until he has the flashlight again. Sophie pulls her knees up, wrapping herself more tightly in her blanket. The corn rustles in a faint breeze; from this angle, sitting on the ground and looking up, the tops of the stalks scrape at the stars.

There's an unzipped sleeping bag spread beneath them, and a thermos of hot chocolate to share. Everything feels perfect and for the moment, Sophie can pretend that she's never been anywhere else. Andrew and his grandparents are her real family; she never has to cross back through the trees that divide their properties to the house that's supposed to be her home.

"Everything around here was farmland back then." Andrew gestures, taking in the house and the barn.

Despite herself, Sophie turns all the way around, and her gaze snags on the trees lining the border of the property. Even through their screening branches, the shape of her house is visible. It's completely dark, her father likely slumped in front of a silent TV, her mother at a local bar.

She turns her attention deliberately back to Andrew—her best friend, her brother, even though they don't technically share blood. Who cares what her parents are doing? After ghost stories, they can watch movies in Andrew's grandparents' living room, and if they get tired, Sophie can snug down in one of his grandparents' many guest rooms. His grandmother has told Sophie she's always welcome here, she's always safe in their home.

"Okay," Andrew says again. "So a farmer is working in his field and he sees a horse outside the fence. It's a beautiful horse, and he thinks surely it must belong to someone, so he chases it. The horse goes into the woods, and he loses sight of it. The farmer is about to give up when he sees a beautiful woman sitting on the ground. Her hair is black and she has very dark eyes. Her feet are bare, and she's rubbing at them like they hurt. He forgets all about the horse and takes the woman back to his home.

The woman doesn't tell the farmer her name. She barely says anything at all, but the farmer doesn't care. By the time they're back at his house, he's already in love with her."

A flicker of shadow between the cornstalks catches Sophie's attention, the light breaking weirdly. Her pulse jumps, and for a moment she's certain there's a tall woman watching them. When she looks again, the woman is gone. Maybe someone wandering away from the party.

"That night, the farmer hears someone moving around in his barn."

"It's not the same barn," Sophie says automatically.

"I didn't say it was." Andrew's tone is defensive and Sophie is weirdly relieved that he seems nervous too. There's a delicious thrill to the thought that he's scaring himself with his own story. It makes it feel more real. Like the Nag Bride has always been here, and he's just telling something that's true.

"There was another barn here before anyway, and stop inter-rupting."

Sophie takes another piece of candy, even though her teeth are starting to ache and she's full. Next month, she'll turn twelve, and so will Andrew. This might be the last Halloween before they're too old for piles of candy and ghost stories.

"The farmer takes his shotgun and goes to look in the barn. It's dark, but he sees someone moving around so he fires his gun to scare them off. He doesn't mean to hit the person, but as soon as he fires, he hears a woman scream. He runs to get a lantern and when it's lit, he sees the black-haired woman on the ground. She's bleeding and her legs are bent the wrong way. Instead of feet, she has hooves."

The back of Sophie's neck prickles, and despite herself, she turns to look at the corn again. A woman stands between the stalks, and as much as she wants to tell herself it's just a guest, deep down, Sophie knows the woman didn't wander away from the party. She's always been right where she is, and Andrew and Sophie are the ones intruding.

She opens her mouth to tell Andrew, but the woman puts a finger to her lips. Sophie's heart flies into her throat. Blood drips from the woman's hand, but even so, she smiles.

"The man ties the woman up and leaves her in the barn. The next morning, he comes back with a set of horseshoes and tells the woman he's going to marry her."

Sophie is still listening to Andrew's story, but she can't look away from the corn. She can't look away from the woman, who shifts without moving, who suddenly seems closer and at the same time, farther away.

"Then the farmer holds the woman down and nails the horseshoes right through her hands and feet.

Dark, coarse hair blows across the woman's face. Only it doesn't look like hair at all. It looks like a horse's mane. There's something wrong with her face—it's too long, her eyes too far apart. The woman points through the trees, towards Sophie's house.

Her father is in the house, all alone. The woman's dark eyes are a question, and Sophie should shake her head—no, no, no. But she doesn't move.

Soph? Are you even listening?" Andrew pokes her arm.

She jumps.

"I saw—" Panic scrabbles at her.

The space between the cornstalks is empty, but something moves too fast between the trees.

"What?" Andrew's eyes widen.

Sophie clenches her jaw so hard it aches. The Nag Bride isn't real.

But a tiny part of Sophie, shoved deep down inside, wishes

she were. A ghost to haunt them is exactly what her mother and father deserve.

"Never mind. I thought I saw something, but I was wrong."

The lie tastes sugar-sharp, sour underneath, like the Sour Patch candies in the dwindling piles between them. Her stomach swoops, hollow and full, and for a moment, Sophie thinks she might be sick.

It's not too late. She can still run and find Andrew's grandparents and tell them what she saw.

And that same, small buried-deep part of her makes itself known again. Her parents don't deserve her help. More nights than not, an endless stream of people rotate in and out of Sophie's house, her parents' supposed friends, coming and going with bright eyes and mouths open in laughter. No one is ever turned away, no matter what time of day or night they show up, because her parents always have time for everyone, except her. They don't even know or care where she is right now, wouldn't know or care if something happened to her. Sophie clenches her jaw even harder, her molars grinding together.

"Are you sure?" Doubt edges Andrew's voice.

"Really." Sophie rises, and deliberately turns her back on the trees, determined not to see. "It's getting cold. Let's go inside."

A man in his late 40s or early 50s and a woman anywhere from her early 20s to her mid-40s stand side by side on their wedding day. A barn stands behind them, a horseshoe nailed to its wall, visible just behind the groom's shoulder. The man wears a dark suit, the woman a simple white shift dress. Her feet are bare. She holds a bouquet of marigolds. The woman's hair is long and black. She wears a white veil. At the moment the photograph was taken, a gust of wind conspired to

pick up both hair and veil and blow them across the woman's face,
hiding the lower half, obscuring her jaw.

Beneath the photo, the text reads: Mr. and Mrs. Everett Moseley,
married September 5, 1969 in a private ceremony at Mr. Moseley's
home on Greenwood Avenue, the historic property originally occupied
by Simpson Horse Farms.

—Napierville Gazette "About Town" September 7, 1969

"Are we really going to do this?" Sophie asks. "We don't know anything about flipping houses."

What she means is: How *can we do this? How can we take the place we grew up in, strip it of everything we love, and sell it to strangers?*

But she doesn't say any of that aloud. This is as hard on Andrew as it is on her; he's hurting too.

The house looks the same—white-painted boards and a covered porch stretched across the front, a peaked roof and gabled windows. It's been just over a year since Sophie last visited, but without Andrew's grandmother and grandfather here to welcome them home, it feels wrong.

"We'll figure it out." Andrew slings an arm around Sophie's shoulder. "Between us, we've probably watched a thousand hours of HGTV shows. How hard can it be?"

"Sure." She tries to match her tone to his, smiling for his sake. "A new coat of paint, plant these beds with some new flowers, and it'll sell in no time."

Marigolds—she pictures them—the beds awash with petals as bright as flame. And, *I hate this,* she thinks. *I don't want the house sold. I don't want things to change.*

When Andrew's grandparents bought their condo in Florida, the intention was always to split their time between here and there. But Andrew's grandmother had gotten sick, and they'd decided the warmer climate and one-floor living with no yard to keep up would be easier on both of them. The cancer had moved so, so fast, though, then Andrew's grandfather had passed scarcely a month after her. They'd been high school sweethearts, married at seventeen; he simply couldn't live without her.

Now the house belongs to Andrew and Sophie knows he doesn't want it. He'd rather have his grandparents back, and Sophie agrees.

Rationally, she knows Andrew can't keep the house. They're only living here for a while—just long enough to fix the place up and sell it. A last goodbye.

Sophie's landlord upped her rent and her firm's biggest graphic design client dropped their account. Andrew was laid off a month ago from the financial software company he'd been working for, a victim of across-the-board downsizing. So it makes sense—they'll live in the house rent free while they clean it out and fix it up. Sophie will still work for the smaller clients in her portfolio from home, while Andrew continues job searching.

And then they'll move on. Sophie will find a new apartment, and Andrew will reclaim the apartment he's currently subletting to a grad student doing a three-month internship. At least that's what Sophie assumes. She knows Andrew isn't limiting his job search; he could end up moving across the country, but she'd rather not think about that. They've never lived more than a few miles apart. Even when they went to separate colleges, they were still only a short drive away from each other.

Ever since Andrew's parents died and he came to live with his grandparents at three years old, they've been best friends, inseparable, together so often that by the time they got to high school people assumed they must be dating. But it had never been like that between them. They'd always been siblings by choice, and now, with Andrew's grandparents gone, he is truly the only family Sophie has left in the world.

By old habit, she glances at the trees along the property line. Her parents' house was razed about the same time Andrew's grandparents moved away. There's a new house there now, but Sophie feels the old one, like a tooth pulled, a rotten hole left behind.

"Come on." Sophie pulls her gaze away deliberately. "I'm hungry. Let's go make dinner."

All her ghosts were buried under the rubble, scraped down to the bone. Not even the foundation of the old house remains. Looking at the new house sitting there—a lovely two-story, four bedroom home painted light blue—you'd never know an ugly brown fieldstone bungalow with a leaking roof used to sit there.

But Sophie knows.

They're barely out of summer, September only just begun, but even so a breeze carrying the first glimpse of October blows across them as Andrew climbs the porch and unlocks the door. Behind him, Sophie can't help but pause. Can't help but look back one last time toward the trees where, for just an instant, a dark shape moves between the trunks, crossing from one property to the next with no one to stop her.

No one knows how the Nag Bride is born. But they know how she dies. Always with iron. Nails through her hands and feet, shod to weigh her down. To slow her when she would run. To break her and tame her and take her power away.

Her skin is made for bruising. Her form invites violence. Too strange. Inhuman.

She is wed. She is killed. She is born again.

The Nag Bride digs her way up out of the ground. Earth beneath her nails and between her teeth, grave flowers in her hands.

She is:
An ancient spirit, bent on protecting her land.
A haunting, doomed to repeat a violent end.
A temptress, drawing out the essential, evil nature of men.
Alone, afraid, in pain.
A curse.
A blessing.

Sophie wakes certain she is eleven years old again. Moonlight falls through the window, so bright it looks like there's a second, elongated window on the floor. Peeling the covers back, she moves to the window, expecting to see again what she saw on Halloween night all those years ago. What she thought she saw.

The sky pearl grey, just before dawn, frost tipping the grass, and a figure running across the yard. At first, she'd been certain it was the woman from the corn, the ghost from Andrew's story. The Nag Bride. But the figure had stopped, turned and looked up, as if feeling Sophie there. Her father.

She'd dropped straight down, ducking out of sight, and when she'd peeked again, he was gone. The lawn was empty and she could pretend she'd only imagined seeing him. She could pretend that the shadows around the barn door hadn't shifted, that the door didn't stand open when she knew Andrew's grandfather would have shut it tight after the last party-goer left.

Sophie presses her hand to the glass now. Her father has been dead for almost five years. She will not see him running across the lawn, but nonetheless, her breath snags as she scans the dark. The barn door is open.

Her breath clouds the glass.

That night, almost sixteen years ago, she'd crept downstairs, just meaning to step onto the porch and check. She'd tried to go back to sleep first, and failed. What if her father really was out there? What if he stole something?

But when she'd reached the bottom of the stairs, Andrew's grandmother sat at the kitchen table, and Sophie froze, as if she'd been the one caught stealing. But she waved Sophie over, pouring her a mug of coffee—more than half milk—to match her own. Sophie's tongue had curled around her confession. Maybe she hadn't seen her father. Maybe there was no reason for concern.

And if she had, what if Andrew's grandmother blamed Sophie? What if she finally realized that Sophie came from bad seed, planted in bad soil, and figured the apple couldn't fall far from the tree?

She'd lied, and told Andrew's grandmother she'd had a bad dream.

"See those?" Andrew's grandmother had patted Sophie's hand, pointing to the space above the kitchen door, then through the hallway to the front door. Horseshoes had been nailed above each.

Sophie must have seen them a thousand times, but she'd never really noticed them and a faint static-electricity feeling, like a storm coming on, ran from the nape of her neck to the base of her spine.

"They're protection," Andrew's grandmother had told her. "Most people think they're for luck, but they're old, old magic. As long as they're there, nothing bad can get in, and you'll always be safe in this house."

Sophie remembers Andrew's grandmother smiling. She remembers her glancing, consciously or not, in the direction of Sophie's home.

She feels the pang of Andrew's grandparents' loss anew, leaning her forehead against the glass. They'd never spoken of it directly, but Sophie had had her own toothbrush here, spare clothes. Sometimes she'd gone weeks at a time without crossing back through the trees planted along the property line, and never once had Andrew's grandparents complained, or suggested she'd overstayed her welcome. She could stay as long as she wanted; she'd always had a place here.

Sophie glances at the barn again, trying to make the shadows resolve in a way to prove that memory playing tricks with her is the only reason it looked like the door stood open. Should she go outside and check? Before she can decide, a terrible cry splits the night. It's the worst sound she's ever heard.

Animal, human, visceral, bypassing her brain and jack-rabbiting her pulse. She's down the stairs and to the front door before she's aware of what she's doing, running barefoot out the door.

She stops on the porch, the boards chilling her feet, grit meeting her soles. The cornfield is dark, half fallen to ruin. The wind shakes the leaves, and the light plays tricks, making shadows reach toward her.

The sound comes again, distant now, and less human. Only a fox, or a night bird. A normal sound. Nothing to fear. Her heart slows to a canter, to a trot. She waits a moment longer, then stiff-legged, Sophie retreats, easing closed the front door.

"What's wrong?" Andrew peers down from the top of the stairs, bleary-eyed with sleep.

"Didn't you hear—" It was a fox or a cat. It was nothing. There are no ghosts here.

"Never mind. I didn't mean to wake you." She's eleven-years-old again, telling Andrew's grandmother she only had a bad dream.

"Go back to sleep," Sophie makes herself climb the steps, shooing Andrew toward his room—his grandparents' old room.

He looks doubtful, and Sophie forces a smile, though something brittle in her chest cracks, a jagged fragment pressing against her heart. She isn't being a coward. There's nothing of value in the barn, no reason to check until morning. She only imagined the door being open.

As she climbs back into bed, she tells herself it's too late to unwind the aftermath of that Halloween night. Too late to undo what is done. She couldn't have stopped it, and it's not her fault. And she tries very hard to make herself believe it.

~

Mrs. Everett Moseley disappeared without a trace in 1971, but even before she vanished, it seems there was something strange about her. In the wedding announcement printed in the Napierville Gazette, she is referred to only as Mrs. Moseley, never by her own name. No one I talked to about the story knew what it was either.

After they were married, hardly anyone even saw Mrs. Moseley, even though Everett Moseley was a familiar face around town. He was a member of the Napierville Volunteer Fire Company, he regularly ate and drank at the local pub, and he belonged to the Moose Lodge.

According to the stories, one day Everett Moseley walked into the hardware store to buy a shovel and cheerfully told the clerk that he was going to kill his wife and use the shovel to bury her. The clerk assumed it was a joke, but informed the police anyway. Walt Standish, who was the sheriff at the time, went to look personally.

He found no evidence of murder, but he didn't find any sign of Mrs. Moseley either. When questioned, Everett Moseley claimed she'd run away. The sheriff did find a large amount of earth dug out of Everett Moseley's lawn, however, about the size and shape of a grave. Moseley claimed it was for a new septic system, though the border had been planted with marigolds.

No official charges were made, Everett Moseley declined to file a missing persons report, and Mrs. Everett Moseley was never seen again.

Various ghost stories grew up following the case. Supposedly, the grave, or the hole, or whatever it was remained on Everett Moseley's property until he moved away. Some stories say he tried to fill it in, but it wouldn't stay filled. Others say it filled in just fine, but it would mysteriously reappear on the anniversary of the day Mrs. Moseley vanished.

I had several accounts from locals who used to drive out to the Moseley place when they were kids. The story went that if you parked in the driveway facing away from the house, and turned off all the lights in the car, you would see Mrs. Everett Moseley standing at the side of her grave in your review mirror. Some people claimed to have been chased by the ghost, and one person swore up and down that Mrs. Moseley had gotten close enough to touch his car. When he and his friends got home, there was a dent in the trunk, just about the size and shape of a woman's hand.

—Spooks, Specters, Superstitions, and True-Crime Tales of the Saratoga Region

The smell of coffee greets Sophie as she enters the kitchen. Gauzy yellow curtains, made by Andrew's grandmother, frame the window above the kitchen sink, pulled wide to let in a flood of sunlight. The house is quiet. Andrew must have gotten up early and gone for a run.

She pours herself a cup from the pot, and a flare of color catches her eye. There's a bowl of marigolds sitting on the kitchen table.

It's so unexpected, so out of place, all she can do is stare. Until the front door opens, startling her, and Sophie jumps, hot coffee splashing her knuckles.

"Hey." Andrew's arms are laden with groceries. "That's barely drinkable." He gestures with his chin at Sophie's mug. "I got desperate this morning and made a pot from an old container in the back of the pantry. I have the good stuff here."

He produces a package smelling of freshly ground beans.

"Did you buy flowers?"

"What?" Andrew plucks Sophie's mug from her hand and dumps the contents into the sink as he starts a fresh pot.

"Marigolds." A chill seeps along her spine, a sense that someone—not Andrew—was in the room just before she entered.

Andrew turns, frowning. "You didn't pick those?"

"They were here when I came down this morning."

"Nobody else has been in here, Soph. I locked the door when I left and unlocked it just now. They weren't here last night?"

She shakes her head. She's certain she would have remembered seeing them, especially since she'd just been thinking about planting marigolds.

"Kitchen door?" Even as Sophie glances at it, it's clear the bolt is in place. She would have heard someone breaking in.

"The caretaker your grandparents hired doesn't still have a key?"

"I don't think so." Andrew frowns.

Sophie rounds the counter to the table, fighting the instinct at the back of her mind that screams *danger* and makes herself touch one of the petals. It's velvety beneath the pad of her finger.

"They're fresh."

"That is fucking weird. But nothing is missing, right?"

"I don't think so?" Everything seems to be in place, but there's a nagging sensation of something she's overlooked, something more than the flowers screaming their wrongness with their bright oranges and yellows.

"Okay, well, I was going to set up home security cameras anyway, but I'll make it a priority. It'll be a selling point when we put the place on the market."

Sophie looks back to the kitchen door, and the answer clicks into place. There are holes in the paint and the plaster where nails should be.

"The horseshoes. Your grandmother used to keep them above all the doors. You don't remember?"

"Maybe they took them down when they moved? Took them with them to Florida?"

The condo in Florida is not the house that needed protecting, Sophie thinks, but she doesn't say it aloud.

"I'm sure there's a rational explanation. So, coffee first, and then we can get started cleaning." Andrew pours for both of them, and Sophie wants to shake him.

Why isn't he freaked out?

But why would he be? She's the one who heard something scream last night, who imagined the barn door was open. The memory, the uncertainty, chills her all over again.

"I can start on the barn."

"Sure, we could—" Andrew starts, but Sophie hurries on, her words running over his.

"You should start with the attic. There's a lot of stuff from your grandparents up there. You should be the one to go through it. If I find anything besides junk, I'll set it aside for you."

"Your funeral." Andrew shrugs.

Sophie listens for doubt in his voice. She's acting suspicious, so why doesn't he suspect her? And why doesn't she just come right out and say that she saw someone or something creeping around the barn? Because she didn't see anything; she just heard a weird sound, and once she double-checks, she can tell him with her mind at ease.

Once upon a time, all a body had to do to own a parcel of land hereabouts was to stake a claim to it, and refuse to move if anyone tried to take it from them. A man who wanted to build a farm set out to do just that.

Every day he worked from sun up to sundown, but it wasn't long before he began to feel like someone was watching him. He would wake to strange sounds—footsteps and someone rapping on the door of the little cabin he'd built himself. This went on for several nights, with the man finding nothing, until one day when he felt someone watching him and he turned around to see a woman standing between two trees. Her feet were bare, and they were very long. Her hair was very long as well and just looking at her, he knew she wasn't human.

He crossed himself and told her to leave. The woman answered him in a grating voice, like it pained her and she was unused to human speech.

"As a child, my grandmother buried me here. She put earth in my mouth, and left me for three days, and when I woke, the land knew me, and I knew it. But you do not belong here."

The man was afraid, so he threw the iron nails at her that he'd been using to fix his cabin.

She took the nails and drove them through her own feet and into the earth saying, "I stake my claim, and I will not be moved."

Terrified, the man fled to one of his neighbors and told him what had happened. Together they gathered more men and when they returned, they found the woman exactly where the farmer had left her. Try as they might, they could not pry the nails from her feet. They threw stones, bruising her flesh and drawing her blood, but she did not move.

They said prayers, and tried all they knew, and at last, exhausted, they laid down to sleep. As soon as they did, the woman began to shriek, ungodly sounds that kept the men from their slumber.

For three days and three nights they endured her wails, then they woke to terrible silence and found that she had died. Her corpse, however, remained nailed exactly where she had stood and still they could not move her.

Then one of the man's neighbors suggested a terrible thing.

"Marry her, and as her widower, the land will belong to you."

The farmer was sickened by the idea, but at last, he allowed himself to be convinced. The men brought a priest, and the groom went to stand by his bride. As the priest began to speak, a wind rose and moaned through the bride's open mouth. The farmer felt such a deep terror that the moment the ceremony was done, he took up a blade and struck off his bride's head. When he did, her body finally fell from where it stood.

He buried her, but did not mark her grave.

In time, the man replaced his little cabin with a farmhouse. With more time, he met a woman he asked to be his wife. Nine months after that, their son was born. And a year after that, a daughter. Eventually, the farmer forgot how he had won the land. And it was then, when the farmer had forgotten, when his first two children had begun to walk, and his wife's belly had begun to swell again, that the farmer's first bride returned.

Sophie pulls her hair into a rough ponytail, listening to the ceiling creak as Andrew moves around the attic. Her stomach butterflies—a strange combination of guilt and unease. She should tell Andrew about the barn, but deep down, she's afraid. The scream, the open door, they feel like part of a story that's been going on for a long time. Her story.

When she could have spoken, she chose silence. She chose to blinker herself to what she did not want to see. The woman in the corn. Her father, freezing partway across the lawn and looking up at her standing at the window.

Until it was too late.

When she finally had crossed back through the trees after that Halloween night, Sophie had found her mother on their battered couch, chain-smoking. She'd told Sophie matter-of-factly that her father had run off. There'd been a bruised quality to her mother's eyes, more wrinkles gathered at their corners than her age warranted. Sophie remembers watching her mother's bony shoulders as she reached for a fresh cigarette. Above the scooped neck of her tank top, Sophie had been able to count the first few bones of her mother's spine.

Life had worn her thin, but with her father gone, Sophie had briefly hoped things might get better. But it had only been a different flavor of neglect, another kind of uncaring. More often than not, the house sat empty, her mother gone for long hours at a time with no explanation, and Sophie would creep through the trees and find herself on Andrew's grandparents' porch or in their kitchen, holding onto her hurt and never speaking aloud all the things that were wrong.

On her way to the barn, Sophie gathers garbage bags and heavy work gloves. She's relieved to find the padlock in place, the chain still wound around the doors, but the relief doesn't last long. The hooked bar isn't pushed in; only rust holds it shut. A gentle tug and the lock opens. Sophie unwinds the chain and lets it slither to the ground.

There's a spot beside the barn door where the wood is darker, unfaded by the sun—the distinct shape of a horseshoe. Sophie rests her hand against it, fingers splayed, touching the nail holes left behind.

Then the farmer holds the woman down and nails the horseshoes right through her hands....

Sophie jerks back, shaking her hand out, pushing open the barn door all at once like ripping off a bandage.

Slats of light coming through imperfect gaps in the wood slice through the gloom. It smells like soil. Like time and waiting. Piles loom in every corner—garden implements, boxes, old farm equipment. Andrew's grandfather was forever buying things at flea markets and antique fairs, claiming he would fix them up one day, but he never did. There are old horse stalls in the barn, hold-overs from a previous owner. Old bicycles and bits of wood and broken furniture fill them now.

Sophie turns in a slow circle, breathing in the dust. She

doesn't know what she's looking for—would she even be able to tell if anything was missing? Or is she looking for something that doesn't belong?

Sophie steps deeper into the barn and her gaze lands on a spot where the packed dirt floor has been disturbed. Her pulse trips. There are garden tools jumbled in a box nearby. She takes a trowel, digging, clearing the rest with her hands. The work gloves remain tucked, forgotten, into her back pocket. Black earth rinds her nails.

Sophie rocks back on her heels, looking at a flat wooden box uncovered by her efforts. There's no lock. And why would there be? She flips it open.

In the same way she expected to see her father running across the lawn last night, the almost overwhelming sensation that she will find her father's cigarette lighter, silver and etched with a stylized horse, overwhelms her. She'd stolen the lighter from her father shortly before he disappeared—a small, stupid act of rebellion. It was the nicest thing he owned, too nice, and he didn't deserve it. More than that, it was tainted somehow, and she wanted to take it away from him. As though stealing it could fix everything that was wrong.

The first time she'd seen him with it, she'd just climbed off the school bus and her father had been standing on their front lawn, fidgeting with something that glinted silver in the sunlight. Sophie had tried to edge past him without saying anything at all, but he'd startled, a violent, involuntary motion, and he'd dropped the thing he'd been holding.

It landed at Sophie's feet and she'd picked it up automatically. She'd barely gotten a look when her father had seized her wrist, hard, wrenching it as he snatched the object back from her.

"Don't touch that. It's a gift from a friend."

His eyes had been wild—red at the edges, whether from drinking, or because he was on the verge of crying, she couldn't tell. Sophie had stepped back, rubbing at her wrist. Her father hadn't even apologized. He'd gone right back to staring at the trees, like he'd already forgotten she was there. Waiting on something or someone.

She hadn't even been looking for it the day she'd found it in her father's bedside dresser. She hadn't even thought about it as she slipped it into her pocket. She'd gone back to her room and hidden it deep in her sock drawer. The next day, the lighter was gone. She'd expected her father to confront her, to yell, to call her a fucking little thief and a sneak and trash, but he didn't. She'd watched him searching for it, frantically, strung-out-looking and afraid as he'd looked standing on the lawn and turning it over in his hands as he watched the trees. Sophie hadn't said a word, and she'd never seen the lighter again.

There's no rational reason why she should expect to see it now, but the feeling is so strong that for a moment Sophie can't make sense of the box's actual contents. The dull glint of metal forms a puzzle she can't sort out until she blinks her vision clear and sees—four horseshoes, all of them broken, three inexpertly repaired.

Weld marks cross the iron like ragged scars, and beneath the horseshoes there's a folded piece of paper. Dirt sifts loose, trapped in its creases, as Sophie draws it out and unfolds it.

Detailed drawings of hands and feet cover the page. Her father trained as an artist—he'd met her mother at art school, where she was studying to be a sculptor. He'd even worked in medical illustration for a while, but together, Sophie's parents fed into each other's self-destructive habits, their talent squandered, uninterested in pursuing their art anymore and doing just enough work to pay for the next round of drinks, the next fix of their current chosen drug.

But even unused, Sophie's father had retained his skill and Sophie has no doubt these drawings are his. Long-fingered hands and long-toed feet, a woman's face, the skin flayed on one side to show the delicate bones of a horse's skull. A woman's hand splayed, the tips of each finger anchored with nails to a horseshoe.

At the very bottom of the page there are words: *This is how the Nag Bride is wed.*

The horseshoes had been in place the night she'd thought she'd seen him running across the lawn. Andrew's grandmother had pointed them out to her. But maybe when she'd seen him he had been intending to steal them, while the Halloween party was going on, but misjudged the time—gotten distracted, gotten drunk—and arrived too late. Or had he come for something else? Come looking for the Nag Bride, and seeing Sophie at the window had scared him away?

Maybe he'd returned later, stolen the shoes and buried them here. Or maybe someone else had. There's so much Sophie doesn't know.

What Sophie does know is that Halloween night was the last time she had ever seen her father. At least alive. And she's spent years telling herself she didn't really see him, that she didn't know anything strange was going on. That it isn't her fault.

During Sophie's final year of college, her father had finally come home. He'd killed her mother, then he'd killed himself. He'd used a nail gun.

Andrew's grandmother had been the one to call Sophie and tell her, and Sophie and Andrew had driven all through the night, back to his grandparents' house, back home. Her father had been gone for eleven years. She'd almost convinced herself she would never see or hear from him again. Then she'd had to identify his body and her mother's in the morgue.

The nails had been removed, but the puncture wounds remained. Sophie couldn't help imagining how it had been. Her mother never bothered to change the locks; her father would have been able to walk right in. He would have been able to sit down in the dark and pour himself a drink and wait for her. Bang, bang, bang.

Sophie pictured her mother lying on the floor in a pool of her own blood, struggling to breathe. She'd imagined her mother reaching toward her father, maybe to beg for mercy, or maybe in a last futile attempt to hurt him.

He'd put just enough nails into her to make sure her death would be slow. Sophie imagined her father pouring himself a second drink—with her mother's hand still reaching for him, always caught in that moment, but never touching him—finishing that one, then putting the nail gun to his own head. Bang.

It's all part of the same story. Her story. And the moments she hasn't been living it, those are the unreal moments. In the morgue, Sophie had realized that even after her father left, part of her had always been waiting for him to return. She'd felt him hanging over their lives, a ghost haunting them, because the circle hadn't been closed. There'd been too much left undone.

Sophie buries her face in her hands, not caring about the dirt. Then she pulls her hands away, smearing her skin, and wraps the horseshoes and the paper into one of the black plastic garbage bags, and tucks the whole bundle under her shirt. She runs across the lawn, and creeps back inside, listening for Andrew, holding her breath and hoping the boards don't creak.

The horseshoes press against her skin. Sweat gathers against the crinkling plastic, slick and uncomfortable. Sophie's heart beats in the roof of her mouth as she buries the horseshoes and the paper at the bottom of her suitcase, and shoves the suitcase all the way under the bed.

Will they still be there in the morning? Or like her father's silver lighter, will they disappear?

A gift from a friend.

A courting gift.

The Nag Bride needs a groom.

Did the Nag Bride take the lighter back from Sophie's room?
Will she take the horseshoes as well?
She's already been here.
She left marigolds behind.
A courting gift.
She needs a groom.
The cycle, the story, never ended. It's begun again.

Image 1: A postcard showing two horses behind a split-rail fence. A gentleman in a suit stands on the other side of the fence, one arm leaning on the top rail. A legend across the bottom of the cardstock reads Simpson Horse Farm.

Image 2: A man in a dark suit stands next to a woman in a wedding dress with an empire waist. Behind them, the wooden wall of a barn, nailed with a horseshoe, is visible. The man's hair is neatly parted and he sports a moustache. The woman's hair is dark and long. The woman appears to have moved partway through the image's exposure; her face is a long, oval blur. In faded ink along the bottom of the photograph is written: Mr. and Mrs. Edward Simpson, September 1932.

Image 3 & 4: A survey map dated 1929 showing the plot of land occupied by Simpson Horse Farm. 30 acres, surrounded on three sides by trees, and bordered on the fourth by the township road. A survey map dated 1989 showing the same land. A 6-acre plot where the original farmhouse and barn stood, surrounded by a suburban neighborhood made up of several single-family homes.

Image 5: The farmhouse at Simpson Horse Farms, surrounded by trees. A flaw in processing the image resulted in a smudge appearing between two of the trees. It vaguely resembles the figure of a woman, and has been used as evidence by those who claim the property is haunted.

—*Napierville Historical Society Archives, Gift of Everett Moseley 1968.10.29.1-5*

～

"Find anything good?" Sophie asks.

She's sore from moving piles and despite scrubbing her hands and face, she still feels dusty.

"Take a look." Andrew points to a stack of photo albums on the kitchen table. "I only skimmed the first one."

Sophie opens the album to a picture of Andrew's grandparents when they were young, standing on the house's front porch.

"They look so young!" Sophie exclaims, and Andrew comes to peer over her shoulder.

"That must be right after they bought the house. Sometime in the mid-70s?"

"I'd say so." Sophie points at the wide collar on Andrew's grandfather's shirt, grinning.

There's no real chronology to the album, the recent and distant past jumbled together. She finds Andrew's father and aunt as children. Andrew as a baby. Various family gatherings. She pauses on a picture of her and Andrew the year they went as robots for Halloween in costumes made from cardboard boxes covered in tinfoil.

"We were such dorks."

She hears Andrew open then close the fridge door behind her. For a moment, everything feels normal. She can almost believe Andrew's grandmother is just in the other room, sitting in her favorite chair, watching one of her nature programs. Andrew's grandfather will walk through the front door at any moment eager to show off his latest treasure.

"Geez, we were never that young, were we?" Andrew carries plates with chips and sandwiches to the table. He reaches back to the counter, and hands Sophie a beer, before sipping from a sweating bottle of his own.

Sophie freezes, her own bottle partway to her lips before her brain catches up.

"Andrew." She points to his bottle.

Realization spread across his face, confusion replaced by alarm as he sets the bottle down on the counter and backs a step away.

"Oh shit. I just opened the fridge, they were there, and I grabbed one without even realizing."

Just over two years ago, Andrew had called Sophie in the middle of the night, his voice shaking across the distance between them. He'd been crying. He hadn't been able to tell her what was wrong, only that he needed her. She hadn't hesitated, taking two subways and walking the remaining damp chilly blocks to his apartment. She'd found him in the bathroom, his entire body curled inward, the arch of his spine pressed to the wall between the toilet and the tub.

"I can't...I don't remember. Soph. I don't remember."

One eye had been bruised, a cut healing on his brow. She'd knelt beside him, wrapped her arms around him, and let him sob. They'd stayed like that on the bathroom floor the rest of the night, Andrew alternately shaking and crying, and in fits and starts, when he could stop his teeth chattering, he'd told her how bad it had gotten. Blackouts. Lost time. Skipping meals to drink on an empty stomach so the alcohol would affect him faster.

Sophie had noticed him losing weight, but told herself it was all the running he did. She'd noticed the sallow complexion of his skin, the bruised quality around his eyes, so much like her mother's, and told herself he simply wasn't getting enough sleep. They talked, but not every day, saw each other regularly, but not as often as they used to.

Sophie gave these things to herself as excuses—why she

hadn't seen it earlier, why she hadn't insisted Andrew get help. She'd told herself she couldn't help Andrew until he was ready to help himself. She told herself Andrew was an adult, he could make his own choices, and if he needed her, he'd let her know. She'd looked the other way, like she had with her parents, and she'd almost lost him.

"You didn't buy them?" The words are out before Sophie can stop them.

Andrew's face crumples, going from frightened to hurt. She knows he didn't buy the beer, of course he didn't. Since that night, he's been sober, worked hard and made the choice every day not to touch alcohol. Until now.

A courting gift.

Cold ticks its way up her spine.

Sophie gathers both their bottles and empties them in the sink. She opens the fridge, repeats the action with the remaining four bottles, flattens the cardboard carrier, and shoves it deep in the recycling bin.

"It's fine. It'll be fine." She's aware of speaking too rapidly, panic fluttering as she tries to push it down.

Andrew's expression remains hurt, and a new fear strikes Sophie.

"I didn't—" she says.

"I'm going out for a run." Andrew pushes his chair back from the table.

She can't tell if he believes her. Struck, unable to make her voice work, Sophie watches him retreat up the stairs. He must know she wouldn't. She would never do anything to hurt him. And besides that, selfishly, she's been avoiding going into town, even to the grocery store. Because she knows it's only a matter of time before someone recognizes her, the whispers buzzing as they do in small towns—there she goes, Carl and Tina's kid, daughter of a murder-suicide, so tragic, I wonder how far the apple falls from the tree....

She hears Andrew come back down the stairs.

"Need any company?"

He doesn't answer. He's wearing his earbuds, looking at his phone, and she tells herself that's why he doesn't respond. Sophie listens to the front door open and close.

Her body goes slack, not quite slumping, but letting the counter take her weight. If she'd told Andrew about the horse-shoes, if she'd mentioned the Nag Bride, could she have stopped this from happening? Sophie rubs a hand over her face, still feeling imaginary grit on her skin from the barn.

After a moment, she returns to the kitchen table. She's lost her appetite, but she's still curious, and she picks up the next album from the stack Andrew brought down from the attic.

Instead of more jumbled family photos, there's a newspaper clipping—a wedding announcement, but she doesn't recognize the names—Mr. and Mrs. Everett Moseley, married in 1969.

Sophie recognizes the barn behind the couple though. It's Andrew's grandparents' barn, only newer. Just behind the groom's head, there's a horseshoe nailed to the wall.

She flips to the next page. There are images copied from the archives of the Napierville Historical Society. When Sophie lifts the book for a closer look, loose pages tumble to the kitchen floor. She finds photocopied pages from a book of ghost stories and legends, mixed in with hand-written pages. She recognizes Andrew's grandfather's hand.

The Nag Bride, over and over again even if she isn't named as such. Women murdered by their husbands. Women with nails driven through their hands. Women buried and digging their way out of the ground.

...said that every night she transformed into a black mare, stole men from their beds, and galloped them all over the countryside until their hearts stopped with fear.

...cursed the land with her dying breath.

The horse spoke with the voice of a woman and said...

...screamed, but it wasn't a human sound...

...drove a spike of iron through her tongue...

Sophie's hands shake, the pages rattling. She's about to shove them back into the album, bury the album at the bottom of the pile when a name on one of the pages arrests her. Carl. Her father's name.

The page is lined loose-leaf, torn from a notebook, torn again at the bottom so only half the writing remains. Sophie recognizes Andrew's grandfather's hand again, but sloppy, as if the words were written in haste, or in a panic.

Carl—

Nettie would kill me if she knew I'd taken these down, but you need them more than we do. Put them over all your doors. I don't know how much you know, how much you think you know from what you've pieced together, but it's important. Do it for Sophie and Tina. Do it for yourself. It's not too late to—

Sophie stares at the ragged edge where the words end, breath rough in her throat, a stinging heat behind her eyes. Andrew's grandfather had taken the horseshoes down. He'd tried to give them to her father, to protect him. To protect Sophie and her mother. *It's not too late,* he'd written, but it had been.

There's a note from Andrew resting up against a white paper bag from the local bakery waiting for her in the kitchen. *Sorry about yesterday. I just needed to get out of my head a bit. I know you didn't buy that beer. I'm starting to think the house is haunted.* He'd drawn a smiley face there, then added a postscript at the bottom of the page. *Meeting Craig for breakfast and a run. Consider this a peace offering.*

Sophie unfolds the bag and finds a chocolate croissant wrapped in bakery paper. Tension she didn't realize she'd been holding slides from her shoulder, defenseless in the face of buttery pastry. She'd waited for Andrew to come home from his run for almost two hours before she couldn't stand being in the house alone. She'd gone for a drive, and briefly considered driving all the way back to the city.

Don't look. Pretend everything is fine. Never look back and maybe all the bad things will go away on their own.

His bedroom door had been closed when she'd returned, and she'd retreated to her own room, slinking down to the kitchen after a while to make herself a sandwich, and eventually going to bed with her stomach in knots.

The smiley face in his note, joking about ghosts, and the fact that he's meeting Craig, his sponsor, eases at least some of Sophie's worries. Maybe not everything is okay. Maybe nothing is okay, but she and Andrew, at least, are okay.

After breakfast, Sophie loses herself in work, shifting piles until her muscles ache, dust and dirt grinding themselves deep into her skin. She leaves her phone inside, plugged in on the bedside table in the guestroom, deliberately not keeping track of time. Even so, she's surprised when she glances through the open barn door and sees the sun on the verge of setting. Only then does she realize it's also gotten cold.

"Hey." Andrew looks up from the stove as she enters. He's stirring garlic and onions in a pan, and Sophie's stomach rumbles.

"You really seemed to be in the zone and I didn't want to interrupt."

"That smells amazing. Your grandfather's recipe?"

"Absolutely. He ruined me for the store-bought stuff."

Andrew's posture is relaxed, his smile easy. Sophie allows herself to sink into one of the kitchen chairs and watch him work. She should take a shower, but the thought of climbing the stairs is too much.

She notes the stack of albums has been moved, and she's

about the ask Andrew about the one with all the clippings, when something catches her eye. A single petal, plastered to the side of the dark blue ceramic bowl in the middle of the table. A marigold petal—orange gold and shading to deep red at the center, the color of heart-blood. All the flowers she found on their first morning in the house were orange and yellow.

"Let me show you what I did while I let this simmer." Andrew's voice jolts her and Sophie turns to face him. "You weren't the only one who was busy today."

He gestures, and Sophie rises automatically, following him into the front room. His laptop is set up on the coffee table, its screen mirrored on the TV—a large flatscreen Andrew's grand-parents purchased before they'd moved.

"I got all the cameras set up."

Andrew drops onto the couch and Sophie watches as he cycles through views, front yard, back, an interior camera looking down the stairs at the front door. There's even one set up to look out over the barn. He backs the feed up, and Sophie watches herself leave the barn and walk to the front door.

The trees sway in the background, at the edges of the screen and something pings at the back of Sophie's mind. It was cold when she came back inside, but she doesn't remember any wind. There's a smudge between two of the trees, a space where the shadows jitter.

"Now we can see everything that goes on around here."

"Can you go back a sec?"

She doesn't look at him, eyes fixed on the screen as she backs it up and she watches herself walk backward into the barn, steps jerky and awkward, as if her legs are bent the wrong way.

"Everything okay?"

Sophie ignores him, leaning forward, squinting at the trees on the screen. They're still; there's nothing between them. Sophie shakes her head.

"Must be dust in my eyes from the barn." She smiles, keeping her voice light.

Why doesn't she just tell Andrew what she saw?

How long did his grandfather wait before taking the horse-shoes down, trying to give them to her father?

How long is too long?

"So, hey, I got a call about a potential job today," Andrew says.

His words jolt her again, careening them back to the normal and the mundane, and it's a moment before Sophie catches her footing.

"That's great!" Her voice sounds brittle, almost falsely chipper, and she's sharply aware of the lag between her response and his words.

For a moment, Sophie thinks she sees a flicker of disappointment in Andrew's eyes. But then he looks down, and she tenses reflexively, braced against his words though she doesn't know why.

"It's in L.A." He looks down. "It sounds like a really great opportunity. They want to fly me out there, which, that's got to be a good sign, right?"

The world tilts further, and Sophie fights to wipe the disappointment off her face before Andrew looks up again. He'd told her he wasn't limiting his job search to local opportunities. She'd known this was a possibility, but now that he actually has an interview scheduled all the way across the country makes that possibility too real. What happens if he gets the job, if he moves away? Daughter of a murder-suicide; a bad seed planted in bad soil—what will she do without the only family she has left in the world?

"The job wouldn't start for a few months, so it wouldn't change anything with the house. I'll fly out and back and I'll only be gone a couple of days...."

He lets the sentence trail. Sophie makes herself breathe,

hating the look in his eyes that seeks her approval, hating the selfish thoughts running roughshod through her head while he's sharing good news.

"No. That's great. I'll keep working here and you'll go there and you'll be amazed at how much progress I make while you're gone."

"You're sure?"

"Yes. Sure. Definitely. We should celebrate." Sophie pushes herself up from the couch, too fast, walking on stiff legs to the kitchen.

Her chest constricts, and she blinks rapidly. What the hell is wrong with her? This is a good thing for Andrew—a fresh start, a new job, a new city.

"Soph?" Andrew touches her shoulder, voice soft and questioning.

She turns, lowering her hand from where she's been subconsciously worrying at the cuticle of her thumb with her teeth. Too fast and the skin tears. Blood wells along the nailbed and drips from her hand and Sophie hisses in a sharp breath.

"Shit." She reaches automatically for the drawer beside the sink, Andrew's grandmother's all-purpose junk repository, searching for a bandage.

"Are you okay? Let me see."

"I'm fine." The words are too sharp, and Sophie jerks away when Andrew reaches again.

She listens to him moving around the kitchen. When she turns, when she finally gets her hitching breath and prickling eyes under control, he's holding a sweating beer bottle in one hand. Sophie gapes at him, stunned for a moment, until fear and anger and adrenaline bubble up and bubble over.

"What the fuck?" She jabs an accusing finger at him and Andrew blinks confusion, lifting his hand and looking at the bottle as if he genuinely wasn't aware of holding it until she pointed it out to him.

"What the fuck?" Again, her pulse galloping, and Sophie shoves him, hands landing in the center of Andrew's chest, leaving drops of blood behind.

Pushing him feels good. She thinks of her parents. The bruises on her mother's skin, the cigarettes burns on her father's arms. The way she tried so desperately to pretend she didn't see them hurting each other, didn't hear them shouting.

They were always the couple everyone wanted to party with, and they never let the fact that they turned into parents along the way stop them. The house was always full of men and women laughing too loud. Empty pizza boxes littering the floor. A constant fug of smoke clinging to the ceiling and walls like a lowering storm.

Once—she couldn't have been more than eight years old—she remembers a hand drifting down her back to the waistband of her shorts and dipping inside, and the laughter getting louder and even more raucous as her face turned burning hot and bright, spilling with tears as she fled through the trees and across the yard to Andrew's grandparents' door.

But in the lapses between parties, her parents were different people. It was like without the laughter and other voices filling up the rooms there was too much space, too much silence in which to realize they hated each other. And Sophie alone wasn't enough to stand between them.

"Hey, calm down, it's okay." Andrew's tone is placating, he holds a hand out, palm up, like he's calming a skittish horse. Sophie realizes that somewhere along the way she picked up the knife he'd been using to chop vegetables. She's clutching it now, tip pointed at him.

Instead of looking alarmed, Andrew looks amused, one corner of his mouth lifted, a strange light in his eyes.

"It's just one beer, Soph. You're the one who said we should celebrate."

He lifts the bottle, takes a deliberately long pull, gaze fixed on hers as if daring her to do something about it. She wants to hit him again. She wants to hurt him. She poured all the beer in the fridge down the drain and she knows neither of them bought new bottles and yet they're here, like the marigolds. Like her father's lighter, which he'd claimed to have received from a friend. A token of affection from a bride to her potential groom. And now again, the Nag Bride, trying to tear them apart, tempting them to violence.

But knowing all this doesn't help, or make it so she can let go of her anger. If anything, it makes things worse. She grips the knife tighter. She's shaking. She reaches for the bottle, and Andrew holds it out of her reach.

"Relax. It'll be fine." Light slides through his eyes.

He's not Andrew. He's a complete stranger. Like her father standing on the lawn looking at the trees, playing with the lighter. Waiting for his "friend", ready to leave his old family behind. Like Everett Moseley walking into the hardware store to buy a shovel to bury his wife. The center of Sophie's chest feels bruised, as though kicked.

"I thought you talked to Craig today."

"I did. He said the occasional drink is fine." That quirk to Andrew's mouth again, shaped like a lie, shaped like he's testing her.

What are you going to do, Soph? Are you going to stop me? Or are you going to look the other way?

"Andrew." She reaches for the beer again.

"Seriously, Sophie. Chill." Andrew's expression shifts, hard now.

The house creaks, a distinctive sound like someone stepping on a floorboard. Heavy. Not a regular footfall. A hoof.

Sophie's head jerks up, tracking the sound across the ceiling. Her knuckles ache on the knife's handle, jaw clenched hard.

Andrew moves, a sudden, darting motion, a feint as if to swat the knife from her hand. But his fingers miss deliberately by a mile, toying with her, laughing at her. She takes a step, her spine bumping against the sink behind her.

"Don't." Her voice shakes.

She lifts the knife's point, but doesn't move as his fingers encircle her wrist. He tightens his grip, wrenching, painful. Her father snatching the lighter from her hand. *It was a gift from a friend.*

The crack overhead is distinct this time, impossible to miss. Andrew's head jerks up at the same time as hers, and they fall back from each other, mouths open, breathing like they've just run a mile.

"The fuck?" Andrew says. "The fuck is happening?"

Sophie can't make herself speak, can't find her voice, like an iron spike has been nailed through her tongue.

"I'm going to check." Andrew is already moving toward the hall.

Sophie lets the knife clatter into the sink. She catches up to him at the foot of the stairs.

"Don't." She touches his arm. He shakes it off, but not violent this time, like a horse shrugging off a stinging fly.

She listens to him climb the stairs, the creak of each step, and can't make herself follow. She can only crane her neck to peer after him, one hand gripping the newel post and her heart in her mouth. She listens to Andrew move down the hall, strains for the sound of a hoofstep.

Her wrist blushes in reverse from red to pale and bloodless, the mark from Andrew's fingers already fading. After what seems far too long, Andrew comes back down.

"Must have been the wind." His eyes are glazed as he says it, pupils widened and cheeks slightly flushed.

He's lying.

She can't stop herself from thinking it.

She stares at him, her best friend, her almost-brother. She

wants to tell him everything, and she can't make herself say anything at all.

~

Sophie steps onto the front porch. The house feels vast and empty, a weight at her back. She'd offered to drive Andrew to the airport, but he'd declined, ordering a car instead. Sophie had at least walked him out and wished him luck, but even that had felt strained.

She wraps her arms around herself, watching the trees stir. She searched the entire house after Andrew left, but she can't shake the sense of someone—something—watching, waiting for her to let her guard down.

Despite herself, Sophie turns her head in the other direction, looking through the trees to the lights of the house that replaced hers—warm and glowing. The bones of the old house —her house—are still there, calling to her. It doesn't matter that the house was razed to the foundation, torn out by its roots; it remains—a ghost beneath the skin.

A shadow-smear of darkness blocks and breaks the light, there and just as quickly gone. She wants to tell herself it's only a branch, swaying despite the lack of wind, and steps back inside, locking the door.

As she pours herself a glass of wine, guilt needles her, even though Andrew is out of town. She switches on the TV, and uses her phone to put the feed from the security cameras on the big screen.

Better to know what's coming for her. Better, if she's being watched, to be able to watch in turn.

She switches to the camera looking down the long drive. Empty for now, but she knows it's only a matter of time. The Nag Bride has marked them, like she marked Sophie's father. She already knows their weaknesses—the loss of Andrew's grandparents, the loss of his job, points of stress and alcohol offered as a balm. And she knows Sophie's weakness, knows from experience that Sophie will turn her head, look away, deny and deny and deny until it's too late.

Sophie leaves the TV on, leaves her glass of wine on the coffee table, and climbs the stairs. She drags her suitcase out from under the bed, digging out the plastic bag wrapped around the horseshoes. She glances out the window and her pulse catches, stutters, and it's a moment before it consents to start again.

The woman standing in the cornfield looks up.

Sophie drops the bundle on the bed and pushes the window up, leaning as far out as she can. There is no mistaking the woman; she is nothing human. Her hair is coarse, like a horse's mane and even though there's no wind, it blows across her face. It hides her mouth, but Sophie feels her smile nonetheless, a visceral, terrible thing that needs no witness to be true. The Nag Bride's smile, like the Nag Bride herself, is rooted in the primal spaces of the world—ancient, recurrent, myth made flesh. She does not require Sophie's belief or consent, she simply is—her teeth flat and wide and too big for her mouth, distending her jaw.

Sophie pushes away from the window, grabbing the horse-shoes and pounding down the stairs. Iron stops the Nag Bride. It's in all the stories crammed into the back of Andrew's grand-father's album. It's in Andrew's grandmother's promise to Sophie all those years ago.

At the bottom of the stairs, Sophie nearly trips as her phone's ringtone pierces the silence. The horseshoes slip from her arms, landing with a heavy clang, just missing her toes. She snatches her phone from the coffee table, the screen lighting with Andrew's name.

"Sophie." His voice slurs.

Instead of a response, Sophie's voice catches in her throat, and all that emerges is a strained hiss.

Andrew sounds wrong. She's certain he can't even have landed yet, let alone have reached the hotel and started drinking.

"I've been checking in on the cameras."

Sophie pulls the phone away from her ear, looks at the number again. It is Andrew's number. It's his voice, but it doesn't sound like him at all.

"I saw you outside, and I saw her in the trees. Is that why you wanted me to leave? So you could marry the Nag Bride and have her all to yourself?"

"No." Sophie finds her voice, but it's small, the denial thick and clumsy on her tongue.

She doesn't want to marry the Nag Bride; she doesn't want anything from her.

But.

But if Sophie doesn't marry the Nag Bride, what if she turns to Andrew instead? She's already divided them, separating them so she can claim one of them.

This is how the Nag Bride is wed.

Andrew's voice comes again, but now it sounds farther away, cut through with a cold wind. He sounds more like himself, but he also sounds afraid, the slurring to his voice not from drink, but from tears.

"Soph, you have to stop it. You have to... I can't—" His voice breaks up, an electronic wash of noise crackling down the line, and inside it, a rhythmic sound, like hooves clopping.

Sophie drops the phone, startled.

By the time she picks it up again, Andrew is gone.

"Shit."

She dials his number, phone pressed hard to her ear. It rings and rings. No answer, not even voicemail.

"Shit!" Louder this time and Sophie throws her phone

against the couch so it bounces off the cushions and ends up back on the floor.

Her breath comes ragged and hard. The house creaks again. Not the walls. The porch this time, as though someone—something— just outside the front door is shifting their weight from foot to foot.

From hoof to hoof.

The weight, the way the boards creak, whatever stands there holds more mass than a single human woman.

A thud, heavy enough to shake the house. Sophie steps back automatically, her heart thundering in response.

The sound comes again, the front door shuddering under a blow, like a horse kicking its stall. She waits for the door to splinter and fly apart. Silence, so terrible and vast that it leaves room for a panicked rush of Sophie's breath. Then, all at once, the restless prance of hooves. The Nag Bride pacing back and forth.

Sophie's chest squeezes, painful and tight. She tries to count, but she can't tell how many hooves there are—two or four. There's a hammer and nails in the kitchen junk drawer, but she can't make herself move.

Thunk, scrape. Thunk, scrape. The door shivers, a horse pawing a question. The doorknob doesn't move. The Nag Bride can't turn it with hooves, but Sophie has seen her long-fingered, bleeding hands. Hysteria tries to crowd the remaining air from Sophie's lungs, and she chokes back terrified laughter. Thunk, scrape, and at last the sound unfreezes her. She bolts for the kitchen, the junk drawer, the nails.

Back into the hall. There's a chair by the door, one Andrew's grandfather used to sit in to put on his boots. Sophie drags it in front of the door.

She grabs one of the horseshoes, inexpertly repaired. Who tried to fix them after they were broken? Her father? Did he repent at the end and try to protect himself, her mother, Sophie, but he was already too late?

Because Sophie turned away. Because she let the Nag Bride cross through the trees and did nothing to stop her?

The chair wobbles as Sophie climbs. Lining up the nail while holding the horseshoe flush is almost impossible. She'll drop the shoe, the hammer, or the nails. She'll accidentally pierce her own hand.

She fumbles the first nail and it falls to the floor. The sound of it striking the wood is the loudest thing in the world. The steady pace of hooves stops. Listening?

Sophie lines up another nail and drives the hammer home.

On the other side of the door, the Nag Bride screams.

It's the sound she heard their first night in the house. The sound of a woman, the sound of an animal, both in unspeakable pain. The sound of a nail driven not through wood, but through flesh and bone.

The hammer slips, and Sophie smashes her thumb. The chair tilts, and she drops the hammer, catching herself before she falls. Pain throbs and she shakes out her hand, the nailbed already turning purple. The horseshoe hangs crookedly, but it stays in place. Sophie scrubs tears from her eyes, climbs down, and goes to the back door to do it all over again.

Her arms shake by the time she's done. Every part of her feels wobbly. The Nag Bride no longer paces across the boards, but Sophie doubts she's gone. The Nag Bride requires a groom. That's the way it's always been. The Nag Bride must be wed.

Sophie returns to the front room where the TV still shows the feed from the security cameras. The Nag Bride stands in plain sight on the drive, and Sophie's body jerks, a panicked, startled reaction. As if knowing the moment she is seen, the Nag Bride moves, walking slowly up the drive. Her head is bowed, dark hair covering her face, but even so, Sophie feels the too-long shape of her jaw.

But the Bride's gait is painful, and for a wild moment, Sophie feels a surge of pity.

She thinks of nails driven through the woman's feet, iron weighing her down. There's a stuttering, halting quality to her steps. Like she isn't meant to walk on two legs, like the legs she walks upon are bent the wrong way.

The Nag Bride's skin invites bruises; her hands and feet beg for nails. She is made to be wed, to be killed, to unbury herself in a terrible cycle. But is she to blame? If she draws violence to the surface of men's skin, doesn't that mean the violence was already there?

If Sophie hadn't turned away, hadn't let the Nag Bride pass through the trees, would anything have changed?

Her father's choices, they were his own. The Nag Bride didn't make him do anything he didn't already want to do.

Sophie drops onto the couch, leaning toward the TV. A shift, the Nag Bride moving a fraction out of focus, and now a horse walks toward the camera, steps slow and plodding. A beast of burden carrying the weight of humanity's cruelty, the weight of the world. Sophie watches until the horse, the woman, passes out of the camera's view. She watches a moment longer, the shadows on the long drive shifting, drawing together and pulling away. She strains, trying to see whether the footprints left behind are shaped like a woman's bare heel, or the rounded moon of an iron horseshoe.

Sophie's legs tremble as she stands, but she makes them carry her into the hall. Thud, thud, thud. Hooves scrape the boards again.

Sophie glances to the horseshoe hung crookedly above the door. As long as it remains in place, she'll be safe. This house is safe. But safe for who?

She thinks of her mother, tortured to death. She thinks of Mrs. Everett Moseley, denied her own name, her husband cheerfully informing the store clerk he intended to bury her.

And what about Edward Simpson's wife? What about the women in all those stories Andrew's grandfather wrote out? The Nag Bride killed and buried, again and again.

And she thinks of Andrew's grandfather, his kind smile, his excitement at showing them his latest flea market find. She thinks of Andrew, her best friend, her brother, the two of them making Halloween costumes and telling stories and always having each other's back. Andrew's grandmother pouring Sophie coffee and drying her tears when she'd come running through the trees, making sure she felt loved. All of them, together, Sophie's family when she couldn't rely on her own, making this a safe place for her.

The Nag Bride with her moon-pale skin, easily bruised, with her long-fingered hands, waiting for the iron nails, is a mirror reflecting the worst and most terrible impulses humanity has to offer. But humanity has more to offer than pain. Sophie has seen for herself that this is true.

Sophie presses her forehead against the door. Hard. Harder, until it hurts. She clenches her teeth.

Behind her closed eyes, she sees the farmer standing over a woman in his barn, driving nails through her hands. She sees her father, driving nails into her mother's skin.

Maybe the Nag Bride doesn't need to be wed or killed. And if she isn't either—unmarried, unburied—then maybe the cycle needn't begin again.

Sophie draws in a ragged breath. She pulls the chair back in front of the door, grabs the hammer. Her thumb still aches, but she ignores the pain as she climbs onto the chair and gouges at the nail, prying the horseshoe free.

Sophie half jumps, half falls, kicking the chair out of the way. She wrenches open the door.

The Nag Bride blinks dark, liquid eyes.

She is the most beautiful thing Sophie has ever seen, and the most terrible.

Her face is long. Not a horse's face, and not a human's either. The lines of her skull are visible through her skin. She turns her head to one side, nostrils flared, and looks at Sophie from one of her wide-set eyes. A prey animal's eyes, rolling and afraid.

Then she turns her head again and she's fully human. A predator again. Except when she smiles, it is pained, her flat teeth never meant to fit a human jaw.

Lashes shadow the bride's pale cheeks as she looks to the horseshoe in Sophie's hand. When her gaze comes up again, it's a question. Will the Nag Bride be wed?

The woman, the horse, both and neither, reaches out a hand. It's already bleeding, rusted punctures where nails have been driven in over and over again. She turns it palm up, waiting for Sophie to place the iron shoe there. Sophie moves closer, until she is on the porch with the Bride and they are face to face.

Breath warms Sophie's skin; it smells sweet, like hay, and it smells old, like earth and flowers—marigolds—on the edge of rot. Sophie places the horseshoe in the Bride's hand.

"I'm not giving it to you," she says, her voice trembling "It's yours already."

Fear pools in Sophie's belly. It trickles along her spine. She is not marrying the Bride, and she will not drive nails through her skin. And she can only hope in choosing not to do so, she is setting her free.

The Nag Bride's jaw shifts, teeth grinding, as if she would speak, but her tongue isn't made for human sound.

"I don't want…." Sophie closes her eyes, takes a shuddering breath. "I don't want to marry you."

She opens her eyes.

"No one here does. This house belonged to a good man and a good woman, and it will again. I—"

A thought takes her, and Sophie releases a shuddering breath, gathering herself before she speaks again.

"This house is safe, I swear it. No one here will hurt you as long as… As long as I'm around. I promise."

Sophie has no idea how she will keep the promise, but she means it, down to her core. She may be making the biggest mistake of her life. If the Nag Bride refuses her proposal, will she pass through the trees, will she go to hunt the family living in the house where Sophie's own house used to stand? Will she continue on until she finds someone else, someone weaker, someone like Sophie's father?

The Nag Bride's hand remains extended, the iron shoe between them. There's nothing protecting Sophie now. The Nag Bride could step over the threshold, whuffing the air. She could kick Sophie in the chest with powerful hooves, cracking Sophie's ribs open with one blow.

The Nag Bride takes a step back. Her mane-like hair stirs, hiding the strange shape of her jaw, then blowing away again to reveal her unnatural smile. Her eyes shine, and they do not look away from Sophie as she continues to walk backward, the iron horseshoe still held out on her palm.

A promise made, and a promise accepted?

Sophie still doesn't know. Has she only delayed the inevitable?

The Nag Bride must always have her groom.

Or will things be different this time?

She leaves the front door open, retrieves her phone from the floor. She dials Andrew's number. He answers on the third ring, sounding out of breath, but like himself.

"Hey. I just landed, and I'm trying to find the shuttle to the hotel." She pictures the crowded airport, Andrew dragging his suitcase behind him. "Is everything okay?"

"I want to buy the house." The words leave her in a rush, given breath, made real.

"What? Soph—What are you—"

"I want to buy the house. Don't sell it. I don't know…I'll figure something out."

Sophie carries her phone back into the hall, out the front door and onto the porch. Ruined cornstalks sway, even though there is no breeze. Footprints trail in the driveway's dust. Hoof-shaped, shaped like a woman's bare heel. A promise in return. The Nag Bride is patient and if Sophie fails, she will be there, waiting.

"We can talk about it when you get home." Sophie hears the weariness in her voice, the strain.

She knows how all of this must sound to Andrew, and she doesn't care. She has a promise to keep.

"Hey, don't even worry about it. Focus on the interview. I know you're going to kill it." Sophie feels herself smile, despite everything.

"Are you sure you're all right? You sound—"

"I know. I'm sorry. It's just…."

Sophie looks to the trees, swaying as though something just passed through them. For a moment, it isn't the new house built where her house used to be that she sees. It's her house, low and narrow, and her father is in there, sleeping, and her mother is gone, and there's no one else to protect it except Sophie.

"I need to do this," Sophie says. "I need to stay here. This is the only place that's ever felt like home."

The trees sway and the wind doesn't blow and somewhere in the darkness a horse wickers. And even though Sophie can't see it, she feels it—the Nag Bride smiles.

TEKELI-LI, THEY CRY

THEY TELL ME THE FUTURE IS BROKEN. WILL BE BROKEN. HAS always been broken.

I was wide awake the first time they spoke to me and have been every time since. They come from *there*, then, when the future is broken. Which is now because the break stretches in every direction. That's what they tell me.

We're time travelers, meeting in some middle distance where they can scream at me, speak in soft, reasonable tones, jibber, weep, and tell me what is to come and is already here.

They're bright, like staring directly into a 100-watt bulb. One that's already broken—jagged but still burning. There are shapes behind them, smearing and blurring and refusing to stay still. It hurts to look at them, so mostly, I just listen.

The voices overlap. Like listening to five radio stations at once. Whether they weep or plead or speak calmly (those are the worst), the one thing they agree on is south. Go all the way south to the pole. Stop the future from being broken.

Why do I believe them? Because of my beautiful baby girl. I've seen her out there on the ice. Even before I came to this blue place full of wind and sleepless sun, I saw her. A skip in time. A scratch on the record of my life. A time, repeating. My past, leaking into my present. Her future, reaching back for her with empty hands.

I know time is broken because I saw my little girl, even though she's been dead for three years, seven months, and twenty-one days.

~

Our eighth day on the ice, James and Risi brought Austin back into the station screaming. He shouldn't have been out there alone. That's the first thing you learn here—the ice is treacherous. It's worse with climate change. Everything is more extreme: the colds colder, the warm periods rotting the ice soft under your feet.

Everything here wants to kill you. Not like a jungle or a swamp with poisonous insects and crushing heat. The cold kills with kindness—or humiliation. It lulls you to sleep. It makes you think you're burning up, so you strip your clothes off. History is full of people who have frozen to death naked in snowstorms.

The wind blows shimmering snow, blinding and tricking the eye. The sun—ever-awake six months and absent the other six— throws shadows all stark on the ground, so we see things that aren't there and miss things that are. If I didn't *know* the world was broken, that there are worse things coming (already here), I would think what happened to Austin was just the landscape fucking with us.

Us. I should say, that's Austin, Ricky, Sheila, Cordon, Risi, James, and me. (And my daughter's ghost.) You wouldn't think I would lose count with only seven, but I do. There should be nearly 200 bodies filling the station. It's peak season. But since the moratorium on climate research, no one cares about the South Pole. They can't afford to. Still, this is where the voices say the future will break. So here we are, funding our own research, stubborn or stupid or frightened enough to run away to the end of the world.

Austin was gathering samples from the ice for me to study. Bacteria. Fungus. Algae. Some of the few things that can survive here. I'm looking for something microscopic in the ice, something people would never notice, being too busy looking at the horizon or the sky for the big, terrible thing, then *bam*. World's end.

When they brought Austin in, he was screaming that something in the ice bit him.

The station has a trauma center. Luckily, it's in the part that didn't burn. Sheila is a surgeon. Was. Like all of us, she came to the end of the world with a bag full of demons. One of them was enough to get her barred from practice apparently. She saved Austin, even though there wasn't much for her to do other than treat him for shock. He wasn't even bleeding. His wound didn't look like a bite; the lower half of his arm had been sheared clean off.

The whirring of the 3D printer woke me up even though it had already been going for hours. It's a waste. All this expensive tech tucked away at the bottom of the world. One government funded a whole bunch of upgrades, top of the line stuff. The next one swooped in and took all the money away, made climate research damn near illegal. Now, all the fancy machines and equipment are rotting away, and private eyes and dollars are on space. Well, it's not a complete waste, I guess. Austin gets a new arm.

(If the government hadn't cut funding, maybe they would have found the poison in the water sooner. I shouldn't complain. Neelie was born with all her limbs in the right place,

300 | THE GHOST SEQUENCES

and no extra ones. Other parents weren't so lucky. My baby girl only had a slight delay in cognitive development. A lag. Sometimes she was miles away, her eyes on some past or future only she could see. But maybe that had nothing to do with the poison in the ground. Just like the nights she woke screaming. All kids have bad dreams, after all.)

Still, I'm surprised the government didn't drag the tech out when they pulled the plug. They could have printed light armor, weapons, and bombs undetectable by scans. Some of the scientists tried to burn the station on their way out in protest. After that, the government could barely be bothered to get the people out. If they wouldn't have had human rights groups from creditor nations barking up their asses, they probably would have left the scientists to rot too.

Anyway, Austin is in remarkably good spirits for someone missing half his arm. He's sticking to his story. Something in the ice bit him. I think time broke, just where he happened to be. Half his arm ended up in some other *when*. It's right where he left it, just a few seconds or years into the future or the past, so we can't see it anymore.

One of the voices (one of the weeping ones) said a city rose, is rising, everywhere and everywhen. There are holes; things can slide through. Sometimes by accident, like arms. People can slide through, but it isn't easy, so most stay put and shout across the distance.

(Oh, I should have said. Time *is* broken. It doesn't matter what we find in the ice. Nothing we do here matters. I lied to Austin, Sheila, Cordon, James, Ricky, and Risi. The voices (some of them at least) really do think there's something we can do to change things, but we can't. I recognize the stages of grief. I'm surprised the other seven (eight?) don't. The voices are bargaining right now. They're pleading with anyone who will listen. Just please take it back. Make it the way it was. Make it okay again. Bargaining never works. That's why it isn't the last stage. One thing it's made me understand that I didn't three years, seven months, and twenty-nine days ago—it's not that no one is listening. It's just that sometimes, there's nothing they can do.)

After I woke up, I went to sit by the printer. It's hypnotizing, all that passing back and forth, building new bones. Out of nowhere, James burst in and said we should be printing weapons, not arms (ha ha). He said there's a fight coming. He said he's seen things under the ice, sleeping. He wouldn't explain. I saw him standing by the window later, staring out at the ice, at the spot where I saw Neelie last time. I wanted to hit him. She's my ghost. Mine. He can damn well find his own.

It's been a couple weeks since Austin's 'accident' and now Ricky thinks he's seen James's monsters, too. Shadows under the ice. Vast, slow things. Turning, he said. I don't know what that means.

Sheila is working with Austin on rehab, even though it isn't her specialty. It'll be a while before he has any kind of dexterity. No one seems to care that Austin is basically useless for field work, except James. Every time James sees Austin, he starts in about weapons again.

Ricky's thing is CERN. He says whatever's going on is probably their fault. He's a good kid. He's supposedly here to keep Risi's notes in order, label things, make spreadsheets and pretty graphs. I think he would be smart under normal circumstances, but Risi only brought him along because she wants something to fuck.

The birds aren't birds. That's another thing Ricky says.

He's been drawing them since he got here. Really detailed, textbook quality. He wanted to be an artist, but he couldn't hack it. So he let Risi pay his way to the bottom of the world.

He's jittery, more so by the day. I don't think he's sleeping. I don't know that any of us are, not real sleep at least. Risi shows it the least.

James going on about weapons got Ricky worked up about CERN again.

"It's when they fired up the Large Hadron Collider," he said. "They fucked everything up. Ripped a hole in space."

Risi looked like she wanted to slap him. Actually, she looked like she wanted to tear him apart with her teeth, right down to marrow and bone. Maybe that's her kink—violence gets her off better than sex. "That's not how it works," she said. "This has nothing to do with science, or if it's science, it's not any kind of science we understand."

She wouldn't explain what she meant; she stalked off and slammed the door. It's the closest I've seen to anything like a crack in her armor. Maybe Risi is human after all.

It's day sixteen, or twelve, or thirty-seven, or two. Cordon and Risi are drinking to cope. I wish I could join them.

I smashed a mirror yesterday. Well, crushed it, really. It was a little pocket mirror I found behind the bookshelf in my room. They're like dorm rooms, except cleaner. Someone before me cared about their appearance, apparently. I broke it in half, squeezed it until it cracked. Seven years bad luck.

(Maybe I should say why I'm really here, now that you know I know we can't stop the end of the world. I came looking for Neelie. Even though I saw her before I saw her out on the ice, I think she wanted me to follow her here. Her ghost is brighter in the snow.)

I think Ricky might be on to something with the birds. I wanted to put that down before I forget.

I could say something melodramatic, like I was looking at

my reflection, and I couldn't stand the monster staring back at me. But I wasn't even looking at the reflective part, just turning the mirror over in my hand like a stone.

(It wasn't until I picked up the broken pieces that I saw Neelie's eye staring back at me, her mouth open to speak. I got scared. I'll admit that. I got scared. I came here to find her; she's my little girl, but she still terrifies me.)

I had all this nervous energy, and I had to let it out somehow. I used to do that with drink. My brain would spin and spin, there was no other way to shut it down. After the accident, I quit, cold turkey. I've been sober for three years, eight months, and thirteen days. A *recovering* alcoholic, mind you; there's no such thing as cured.

I saw Neelie inside the station yesterday. Every other time, she's been out on the ice. Ricky was drawing, and she was looking over his shoulder. It reminded me of the way she used to watch me cook, not asking questions but intently studying everything I did and recording behind her eyes, chewing on the ends of her hair the whole while. I didn't hit Ricky. I wanted to.

(I've waited so long for her to come inside, and when she did, I ran away. Her eyes recorded everything; what if she doesn't forgive me for the last moments of her life? My little girl turned and stretched out her hand, and I ran away.)

Could I have stopped the car? I wasn't drunk, only buzzed.

It was late, foggy; Neelie shouldn't have been out of bed. The babysitter should have been watching her....

No. I can't shift the blame. Neelie liked to run out to meet my car. It didn't matter whether I'd been gone an hour or a whole day. I knew that. *I* should have been paying more attention.

(I was.)

(Neelie…I could never get over her eyes. Deep down, in the truest and darkest part of myself, love wasn't enough. I couldn't get over her eyes. I was one of the lucky ones. All her limbs were in the right place, but her eyes…she was out of phase with my reality. Can poison in the ground do that? Sometimes, she looked just like a normal little girl, like the other children on our block after we moved. And sometimes, her eyes were flat black. Polished stone. Static-shot. She would look at me like she was tuning in something very far away or sending everything I was doing elsewhere. Did she know? Was she always judging me for what happened in the last moments of her life, or was it that I thought she was judging me that caused my decision?)

The car. There was a heartbeat's worth of space. Two. I took a breath, let it all the way out with her frail body pinned in the headlights. The fog made tendrils, swirling around her. She looked right at me with those eyes. Recording. She didn't look human. I wasn't drunk. I was scared, scared of my little girl.

I took a breath and let it all the way out, and my foot didn't move from the gas to the brake. Neelie bled out a few feet from our door. I didn't cry. I just cradled my baby's head in my lap and stroked her hair.

The voices gibber and whisper and weep. Last time they came, I looked at the light behind them for as long as I could. The spaces behind them, between their silhouetted bodies and the jagged edges marking my world. Things slid and dragged— amorphous shapes. Too many eyes, too many limbs. Some of them used to be human, I'm sure.

I lied to Austin and Sheila and all the rest. I came here because if the voices can come through, other things can as well. A ghost. A little girl already out of time. I'm not here to save the world, just to take responsibility for what I did, will do, have always done.

The smell made me look through Ricky's door. He spends 20 out of 24 hours in his 'lab', birds pinned down, so he can draw the mechanics of their wings. Like we don't know how birds work by now. (Except the birds aren't birds.) It's okay; drawing keeps Ricky out of the way. It keeps him from going off screaming onto the ice like Austin did.

Did I mention Austin disappeared? We found the arm Cordon printed for him and nothing else. He went out into the snow and vanished. Or maybe he's still here in another *when*, reunited with his original arm.

I thought maybe Neelie would be looking over his shoulder again. She wasn't, and Ricky wasn't at his drafting table either. He was crying, wiping at his face and smearing blood all over. Did I say about the blood already?

Ricky was covered in it. His hands, his clothes, all the places he'd tried to wipe the tears away. Only some of it was red. The rest…there isn't a word for the color. Green, but purple. Iridescent: beetle shell, crow feather. The color itself made the stench, clogging up my mouth and nose.

"I needed to see inside," Ricky said. "The birds aren't birds. I told you so."

He held a scalpel, probably nicked from Sheila. He'd made a real mess of the bird pinned to the table, a storm petrel, I think, but not like someone inexperienced at dissection. More like he got scared and tried to stab what he saw out of existence.

It buzzes. The picture of the bird in my mind buzzes, like flies going all at once. It drips, melting wax too close to the sun. Icarus is falling and drowning and drowned, and the world is ended, always ending, has been ended since the beginning of time.

Okay, I just read back, and I'm letting that sentence stand. Some things are just true. It isn't my fault if anyone reading this doesn't understand.

I don't know much about the biology of birds, but I know what they're *not* supposed to look like inside. Nothing living should look like that inside.

Picture a city with angles folding inward and protruding outward at the same time. A city made of bone and flesh, intestines and organs, sinew and blood. Picture something like a starfish. Picture all of that and throw the picture away. Remember the worst migraine you ever had. The inside of the bird on Ricky's drawing table was like that but moreso.

I pulled Ricky out of there and hid him in my room. I had to get him away before Risi saw what he'd done because then she would kill him for sure.

Ricky cut his throat. Probably with the same blade he used on the bird. He bled out in one of the showers, slumped against the wall. Or maybe Risi killed him, a murder-suicide. No one has seen her for two days.

I found Ricky's notes after we burned his body. We dragged him to the ghost part of the station and set him on fire. Nervous energy. We needed something to do. He was probably too young to have a will. Kid like that thinks he's going to live forever. Hopefully he wanted to be cremated.

After we burned him, I went through his stuff. Clothing. Razor blades. Deodorant. Cologne. A dildo, tucked down in the bottom of his bag under the socks and underwear. He'd never unpacked. He'd left everything in a duffle bag, like he'd be going home any day. A family portrait: mother, father, daughter, golden retriever, cute as hell. No one in the picture looked anything like him. His drawing supplies.

I found his notes wedged between the mattress and the bed frame. Crumpled, like he wanted to destroy them but couldn't quite bring himself to do it. There was a notebook filled with gibberish; each entry was neatly labeled with the date and location. The sketches were perfect. Gorgeously rendered in accurate scientific detail. Until they started to bend. Until you could tell from the outside that what I saw when Ricky cut open the bird was lurking just beneath the feathers and skin.

I keep a picture of Neelie in my room. Yesterday, Neelie was gone. The picture was still there, showing our yard and the swing I built for her hanging from the old maple tree. The arrested motion of the swing made it look like she'd jumped out of the frame. She used to pump her legs as hard as she could and jump when the swing was at its highest point. It put my heart in my throat when she did that. There were days when I expected (wanted) her to fly, keep going up forever.

I turned the picture over, like I might see her on the other side, giggling. Hide-and-Seek post-mortem.

It's proof. Time is broken. It's always been broken. A vast, cyclopean city rose everywhere and everywhen. Neelie isn't in the picture, but she's out there waiting for me. I'm coming, baby girl.

I woke up outside. Sleepwalking, I guess, though no one really sleeps anymore. I'd thought to put a coat on but not button it up. Boots, but I was still wearing a nightgown.

(Neelie was wearing a nightgown when she died. Maybe, I wasn't sleepwalking. Maybe, I went looking for her.)

Neelie was patting my cheeks when I woke up. She was crying. "Don't go to sleep, Mommy." My dead daughter saved my life. After I could have hit the brakes but didn't.

"I'm sorry, baby. I'm so sorry," I said and threw my arms around her. Not a ghost. Solid and real.

She looked at me. Her eyes just the way I remember them: flat, black, seeing everything. I almost took it back. I almost pushed her away and ran across the ice, begging it to take me, like it took Austin. Can I live with my dead little girl looking at me like that, knowing? Yes. I have to live with it—the choice not to hit the brakes, and the choice to find Neelie again. There are no third chances.

Funny (not ha ha), but it wasn't cold. The ice groaned. An old sound. A deep sound. "Don't be afraid, baby girl," I said. The birds circled between us and the sun, throwing harsh shadows on the snow. Piping while the ice groaned. Almost a song.

The voices were there, too. Begging, screaming. *Why did you stop*, they asked. *Why didn't you do more to fix the future that has always been broken?* I didn't answer; they already know. Acceptance is a stage of grief, too.

"Look, Mommy," Neelie said. She pointed to the thing in the ice that James had talked about.

Did I say what happened to James? I don't know. I don't know if I said, and I don't know what happened. We're the only ones left here, me and my little girl. And the voices. And the thing in the ice. Not *things*, despite the multitude and the vastness of it. One thing, stretching all the way out under ice that's clear and blue and shining. It turned while the birds sang. Waking up.

Haruspex. I always liked that word. I read to Neelie about ancient Rome. She liked stories about soldiers. I didn't tell her about the bloody prophets who dug their nails in the entrails of birds to spell out victory and doom.

Ricky was right about the birds, even though he wasn't scrying the future when he cut one open. Somewhere, a city is rising, has risen, will always and forever be coming up from the waves. The future, as a concept, is obsolete.

I stood with my daughter, and we watched a vast thing turn in the ice. We listened to the birds whose bodies are cities and angles and impossible, multi-limbed things. This is the new shape of the world. This is the shape it's always been. We listened to the birds-who-aren't-birds weep in their weird, piping way. This is where it begins, where it began.

Ricky was right about the birds. They're an omen but not in the way of a warning. Voices crying in the wilderness, heralding what has already come.

THE MEN FROM NARROW HOUSES

THE MEN FROM NARROW HOUSES COME UP THE STAIRS WHEN Gabby is sleeping. They sit on her bed, place their long fingers on her coverlet, and say, *Tell us, love, tell us everything. We've been gone for so long.* Except sometimes it sounds like *You've been gone for so long.*

The men from narrow houses have voices like Halloween. Dead of night voices, blown in on a cold wind. They talk almost until dawn, leaning this way and that, their tall hats never slipping from their heads even when they stir like restless trees in a breeze. They pluck at Gabby's coverlet and say, *How interesting*, and *Tell us more.*

When the sun comes up, the men from narrow houses are gone, but they always leave her with the same nonsense rhyme: *Count your fingers, count your toes. Count your buttons, count your bows.* Before they vanish, they lean forward and put their lips next to Gabby's ear. Sometimes the men are only one man and she's certain she's seem him somewhere before. He's an uncle, the kind who does magic tricks. His face is in an old family portrait hanging on a wall she can never quite find. *Tell me, love,* he says. *Where were you before you were here?* Except when he says it, it sounds like *before you were her.*

Fred loves Gabby. He's told her so a thousand times. He is perfect for her, and they are perfect together, and everything will be perfect and happily ever after for all time. Gabby isn't so sure.

Fred is sweet, but Fred is dull. He is safe, and sometimes Gabby wishes she was the kind of person who could love him the way he loves her. Other times she looks at Fred and doesn't know him at all. Fred is always talking about building memories. He brings Gabby trinkets to commemorate every little thing—their first kiss, the sailing trip they took where she taught him how to fish. She has crystal figurines in the shape of lips and fish for these two things.

On their first date, Fred took Gabby to a carnival. She won him a stuffed pig, and he bought her sweet, sugared pears. They rode the Ferris wheel, and he held her hand. A delicate crystal pig, a pear, and a wheel sit lined up along her bookshelf. The latest crystal is actually a diamond, sitting in a ring on her left hand. Not a memory, but the promise of a memory waiting to be born.

Sometimes Gabby thinks there is something to be said for memories made solid, ones she can pick up and hold in her hand when she feels like she's lost or suffocating inside her own skin. And it isn't just her. Sometimes Fred looks at her like he's trying to remember a name on the tip of his tongue, a recollection forever sliding away from him.

Gabby steps onto Fred's balcony while Fred is in the shower. At the horizon, the sky is orange, stained with city lights. Above, it purples, and in-between are tattered clouds. The orange reminds her of flames. Gabby holds up her hands and counts her fingers against the smeary light. She isn't sure the hand belongs to her at all. A question lingers like the afterimage of a dream.

Where were you before you were her?

The men from narrow houses have smiles like melon rinds, white slices of apple, the sliver of the moon before it disappears. Their clothes smell like earth, and their eyes shine like old coins —copper, silver, and gold. As the wedding draws closer, Gabby begins to see them during the day. They pluck at her with long fingers, like a hard wind worrying at her clothes. They slide around her in subway cars on her way to work; they ride behind her on the elevator on her way to the fifth floor; they lean over her shoulder as she studies spreadsheets on her computer; they dangle their legs over her cubicle wall. They are like reflections on water, always whispering, *Tell us, love, tell us everything you've seen. You've been gone for so long.*

The distraction makes Gabby type the wrong numbers into her spreadsheets and turn in reports that cause her boss to look at her with concern.

Her boss gives her well-meaning advice about eating right and going to bed at a reasonable hour. There's nothing about men whose clothing smells like earth, men with fruit-and-sickle-moon smiles. Nothing about eyes like coins vanishing up a magician's sleeve. Gabby avoids looking at the men standing just behind her boss's shoulder, leaning forward like they're starving, like they're expecting her to perform some trick, something worthy of their applause.

Tell us, love, their smiles say. *Tell us every little thing.*

Gabby dreams of a house underground. She moves through the house at the same time she sees it from the outside, a cross-section diagram. The house is wide at the top, and narrow at the bottom, the attic branching like roots, while the basement sprouts leaves to push up through the ground.

Tunnels connect the rooms, low enough that sometimes Gabby has to crawl. She slinks like an animal on her belly until she gets to the next room where she can stand again. She tastes dirt at the back of her mouth, and sometimes blood—hot and straight from the heart, and marrow cracked free from delicate bones. Sometimes she moves faster on all fours than she does on two legs.

The rooms are filled with familiar objects that don't quite belong to her. She picks them up and puts them down again and moves on. Not all of the rooms are furnished. Some bear circles beaten into the earth, as if an animal paced there before settling down. Others hold piles of feathers and bones—nests, or the remains of a satisfying meal. There is a formal dining room with a crystal-dripping chandelier, and a parlor with high-backed silk-upholstered chairs.

In the parlor, there's a picture of her uncle above the fire-place, the uncle who is a magician, the uncle she can't quite remember all the time. He himself sits underneath the portrait, in front of the cold hearth, which holds ash that looks suspiciously like more bones.

"Sit down, love," her uncle says.

He wears a tall hat like the men from narrow houses, but his clothing doesn't smell like earth. Not yet. There's a sheen to his lapels, like satin, and Gabby knows she was right about the magic tricks all along. His long-fingered hands shuffle cards, vanish coins the color of eyes. They pull scarves from his sleeves, but never doves, and his cuffs are spotted rust-red.

"Let me tell you a story," he says.

Gabby leans forward, but bites her tongue before she can say, "Tell me everything. I've been gone for so long."

"Before I was buried, I knew the best magic trick a magician can know. Do you remember?"

Gabby shakes her head. It all sounds achingly familiar, like the taste of blood on her tongue. Her uncle holds up one hand, then the other, twitching his cuffs to show sleeves as empty as the sky.

"I knew how to turn a girl into a fox, and back again. Isn't that clever?"

He holds up a card, not a playing card, but a brightly-colored tarot card. It's The Magician, except the image looks more like the magician's assistant, a woman in a spangled leotard and fishnets, a top hat and a bright smile. Gabby's uncle flips the card and the woman becomes a fox, flips it again, faster and faster, like the card trick that closes the cage around the bird, blurring woman and fox into one.

Across from her, her uncle grins. He splits into one, two, three, until the whole array of men from narrow houses fans out before her.

Tell us, love, they say. *Tell us how the trick is done.*

Sometimes, Gabby thinks the men from narrow houses are all the same man spread out at different points along her lifetime. She sees them whether she's awake or sleeping now. They trip around her heels, like leaves on the sidewalk. They follow her up and down the steps of her brownstone building to her third floor apartment. She rides the elevator to the top of Fred's eleven-storey building, and they are waiting for her when Fred opens the door.

Fred takes Gabby to buy furniture for the new house they don't own yet. Fred has told her about the house a thousand times. It is the house of his dreams. When he talks about it over eggs and bacon at his kitchen table, she sees the blueprint beneath his skin, sees him in cross section—each room occupying a different part of him in place of his heart, his liver, his lungs. The house will be perfect, he tells her, just like them.

In a lonely corner of the furniture warehouse, a single light shines like a full moon, a magician's spotlight, illuminating a cabinet taller than she is, but narrower than her outstretched arms. The men from narrow houses cluster around the cabinet, hanging from its edges, perched on its top. Their smiles say *ta-da*, the magician's reveal, but their midnight-cold-wind-Halloween voices say nothing at all.

The cabinet is black, spattered with copper, gold, and silver stars. Looking at it, Gabby remembers her spangled leotard. She remembers her top hat, like the hats worn by the men from narrow houses, but not quite as tall. She remembers her smile, bright and white as she faced the crowd. Beneath the tails of her coat was another tail the color of fire, with its tip the color of ash, the color of smoke, the color of the wood left over when the flames burn down.

Memory is like dropping into a hole in the earth, falling into the house buried upside down. The men from narrow houses—though maybe it was only one man then—take her hand and help her step inside the cabinet spangled with stars while the audience holds its breath and leans toward them. The men from narrow houses seal the box up tight, rapping it with their knuckles, turning it round and round so the audience can see there are no hidden levers or doors.

Gabby breathes the scent of cedar and earth. She breathes the scent of being buried alive. She holds it in her lungs like the memory of a thing that hasn't happened yet, but will. Outside, the magician speaks the magic word.

Gabby flickers, she blurs like flame—two feet and then four paws. When the walls of the cabinet fall away, she's a fox, and the audience *oohs* and *aahs*. Gabby runs a lap around the stage, calling high, strange barks into the air. The audience thunders. She wants to leap over the footlights and tear their throats out, each and every one. After the performance, her uncle feeds her the doves hidden up his sleeves.

"Tell me," the men from narrow houses say, their voices trebled and doubled and trebled again, but spoken from a single mouth. "Tell us how the trick is done."

Gabby opens her mouth. She almost remembers. But a hand touches her arm and everything she almost knew drops away.

"There you are," Fred says. "I thought I'd lost you."

Gabby chokes on a breath, clawing up from deep underground.

"I thought...." she says, looking at the cabinet, feeling the blur, the softening of her bones. Remembering skin like fire and doves crunching copper-sweet between her teeth.

Fred's fingers, short and blunt, tug at her sleeve, leading her away before she can remember what she thought she wanted to say.

Walking through the rooms of the upside down house, Gabby remembers everything. Once upon a time, she was a fox stitched into the skin of a girl. She was a girl wearing a fox's clothes. The men from narrow houses buried her underground and dug her up again, their long fingers plucking grave-dirt from her sleeves. Their smiles smelled of apples and the cold slice of the moon. They drank her in with their burnished coin eyes—hungry, so hungry, asking again and again, "What do you remember? What did you find? Tell us every little thing."

The wedding is three months away. Yesterday, Fred put an offer on the house of his dreams. Gabby looks around her apartment at the clutter of objects and the piles of moving boxes waiting to be filled and tries to skip over all the spaces where the men from narrow houses are tucked away. They dangle their feet over the top of her refrigerator, peek out from behind the futon and under the bed. They fold themselves into corners and behind her potted Amaryllis and curl around the blades of the now-still ceiling fan.

Gabby moves around the apartment, lifting things and putting them down. They're all familiar, but did they ever really belong to her?

Where were you before you were here?

Gabby breathes condensation on the window and writes the words with the tip of her finger. Then she crosses off the last 'e'.

She must have a good reason for marrying Fred. But no matter how she tries to jam them together in her mind, the pieces don't fit; she is jagged where Fred is smooth, she is hollow where he is full. He is safe, which is something she thought she wanted to be, but now she isn't so sure.

In the kitchen, Gabby opens the junk drawer and upends it on the table. The men from narrow houses peer over her shoulder, watching her with hungry, precious-metal eyes.

Gabby sorts elastic bands and thumbtacks, boxes of matches and spools of tape. It's the least important part of her life to deal with as she prepares to pack up and leave, and thus the only one that interests her now. She imagines Fred tsking at her when he arrives to cook her dinner, after she spent all day filling boxes and hauling things around.

Gabby finds a skein of ribbon the color of rust, and a scatter of buttons that aren't just the color of old bone.

Count your fingers, count your toes. Count your buttons, count your bows.

She winds the ribbon around her hands. Over and under,

finger to finger, finger to thumb, binding them tight. No longer a hand, more like a paw. Gabby has the urge to knot the ribbon around her toes, wrapping them in silk, changing their shape and coloring them dark as old blood. She wants to press the buttons into her skin, a line of them like teeth, waiting to be undone. A magic trick; what will step out of the girl's skin when the doors of her ribs are opened, the secret revealed?

Once upon a time she was a fox inside the skin of a girl, or the other way around. Both. Neither. She knew how to change, flicker quick, no need for a magician and his star-spangled cabinet. She buttoned herself into her lovely fox skin and strutted around town with a ribboned top hat and a wicked grin. Fox and girl, one and the same. Until she met the men from narrow houses on the road.

Except they were only one man then. They hadn't learned to split themselves infinitely yet. Their eyes weren't old coins, and their smiles weren't sharp slices of fruit.

They were hurt. They were broken. She would have passed by, tipping her hat, swishing her tail, but they cried. Oh, how they cried, a piteous, yipping thing. They smelled like kin. An uncle with flame-colored fur.

"Help me. Oh help me, please," they said with only one mouth, reddened with blood. They looked like a man, but she could see the fox inside them.

"What do you need, uncle?" She doffed her hat, holding it in one hand and sweeping a low bow.

"My skin, oh my skin," he cried.

He smelled like her, but wrong—blood instead of flame, stillness instead of flicker quick change. He stretched out a hand, pointing. Dirt under his nails, earth streaking his arms.

"My skin, my skin," went his yipping cry, fox and human, sobbing both.

Where he pointed she saw something snagged in a tree. Skin in the shape of a fox, but burning, like a leaf clinging to the branch, colored with autumn flame. Already turning from bright to ash, charcoaled bits streaming in the wind.

"Who did this to you, uncle?" She crouched low.

"They were frightened of me," he said, his voice smoke-hoarse. He wiped blood from his lips with the back of his hand. "They called me devil, but they killed me all wrong. They buried me upside down, and burned my skin. They should have buried my skin and burned my bones. I dug myself back out of the earth. Oh, it was a long crawl, and I lost so many things along the way."

He held his hand up again, pleading, showing her again the crescent-moon smiles of dirt under his nails. She placed her hat on his head, and took his hand.

"Lean on me, uncle," she said and helped him stand.

"You could do it," he said, his eyes fever bright as his skin-burning-into-flame. "You could help me find the things I lost underground. You could help me remember how to change."

She let him lean on her, kind when she could have been cruel. Even tricksters weary of tricks sometimes.

"Memory is a house," he whispered. "If I could only walk though its rooms once again, I would know who I am. I would know what went wrong."

With the ribbons wrapped around her hands, with the buttons like bone pressed against her skin, Gabby remembers. She was a fox and a flame and a girl. She traveled with her uncle, playing at magician and assistant, conning coins, making money disappear. But the thought of what he'd been before gnawed at him, leaving him hollow and hungry. The more he forgot, the more he need to know. Plucking and plucking at her with desperate fingers.

Tell me, love. Tell me everything you remember. I've forgotten so much. I've been gone for so long.

He fed her doves. He brought her buttons for her boots and ribbons tied in bows. They were kind to each other for a while.

That was before he buried her underground. Before he split himself again and again, trying to find his way back to what he'd been. Before he dug her up with long-fingered hands, leaning over her with his ripe-melon smile, whispering, *Tell us, love, tell us everything.*

She'd gone underground and come up, coughing dirt, shivering cold, and always the men from narrow houses were there, waiting. Until the day she buried him instead.

Gabby's fingers ache, tingling with the flow of blood cut off by the sharpness of the ribbon. She lets go, lets out a breath as blood flows back again. Keys jangle in the lock. There are sharp teeth behind her smile, the crunch of hollow bones between them; she tucks them away just in time.

Fred carries in grocery bags, glancing around in dismay at how little she's done—the still-empty boxes and the scatter of junk across the table. The men from narrow houses crowd behind Fred's shoulder. They wink copper, silver, and gold. They put their long fingers to their lips, sharing a secret, and they grin.

Something glints in Fred's eyes, a reflection slipping out of the frame.

"I know you," she says.

Fred's expression changes to one of concern.

"Of course you know me." He puts the groceries down, feeling her forehead. "What's wrong?"

Gabby remembers shaking clods of earth from her hair. Climbing out of the ground and gasping in the fresh air. She remembers wanting to run.

Fred starts to move away, but Gabby grabs his arm, holding him still.

Where were you before you were here? Before you were her? Tell us, love, tell us everything.

Once upon a time, she was a magician's assistant. Once upon

a time, there was a man in the audience who looked very much like Fred. Safe and dull.

"I need an assistant from the audience," she'd said, even though that was the magician's line.

She held out her hand, and Fred climbed up on stage, ignoring the blood on her cuffs and the dirt in her hair. Dazzled by the lights and by her smile.

"I'll show you a trick," she whispered in his ear and led him to the cabinet spangled with stars. "It's a really good one."

She helped him climb inside. She sealed him up tight, rapped her knuckles against every seam.

"Abracadabra," she said, and at the last moment, she jumped into the cabinet with him and pulled the door closed.

When the magician opened the cabinet, they were both gone.

"I'll show you a trick," she said, and changed into a fox with sharp teeth and flame-colored fur. "It's a really good one," she said, turning back into a girl. "I'll teach you another trick, too. I'll teach you how it's done if you do a little favor for me."

She nipped at his skin with sharp-glittery teeth. She made a little hole, and buried a fragment of trickster inside. She unzipped her skin, winking as she put her coat the color of fire into his hands.

"Hide it," she said. She caught his hands and kissed him. "And kill the magician when he comes after me. Help me bury him deep underground, and I'll marry you. When we wake up, all of this will feel like a dream."

Fred blinks at Gabby, her hand still on his arm. When she lets go, the pale mark of her fingers remain on his flesh like a ghost. In the morning, he might have a bruise. Over Fred's shoulder, the men grin their apple-slice grins.

"Where is it? Where did you hide my skin? I need you to remember everything."

Fred stares at her, bewildered. "I don't know what you're talking about. I don't even know who you are."

Gabby looks at Fred, really sees him for the first time. Sweet and dull. He did her a favor once upon a time, but that isn't a reason to stay.

"It's okay," she says with a grin, and drops a kiss on Fred's cheek. "I know enough for the both of us."

Then she's gone.

Memory is a house, Gabby thinks as she runs down the stairs. It should be a simple trick to find her way through to the room where Fred buried her skin. Past the second floor, past the street level, and down to the basement.

The men from narrow houses buried her again and again, and Gabby is oh so good at remembering, walking from room to room, trying to gather up everything they lost and left behind. She learned the trick of it, but they never did.

She finds her way by the blueprint inside her skin, like a negative image of Fred's perfect dream house, all twisted and strange, but wholly and utterly hers.

Beyond the furnace is a tiny door barely as high as her knee. When she moved into the building, the landlord told her they used to store firewood there. Or maybe there was never a door here until now, until Gabby needed there to be.

Inside, it smells like wood and earth, like moonlight and apples. It's a small space made for storage, nothing more. It's an endless space where the men from narrow houses emerge to creep up the stairs.

Gabby gets down on her belly, and crawls through the door. It's not big enough for a grown woman, but it's just right for a fox.

The walls narrow until they aren't walls. Until she's falling into the house built upside down. She tumbles into the parlor where her uncle sits shuffling brightly-colored tarot cards. In the fireplace, flames lick around a pile of bones.

As she crashes to the ground, he reaches for her, dirt beneath his nails like he's been digging at the walls, and blood inside his smile.

"Take me with you, love," he says. "Oh please, show me the way."

His legs tangle as he runs after her, but Gabby is faster, crawling through the rooms to the attic which is a basement in the house turned upside down. There, beneath the floorboards, is a star-spangled cabinet just the right size to hold everything she's been. She picks the lock with nails that were always too sharp for human hands. The lid falls back; inside her skin glows like flame.

A footstep creaks at the top of the stairs. Her uncle barks a high, piteous cry. A shadow paints the wall. A shadow divided again and again.

The men from narrow houses creep up the stairs, up from the attic, down from the basement. Their long fingers, like bone, are ready to catch at her hair, at her clothes. Ready to bury her and dig her up again and again. Ready to whisper their grave-cold voices in her ear, *Tell us love, tell us everywhere you've been.* Her uncles, her magician, the fox she saved once upon a time. Step, step, step, go the men from narrow houses, slinking up and slinking down, their hungry eyes like coins.

"Tell us, love," they croon as they slip and slither and creep toward her.

Gabby doesn't let them finish. She knows, and she remembers, and she's going to keep the secrets she found under the dirt all to herself this time. Up and out, she unburies herself. The men from narrow houses are coming for her. It's time to be fleet, to flicker-change. It's time to run.

THE GHOST SEQUENCES

The 2017 Annual Juried Exhibition at Gallery Oban consists of a single winning entry in four parts titled "The Ghost Sequences." Although they dissolved their artist collective shortly before the opening of the show, two of the members, Georgina Rush and Kathryn Morrow, worked closely with the gallery, providing specific instructions for the exhibition's layout, and further stipulating that any subsequent showing should replicate the original conditions—four rooms in the order Red, Black & White, Mechanical, and Empty—and that the works never be shown separately.

Red

A haunting is a moment of trauma, infinitely repeated. It extends forward and backward in time. It is the hole grief makes. It is a house built by memory in-between your skin and bones.

— *Lettie Wells, Artist's Statement, 2017*

326 | THE GHOST SEQUENCES

The red room contains a series of abstract paintings by Lettie Wells. The paint is textured, thick, the color somewhere between poppies and oxidized blood. On each canvas, the paint is mixed with a different medium—brick dust, plaster, wood shavings, ground glass.

Upon entering the room and turning left, the first canvas the viewer encounters holds a single drop of black paint against the red. With each subsequent painting, the drop grows—a windshield pebble-strike, a spider web, a star going supernova. Something coming closer from very far away.

There is no guarantee, of course, that the viewer will turn left through the doorway. As a result, the thing inside the paintings is constantly retreating and approaching, drawing nearer and running away, depending on the sequence in which the works are viewed. The room, however, is a closed circuit; there is no escape. The thing in the paintings must circle endlessly, trapped beneath layers of red, always searching for a way out.

∽

Studio Session #1 - Ghost Stories

"Family meeting!" Abby calls, her little joke as she enters the shared studio space where their artists' collective of four works and lives.

She deposits grocery bags on the counter as the others emerge: Lettie paint-spattered, Georgina smelling faintly of developing chemicals, and Kathryn twisting a spare bit of copper wire around her left hand.

"What are we going to do about this?" Abby slaps a bright yellow flyer on the counter beside the bags.

Lettie picks it up, and Georgina and Kathryn read over her shoulder. The skin around Lettie's nails is as stained as her clothes, a myriad of different colors.

"Gallery Oban." Kathryn looks up. "Is that the one on Prince Street?"

"No entry fee for submissions." Abby grins. "The winner gets a three month exhibition."

"I haven't finished anything new in months." Lettie's thumb drifts to her mouth, teeth working a ragged edge of skin. Kathryn gently pushes Lettie's arm back to her side, but not before she leaves a smear of paint behind.

"And no one wants to buy the crap I'm producing," Georgina says as she unpacks the grocery bags, laying out packages of instant ramen, and setting water on to boil.

"Then this is the perfect thing to push us out of our ruts," Abby says. "We could even work on a central theme, each in our own medium."

"Do you have a theme in mind?" Georgina asks.

"Nope." Abby grins. "We'll brainstorm tonight. This should help."

She retrieves a bottle of cheap wine from the last grocery bag and hunts for a corkscrew. Georgina dishes ramen into four bowls. As she hands the over last bowl over, the power flickers and goes out.

"Shit."

"Think Mr. Nanas *forgot* to pay the electric bill? Or maybe the rain is really to blame?" Abby strikes a pose, doing her best Tim Curry from *Rocky Horror Picture Show*.

"I'll get candles." Kathryn leaves her bowl on the counter while Lettie sits with hers cupped between her hands, steam rising around her face.

"We should tell ghost stories," Kathryn says. The last candle lit, she joins the others around a low coffee table they rescued from the trash. "That's what my sisters and I used to do when the power would go out."

"Oh." Abby sits up straighter. "That's perfect. Ghost stories. That can be our exhibition theme!"

Lettie, Kathryn, and Georgina exchange a look, and Abby throws up her hands, flopping back against the futon.

"We're artists! Our whole job is to make the unseen visible."

"Actually, I might have an idea." Georgina taps her spoon against her lips. "You know Morgan Paige?"

"The director?" Lettie sets her bowl aside, sitting on her hands to keep from gnawing at her skin. Georgina nods.

"Most people think *Cherry Lane* was his first movie, but there's an earlier one that was never released. He made it right out of film school with a couple of friends. It's practically a student film, but..." Georgina shrugs. She looks around and, seeing no wandering attention, continues.

"It's called *The Woods*. It's about a group of high school kids who try to create their own version of the Suicide Woods in Japan by driving one of their classmates to kill themselves. They're testing the idea that they can create a haunting through a single traumatic event that spreads until it effects the whole school. It's supposed to be an examination of depression, apathy, and mental illness." Georgina reaches for the wine and refills their glasses.

"Anyway, that's not the weird part. You know the woods over by Muirfield Farm?"

Nods all around, and Lettie shifts in her seat.

"That's where Paige and his friends shot most of the film. On their last day of shooting, something went wrong with the camera and while Paige was trying to fix it, he saw something on the film that shouldn't have been there."

One of Lettie's hands creeps free, and she chews at the side of her thumb. A faint smear of red marks her lips, not matching any of the paint under her nails.

"He sees a girl standing between the trees, barefoot, wearing strange clothes. She could just be some local kid, but Paige is convinced he's caught a ghost on film. He freaks out and scraps the movie. Eventually, he takes the frames he has and buries them, and doesn't make another movie for nearly five years. According to the rumors, the raw footage of *The Woods* is under the freeway overpass somewhere near Clover Street."

"No one's ever found it?" Kathryn asks.

Georgina shrugs.

"Maybe if they ever do those repairs they've been promising for years...." She finishes her wine and shrugs. "Anyway, maybe I could do something with that for my part of the exhibition."

Abby stands.

"I have a story, but give me a sec."

There's a slyness to her expression as she disappears into her studio. She and Kathryn have spaces on the first floor, while Lettie and Georgina have studios on the half floor overlooking the common room. The whole building used to be industrial storage space, renovated during the city's renaissance in an attempt to attract artists to the region and create the next big hipster neighborhood. Abby returns with a second bottle of wine.

"You've been holding out on us." Georgina nudges her as Abby opens the bottle and pours. Lettie covers her glass.

"This is something that happened at my grandmother's school when she was in tenth grade," Abby says as she settles back down. "There was this group of popular girls. Everyone called them "the pack", though not to their faces. Even the teachers were afraid of them.

"Anyway, halfway through the school year, a new girl named Libby joins the class. She's painfully shy. Her clothes are out of style, like maybe her family doesn't have much money. Basically, she's that kid that every class has, the one with *victim* written across their forehead.

"The leader of the pack is a girl named Helen. One night when her parents are out of town, she invites Libby to join the pack for a sleepover. Libby's never slept away from home before, but Helen won't take no for an answer. All the other kids in the class know the pack is planning something, but they're too scared to warn Libby in case Helen turns on them instead."

Abby takes a slow sip of her wine, reveling in the attention as she unwinds her tale.

"Anyway, Helen finally convinces Libby. The night of the sleepover arrives and Libby pulls an old-fashioned nightgown with long sleeves and a skirt that almost touches the floor out of her overnight bag. As they're all getting changed, Susannah catches a glimpse of bruises on Libby's thighs and arms, just a quick flash before the nightgown covers everything. She tells Helen, but not the other girls.

"After they're all dressed for bed, Helen tells them how the woods behind her house are haunted, then she insists they play truth or dare. When her turn comes, Libby picks truth, and Helen asks, *Who do you love more, your mother or your father?* Libby's eyes go wide, she looks scared and won't answer, rubbing at her arms through the sleeves of her nightgown. *If you won't answer, then you have to do a dare*, Helen says. The other girls start chanting *dare, dare, dare*, until Libby gives in.

"*I dare you to go into the woods behind the house and play the hanging game*, Helen says. She grabs a pair of her mother's silk stockings and drags Libby outside. The other girls stay inside and watch through the window as Helen makes Libby stand under one of the trees and wraps one leg of the stocking around her throat and the other around the lowest branch.

"*Now close your eyes and count to one hundred, then you can come back inside*, Helen says. Libby closes her eyes and starts counting aloud while Helen walks backward toward the house. When she gets to the door, Helen is planning to lock it behind her, and then she'll make the rest of the pack hide. But before Helen can get to the house, Libby screams, and Helen freezes. Libby is thrashing, clawing at the stocking. By the time the other girls run out of the house, it's too late. Libby isn't breathing. It's as if something pulled her into the tree and left her there to hang."

"That's a horrible story," Kathryn says.

Abby opens her mouth to protest and at that exact moment, something hits one of the windows. The sound is like a gunshot, and Lettie jumps, knocking over her wine. Georgina scrambles up to get a towel. She hands it to Lettie, but Lettie only twists it into a rope between her hands. Then she speaks, staring straight ahead.

"When I was eleven years old, my big sister and I came home from school and found my mother sitting in the middle of the kitchen floor. She'd smashed some of our plates, and she was putting the pieces in her mouth one by one." Lettie takes a breath, and Abby leans forward slightly. Kathryn and Georgina go still, staring at Lettie who continues to look straight ahead. "We screamed for her to stop, but it was like she couldn't hear us. My sister grabbed her wrists, and then hit her to make her stop. When my mother finally looked at us, it was like she didn't know who we were."

"Lettie." Kathryn touches her arm. Lettie blinks, and slowly turns her head. The candlelight plays tricks with her eyes, turning them to glass.

Kathryn's hand slides from Lettie's arm as though pushed away.

"Honey, you don't...." Kathryn starts, but Lettie ignores her. Georgina frowns, and Abby scoots forward so she's sitting on the edge of her chair, but she doesn't reach for Lettie or her restless hands.

"As long as I can remember, my mother thought she was haunted. She would go on binges of eating, trying to fill herself up so there was no room for ghosts inside her skin. But other times she refused to eat at all, nearly starving herself and begging the ghosts to take her."

Lettie looks at each of them in turn, still twisting the towel in her hands.

"On my sixteenth birthday, I came home from school and

found my mother and my sister dead. My mother was lying on her bed. There were clothes scattered on the floor, a lamp knocked over, like there'd been a fight. There were empty pill bottles with the labels peeled off. My mother's hands...it looked like someone had bitten her. They were all bloody and there were teeth marks on her skin. I screamed for Ellie, but she didn't come. Then I found her in my mother's bathroom. She was lying in the bathtub with her clothes on. It looked like maybe she'd hit her head. There was blood around her mouth. I don't know if my mother killed her, or...I don't know."

Lettie wraps her arms around knees, hugging them to her chest. She rocks slightly, then puts her head down, her voice muffled when she speaks.

"My sister is starving, and she wants to come home."

~

Interlude #1 - A Room with One Door

There was a game my sister and I used to play when we were little. When our mother was having one of her bad days, we'd go into the crawlspace under the basement stairs. It was just big enough for us on our hands and knees, or sitting down, and there was only one way in so it felt safe.

The game was called Brick by Brick. There was a deck of cards, each with a picture of a different room. In the real rules, we were supposed to play against each other, but Ellie and I always changed it so we took turns drawing cards and building the house together. We were born only eleven months apart, so really we were more like twins than sisters.

In the game, there were little plastic figurines that came with the cards—red, yellow, green, and blue for the people, and white for the ghost, or the monster. The idea was to move through the house as fast as possible, so the monster wouldn't catch you.

The trick was, if you built a secret passageway, or a hidden staircase to get through the house faster, the monster could use it too.

Sometimes Ellie would make up stories about the house while we played. She'd tell me about all the things in the rooms, and the lives the little plastic versions of us lived there. The monster was in her stories, too, but there it was nice and it wasn't trying to hurt us at all.

The little plastic figures got lost at some point, but I still have the cards. On nights when I can't sleep, I take the deck out and arrange the cards different ways. If I close my eyes just a little bit while I'm doing it, I can almost see Ellie moving around inside the card house. If I manage to get the sequence of cards just right, she'll be able to find her way out and come home. The trick is, what if the monster finds the way out first?

∼

Black and White

The second room in the gallery contains a series of black and white photographs by Georgina Rush. One grouping is labeled *The Tomb*, the other, *The Woods*. *The Tomb* photographs depict a spot beneath a highway overpass—graffiti, empty bottles, a half-finished meal in a Styrofoam container. Even so, there's something mystical about the images. They suggest a sacred site, an archeological dig. Something is buried here, and the artist is documenting its unearthing.

The Woods depict rows of trees on the far side of an empty field. Rather than a wild forest, these trees are planned and planted, and Rush achieves a stunning effect with the light coming between the trunks. Despite the regularity of the rows, there is something uncanny about the trees. The spaces between them are full of waiting. One cannot help feeling the woods, and perhaps the photographs themselves, are haunted.

In the center of the gallery there is a pedestal holding a laptop with files that visitors are encouraged to explore. These are raw, unprocessed images, outtakes from the exhibition. The one incongruity is a video file titled "Overlapping Voices (Abby's Possession)." The film appears to be shot in the studio shared by the four artists. It's unclear how it fits with the photographs on the wall, however it's possible the film is another outtake, a dress rehearsal for the performance piece Abby Farris had planned for the show.

Studio Session #2 - The Ghost in the Machine

There's a tapping sound so soft Kathryn barely hears it. When it finally registers, her first irrational thought is that there's someone in the walls. Then she realizes the sound is at her studio door and opens it to see Lettie's face, just a slice between the door and the frame. There's darkness under her eyes, like she hasn't been sleeping, and the rest of her skin is paler by comparison.

"Sorry, can I come in?"

Kathryn opens the door wider before Lettie even finishes, and Lettie steps inside, glancing over her shoulder.

"Sorry, I just…." She rubs her arms. When Kathryn closes the door, Lettie relaxes visibly, then offers a self-deprecating smile and shrugs. "You know how it is when you get in your own head sometimes."

"Sure." Kathryn gestures to her work table.

The frame for her piece is mostly complete. Wires trail across the table's surface like a mat of tangled hair.

"I was actually just finishing up this part. Wanna see if it works?"

Kathryn clears space around the machine, bits and scraps she ended up not using. Most of the parts were bought at the local hardware store, but the crown jewel she found on eBay—a Ouija board in good condition, but showing signs of use, which is exactly what she wanted. The letters are a bit faded, and the felt pads on the planchette's feet have worn away. The board sits in the center of a frame, and a thin metal arm runs from the planchette to the frame, hinged to allow a full range of motion. It can reach every letter and number on the board, along with Yes, No, and Goodbye.

"Wait." Lettie touches Kathryn's wrist as she reaches for the power switch.

A bandage wraps Lettie's thumb, the edges dirty and peeling. There's a dark red stain along one side, fading to brown.

"Can it really talk to ghosts?" The way Lettie says it, almost hopeful, gives Kathryn pause.

She lowers her hand. As a kid, she wanted so badly to see a ghost. All those stories she and her sisters told, gathered around a flashlight under sheets strung over chairs—if she could just see one of those ghosts for real it would make her special. But what she sees in Lettie's eyes is completely different. Raw need. Loss. The room goes colder, air dropping out and goose-bumps rising on Kathryn's skin.

"We don't have to." Kathryn fights the urge to rub at her arms the way Lettie did. This whole thing was a terrible mistake. "It can wait until some other time."

"No, I want to see."

The chill goose-prickling her arms crawls up the back of Kathryn's neck. There's someone standing in the corner. Someone just behind her. If she turns to look, it won't be there. The corner will be empty. But if she doesn't look, the thing will continue to stand there. Not breathing, not moving. Just watching her. Always.

Lettie stands beside her at the table, close enough that their arms almost touch. Yet Kathryn is filled with the sudden, irrational feeling that Lettie is also standing behind her in the corner of the room. A shadow moves in the hallway, just visible through the crack in the door even though Kathryn is certain she closed the door after Lettie entered. Her heart thumps, and she bites down on her lip. A moment later Georgina peers through the gap.

"We heard voices. Is your piece finished? Can we see?"

Kathryn nods, her throat dry. Georgina pushes the door wide, and Abby follows her inside. The studio feels crowded with all of them there. Lettie moves around the table holding the machine like she's sleepwalking and flicks the switch that turns on Kathryn's machine.

The EMF detector attached to the frame lights up, lights cycling from green, through yellow, to orange and red before settling back down to a single green pip. The readout on the thermometer beside it shows the room at 70 degrees, slightly higher than normal with their body heat.

Nothing is going to happen. Nothing is going to happen and this is stupid and Kathryn wants everyone out of her room now. The lights flicker from green to red again and the mechanical arm holding the planchette jumps.

"Oh shit," Georgina says, then laughs, a nervous sound. "Is it programmed to do that?"

Kathryn's throat is tight. She wants to squeeze her eyes closed, but she can't. For a moment, nothing else happens, then lights on the EMF detector spike and the arm moves again. The planchette scrapes to the left. The un-felted feet on the board shriek, worse than a chalkboard and nails. Then the planchette swoops down to the bottom of the board.

Yes. Goodbye. I-B. No. Goodbye. B-B-B. Kathryn tracks the

motion, her mouth open. The machine is working as designed, but it isn't supposed to do that. There's no such thing as ghosts; rationally, she knows that to be a fact. EMF detectors can be set off by microwaves, cellphone towers, or maybe she wired the machine wrong.

Beside her, Lettie watches the board, rapt. The planchette moves faster, screeching as it does. *Yes. Goodbye. Goodbye. L-B-I-I. No. I-L. No. L-I-B-I. L-I-B-I.* The planchette whips through the letters, a blur repeating the last four with sharp insistence.

"Oh shit," Georgina says again. "It's spelling Libby. Like the girl in Abby's story."

Lettie makes a sound, not quite a breath, not quite a sob.

"What did you do?" Kathryn rounds on Abby. Her fingers clench and unclench at her side.

Abby's mouth drops open, and she holds up her hands. If her shock is an act, it's convincing. An ache makes itself known between Kathryn's eyes, and she shakes her head once to dislodge it. What makes her think Abby had anything to do with this? Just because she told a ghost story about a girl named Libby? Besides, Georgina is the one who pointed it out so quickly, couldn't it have been her? Or none of them, because no one has touched the machine except for her. It's just a weird coincidence, and Kathryn is being paranoid.

"It's something wrong with the wires," Kathryn speaks quickly. Instead of turning off the switch, she yanks out the whole bundle of wires in one go, and the arm and the planchette fall still.

Lettie continues staring at the machine, willing it to move again, to speak. Her face is bloodless, except for one spot of color high on her cheek as though someone slapped her.

"It isn't Ellie." Lettie shakes her head. She turns to Kathryn, stricken. "It's the wrong ghost."

Kathryn pulls Lettie into a hug, but it's too late. She can't shake the feeling that she's ruined everything. Something terrible is in the room with them, and she's the one who let it in.

～

Interlude #2 - A Room with No Windows

Georgina let me help her with her photographs. ~~I don't want to be in my studio alone.~~ The red light in her darkroom is peaceful, and there are no windows. It reminds me of the crawlspace where Ellie and I used to play. Safe, except when the ghosts would tell my mother where to look and helped her make herself small enough to crawl into the darkness after us.

I watched Georgina make images out of light, then she showed me how to bathe the photo paper in the chemical wash. It's like a magic trick, watching the picture fade into place. While I was watching her trees, they suddenly weren't trees anymore. They were the wooden frame of a house still being built. A skeleton without windows, or walls, or doors. Then the chemicals finished their work and it was just woods, but there was someone standing between the trees.

I was so startled I knocked the whole tray over. It ruined Georgina's picture. She told me not to worry, she could make another one, and she did, but there was nothing between the trees the second time. No house. No figure. Just shadows and light.

I think Georgina was afraid of upsetting me. Everyone walks on eggshells around me since the night the power went out. Except for Abby. The other day I walked into the kitchen and they were all there. I'd been in my studio with my earphones on, so I didn't hear them until I opened my door, then Kathryn said, "So who moved it? A ghost?" But they all stopped talking the second they saw me. Kathryn and Georgina exchanged a look like they wanted to say something, but they didn't know who should go first. Abby smiled, but in the end no one said anything. They just watched me get a glass of water and go back into my studio. Am I so fragile they all have to tiptoe around me? Or are they scared of something else? ~~Do they know about the house I'm building with the cards? Or how badly I want to open the door?~~

~

Mechanical

Is it possible to build a machine to capture a ghost? That is the question at the heart of "Séance Table." Ghost hunters have used a variety of equipment to detect paranormal activity for years— electromagnetic field detectors, voice recorders, infrared cameras. "Séance Table" makes use of some of those tools of the trade, specifically an EMF machine and an extremely sensitive thermometer. The goal of the piece is to mechanically facilitate communication with the paranormal world. A spike in EMF readings, or a drop in temperature, will trigger the arm attached to the piece's frame, causing the planchette to move. Even though the motion is mechanically aided, the prime mover, the trigger if you will, is the ghost.

Is it possible for the random motion of the arm to spell a word, or impart a message with specific meaning to visitor? If my machine does capture a ghost, is it because the ghost was always there, or do the conditions of the machine itself—an open phone line, an invitation to speak—cause the haunting? I am certain you have questions of your own as well, and I invite you to write them on the provided note cards and drop them in the box affixed to the base of the machine. Perhaps a ghost will answer. I also invite you to take your time in the gallery, and keep an open mind. Let's explore the questions of the afterlife together.

—Wall text by Kathryn Morrow, 2017

∼

Studio Session #3 - Overlapping Voices (Abby's Possession)

Georgina wakes to Kathryn leaning over her, gesturing for silence.

"What—"

"Shh. Here." She presses Georgina's phone into her hands. "Something's wrong."

"I don't—"

"Come on." Kathryn tugs her, and Georgina stumbles after her.

"What's going on?" Lettie joins them, her eyes wide in the dark. They look like they've been wide for a long time. Sleepless.

The door to Abby's studio stands ajar, the murmur of voices emerging from within.

"Turn your camera on." Kathryn indicates Georgina's phone.

Confused, Georgina obeys. Her mind is sleep-numb, dazed. She lifts the phone regardless, watching the screen as Kathryn pushes open Abby's door.

The room is a mess. The sheets on the empty bed are rumpled; Abby's clothes are scattered on the floor. It looks like someone tossed a deck of playing cards in the air and left them wherever they fell. As Georgina's eyes adjust, she sees they're not regular playing cards. There are pictures of rooms on them, stairs, hallways, broken pieces of a house in random order.

Georgina lifts the camera higher, going cold as her eyes and her screen make sense of the image at the same time. Abby stands in the corner, facing away from them. She's wearing a nightgown with a long skirt and long sleeves. Her hair is loose,

THE GHOST SEQUENCES | 341

and she's rocking back and forth on her bare feet, muttering words Georgina can't quite hear.

"Abby?" Kathryn speaks softly behind her. Lettie makes a distressed sound, so small it's almost lost as Georgina and Kathryn move closer.

Georgina finds herself speaking, like a narrator in a documentary film, before she's fully registered what she's doing. Kathryn told her to film this, so she'll do it right.

"Abby is standing in the corner. She's barefoot and facing the wall. She's wearing a nightgown none of us have ever seen before."

"I don't like this," Lettie says.

Georgina inches closer, and Abby's words either grow clearer, or she's speaking louder, pitching her voice so her audience will hear.

"In the trees. In the woods. Buried under the road."

Even if it is a performance, and Georgina really isn't sure, the skin on her arms tightens, puckering around each hair, and some primal instinct tells her to flee. This is wrong. The voice doesn't sound like Abby, but there's no one else it could be.

"There's something wrong with her spine. The way she's standing looks wrong," Georgina says.

If she keeps narrating, it'll keep what's happening at a distance. It's just a movie. She plants her feet, refusing to run, and forces herself to breathe.

"Abby, can you hear me?" Kathryn stops just short of touching Abby's shoulder. On Georgina's screen it looks like her hand actually bounces away.

"In the woods. In the woods. In the." Abby's voice grows louder.

"Make her stop." Lettie's voice cuts in over Abby's.

"Abby." Kathryn finally succeeds in touching her and Abby jerks around to face them, her lips pulled back in a snarl. It's definitely Abby, but at the same time it looks nothing like her.

"In the woods in the trees in the woods." It's almost a chant, and Georgina has the odd sensation Abby's lips don't move.

Abby pushes Kathryn, and Lettie catches her. Georgina jumps out of the way, and the image on her screen jumps with her.

"Bury me. Bury me." Abby's voice gets louder, closer. Georgina's head snaps up, looking away from her phone, and somehow Abby is beside her.

Abby grins with her peeled-back lips, a nasty smile. Her gums look wrong, bloody, and Georgina looks away. It's a moment before she can force herself to follow Abby into the hall.

"Bury me." The words trail after Abby, but the voice sounds like Lettie's.

"She's going to the kitchen," Georgina whispers to her phone.

A crash reverberates, and Georgina flinches, jerking the screen again. Kathryn pushes past her, and Georgina hurries after her, their footsteps almost, but not quite, covering Lettie's sob.

There's just enough light to see Abby standing in the center of the kitchen. Shards from a broken plate radiate around her like the scattered cards in her room. Her eyes are closed now, head tilted at an angle that looks almost painful. Her neck is broken, Georgina thinks, and immediately pushes the thought away. One of Abby's feet is bleeding; she must have stepped on a piece of the plate.

"It's my fault." Lettie speaks so close to Georgina's shoulder that she nearly drops her phone. "I used the cards to try to build Ellie a path through the house, but the bad thing came through first."

"Abby, stop it. Now." Kathryn grabs Abby's arm, shaking her. Abby lets out a whimper, but doesn't open her eyes.

"Bury me! Bury me!" She shrieks.

Then her eyes do snap open and she drops to the ground. Kathryn jumps back, kicking a shard of plate that spins away from her. Abby crouches, her feet arched so she balances on the balls of her toes and the points of her fingers. Her mouth opens, and one hand creeps forward, a spider-walk across the kitchen floor, reaching for a broken piece of plate. Georgina's pulse thumps, her throat too thick to speak.

"No!" Lettie throws herself forward as Abby's fingers brush the broken plate, and she slaps Abby's hand away.

Abby snarls, swaying, and Lettie hits her, knocking her back. There's a painful thump as she hits the ground, but Georgina can't tell if it's Abby's back or her head striking the floor. Lettie scrambles on top of Abby, pinning her down and hitting her again. Abby's hands come up to defend herself, and Georgina and her camera catch sight of Abby's face in profile; she looks scared.

Fascination holds her in place. It's Kathryn who finally grabs Lettie's wrists and pulls her away. Abby and Lettie are both breathing hard, Abby's breath hitching on the edge of hyperventilation.

"Turn it off," Kathryn snaps, and its only then that Georgina fully realizes she's still filming.

Her thumbs shakes as she taps the stop button. Kathryn puts her arm around Lettie's shoulder, leading her away. Lying on her back, Abby turns her head toward Georgina. She's still holding her phone, and she has the sick urge to take a picture of the scene. Abby's nose is bloodied where Lettie hit her, and red smears her lips and chin, looking black in the dark. Abby's eyes meet Georgina's, shiny and wet. Her lips move, mouthing words which might be "I'm sorry" or "Help me", Georgina can't tell.

Interlude #3 - A Narrow House

There's another game Ellie and I used to play. We would lie perfectly still in the dark, our bodies straight, our feet together, our arms pressed at our sides, like we were lying in invisible coffins. If we were good enough at pretending, the ghosts would think we were one of them. We called it The Dead Game.

Last night, I came into my studio and found all my paintings for the show rearranged. At first I thought maybe one of the others had been in my room, but I know Georgina and Kathryn wouldn't do that. I don't know if I don't think Abby would either. I realized it had to be a message from Ellie. The deck for Brick by Brick isn't in my room anymore. I don't know where it went, but I haven't seen it in almost a week, and I've looked everywhere. Without it, Ellie had no other way to reach me. She had to use the paintings. The canvases are walls in a house that is always being built. It still isn't finished.

I looked at the paintings for almost an hour, but I couldn't understand what she was trying to tell me. Then I thought if I played The Dead Game, she might talk to me directly. I lay on the floor and put my arms at my sides, keeping as still as possible. The room was quiet and dark, but I kept smelling paint, and something like sandalwood. Maybe Abby was burning incense in her room. The smell comes under her door sometimes. It's so strong some days the scent stays on her clothes and in her hair and trails behind her so we can always tell where she's been.

I tried to hold my breath. Ellie was always better at that part of the game. One time when we were in the crawlspace playing, I got really scared thinking she wasn't breathing at all. I kept shaking her until she finally opened her eyes and smiled at me. There was someone else inside her looking out at me. I broke the rules then, the ones we'd made up for Brick by Brick, that we'd always help each other and stick together so the monster wouldn't catch us alone. I ran, and I left Ellie in the crawlspace behind me.

Lying in my studio, I listened for Ellie as hard as I could. I kept holding my breath until my head pounded. Until my lungs hurt. Then I let it all out at once, and the sound was like a train thundering over the tracks. Black smoke hung over my head, like I'd breathed myself out entirely. Then there was something else in the smoke. It turned and looked at me and I was so surprised, I gasped. I didn't mean to, but I breathed it in. The dark thing is inside of me, and now I don't know how to let it out again.

~

Studio Session #4 - In the Trees

Lettie starts, gasping in a breath. Someone is in her room. Someone is leaning over her. She's playing The Dead Game, and she is a door and something is stepping through.

"Are you awake?" Abby's voice jolts her.

Lettie crashes back into herself, but her body feels like a collection of loose bones—an unfinished construction—only barely joined by skin. Her studio resolves around her, the canvases lined against the wall smelling of paint and turpentine, even though she opened all the windows. Abby's scent is there, too, sandalwood threaded through and beneath everything.

"What's wrong?" Lettie sits up; it's a struggle.

"The others are asleep," Abby says. "I want to show you something."

Abby goes to the door, looking back over her shoulder and beckoning. Lettie follows. She shouldn't. She doesn't trust Abby, but there's no reason not to trust her either. Only there's something different about her tonight. It's not like when she spoke in strange voices and Lettie hit her, that night they still haven't talked about. Now, Abby almost seems to glow. There are hollow spaces inside her, places for ghosts to fill.

"Oh," Lettie says, and hurries to follow Abby into the dark.

Once they're outside, she asks, "Where are we going?"

Her feet are bare, but it's too late to go back for shoes. She picks her way carefully over the warped asphalt, following Abby down the narrow alleyway between buildings.

"I borrowed my brother's car," Abby says. "I need to get some things for my performance."

"At night?"

"They accepted our proposal. Didn't you hear? We made it into the show. We *are* the show."

Lettie stops. As far as she knows, Abby hasn't even started working on her piece. Any time any of them ask her about it, she changes the subject. And she certainly doesn't remember assembling images of her own paintings to submit to the jury. Surely she would remember that. Unless Georgina did it, with her camera, got everything ready. Of course that's what happened. How could she forget?

At the mouth of the alley, Abby turns back to look at her. There's something disdainful in her expression, but something pitying as well, as if she's sad that Lettie doesn't understand. That's when Lettie sees it, a faint ribbon the color that moon-light would be if it could be made solid. It twists away from Abby, a path, a thread, beckoning Lettie to follow.

She climbs into the passenger seat as Abby unlocks the door of an ancient Dodge Pinto, the car she borrowed from her brother. The rubber floor mat is gritty under her soles. Light slides over them as Abby pulls away from the curb. Everything is sodium orange and bruise-colored, bloodied at the stoplights, drowned green for go. Abby looks at Lettie sidelong, like she's testing Lettie, like she's asking a question.

"Do you believe in ghosts?" Lettie says.

The vents in the dashboard rattle, exhaling air smelling of burnt toast. Abby started this whole thing, but Lettie still doesn't know if she believes. The story she told; Lettie suspects Abby made it up on the spot. Why would Abby's grandmother admit to such a thing, because how else would she know about it unless she was one of the girls involved? And why would she tell her granddaughter about it if she did?

Depending on how Abby answers, Lettie will know whether Abby knows about the moon-colored glow surrounding her, whether she knows about the ghosts, or whether they're just using her as a vessel to send a message.

"I'm building a suicide tree," Abby says instead of answering her. "For the show."

She turns off the main road where there are fewer street-lights and shadows stick to her skin.

"During my performances, I'll stand under the suicide tree with a noose around my neck and invite ghosts to prove themselves by making me into one of them, if they can."

Abby's eyes cut right, looking for a reaction. Lettie watches the lights instead, the pattern of shadows. She has the strange impression that the car is moving backward in time. She's heard everything Abby has to say somewhere else before. She watches through the windshield for the place where the glowing ribbon ends, the place it's leading them.

"We're here." Lettie says it so suddenly Abby hits the brakes without engaging the clutch and the car stalls.

The Dodge's headlights wash over browned grass, showing the expanse of a field. Beyond the field, trees stand like sentinels in eerily perfect rows. Abby's mouth opens; Lettie smiles to herself. Her suspicion is confirmed; Abby doesn't know where they are. She isn't the one in control.

Abby recovers quickly, scrambling with her seatbelt, but Lettie is out of the car first, walking toward the trees. She looks over her shoulder. Abby is very small in the darkness, dwindling. Her mouth is a perfect circle, her eyes smudges of black. It's time.

Abby is a house, waiting for a ghost, so Lettie slips inside, looking out through Abby's eyes and watching herself walk across the field. Brown grass crackles under her bare feet.

Abby blinks, feeling like she's waking up from a long dream, disoriented and unsure where she is. She doesn't remember leaving the studio, but she's outside and the trees ahead of her are unsettlingly familiar. Georgina's photographs. And Lettie. Lettie is with her. Panic beats a tattoo against Abby's skin.

She blinks again, and there's something between the trees. Someone. There and then gone. Afterimages of Lettie trail behind her leaving luminescent footprints on the grass, except Abby can't tell which direction they're going. She has to catch up before it's too late. She breaks into a run, tripping, and Lettie is even farther away by the time she gets her feet under her again.

This was a mistake. She came here to…. Why did she come? She wanted…. She honestly doesn't know.

Something is terribly wrong. Something she can't quite remember. Like a story someone told her a long time ago.

Lettie is almost at the trees. At the edge of the field, Lettie stops. Relief crashes through Abby. She bends over, hands on her knees, gulping deep breaths. She straightens just in time to see Lettie open her mouth, but before either of them can get out a word or a name, something dark surges from between the trees. It's there and then it's not, and Lettie isn't there either. She's gone. Pulled into the trees. Vanished.

Abby screams. She plunges forward. Trips again, biting her lip and tasting blood. She calls Lettie's name and her voice echoes back to her, overlapping, a cacophony. There's no answer but she keeps shouting, on her hands and knees at the edge of the field, calling Lettie's name until her throat is raw.

Empty

The last room in the gallery is empty. The walls are freshly painted. The special lighting installed to cast shadows from an assemblage in the shape of a tree remains switched off. The room was originally intended to host a performance piece by Abby Farris, but now it is a space defined by absence.

Mostly. A week after the opening of "The Ghost Sequences," a visitor brought something to the gallery owner's attention. Along the baseboard near the door, there are words written in blue ballpoint pen, in lettering so small it is almost illegible. The words were not there on the day the exhibition opened. There are two sentences, which almost overlap, possibly written in two different hands, but it's hard to tell. Rather than retouching the paint to cover the words, the gallery owner let them stand as though they were always meant to be part of the exhibition after all.

I'm sorry Lettie. Ellie I'm still building the house come home.

PUBLICATION HISTORY

"The Nag Bride" is original to this collection.

"How the Trick is Done" originally appeared in *Uncanny Magazine #29*, July 2019.

"The Stories We Tell About Ghosts" originally appeared in *Looming Low Vol. 1* (Sam Cowan & Justin Steele, eds.) 2017.

"The Last Sailing of the *Henry Charles Morgan* in Six Pieces of Scrimshaw (1841)" originally appeared in *The Dark #14*, 2016.

"Harvest Song, Gathering Song" originally appeared in *For Mortal Things Unsung* (Alex Hofelich, ed.) 2017.

"The Secret of Flight" originally appeared in *Black Feathers: Dark Avian Tales* (Ellen Datlow, ed.) 2017.

"Crossing" originally appeared in *LampLight Magazine, Vol. 5*, 2017.

"How to Host a Haunted House Murder Mystery Party" originally appeared in *Bourbon Penn #12*, 2016.

"In the End, It Always Turns Out the Same" originally appeared in *The Dark #37*, 2018.

"Exhalation #10" originally appeared in *Final Cuts: New Tales of Hollywood Horror and Other Spectacles* (Ellen Datlow, ed.) 2020.

"Excerpts from a Film (1942-1987)" originally appeared in *Tor.com*, 2017.

"Lesser Creek: A Love Story, A Ghost Story" originally appeared in *Clockwork Phoenix #4*, 2013.

"I Dress My Lover in Yellow" originally appeared in *The Mammoth Book of Cthulhu: New Lovecraftian Fiction* (Paula Guran, ed.) 2016.

"Tekeli-li, They Cry" originally appeared in *Tomorrow's Cthulhu: Stories at the Dawn of Post Humanity* (C. Dombrowski & Scott Gable, eds.) 2016.

"The Men From Narrow Houses" originally appeared in *Liminal Stories #1*, 2016.

"The Ghost Sequences" originally appeared in *Echoes: The Saga Anthology of Ghost Stories* (Ellen Datlow, ed.) 2019.

ACKNOWLEDGEMENTS

The collection you hold in your hands owes its existence to many people, and I am extremely grateful to them all. First and foremost, thank you to Michael Kelly for editing and publishing the collection and making it look incredible. Thank you to Olga Beliaeva and Serge N. Kozintsev for their art, and Vince Haig for his design work—I could not have asked for a more gorgeous cover! This collection certainly wouldn't be here without all the editors who gave the reprinted stories their first homes. Mike Allen, Ellen Datlow, Scott Gable and C. Dombrowski, Paula Guran, Jacob Haddon, Alex Hofelich, Shannon Peavey and Kelly Sandoval, Erik Secker, Justin Steele and Sam Cowan, Lynne and Michael Thomas, and Sean Wallace and Silvia-Moreno Garcia—you are all wonderful! Thank you for all your hard work and everything you do for the genre. As always, thank you to all my critique buddies and con buddies for years of friendship and story-swapping. Even though the writing itself is usually a solitary pursuit, it's nice knowing that I'm never really doing it alone. Thank you to my family, human and four-legged alike; I could not do any of this without you.

Thank you to all the ghosts who inspired these stories and the ghost story writers and tellers too. And last, but absolutely not least, thank *you,* yes you, the person reading this right now; go do something amazing today.

ABOUT THE AUTHOR

A.C. Wise is the author of two collections published by Lethe Press, and a novella published by Broken Eye Books. Her debut novel, *Wendy, Darling* was published by Titan Books in June 2021. Her work has won the Sunburst Award for Excellence in Canadian Literature of the Fantastic, as well as twice more being a finalist for the Sunburst Award, twice being a finalist for the Nebula Award, and being a finalist for the Lambda Literary Award. In addition to her fiction, she contributes review columns to *Apex Magazine* and *The Book Smugglers*. Find her online at www.acwise.net.

ALSO BY A.C. WISE

The Ultra Fabulous Glitter Squadron Saves the World Again
The Kissing Booth Girl and Other Stories
Wendy, Darling

Lightning Source UK Ltd.
Milton Keynes UK
UKHW040747131021
392136UK00001B/143

9 781988 964331